NO L[illegible] DREAMS

An Anthology of Horror, Fantasy, and Science Fiction

Edited by

Danielle Ackley-McPhail
L. Jagi Lamplighter
Lee Hillman
Jeff Lyman

Lite Circle Books
Baltimore, Maryland

This volume is a work of fiction and poetry; any similarity to actual individuals, locations, or events is strictly coincidental.

First edition published in 2005.

The Lite Circle, Inc.
a non-profit literary organization
P.O. Box 26162
Baltimore, MD 21210
www.litecircle.org

Library of Congress Cataloging-in-Publication Data

Library of Congress Control Number: 2005923139
ISBN: 0-9641622-7-X

First Printing

Printed in the United States of America by Vicks Lithograph, Albany, NY.

Cover Art by Theo Black
Interior Illustrations by
Theo Black, Ruth Lampi, Edward J. Reed, Travis Ingram, Kirsten Edwards, Adam Gillespie, Jesse Foley, and Erica Henderson
Book and Cover design by Danielle McPhail/Sidhe na Daire Multimedia
Text edited by Lee "Gwen" Hillman/Sidhe na Daire Multimedia
Art edited by Mike McPhail/Sidhe na Daire Multimedia

Prints of all artwork contained in this volume are available for purchase from the individual artists.

DEDICATION

To those upon whom we built our dreams,
and those who will be lifted up by them.

ON DREAMS AND DREAMERS...

THIS PROJECT ORIGINALLY BEGAN AS A WAY TO CELEBRATE THE PROGRESS of the writers on my internet newsgroup, Yesterday's Dreamers. It has far exceeded those expectations, as have the members themselves. The group was started as a support structure; a way for beginners to benefit from the advice and experience of those who have already gotten their start.

In a recent topic discussion, a new member asked what the group was all about. Carrie Lynn Lyons—long-time member and author of the upcoming *Dream Pictures*, from Mundania Press—posted this response, "Danielle calls it [Yesterday's Dreamers] cause she and this bunch have a way of yanking you into today and helping build dreams into a reality."

I was touched by Carrie's response, but in truth, it is the members themselves that have made this and all of their own dreams possible. Their hard work and dedication to their craft is quite an example to all those out there who just aren't sure if it is really possible.

We are here to say, "Yes, in deed, it is."

Taking small steps to realize big dreams,

DANIELLE ACKLEY-MCPHAIL

Senior Editor, *No Longer Dreams*
and Author of *Yesterday's Dreams,*
Tomorrow's Memories, and
Children of Morpheus

CONTENTS

Horror

NO LONGER DREAMS
poem by Danielle Ackley-McPhail (illustration by Ruth Lampi) 7

FAT TUESDAY
by Dan Foley (illustration by Jesse Foley) 9

FERAL
poem by Jeff Lyman (illustration by Ruth Lampi) 16

KVETCHULA
by Darrell Schweitzer (illustration by Travis Ingram) 17

WAITING IN THE GARDEN
poem by Tony Ruggiero (illustration by Ruth Lampi) 26

THE QUARTERED MAN
by Jeff Lyman (illustration by Ruth Lampi) 27

WEEKEND AT POCONO MOUNTAIN
by Robin M. Buehler (illustration by Ruth Lampi) 39

THE FOREST OF A THOUSAND LOST SOULS
by Danielle Ackley-McPhail (illustration by Travis Ingram) 49

REALITY CHECK
by Tee Morris (illustration by Ruth Lampi) 59

THE PAXTON BOYS
by Den Wilson (illustration by Adam Gillespie) 67

TRICK
by James Chambers (illustration by Travis Ingram) 77

THE DOOM THAT CAME TO NECROPOLIS
by Steve Johnson (illustration by Travis Ingram) 81

MEAT
by Adam P. Knave (illustration by Travis Ingram) 97

TINY DOLL-FACE
by Mattie Brahen (illustration by Travis Ingram) 105

Fantasy

AUTUMN OF IMMORTALITY
poem by Jeff Lyman (illustration by Ruth Lampi) 108

THE KINDRED
by John C. Wright (illustration by Ruth Lampi) 111

TO THE BEAST
by C.J. Henderson (illustration by Erica Henderson) 119

SWEET LIAM ROANES
by Danielle Ackley-McPhail (illustration by Ruth Lampi) 132

THE GIFT
by Melanie Florence (illustration by Edward J. Reed) 133

HOLLOW GROUND
by Danielle Ackley-McPhail (illustration by Edward J. Reed) 141

WHERE EAGLES CRY
by Patti Kinlock (illustration by Theo Black) 146

THE POPPET
by L. Jagi Lamplighter (illustration by Ruth Lampi) 147

PREMONITIONS
by Dan Foley (illustration by Adam Gillespie) 155

DESERT NIGHT
by Patti Kinlock (illustration by Ruth Lampi) 162

FRANKIE'S WISH
by M.J. Harris (illustration by Kirsten Edwards) 163

Science Fiction

SELF-REFLECTION
by Danielle Ackley-McPhail (illustration by Ruth Lampi) 173

FATHER'S MONUMENT
by John C. Wright (illustration by Kirsten Edwards) 175

CHIMERA
by Mike McPhail (illustration by Travis Ingram) 187

WEZLESKI TO THE RESCUE
by C.J. Henderson (illustration by Erica Henderson) 199

ADRIFT IN THE MAELSTROM
by Will McDermott (illustration by Travis Ingram) 209

LAW OF THE KUZZI
by James Chambers (illustration by Ruth Lampi) 223

NOT BORN A MAN
by John C. Wright (illustration by Ruth Lampi) 243

ACKNOWLEDGEMENTS

No Longer Dreams, by Danielle Ackley-McPhail previously printed in *Children of Morpheus*, a collection of poetry and short fiction published by Lite Circle Books. It also appears on-line at Darkwalls.com.

Kvetchula, by Darrell Schweitzer originally published in *Marion Zimmer Bradley's Fantasy Magazine* #36, Summer 1997. Copyright ©1997 by Marion Zimmer Bradley Living Trust. Reprinted by arrangement with the author.

Weekend at Pocono Mountain, by Robin Buehler previously printed as *Weekend at Pocono Manor* in *Sacred Twilight*, published by Selorian Press. It also appeared online at both Darkwalls.com and GothicReview.com.

Little Doll-Face, by Mattie Brahen originally published in *Fantastic, Stories of the Imagination*, formerly *Pirate Writings*, No. 19, Spring 2000.

To the Beast, by C.J. Henderson originally published in *Pegasus Magazine*, 1982.

Premonitions, by Dan Foley originally published in *Nocturne Magazine* issue 1.5, March 2005, United Kingdom, Lighthouse Media One.

Wezleski to the Rescue, by C.J. Henderson originally published in *The Nth Degree Magazine*, June 2003, issue 6.

Not Born a Man, by John C. Wright previously published in *Aberrations*, Issue 25, 1994.

POETS' AND ARTISTS' BIOS

PATTI KINLOCK'S poetry has appeared in *The Baltimore Sun, Dreams of Decadence,* the anthologies *Lower Than the Angels* and *Through a Glass Darkly* (Lite Circle Books) and other literary publications.

TONY RUGGIERO'S science fiction, fantasy, and horror stories and novels have appeare in both print and electronic mediums. His published novels include *Team of Darkness, The Min Trilogy* (*Get Out of My Mind, Mind Trap,* and *Innocence of the Mind*), and *Aliens and Satani Creatures Wanted: Humans Need Not Apply.*

THEO BLACK attends the masters program at the School of Visual Arts. His work ha been used by Maverick Ltd., White Wolf, and Dragon Moon Press.

KIRSTEN EDWARDS is a librarian, writer (*Teen Library Events, A Core Collection for Youn Adults*) and illustrator. She lives with her husband, daughter and dogs at Foxholt in Washingto State's Snoqualmie River Valley.

JESSE FOLEY lives in Meriden, CT. She attended Paire School of Art, in Hamben, CT Her dream is to illustrate childrens books, as well as her father's tales.

ADAM GILLESPIE lives in Portland, Oregon. He has worked as an illustrator wit *Night Light Graphics* for over ten years. You can always find more of his work www.nightlightgraphics.com.

ERICA HENDERSON is and art student and the illustrator of *Baby's First Mythos*, project she co-created with her father, C.J. Henderson.

The creative mind behind www.projectzero.net, TRAVIS INGRAM has been drawing mo of his life. He has done illustration work for various comics, publications and gan ing companies.

RUTH LAMPI is a BFA student at Moore College of Art and Design. To find out mo about her work, visit www.thefivewits.net.

EDWARD J. REED is an artist who teaches portrait and figure painting at The Art Leag School in the Torpedo Factory in Alexandria, Virginia. He moonlights as a freelance fanta horror, and science-fiction illustrator.

HORROR

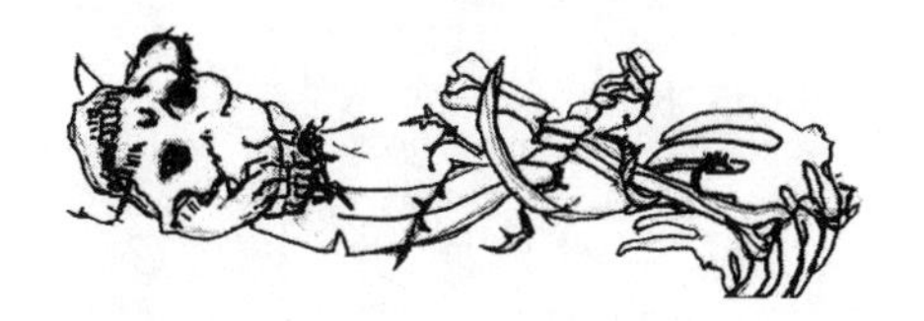

NO LONGER DREAMS

Danielle Ackley-McPhail

In my troubled sleep I thrash—
sweat-soaked blankets and I entwine.
At my throat claws ragged breath,
and deep and low, in fear I whine.

Wisps of fog obscure my view
and twist my thoughts with every breath.
Hurry on without a chance!
It matters not—there is no path.

The Whisperer, keeping pace,
does not relent but lengthens stride,
Sounds the cry that chills my blood,
which echoes 'round from every side.

Cannot tell from where he'll strike
It is a game he loves to play—
Tracks me by my stench of fear,
draws close to taunt, then falls away.

Waking from my tortured sleep,
relieved for now (the hunt is done),
Stretching muscles tense with fright,
and wearily I greet the sun.

Yet too soon have I relaxed—
I open eyes and choke on screams.
There before me, staring back
The Whisperer—No longer dreams.

FAT TUESDAY

Dan Foley

MARDI GRAS. FAT TUESDAY. THE QUARTER WAS PACKED, WALL TO WALL people from Canal Street to Jackson Square. Most of them were drunk or well on their way to getting there. Not Jean-Paul though; he was working. Pretty soon, some college girl would lift her top, show her tits to the cheering throng, and, depending on how drunk she was, some lucky guy or gal might get a free feel. Then he would be in business. When the inevitable hooting and whistling started, Jean-Paul darted in, slipped the mark's wallet out of his pocket, and disappeared back into the crowd.

Jean-Paul was the best pickpocket in New Orleans. He was a small man: five-feet, three inches tall and a hundred and thirty pounds dripping wet. His size, or lack thereof, was an added benefit in the streets of the Quarter. He could dart through a crowd like a mouse through a maze on the rare occasions that warranted it. Usually it happened when he was ducking a cop or someone else he didn't want to encounter.

Jean-Paul considered himself more than just a pickpocket. He thought himself as much a part of the New Orleans experience as the street performers and artists in Jackson Square, or coffee and biegnets at Café Du Monde. Something the tourists could tell their friends about when they got home.

"I never felt a thing! One minute my wallet was in my pocket, and the next time I looked for it, it was gone. I didn't lose it, someone must have stolen it."

He was a legend in the Quarter, but he never hit the locals. He had two reasons. First, many of them knew who he was. Second, since they knew they were immune to his touch, they considered him one of their own, part of the Quarter's extended family, sheltered under a communal umbrella of mutual protection and respect.

He worked the entire city of course—the Super Dome, the busses, the airport occasionally—but he loved the Quarter. From its plant-festooned, wrought-iron balconies to its seamy strip clubs, the Quarter was his universe. He left it reluctantly, and felt like he was returning to a lover when he came back.

Jean-Paul hadn't even extracted the cash and credit cards from his latest score when he picked his next mark out of the crowd. The guy didn't look like a tourist, but he was too good to pass up. He was an ancient looking, tall, thin black man dressed in an old-time white suit that made him look like a black Mark Twain.

He watched as the old dude took a cigar from his breast pocket, reached into the voluminous (to Jean-Paul) side pocket of the coat and withdrew, first, a very thick money clip, and then a jewel encrusted lighter. After lighting the cigar, both went back into the pocket.

This is going to be too easy, Jean-Paul thought as he approached the man. Hell, with a pocket that big he could probably climb in, pick out what he wanted and stroll back out like bargain hunter at a flea market. He'd just get close to the guy, wait for someone in the crowd to bump into him, and then take care of the rest.

He followed the old man through the crowd, staying just a few steps behind his right shoulder, waiting for an opportunity to strike. With the size of the crowd, and the way people were packed in shoulder to shoulder, it shouldn't have been a problem, but the masses seemed to part for the old man like he was Moses leading the Jews out of Egypt. Then suddenly, the man stopped and looked off at someone to his left who was throwing party beads from a wrought-iron balcony above the street.

Jean-Paul seized the opportunity. He walked calmly past the old man, dipped his left hand into the cavernous right pocket...and something bit him!

Being the pro that he was, Jean-Paul did not yell or jerk his hand away from the mark. Instead, he quickly but smoothly extracted his hand from the pocket. He glanced down as he did so and saw two small, red eyes staring back at him.

Jean-Paul's middle finger was stinging like it was on fire—as if the mother of all wasps had stung him. Two tiny drops of blood glistened at its tip. Instinctively he stuck the finger in his mouth to ease the pain. As quick as it went in, it came back out even faster. It tasted like acid and burned his tongue. He wanted to spit but couldn't afford the attention that would attract.

Before he could retreat into the crowd, the old man turned to face him. Jean-Paul looked into the man's eyes and froze. They were so pale it appeared they had rolled back into his head. When the man grinned at him, he felt as if he were about to be eaten, devoured in the middle of Bourbon Street. And then it passed. The man blinked and his eyes were dark brown. His smile faded and he stared past Jean-Paul into the crowd, his attention elsewhere. Freed from the man's gaze, and his own paralysis, Jean-Paul slipped into the refuge of teeming bodies that was Mardi Gras.

Shaken by the encounter, Jean-Paul sought the solitude of the river. It wasn't until he was sitting on its banks, staring across the muddy, swirling water that he realized exactly who the black man in the Mark Twain suit must have been—Old Mose, the voodoo priest, another legend of the Quarter. Jean-Paul had never seen the man, had always thought he was a myth. But who else could it be? Who else would carry something in his pocket that would bite—something with red eyes?

The mark was a fool; a big, hulking, football-player type with baggy pants Jean-Paul could have lived in without the guy knowing it. To Jean-Paul, the pick was routine: wait for the right opportunity, hand into the pocket, get the goods, hand out of the pocket, disappear. Like an athlete or a musician, it was all touch, timing, and muscle memory. He could do it in his sleep. But this time one of the muscles forgot what it was supposed to do. One of them changed the routine. On its way out of the marks pocket the middle finger reached out and snagged the material of his pants. That's when all hell broke loose.

Jean-Paul never felt the finger move, never knew anything was wrong until his hand stopped moving and he was tugging on the mark's pants. The guy, drunk as he

was, took a minute to realize what was happening, but when he did he reacted it was with brutish predictability.

"What the fuck are you doing?" the giant roared as Jean-Paul frantically tried to get his hand out of its unexpected prison.

Panicked, he wrenched his hand away, felt fabric rip, and fled into the street with the brute staggering behind him, trying to push his way through the crowd. He had no trouble losing the man, but his heart was in his throat and his confidence shattered. His hand, the pride of his life and the source of his fortune, had betrayed him.

Sitting on a bench on the river-walk, Jean-Paul stared at the traitor and wondered what the hell was going on. A piece of the mark's pocket was still trapped in his hand, held captive between the middle finger and the palm of his left hand. And, try as he might, he couldn't get the finger to release it. He finally wound up tearing it free with his right hand, almost breaking the rebel on the left in the process.

Jean-Paul tried everything short of cutting his finger off to get the thing to relax or straighten out. Then, as if defying him, the digit unfolded itself and lay limp between its brothers. Jean-Paul then flexed his hand, and the other fingers responded, but not the middle finger. It stayed extended, giving him the 'fuck you' salute he had used to flip off so many others in the past.

Bewildered, scared, and shaking with uncertainty, Jean-Paul took the unresponsive digit between the thumb and forefinger of his right hand and examined it in minute detail. Even then he almost missed the two black dots at its tip.

What the hell? he thought, and then remembered the two bright-red eyes that had stared out at him from the old man's pocket two days ago.

Jean-Paul first noticed the discoloration at five o'clock. By midnight the entire tip of his finger was black and the discoloration was spreading toward his hand. Most of the finger was already dark gray and it was a sick, ashen shade where it joined the palm.

Worse than the color, to Jean-Paul's mind, was the lack of control he had over the thing. It completely ignored his attempts to do anything with it. Instead, it twitched and wiggled as if it had a mind of its own.

Jean-Paul, awake from his whisky-induced stupor, slumped over the table, resting his face in a puddle of Jack Daniels. "*Merde*," he swore, trying to remember where he was, when he realized his hand was moving across the table toward his face. He couldn't feel it as it inched its way toward him, 'walking' on its fingertips like some weird yellow pages add, and that made it all the more frightening.

Almost as if it knew he was awake, the hand stopped where it was, and Jean-Paul doubted what he had seen. It couldn't really be moving on its own, could it?

In answer to his unspoken question, the hand finger-walked another six inches toward his face, leaving it a scant two inches from his eyes. Jean-Paul jumped up from the table, but he couldn't flee the hand that now hung at his side, clenching and unclenching itself into a fist.

"*Merde!*" he swore again and paced the room, as if by walking he could get away from the damn thing. Eventually his pacing brought him to the balcony that overlooked Barracks Street. Jean-Paul stood outside, listening to the crowd noise coming from Bourbon. He was breathing in great gulps of night air, trying to calm himself, when he saw the lone figure standing in the street below him. In the dark it appeared to be just another shadow until it moved.

Jean-Paul froze. He had no idea who it might be. But whoever it was, he sent chills up Jean-Paul's spine and he didn't want to be seen by him. They stood like that in the dark, neither of them moving, as if waiting for something to happen. And then the figure tilted its head upward and Jean-Paul stared into a pair of pale, white, eyes that seemed to glow in the dark.

It was Mose, the old man from Bourbon Street. Once again Jean-Paul remembered looking into the pocket with its bright red eyes. Jean-Paul tried to slip silently back into his room, but his left hand was clutching the balcony rail in an iron grip.

He didn't remember grabbing the rail and now he couldn't break his hold on it. The hand, now blacker than the night, was invisible in the dark and his arm seemed to disappear at the wrist. He was trying to pry the hand loose with his good right hand when a deep, evil-sounding chuckle drifted up to him from the street.

"Dat hand ain't yours no more, Mister. Dat hand be mine. You tink you can steal from old Mose? Well, old Mose gwan steal from you. Old Mose gwan steal your mind."

Jean-Paul's heart leapt into his throat when he heard the old man's threat.

"See dis?" the voice said, and Mose raised his clenched fist in front of his face and shook it at him. In answer, Jean-Paul's hand shook the rail of the balcony so fiercely he feared it might rip it from its foundations.

Jean-Paul stood at the balcony rail looking down at the man, trying to take it all in, not wanting to believe what was happening to him.

"Now watch dis," Mose said, and spread his hand wide, splaying the fingers for Jean-Paul to see. Immediately his hand responded to the man's unspoken command, mimicking the motion.

With his hand waving to the sky, Jean-Paul stumbled backward into his apartment, chased by the unnatural laughter coming from the street below.

"I be back for you later, Man," the voice promised, and then silence claimed the night.

Sunrise found Jean-Paul sitting at his kitchen table, nursing the last of his Jack Daniels. And even though he couldn't feel the hand at all, he quailed at the pain he knew was coming. Assembled on the table before him, all within reach of his right hand, was a leather belt, the empty Jack Daniels bottle, a very sharp filleting knife, a hammer, and a dozen rusty nails he had found in the back of a kitchen drawer.

Jean-Paul looked at his once beautiful hand, the hand he relied on for his livelihood, and knew it would have to come off. He just had to stop crying long enough to do what had to be done. Finally, steeling his resolve, he wiped away tears born of anger, frustration, and depression, picked up one of the nails and rammed it through his hand like a dagger. Then he grabbed the hammer and struck at the nail until he almost drove it all the way through his palm. Fresh tears flooded his eyes when he realized he hadn't felt any of it. Not the nail or the blows that had surely broken most of the bones in his hand.

Jean-Paul hammered three more nails through his palm before he managed to work up the nerve to pick up the knife. On his first try, all he managed was a shallow scratch on the inside of his wrist that didn't even bleed.

"Do it, you fucking pussy," he told himself, trying to work up his courage.

His next attempt was the real thing. The knife cut deep into his wrist, severing veins and tendons. Jean-Paul pulled it toward himself and felt it drag across the bones. Too late he remembered the belt he had intended to use as a tourniquet. He had never wrapped it around his arm! It was still lying useless on the table, and now he had no way to stop the bleeding. Then he realized he didn't need it—not for this cut anyway, the wound wasn't bleeding. It was halfway through his wrist all right, but it was like he had cut through a dried-out corpse. What fluid did leak from it was a dark brown, muddy ooze.

"Oh *merde*," he moaned, and dropped the knife on the table. He glanced longingly at the empty bottle of Jack Daniels as he reached for the belt. He fumbled with it, but managed to get it fastened around his arm and snug it tight just beneath his shoulder.

When he picked up the knife this time he attacked his arm at the elbow. This he felt, and if the belt hadn't been in place an ocean of blood would have erupted from the wound.

New tears streaming from his eyes, Jean-Paul hacked and sliced his way through the joint. Then, without a backward glance at his severed hand and forearm, he staggered from the room and down toward the street.

Jean-Paul awoke to the sounds of a hospital ward. A television set tuned to a soap opera blared from somewhere and call bells dinged in a vain attempt to summon one of the overworked nursing staff. He had no idea why he was there, but gradually, memories from the previous night crept into his mind like sewage from an overflowing septic system. The blackened hand, the old man, the pain. The pain! He could still feel the pain. His hand was on fire. It was still there!

With fear and hope tearing at his emotions, Jean-Paul raised his left hand in front of his eyes. And, even though the pain was very real, his bandaged arm ended at the elbow. Looking at the bandaged stump, Jean-Paul was overwhelmed by a flood of emotions, relief, regret, rage, helplessness, self-pity, and a dozen others he couldn't identify if he tried.

He was rescued from his mental turmoil when a nurse came into the room to check on him.

"Oh, you're awake," she said when she saw him staring at his ravaged arm.

Jean-Paul started to answer, but his tongue moved like a stranger in his mouth; he couldn't make it form the words. And then, without intending to, he started laughing.

Maybe it's the drugs, he thought.

Then, as the raucous laughter continued out of his control, Jean-Paul remembered sucking on his finger and the burning taste of acid on his tongue.

Dan Foley lives in Connecticut with his wife Tere. Dan has worn many hats in professional life, including Sailor, Licensed Senior Reactor Operator, Nuclear Operations Consultant, and more recently, an Insurance Agent. Dan started writing late in life, publishing his first short story at the age of fifty-seven.

Dan has three daughters, all of whom enjoy a good horror tale. His four grandchildren are not old enough to read his stories yet.

RECENT PUBLICATIONS:

It's In The Bag, Cyber-Pulp's Second Annual Halloween Anthology
Talking To Robert, Be Mine Anthology, February 5, 2004.
Friends, Maelstrom 1 Anthology, Lighthouse Media One, September 27, 2004.
The Sixth Victim, Dark Notes From NJ, March, 2005
Premenitions, Nocturne Magazine issue 1.5, March 2005, United Kingdom, Lighthouse Media One.

FERAL

Jeff Lyman

The moon summons me up
from the dust of my father
and the rattling wind of my
mother's voice.

So full tonight so I
can see the way home.
Sunlight has eluded me.
A long time gone. I hurt.

Arthritis hurt, and the deep
ache of flu. It's warm.
That's something. Sometimes
when the hurt comes, I shiver.

My homeward journey is made
by feel, and curious scent.
The way may bleed moonshadows,
but I can smell the imprint of hooves.

The scent is old and the trees
are taller than I remember.
I have been away for three
lifetimes, with the moon for a wife.

The pain deepens now to
bone rattling cramps. My legs
shorten because they have to.
I lie down. It's better lying down.

Jerking and panting in ripple
moonlight, I want this moment to end.
Moments never do. They can be
like lives: long and uncomfortable.

So I run on all fours, tail
behind like my standard.
Nose pointed and ears up.
It's not enough. Pain follows.

Until I'm too animal to think.
Then it stops.

KVETCHULA

Darrell Schweitzer

RUTH," MY GRANDMOTHER ESTHER ONCE EXPLAINED TO ME, "THERE'S NO helping it. You're a born *kvetch*. A *kvetch* is a complainer, a person who complains and complains all the day long and all through the night, because *kvetches*, they don't have peaceful dreams. A *kvetch* can't stop *kvetching* no more than they can get rid of the damp when it rains and soaks everybody to the skin. The *kvetch* just *kvetches* about being wet; then she sneezes, and then *kvetches* about sneezing, because a *kvetch kvetches* plain and simple. The woid is both a noun and a voib, depending on where you put it."

Grandmother Esther said "woid" and "voib" 'cause she's is not sophisticated like me, though she did go to school.

So I am a *kvetch*. The world needs its *kvetches*, or else why would God make so many of them? A dirty job, but somebody's got to do it.

I tell you, it keeps me constantly busy.

There's my husband Morris, whom I married out of pity, and that's the truth, because he needed looking after so badly. *Every* moment of the day he keeps me hopping.

"Morris, your spectacles are on top of your head, so stop tearing the place apart," I have to tell him, and "Morris, did you change your shorts?" (and this *in front of people* sometimes, but I've got to remind him), and also "Morris, stop wearing those *awful* ties!"

The ties are the worst part. I don't know where he gets them. It's no use if I throw them out, because he always gets more. I swear they've got a whole department of devils in Hell just working full time to keep my husband supplied with ties, for the sole purpose of trying the patience of Ruth Leibowitz.

And my patience has its limit, to tell you the truth.

The glaring, puke-green silk one, that one I can live with, or the day-glo pink one with the eyeball, even the one with the hula-girl under the palm tree, and I refuse to take seriously the plain white one he wears with a black shirt so he looks like some Mafia don. But his warped idea of class is going to our fancy 20-year high school reunion banquet showing off a tie with a picnic-table pattern that's got *enormous ants all over it!* With that one, he goes too far. That one I took to the office and fed into the shredder, but it did me no good, he has more of them. Maybe they grow in his closet. I swear he wears them just to torment me, such an ungrateful man.

Then there are the vampires. Morris, he's partial to wolf-men and mummies and Frankensteins like he is still a little boy, but he is really loves are these vampires, especially the young and sexy ones he watches over and over again on our VCR. Every vampire movie ever made, my Morris he's got them all, and he sits all day and watches them when he should be mowing the lawn or changing his shorts or *something*.

Once, just to make a joke, I ask him if he's ever seen *Mein Yiddishe Dracula*, and he doesn't blink, and starts rummaging among his Mount Everest pile of tapes and says, "I think it's in here somewhere, Honey Love."

My Morris, he's totally nuts about vampires and such.

So I'm not surprised—but this is not to say I'm not appalled—when he says, "Honey Love, guess where we're going for vacation. To Transylvania. I've saved up. I've already bought the tickets. So we're going on the Deluxe Vampire Tour." And then he adds, "There's no refunds."

You could hear my jaw drop in Brooklyn. We live nowhere near Brooklyn.

Morris, he's all smiles, like some kid who's got an "A" on his report card or something. He's even gone and bought a new tie for the occasion. It's all black with a glow-in-the-dark bat with motorized wings that really flap. He's particularly proud of that.

And the noise it makes. Whir . . . flap, flap. Oy!

Kvetch? Maybe you think I should celebrate?

So the summer arrives and off we go to the airport with Morris wearing his stupid tie, which delays us because its tiny motor makes the security machines bleep, and the guards look at Morris like he's a mad bomber with an exploding tie, but finally we get through, and he babbles all the way about Vlad the Impaler, who was not a nice man at all, and *nosferatu*, a word which could never fit into the crossword puzzle I'm doing to occupy myself with and hide my embarrassment.

Then we're in Bucharest and everything gets much worse. Our tour group is forming up, and now there's a whole busload of people just like Morris. They jabber and jabber things like, "Listen to them, the children of the night, such beautiful music they make," but I don't hear no music, and I don't care, it's so awful, because everyone one of them is wearing that same damn tie!

Now I have to admit those mountains are pretty, the Balkans or Carpets or whatever they are. (*"Carpathians,"* Morris whispers in a tone like it's some crime to make a little mistake in geography, even if I did graduate almost thirty years ago and how many of these Romanians know *their* way around *Jersey City?*)

So they've got nice mountains. Almost like the Catskills.

But the tour, it's not so nice. Their buses are always late and you can't find a decent bathroom, and the food is, to talk like Morris for a minute, an unspeakable blasphemy of indescribable horror, which is a pretty accurate description.

So there they are, all these middle-aged Children of the Night—that's the name of the fan club, I finally discover—all of them wearing those awful ties, with only me to take care of them, such other such wives as are dumb enough to come being as wacked-out as their husbands, some of them actually wearing flapping bats in their hair, which is something, I swear to you, you will never see Ruth Leibowitz ever do. We traipse all over these Carpathians, go into this crypt and out of that vault, and we listen while long-winded tour guides lecture us as we stand around one more pile of rocks. The guide keeps going on about how only goodness can stop a vampire, like waving crosses and all, so finally I can't stand it any longer. I ask him a historically challenging question.

"Well, what did you Commies do, wave a hammer and sickle at them?"

You see, I know this guide works for the government and since he's not a kid, I know he's been doing this for years, that makes him a Commie.

And Morris he looks like he's just swallowed a live poodle, and everybody else turns away and groans, with their little plastic bats fluttering like sick birds with no feathers.

The guide, he says in a low, nasty voice, all the time pretending to be polite, "Madame, I assure you, there are ways."

Like the bad guys say in the movies, "Ve haf *vays* to make you talk."

Right now I want him not to talk, but to shut up.

Morris yanks me away and whispers, real mortified like, "What do you think *we* do? Draw a Star of David on the vampire's forehead with a magic marker?"

Which is probably an interesting question, but just then I don't feel much like being interested.

That same night at Castle Bran we're all gathered in the floodlit courtyard for some kind of theatrical number. "Do they really make bran flakes here?" I kid Morris, who has no sense of humor. Then I notice him noticing that *other woman*, the pale and slinky one with the long black dress and awful black fingernails, and he notices me noticing him noticing—here I am looking out for his best interests, as if he could see something in a creature like that—and his expression is downright defiant, like he's been this whole trip. So I decide to give the both of them a piece of my mind, but then *she* notices all this noticing, and our eyes meet, and her look I can't describe. Cold. Empty. Those huge dark eyes of hers look like two subway tunnels that stretch all the way down to nowhere and you know there's never going to be any train coming on those tracks, because they closed the station down before Moses parted the Red Sea. Only the tunnels are somehow evil and sucking me in.

They give me goosebumps, those eyes, so I jerk away and look at something else, and don't say anything to Morris for a while.

About midnight, in our crummy hotel, Morris gets up to go to the bathroom—For God's sake there isn't even a bathroom in the room, it's down the hall, it looks like some 14th-century dungeon maybe!—and he's gone so long that when he comes back, I say half-asleep, "Did you fall in?"

Right then and there he starts making love to me. I say, "Not now, I'm tired," but that doesn't stop him, and *Oh my God!* he hasn't been like that in years, and it's so ridiculous, fat, balding Morris in his glow-in-the-dark bat pajamas all over me, just *exploding* with passion like he's a Don Juan or something, and *Oh!* he's *never* been like this, and I say, "Morris, what's come over you?" and I could almost get to like it, he's such a changed man. Except for the pajamas, I might have thought he was some other man snuck into my bed!

But then I come fully awake, and I say, "Morris! Your hands are so *cold!*" but he doesn't say anything. He just bites me on the neck and I shriek and sit up with Morris hanging onto me like some enormous tick, and switch on the light and see myself in the mirror and there I am all wild-eyed, with *blood* on my neck, but there's no reflection of Morris at all. He and his pajamas have both turned invisible. And, as I watch, I seem to turn invisible too.

Then I wake up in a coffin, but that's not the worst of it, because now I'm in the *real* 14th-century dungeon that's just below the bathroom and it's muddy and my nightgown is ruined, and they've buried me with my curlers half falling out—which would mortify me, if I weren't already dead. Me, such a neatnik, laid out with curlers in my hair!

So now we're vampires, Morris explains, and I think he has made me a vampire too because he can't live without me, even if he is dead. So we wander around the hotel a bit we jump on one of the bellboys and drink his blood—which doesn't taste *good*, but I've had worse to eat on this tour—and then a clerk comes and taps us on the shoulders and says we have to go down into the dungeon for the Vampire Orientation Course, because they've got a lot of forms to signed and fill out, and we fill them out. The Vampire Welcoming Committee finally gives us new ID's, but you have to stare at the photo cross-eyed for a long time do you see anything, like one of those holographic pictures.

Most of the people from the tour are there, and the bellboy, and the guides, and then that slinky woman comes up and tells us what we *have to do*. She thinks she's some important vampire; her name is something weird Zora or Gavora or something. We have *responsibilities* she tells us. Vampires secretly run the world, undead hands hold the levers of power, she says. We are in charge. We've been in charge for a long time. When the Archduke Ferdinand got killed in Sarajevo, she explains, there was one story put out in the newspapers, but *we actually did it*. In fact, Miss Slinko, Zora or whatever the smug bitch's name is, hints she killed him personally.

Now she brings on this whiskery old duffer in a band costume who says he's the Archduke, and he tells how it was, having some trouble being understood what with his whiskers and his long teeth and his accent. I want to ask him if he really is the long-lost missing link between Colonel Sanders and Santa Claus, but I do not.

Miss Slinko continues the lecture. As for the Commies, she explains, nodding to me, they weren't a problem, because Ceaucescu was one of us, and when they showed him dead on television he wasn't just shot, he had a stake through his heart, just outside of the frame of the picture.

So off we go across Europe, me and Morris and the rest of the Vampire Graduating Class of '96, with our coffins loaded on trucks and driven by drunken Gypsies who seem to find the bumpiest roads they can exceed the speed limit over,

but when I complain Slinko says they've been in the hauling vampires almost as long as she's been slinking. ("But you don't look a day over five hundred," I assure her.)

Every night we go out and bite people, it's our job, and if we drain all their blood they become vampires too, otherwise they wake up in the morning with a worse hickie than my cousin Alma's teenage daughter after a date. Then they *really* have something to *kvetch* about.

Me, I still care about the company I keep. Some people I won't let Morris drain entirely because I wouldn't have them sharing the same truck with me, yak-yak-yakking in their coffins. One *yenta* is enough.

Still, Morris is having the time of his life, if I may use that expression. Such an exhibitionist. He even got himself a black cape, a white vest, and a medallion, the whole nine yards, and he likes to go swirling off into the night where I can't look after him. He prefers the showy entrances, oozing into someone's room under the door as a mist, or flapping at their window until the victim lets him in. I'm ashamed to say he's *particularly* fond of looming over ladies in their beds with those glowing eyes of his, making all sorts of funny gestures before he drops down and covers them up with his cape.

But worst part is he still sleeps in those bat pajamas, in his coffin next to mine.

And, just to torment me, he still wears those ties, even if they don't go well with the rest of his outfit. He wears them with his pajamas too. The man is still ungrateful after all I've done for him.

Plus, I've got good reason to envy Miss Slinko with her the sexy shape, because for all I'm a vampire too, this doesn't make me *svelte*; I am stuck through all eternity with a *zaftig* figure no fat farm can save me from now. And I still have to spend hours with my make-up—you just try putting it on when you can't see yourself in a mirror. Then it's work, work, work, sidling up to frumpy tourists, pretending to ask directions as I get out a map and lead them aside, ignoring their saying, "Lady, what good is a map of Bucharest? This is Paris." Or it is Rome or Vienna or London. Before they can figure it out, *chomp*, I get rather attached to them.

You know, most people's blood tastes like weak, badly-curdled borscht. The other vampires agree, but nobody knows how to improve it. When I suggest maybe we should popularize some kind of flavored food-additive for the living, Morris cocks his eyebrow, swirls his cape, and runs off with the Children of the Night to make beautiful music. Actually he can't carry a tune in a bucket.

Work, work. We certainly get around. It is a little-known fact that when certain prominent people die, who are already vampires, or about to be vampires, we already-vampires have to dig them up for the first time, to show them around. Morris and I get drafted onto the Exhumation Detail. We dig up Mitterand, and then Andropov, who got forgotten for a few years because of politics, and we welcome them to the club. Nixon too, and Mrs. Thatcher, even though she isn't dead yet, she just fits in so perfectly.

Still, we mostly make tourists into vampires, me with my very tattered map of Bucharest, all of us bumping around and around in cheap wooden coffins with no conveniences. We have to listen to stale Gypsy jokes more than once, while the trucks break down more often than not. Once in Bulgaria we're all off-loaded and on our way to the trash-compactor before fortunately the sun goes down and I am able to take matters in hand. Afterwards, we spend the whole night scrounging up an additional truckload of coffins for all the Bulgarian officials that needed convincing.

In short, for all that my husband may think this is a fine way for a grown-up dead man to occupy himself, *I* can certainly see room for improvement.

For one thing, Morris doesn't call me Honey Love anymore, and I miss that.

So, when I finally can't stand it anymore, I grab Morris by the scruff of his cape and say, "Look, we're going to *complain* to whoever's in charge here," and when he's horrified and says, "But you *can't!*", I tell him I certainly can. I will speak to the boss. My mind is made up.

"You mean to Count Dracula himself?"

"Is that who the boss is? Then he's getting a piece of my mind."

Oh, he flusters and he flutters and he gnashes those big fangs of his, but Morris was never a match for me when my mind's made up. So, just before dawn, as all the other vampires are going beddy-bye and the sun will come shining up within minutes, Morris and I drag our coffins away from the others, and just in the nick of time hypnotize two Gypsies, who steal a nearby crumbling Volkswagon minibus left over from the '60s—it's got purple flowers all over it, in fading, peeling paint—and load us into it. Off we go, faster than ever, over even bumpier roads than before, all the while thanking God or maybe someone else that the bus doesn't break down and that I don't have to convince too many officials to let us pass.

Deeper and deeper into the wild Carpathians our Gypsies drive us as we slide around inside our splintery coffins, and more than once I have to bang on the lid to yell, "Hey! Slow down! You trying to kill us?" Which is funny, because we are already dead, but the Gypsies can't hear us and go on telling their own tired jokes. When they don't know which way to turn, I have to get out of my coffin and tell them that too, because we vampires have a fine sense of direction, but it is a miracle we ever get anywhere.

Naturally, Morris is having a wonderful time. Each night, we pull off to the side of the road, and while the Gypsies snooze in the trance I put them in, Morris and I go terrorize the countryside. Wolves howl all around us and sometimes come up to us as friendly as my brother Max's German Shepherd, to lick my hands, but I have to stop them from ruining my nails.

Now the Gypsies are afraid, and even *I'm* getting the creeps as we drive across empty landscape, wolves howling like a chorus out of Hell, blue lights flickering in the dark forests, the Carpathians rising up and up around us, all black and jagged. Morris points out this or that place from the tour, but even he doesn't seem to care any longer.

We're all solemn as we pull into the courtyard of Castle Dracula. Even the wolves are silent, streaming around us like a dark tide, filling the courtyard, wriggling into the castle through countless holes and crevices—I mean this place is a *ruin.*

Haven't these big-time vampires any pride?

Morris and I climb out of our coffins, and we speak to the wolves in their own language. We tell them to leave our Gypsies alone for now, and we go inside.

The enormous doors swing open all by themselves, and more wolves run in. I'm sure they'd ruin the carpeting, if there was any. Overhead, bats swarm like a bunch of starlings. Outside, the wind howls, louder than the wolves ever did. Inside, it seems to *hum* in the rafters, like we're inside some huge pipe organ, and it really does give me the shivers, even if I am dead, and Morris is the wide-eyed tourist again, and all the big dope can say is, "Gosh, Honey Love, I always knew it would be like this."

I take him by the hand reassuringly, and say, "It's all right. I'm with you." And we walk through the cobwebs without breaking them, down into the castle's crypt.

But in the crypt it's very different: low ceilings, flickering electric lights, coffins wired for cable, and one of them open, with CNN going on a screen set into the lid. Newspapers everywhere, the *Times* of London, *The Wall Street Journal*, a bunch more, in Russian, Japanese, whatever, and finally, after we walk past rows and rows of filing cabinets, there, behind a desk covered with computers and phones and piles of paper, is the vampire king himself, Count Dracula, lord of the undead, once Voivode of Wallachia, called the Impaler, the perpetrator of so many horrors.

And I give him a piece of my mind, just like I came there to do, telling him *all* about Morris's ties and the smarmy tour guides and Miss Slinko's nails and the uncomfortable, cheap coffins, and the bumpy roads and how awful the Gypsies drive and how bad their jokes are, how I'm missing all my soap operas from having too sleep in the daytime, and *tired* I am of accosting tourists with that stupid map of Bucharest while my husband thinks he's in some old-time horror movie and —

The Count rises, his face contorted with rage.

I grab Morris by the bat-tie and yank him forward.

"Just look at this, will you?" I say to the Count. "Look what I have to put up with!"

"Madame," says the Count in a low, terrible voice, like the Crack of Doom heard through double-lined thick earmuffs, "I have *a great deal of evil to orchestrate in the world.* What makes you think that among all the legions of the damned I have time for *you?*"

Morris and I both stagger back from the awful power of his glare, but then I can't help myself. I've got to *laugh.* I mean, where is *the* Count Dracula, and is he wearing his medallion or even his cape? No, he's got on a plain white shirt like any office clerk, and his sleeves are rolled up and there's ink-stains on the pocket and he's got a pencil behind his ear. I am not sure, but maybe he wears bifocals. He's just haggard and his hairline is receding to a point, and he's no more impressive than Morris, really, only taller.

But Count Dracula is shaking and screaming and the whole castle seems about to come down around our ears, so before he can ask what is so funny, I tell him.

"I'm sorry . . . forgive me, but...*you don't look one bit like Bela Lugosi!*"

He screams some more. He is not listening.

I have to continue giving him pieces of my mind. The place is a mess. I pick up a bunch of papers. It is requisitions for coffins, from Russia in 1917. If he hasn't got them now, why bother, I want to know. Then there's the meeting of the Trilateral Commission he was supposed to be at, a letter from Henry Kissinger that didn't get answered in twenty-five years, and some famous rock star who was supposed to get bitten and didn't get bitten. So much work is not getting done. I start to straighten up. I tell him, "Look at you. You got ink-stains all over you. You don't brush your clothes. You can't be so sloppy. If you're going put your undead hands on the levers of the world, you got to wash them first. I'm telling you. I don't know how you ever got along before I arrived. You need someone like me around here to manage things."

That's it. *That's the end.*

I *think* the very last thing I hear is Morris burbling, "Gee, Mr. Dracula, Count, Sir, can I have your autograph?" but I can't be sure because everything gets confusing after that.

The Count raises his arms and I *imagine* he's got on the black cape like you'd expect, and he's a huge, snarling bat with legs. Then his minions are all around him, minions of minions, a world monopoly on drooling hunchbacks, an excess of glow-in-the-dark dwarves, slinky, barefoot vampire wives wearing just *rags*, (the Count should be ashamed!) not to mention all those wolves, most of which are human; and they just *sweep* us straight out of Dracula's office, down, down into lower crypts, into the uttermost abysses in the Earth's bowels (as Morris would put it) and then we're in our coffins again, with the lids hammered down so we can't get out.

Of course they had to bring in the Gypsies to do the dirty work. Silver nails. Only the Gypsies could touch them.

Okay, so maybe I have *kvetched* once too often, but what else was I to do? When something isn't right, it isn't right.

Grandma Esther would understand if she were here. Now I lie in the dark, and the only way I can go anywhere is in my dreams, and in my dreams I search for Grandma Esther, to explain everything and ask her what I should do.

Morris lies beside me, not too happy right now, but he is trying to be brave, and he whispers, "Don't worry, Honey Love, maybe Grandma will come and let us out, or a hundred years will pass and the coffin wood will rot, or even the Count will forgive us if we are patient enough."

What can a vampire do under such circumstances, but be patient?

I know Morris is trying to help, and he even called me Honey Love, but still I can't forgive him. I know he's lying there, right beside me, still wearing one of his stupid ties.

DARRELL SCHWEITZER IS THE AUTHOR OF *THE MASK OF THE SORCERER*, *The Shattered Goddess*, *Tom O'Bedlam's Night Out* and others. He has been nominated for the World Fantasy Award three times and won it (shared with George Scithers) once, as editor of *Weird Tales* (now *World's of Fantasy & Horror*.)

WAITING IN THE GARDEN

Tony Ruggerio

The old man sat in his garden waiting.
His hand held onto a rose,
its thorns unable to pierce the skin.
His hands were worn and rough
from years of work in the unforgiving soil.

He sat there waiting,
his old, yet sharp eyes gazed upon the beauty
which had been cultivated with those hands,
all through the countless years of his life.

His garden was old as was he.
its age shown in gracefulness,
his age shown in frailty.
He sat there patiently waiting,
his visitor unknown, yet anticipated.

A soft breeze tickled at his skin,
and taunted the delicate petals
of the rose that he had picked.
The sun's warming effect dissipating
with the ending of the day,
leaving him cool and longing
for the warmth of life.

Darkness began to unfold itself
upon this part of the earth.
The soft breeze changed its demeanor,
insatiable and searching,
it swept over the area,
seeking for that in which it came.

The last petal detached and
floated from the rose,
plummeting downward.

Defiant to the wind that would
take it elsewhere,
it obediently landed
at the feet of the old man.

The wind departed,
leaving the lifeless hand
holding onto the bare stem.

THE QUARTERED MAN

Jeff Lyman

I WAS NINE AND MY COUSIN WAS ELEVEN THE FIRST TIME I SAW THE CROSSROADS. Father had ridden out to the trading camp a few days ahead of us while we waited for more pieces of tinker's ware from my uncle.

About halfway through the three-day ride, Jack brought his horse to a stop. I came up next to him. We were riding through countryside of sparse cottonwood trees, whispering grass, and rolling hills.

"Why'dja stop?" I asked him impatiently. Black birds croaked at us and the winter-bare branches of a nearby tree crackled in the breeze.

"You see that?" He pointed.

There was a crossroads about a hundred yards down the dusty lane. A stone cairn stood where the two roads met.

"The rock pile?"

"Um-hm. And you see that?" He pointed a little to the right.

I squinted, and noticed for the first time a detour around the crossroads. A track had been weathered into the dirt. It bowed south just enough to miss the cross, rejoining our road on the far side. It had seen a lot more use than the main cross.

Jack led his horse onto the detour and I followed.

"Why are we avoiding the crossroads?"

He shrugged. "I don't know. But when you see these detours, you take them."

I was silent for a moment. This was my first long trip outside of the village. Jack had been out dozens of times on trading runs with my father, so he knew things. But this crossroads detour seemed ridiculous. We were passing not ten feet from the crossing and the quiet stone cairn. "It's a pile of rocks," I said.

Jack brought his horse to a stop, and I clamped my mouth shut, fearing I had annoyed him. The sound of black birds replaced the sound of leather and hooves.

"We avoid it because the locals avoid it. They have a reason." He nodded at the cairn. "Most likely someone's buried there."

I felt a chill. "Why would they bury someone in the road?"

Jack leaned towards me and spoke low, like he does when he's trying to scare me. "Sometimes, if someone's been bad, they'll bury 'em head down to send 'em straight to Hell. But sometimes, when a fellah's been really bad, and folks suspect he's got a deal with the Devil, they don't want him going to Hell. He'll just come back up and cause trouble. So they cut him into four pieces and bury him at the four points of a crossroads. Then his ghost'll be too confused to know which way's Heaven and which way's Hell. And he cain't haunt nobody, because he cain't find his way back to town." Jack sat back up and nodded to the cairn. "His head's probably in there."

"And you believe that?" I asked, sneering as best I could, but it sounded weak. My heart beat a little faster when we kicked our horses and moved away from the crossing.

"If the local folks are gonna ruin a perfectly good crossroad," Jack said without turning to look back, "they must've had a reason."

"What happens if I touch it?" I asked, looking back at the cairn that still looked like an innocent heap of rocks.

"Your father told me the ghost is looking for someone to give it directions. If it can grab you and make you tell, it will. Or maybe it'll trick you into pointing out where the village is. Your father says it'll promise you the world too, but don't believe it."

I wanted to laugh, to show my older cousin I wasn't scared, but my throat was dry.

We met up with Father later and had a busy time at the trading camp by the river. I mostly kept my mind off the stone cairn while working, but at night, going to sleep under my blanket, I kept imagining spooks and haunts coming for me out of the long grasses of the hills. A lot of people were about because trader camps never really sleep, and twice I sat up wide-eyed when someone walked by with a horse or a dog. Then Father ordered me to go to sleep and I didn't dare sit up again.

We took a different way home two days later because Father wanted to pass through the villages up north. We still had some tin-ware, and he intended to sell it all. I was disappointed that we didn't see the crossroads again, but not too disappointed.

Jack and I came back through a number of times as the years passed, and we always rode around the crossroads. Then one day, when I was about twenty, I came through alone. Jack was already at the trader camp with his son, and I was joining him with a few more pieces Father had hammered out. Father's leg was bad, so he couldn't come with us anymore, but Jack and I had done this enough times that we haggled as well as he did. This he finally admitted, but he still hadn't allowed as our tin-ware was comparable to his or my uncle's.

I stopped my horse as I came to the top of the hill above the crossroads. The site looked gentler than when I was young. The cottonwoods were swelled large with green and the tall grass and wildflowers rolled with the breeze. The bypass around the crossroads was much more defined now. There were wheel ruts, and the grass had been worn away to twice the width of a cart. The cross itself was a diminishing scar of hardy weeds that had crept out onto the packed dirt. Eventually the prairie would take the crossing back, but not for some years.

I nudged my horse, Addie, down the hill, riding easily. I didn't believe the crossroads was haunted but wanted to prove it to myself. The ever-present blackbirds filled in the silence when I stopped. I swung down and left the horse standing placidly as I walked over the seldom-trodden earth to the cairn. I wondered if there was a skull in there. Who knew how these rumors started?

Praying quickly, and assuring myself that late morning in the bright sun was the very best time to confront ghosts, I lifted the top rock off the cairn. There was nothing below but the next layer of stones. I set the first rock on the ground, annoyed now at the hollowing whisper of the wind and the calling birds. I removed the next few stones, then the next few. And lifting off a large flat one, I stepped back in mild surprise to see the round, white top of something that certainly wasn't a rock. So there *was* a skull in there.

I pulled away the rock in front of the face to be confronted by a water-stained skull with rotten teeth. Water had collected in tiny puddles in the hollow eye sockets from last week's rains. There were broken vertebrae nestled below the skull. Who ever he was, they had chopped his head off.

Having eased my curiosity, I diligently replaced the stones around the dead man's head. I had set them on the ground in order, so I tried to pile them back in the same way. I set one stone down a little hard on the skull. I picked it up again quickly, but I hadn't broken the bone. As best as I could gauge, the rebuilt cairn looked as it always had, and no one the wiser.

Clapping my hands together to rid my gloves of dust, I turned back to my horse and stopped in surprise.

A middle-aged man stood next to my horse. He was dressed like a farmer, with a bushy beard like the local farmers wore. The skin of his face and hands was leathery from long hours in the sun, and he had a red bruise on his forehead. He was running his hand along my horse's side, saying softly, "Easy girl. Easy girl." I hadn't heard him come up. How had he walked all the way down the hill without me noticing?

"Mornin'," I said guardedly. It was likely he would take offense at my rock moving. It was equally likely it was his grave I had disturbed. Maybe that knot on his head was from my careless rebuilding.

"Mornin'," he returned amiably.

"I was just curious about this pile of rocks here," I said by way of explanation.

"That's okay," he said, continuing to run his hand along Addie's flank. She didn't seem bothered by him. "There's nothing to the stories anyway."

"That so?"

"Yeah. It's to scare the wee 'uns to make 'em do their chores."

"Somebody's head's in there, so it's not all stories."

"Somebody's head's in there, sure. But no ghost."

"Who's head?"

He shrugged. "I couldn't say. It's been here since afore I was born."

"Really?" I looked back down at the rocks. They sat quietly like they always had; only now I knew what they concealed. I could see the skull in my mind, under the rocks, looking up at me.

"Where you headed?" he asked.

I had been waiting for a question along these lines, and had been trying to think of an answer. If he was a local farmer, it was appropriate for him to want to know my business. But if he was the ghost, he would try to get me to tell him the way home. There was no way of knowing, so I had to be coy. Not that I believe in ghosts, mind you, but it's best to be careful after you've just seen a skull.

"I'm a tinker," I said, pushing enthusiasm into my voice like I wanted to sell him something. I marched forward and pulled out the belt loop that held the pack of pots and pans on Addie's back in place. With a clash and a rattle, the pots swung down from their strings and hung along my horse's side. "And I'm here to sell to anyone and everyone who has need of a good pot."

He pursed his lips and came around the horse to look at the wares, lifting first one and then another. Looking at the craftsmanship. He still could have been alive or dead, for all I knew.

"Nice work," he said finally. "Yours?"

"My father's."

He nodded. "He does good work, but I don't believe I need any pots just now."

I shrugged and began the loud task of resetting the pots in their bag.

"You heading into town to sell those?"

"I'm headed to the trader's camp. They set it up once a month and I head over when I have something to sell."

"Yeah. Trader's camp. I been there myself once or twice, but not in a while. Not in a couple of years. You been riding long to get here?"

"Not long. A few days. Been taking it easy on this old horse." Trying not to be rude, I swung up onto Addie's back. The farmer didn't seem to mind my elusiveness. He just kept smiling faintly and started walking along beside me as I nudged Addie into motion.

"Treat your animals right," he said, running his hand along her flank again. "They stick by you."

I nodded. This was getting weird. I passed the cairn and moved out onto the outgoing western road.

"You know what time it is?" he asked, stopping about five paces from the cairn.

I kept riding until I was fully on the western road, then stopped and turned to face him. That was a ridiculous question. The sun had passed its peak and was beginning its descent, so it had to be early afternoon. There was no way he couldn't know that, unless he didn't know what direction he was facing and didn't know if the sun was rising or falling. I pondered challenging him. He didn't look like I thought a ghost should look.

"There are some would say you're a ghost," I said finally. His smile didn't fade. "And there are some would say you're not. But I'm not gonna tell you directions or times or where I'm from or where the trader's camp is setting up. If you aren't a ghost, then I'm sorry, but you can't be too careful."

I tried to make it sound apologetic, and he nodded to me once. "You can't be too careful," he said. I started to turn my horse to be on my way, but he wasn't done. "I'd like to see your pots again."

He made no move to advance, so I stopped the horse, facing him at an angle. "You don't need any pots just now, and I haven't got anything else you'd be interested in."

"You could tell me the time."

I grew annoyed. So this was the spirit of the dead man, condemned to stand at the crossroads until someone told him the way home. At least he could be more creative in his requests. My cousin had told me that the ghost would try to trick me into helping him, and failing that, would offer me fabulous trophies. This guy was barely trying. "I haven't got anything else you'd be interested in," I said more forcefully, and turned my horse to go.

"I might have something you'd be interested in," he said, and I stopped once more. I admit I still had no fear of him. He had not done anything to make me afraid.

I tugged Addie around to face him fully, put on my best expression of waiting, and said nothing. He also remained silent. The quiet wind drifted through the grass. A bird croaked in the tree to the north and was answered from another tree down along the road to the south. Crickets hummed.

He inhaled and reached into his pocket. I watched with interest as he pulled out a silver-headed hammer. It was a good hammer. Much nicer than the one I owned. "This is a very special hammer," he said, and I kept waiting, refusing to let out my emotions. "With it you can tap out the most wondrous pots. Better than anything your father ever made, and better than anything you cousin ever will. You'll make a fortune at the trader's camp."

I shrugged. I already knew I was as good as my cousin or my father and had no aspirations for more. And wealth meant little to me. I bought this horse when I was young, and when it died, I'd have enough to buy another. I did enjoy a cup of beer and the ham the town inn served, but I had enough money for those things, too. My clothes I made myself, and I was proud of them.

And besides, there was no telling what a charmed hammer might make. All of my pots might spring leaks, or they might bite their owners. I could be reasonably sure none of my current pots would do that.

He must have felt my indifference, because he slipped the hammer back into his pocket and came up with a rolled parchment and a small cloth sack instead. He lifted the parchment high like it was a torch. I didn't expect much, since I can't read.

"This is a map," he said. "A special map to show you all the beautiful women of the land. And this," he held the cloth sack up, "contains the Powder of Allure. You could find a wife. You could find a dozen wives. You could visit a different woman every night and they would all love you." He grinned a knowing grin.

But again I wasn't all that impressed. I had visited my share of women while traveling the circuit. None of them could rightly be called beautiful, but then I'd never seen what the storytellers call a beautiful woman and figured that was for the best. Men were always getting enchanted by beautiful women in stories, or trying to do courageous things and getting killed. Anni at one of the villages two days' ride north had only one eye and a bad temper, but she wouldn't make you fight a dragon. I was more comfortable with her than I ever would be with a princess.

"No thank you, Sir," I said.

Without seeming angry, or dwelling on this second failure, the ghost put the map and powder sack away and pulled out an open-topped sack that jingled with coins. But he pulled it out too quickly and the coins tumbled out before he could catch them. They bounced and rolled and he cursed angrily. A couple of coins reached as far as Addie's hooves and she stepped back nervously, dropping her head to sniff them.

The ghost, all cross now and muttering things to himself that Mother used to box my ears over, bent down to gather the coins and drop them back into the sack. He wasn't too careful, and I saw grass and dirt go in with the money. I just watched him, still not saying anything. If he was clumsy, well then, that was his problem.

But after a little while, when he had gotten up the coins that were piled close to him and he had to start walking around to fetch the ones that had rolled, he stopped and looked up at me. "You know," he said, still mad, "this would go a lot faster if you'd lend me a hand."

I leaned over and looked down at the three small gold circles below me, then sat back up. If I picked up what wasn't mine, then it might become mine under the rules of Finders Keepers, Losers Weepers. And if I accepted a gift from him, then I was beholden to him and maybe he could jump across that circle and grab me and make me tell him which way was town. It was a possibility, and I wasn't taking chances. So I climbed down off the horse and flipped the three coins back to him with my toe.

I mounted Addie again. "I have to be going," I said, tipping my hat cordially.

He straightened from where he was picking up the last of the gold. A forlorn expression came across his face, driving away his angry scowl. "There must be something I could give you for my freedom."

I shrugged. I couldn't think of anything I wanted that was worth releasing him. "I doubt I'm smart enough to come out ahead in the bargain. It's only in the stories where the hero outwits the ghost, so I'll be going."

"You disturbed my sleep." He rubbed at the deepening bruise on his forehead. "You can't leave. We *must* bargain for something."

I tipped my hat to him a second time and headed out of the valley. I looked back when I reached the crest of the hill that would hide the crossroads from my sight. He was still standing there looking up at me. An uneasy feeling wiggled into my belly, and I hurried on to meet with my cousin.

A day later, after a restless sleep in the fields, I rode up the last of the rolling hills that preceded the river. I hadn't smelled wood smoke all morning, but dismissed this as an odd effect of the wind. I hadn't seen any other horsemen or wagons on the hills either, and hoped that I had arrived at a lull in trading. But coming up the last hill, I couldn't hear the dull rumble of hundreds of people and animals or the clank of metal. I grew more and more uneasy until I crested the hill and saw nothing.

There was no camp. The grass was long and untrampled, so no camp had been here in the past few weeks. Why would they have moved? This spot was a day's ride from three large towns and right on the river.

I rode down to the wide river and let my horse drink while I looked over the road that ran along the bank. It was dusty and well used, but there was no arrow pointing to tell me where the camp or my cousin might have gotten to.

I remounted and rode north for several hours to another flat place where they might have gone. Because I hadn't seen another living soul on the way, I knew long before I got there that I would find no camp.

The closest village was another four or five hours ride, so I continued on. They should have news of what had happened. If they didn't, I would take the north circuit home and sell my pots. Father would be furious if I came home with everything unsold. My cousin and I usually took the north circuit home because there were more villages. He was probably up there now, taking all my sales. I should reach home three or four days after him.

A few hours later, as the sun dropped, I once more passed cultivated lands. I looked for farmers, and sure enough, I soon saw a man looking down at me from atop a hill.

I waved and turned off the track and rode up to him. He waited without moving, leaning on a rusty old pitchfork with one tine missing. I stopped Addie just out of stabbing range and spread my hands to show they were empty.

"Good afternoon," I said. He nodded to me. There were more fields down in the valley behind him, and a number of people working. This man was their lookout. Perhaps there had been trouble with raiders. Maybe that's why the trader's camp had moved.

"I'm a tinker," I said. It was all the introduction I needed out here. His eyes stayed locked with mine. "I went to the trader's camp a few hours down the river, but there's no one there. Do you know where they moved it to?"

He shook his head faintly. "Hasn't been a trader's camp there for a good long while," he said. "They moved down closer to Brillain when I was a boy."

"The city? But I was at the trader's camp last month."

He shrugged and didn't bother to defend his statement. I stared at him a few moments longer, then started to ride into the valley to ask someone else. He lifted his pitchfork and pointed it at me. "We don't need any pots, Tinker," he said without malice. Something bad must have happened to have spooked him.

"Have the farmers had trouble?"

"Not this month, Tinker, but you have to be careful."

I nodded and returned to the river road. I could easily have ridden around him, but I sell to a lot of the same people over and over again, and it's best not to get a reputation for causing trouble. Besides, I would reach the village before nightfall. They should be friendlier there. The raiders might attack lone farmsteads, but they had never been numerous enough to bother the towns.

Two hours later, as the sun touched the horizon, I turned east when the road forked away from the river. In minutes I was back in hill country and the river was lost from sight. This whole situation was odd, possibly the oddest thing that had ever happened to me. It had gotten my thoughts all wrapped up and twisted around so that I didn't notice what was in front of me until I was half-way down the hill.

Looking up I yanked my horse to a stop. The crossroads lay in front of me, and the ghost still stood at its edge, smiling faintly. I looked behind me, but there was nothing to see. There were at least ten hills between me and the river.

A little angry, I rode down into the valley, this time taking the branch track that skirted the crossing like I should have the first time. The ghost walked beside me and again stopped at the edge. Glaring at him, I rode on and up the hill. Cresting it, I saw the crossroad in the next valley. The ghost was standing at its edge looking up at me. I turned around and the crossroad was also in the valley behind me. The ghost down there looked up at me. For a moment I was surprised that I couldn't see myself standing on the crest of the next hill.

Resigned, I rode down. "What do you want?" I asked, knowing his answer.

"My freedom, of course," he said. "I offered you skills, women, and money, and you didn't want it. But you woke me up, and now we must bargain. You are trapped here until we do. It seems I finally have something you want."

"There's got to be a way out of this valley. One of these directions."

"Oh, sure," he said. "There's one or two ways out. Maybe you'll find them before you starve to death, but it won't do you any good. Fifty years have passed since you set out. Your family searched for you, and then mourned your death. Your cousin grew old and died, and his children are old now. Everyone you knew is dead."

"Dead? Everyone?" My father and uncle, my cousin and his family? How could they be dead? I had just seen them a few mornings ago. Why had I been so stupid? I only wanted to see what was under the cairn. Why didn't I listen to my father's advice? "How did I get fifty years ahead?"

"Strange things can happen in a crossroads. If you're willing to deal, I can take you back to the moment you left."

"You can?" I instantly knew I had spoken too eagerly. That was a bad way to begin bargaining. I had to think of a plan. I saw that the red lump on his head was gone. "I want more than to just go back."

"Tell me what you want and I'll consider it."

"Let's see." I began to tick off on my fingers. "After you take me back, release me from this valley unharmed. Then don't ever hurt my family, or me, or anyone I know. Don't harm their animals or crops either."

"I can agree to that. Would you like the gold too?"

"No gold. Everything comes from somewhere, and I don't want to know where your gold comes from."

I climbed down off my horse and stepped up to him, standing just a foot away from his face. It struck me as funny, that he looked so normal. They had gone through a lot of trouble to keep this man from coming back, and he looked the same as any other farmer. Probably my cousin was right and he had a contract with the Devil.

"What happens if I break my side of the bargain?" I asked.

"If you lie to me, I am free to do to you as I please. You named your family in the contract, so their fate is on you. I can kill them in a second if you're not careful."

I reached out across the border of the crossroads and he reached back and grasped my hand, though I didn't want to touch him. Now the grin really consumed his face, and I thought a human shouldn't be able to grin that wide or show that many teeth. He let me go and I wiped my palm against my pants.

"Now, Tinker," he said, "tell me the way home."

He stepped right to the edge of the crossroads, waiting on me to give him a destination and free him.

"Am I back to the day I met you? The same hour, the same minute?" I circled around to the inside of him, acting like I was afraid and trying to keep my distance.

He looked at me a moment, then said, "Yes."

"And am I free to go?" I took a big step back.

Again he hesitated, then said, "Yes, and I will honor the remainder of our agreement." He stood there waiting, having fulfilled his side of the contract. I didn't doubt he had fulfilled it and we were back, because they always say in the stories that demons must bow before contracts and obligations.

I took three more steps back, until I was near the cairn. My memory of this place was made complete as the wind whispered across the grass and a black bird called.

Pointing left with my gloved hand, I lied, "That's the north road."

Cackling and laughing and howling, the ghost leapt into the air higher than a house. Gray mucous streamers bled from his skin and twirled around him. Addie bolted, but there was nothing to be done about that. I let her go.

Quickly, while he was celebrating, I turned and kicked the cairn as hard as I could. Rocks tumbled. The ghost shrieked and descended, but I already had his skull in my hands. I rapped it sharply against a rock so that it cracked across the back. That old ghost flopped to the ground, screaming and holding his head like a big man who's just lost a bar fight. I was mighty pleased that I had guessed right. I could hurt him. That first bruise on his head had pointed my way.

"We had an agreement." His voice was icy, furious. "Your family will die now because of you."

"Let's make a new agreement," I said. I ground my finger into the spine hole in the base of his skull. Flecks of bone crumbled off and the ghost doubled over again, howling and thrashing.

I pulled a sack from under my belt and dropped his skull into it. Then I twirled the sack above my head until the ghost staggered back and forth, dizzy.

"That's not fair," he said.

I continued to twirl, keeping him off balance.

"It's not fair," he said again. "I'll trap you here again if you don't release me. Then you'll starve to death and your ghost will haunt this crossroad with me."

"I told you, we need a new agreement." I let the sack fall limp while I fetched Addie. I dragged her back to the edge of the crossroads and remounted. The ghost stood angry and silent the whole while. Suddenly I was consumed by a great itching from feet to head. I couldn't get down fast enough before I fell off, writhing around on the ground trying to scratch away this mind-numbing pain. Then it was gone and I was left gasping for breath, with a newfound appreciation for the damned.

Crawling to my feet, panting, I found that he was at the edge of the circle, feet from me. "I can curse you in so many ways that you'll kill yourself in an hour. Now tell me the way home or your cousin dies! That is the only new bargain I will make."

My heart was pounding and my skin blistered as I yanked his skull from the sack. His lower jawbone fell off as I struggled to get the skull free. The blistering stopped the moment I broke an upper molar off with my thumb. He howled and clutched his mouth. I broke another tooth off. Then a third.

I let him recover, all the while holding the skull out in front of me with my thumb pressed against a fourth tooth. He was trembling, and I could finally see fear

in his eyes. As I had hoped, he was a coward. Even with all his power, he was a coward.

I drew my tinker's hammer from my belt. "I need a better bargain, or I start using my hammer."

"It's not fair. You lied."

"That's the benefit of being alive. I can cheat. You've got to follow your promises. For this new bargain, I want everything you promised last time. In return, you only get your skull back."

"No! Tell me the way home."

I tapped his cheekbone expertly with my hammer and a tiny flake chipped off.

"No no no," he howled around broken teeth and a rapidly swelling cheek. "I promise. I promise everything."

So we shook hands much like the first time, only less cordial. I fulfilled my end of the new bargain by tossing him his skull. "I'd bury that in the cairn if I was you. It's not safe out here."

"I will kill you," he muttered as he began stacking rocks. "Somehow. You broke our bargain."

"The first one, not the second. And you didn't make such a good deal the second bargain either." I pulled his lower jaw from my sack. "You only bargained to get your skull back. If I ever feel so much as an ounce of pain from you, or if one of my friends or family comes down with a curse, then I'm starting in on your jawbone. I can make it last a long time if I only take off tiny bits." I waved the hammer back and forth. "You remember that."

And there I left him, standing angry and afraid and damned. This time I didn't look back as I rode away. I headed west to the trader's camp and my cousin. And I did end up with a boon after all. It turns out the jawbone can talk, and doesn't like the old ghost very much. It tells me all kinds of wonderful stories and I feed it sweets.

JEFF LYMAN IS AN MECHANICAL ENGINEER AND WOOD SCULPTOR, AND HAS BEEN writing short and long fiction for about ten years. He recently attended the Odyssey Writing Workshop 2004, and is currently seeking a home for his first novel.

WEEKEND AT POCONO MOUNTAIN

Robin M. Buehler

WE SHOULD HAVE KNOWN IT WAS GOING TO BE A DISASTER. GETTING LOST on our way to the Poconos was the first indication. The second was the Pocono Mountain Resort itself. Tucked away among the Pocono Mountains, surrounded by blue spruce, red oaks, and maples, the ski resort rose above Marshall and me reflecting the sunset like a towering inferno against the ashen night sky.

"This looks more like *Hotel California*," Marsh said.

"Or the Tower of Terror," I quickly offered, wondering which of the two our ski excursion would become. I had to admit, "This place gives me the creeps. Maybe we should go to another ski lodge?"

"And do what? Waste more time driving? I don't think so, bro!" Marsh was right. Poor directions given to us prior to the trip actually had us going away from the resort at first. Signs for New Jersey alerted us, and, twenty minutes later, we were back on track toward our final destination. Even so, it took us nearly five hours driving here, when it should have taken us only two.

Neither one of us were real happy about that. All we had done the last hour was bitch.

"All this time, wasted," Marsh grumbled. "We could have been on the slopes by now."

When the manor came into view, we both whistled and hollered with excitement. Or we did until we pulled up the drive and saw the hotel. It did remind me of Tower of Terror. I shivered at the thought of staying here, but Marsh reminded me we already had reservations. Going to another hotel—if any had room—would mean losing our deposit and more time away from the slopes.

"Besides, the place may not be as bad as it look," he suggested. "C'mon," he added as he approached the front door. "Let's go and check in."

The lobby was large and sterile, an impression encouraged by the white padded, mirrored walls. The ceilings rose twenty feet above us. A crystal chandelier hung over the middle of the room, casting dazzling beads of light across a bearskin rug. Its head, with its mouth forced open from the hunt, bore teeth that snarled up at us as we walked past it.

"Are you sure about this?" I asked, looking around nervously. "This place is *sooo* not happening. Like that circus Uncle Rey took us to when we were kids," I rambled, "with all the trick mirrors and the pet bear that was actually a dog in drag...."

Marsh laughed. "Those mirrors were a blessing, shaving twenty pounds off of me...."

"And onto me," I replied. "Only time in our lives we've been the same size."

Still laughing, Marsh approached the front desk and rang the bell to announce our arrival.

We both jumped back a step when the concierge stood up from below the counter. With a deep, raspy voice, he apologized. "So sorry. Didn't mean to frighten you on this fine evening. May I help you?"

"We have reservations," Marsh spoke up after a long, drawn out pause. "The name's Bruckler."

The man ran a long, bony finger along the edge of the reservation book. "Oh, yes. Here we are. Marshall and Ronin Bruckler.

"You have adjoining rooms; 231 and 233 are located on the second floor," he added, handing us the keys to our suites. "I hope you'll enjoy your time with us, here at Pocono Mountain Resort."

"I'm sure we will," Marsh responded. "But before we go, could you tell us what amenities you have here, besides the slopes?"

"We do have a pool, located on the lower landing," he replied. "Can't say there's much of anything else this time of year. Unless you count the other guests, of course."

"Yes, of course," I repeated, smiling a worried grin.

"Dinner is served from five to eight each evening, if you care to join us," the concierge continued. "There isn't a dress code, but we do recommend you dress as you would at any upscale restaurant.

"Additionally, when you retire for the evening, we suggest you lock your doors and windows," he advised, before slithering back below the counter, "Things have been known to happen at night."

I swallowed hard, feeling a pang of anxiety swell in my breast. I had a desire to flee, but was kept grounded by my brother's tight grasp on my arm and the desperate plea in his eyes.

We had come here for some rest and relaxation. We had both graduated several weeks earlier and gone into jobs that were tedious, unchallenging, and uneventful. This ski trip was an early Christmas gift from our folks to celebrate our transformation from mere children to professional, responsible adults.

Friends of our parents had recommended the place. No brochure or word of mouth would have prepared us for what we were about to experience.

The Pocono Mountain Resort was once a premiere luxury hotel. With over 300 guestrooms, the main building was of a Tudor design that had seen better days. Few guests, from what we saw, were actually staying over like we were. The hallways were uncannily quiet for a holiday weekend. We could hear our own footsteps beating upon the wooden floorboards. And there was a stale, dingy smell that reminded me of old Cuban cigars.

"Maybe we should bunk together," I suggested as we ascended up the stairs to the second landing. Our rooms were on the far end of a narrow and ill-lit corridor. The walls were covered in a brown, mahogany wood. A few lamps were bolted to the walls, and those at long intervals, barely lighting the way to our rooms.

"Don't be silly. That desk clerk was just trying to scare us. What could happen in an old place like this?"

NG

I looked at him disapprovingly. "Have you ever watched *The Addams Family* or even *Psycho*? What about *Hotel California*? I remember the lyrics talking about being able to check in, but never getting to leave."

"You're letting your imagination get the best of you," Marsh chided. "Besides, like I said, Sport, what could happen in an old place like this?"

"Plenty!"

Marsh shook his head as he fiddled with the keys. "Here," he said handing over mine. "Let's just settle in for the evening. Catch some TV; shower. In an hour or so we'll go down and grab a bite to eat and then, we can check out that pool."

I agreed, reluctantly.

In the room, I gazed around. It was elegantly furnished with rich, velvety curtains and matching bedspreads. It was floored with the same hardwood from the hallway, spread with an area rug that had specks of red to match the curtains and bedding. "This is bitchin'," I said to myself. I unlocked the door between our rooms and stretched out on the bed for what I hoped would become a quick nap before dinner. I knew Marsh would be preoccupied until then with channel surfing.

I woke hours later to tapping outside my window. From what I could hear, the wind had kicked up its heels, whirling a fresh batch of Christmas snow across the Pennsylvania countryside. I could imagine Marsh getting excited in the adjoining suite, knowing we would have fresh powder to ski on the following morning.

I wished I could share his enthusiasm, but something about this place kept nagging me. Something just didn't seem right. And, as if on cue, the windowpane shot up, allowing snow to flow into my room carried by a howling wind that sent a frigid chill through me.

"Is everything all right in there?" a shout came from the adjoining room. "Ronin? Come on. Answer me! Unlock the door!"

"What are you talking about? It's not locked," I called back and went to the window to shut it before turning to the door that connected our rooms. "What the hell? I know I unlocked it."

Marsh forced his way through the door; his eyes widening. "What on earth happened in here? It looks like a blizzard!"

"It might as well have been," I replied. "The window shot open and the snow came flying in."

"What have you been sniffin'?"

"Very funny...You're just lucky we'll have some new snow to ski on tomorrow."

The comment, as expected, brought a smile to Marsh's lips, but it didn't last as long as I had expected. "What's the matter," I asked.

"I've been tapping on the door for the past twenty minutes. What kept you?" he demanded.

"I...I didn't hear you; well, not at first, anyway. I must have sleeping harder than I thought." I looked at the door he came through with a puzzled look.

"It's really weird. I unlocked that door before I laid down but when I came to open it, it was locked. I wonder if it had anything to do with the tapping I heard when I came to. I thought it was on the window...tree branches...What if it was inside?"

"There aren't any trees on that side of the hotel," Marsh said, going to the window and peering out. "At least, not for 30 feet or more." Turning back toward me, Marsh narrowed his eyes. "But somebody in your room? What kind of game are you trying to pull, Ronin? Are you doing this just to scare me? To get me to go to another lodge?"

"Why would I do that?"

"Let's see...from what I recall, you didn't want to come. You certainly didn't like the looks of this place when we arrived..."

"And the concierge did say unexpected things were known to happen," I concluded.

Marsh just shook his head in defeat. "I don't know about you, Ronin. Sometimes, I wonder if we're even related. Only you would come up with some wild story like this, or even suggest this place is haunted just because of the way this place looks, and what the front desk clerk said."

"How else would you explain it?" I asked, reminding him about not hearing him knock. "Yet, I heard tapping on the window. Are you going to say that it was a figment of my imagination?"

"*Hello!* That was me...tapping on the door!" Marsh looked at me like I was dense. "Never mind." He shrugged it all off. "I'd rather settle on getting something to eat. Game, bro?"

Of course, I was. My stomach ached for something fulfilling. Sitting here the entire night and not eating would kill me.

It was nearly 7:30. The dining room was empty except for the dozen or so tables. Only a couple were occupied. But what caught my attention more than the lack of people dining were the white jackets worn by those that were there.

"Does it seem odd that we're the only ones not wearing white?" I asked.

Marsh disregarded my inquiry and instead said, "We'd better take a seat and order. The kitchen closes in a half hour."

"Did you hear what I just said?"

He barely looked at me, his eyes searching the room for a waiter. "What?!"

"Everyone else is wearing white!"

"So?"

"Don't you think that's rather odd?"

"Why should I?" He asked. "This might be the employees' dinner hour."

"I...I'm not so sure about that...Their clothes don't say chef or wait staff to me."

"You're nuts, man."

"You think I'm making this all up?"

"You could," he responded, more quickly than I anticipated. "You didn't want to stay here when we first arrived. Then the whole thing upstairs." His tone was accusing. "You're probably going to tell me next that those people are actually inmates."

"Well..."

"C'mon," Marsh continued. "Let's order before the kitchen closes. You'll feel better," he insisted.

Marsh ordered the chicken platter. I, on the other hand, ordered the snapper soup with a side order of pasta.

We talked about our plans for tomorrow until our meals arrived. Marsh remarked how quickly we were served.

"They may have had some dishes already prepared beforehand," I suggested, but regretted saying it the moment Marsh removed the lid from his chicken. The bird, with its feathers still intact, stood up and squawked at us before flapping a short distance away and strutting into the next room.

I couldn't help laughing at the horrified look on my brother's face. He returned the favor when my soup had more of a bite to it than I had bargained for.

I looked down at the large bowl in front of me and saw a small snapper paddling around in circles. I closed my eyes and shook my head briskly when I imagined it had smiled back at me and waved.

"No wonder our meals arrived so quickly," I said. "They weren't even killed, let alone cooked!"

"I'm sure there's a logical reason for this."

"Like what?" I demanded. "They serve everything 'fresh'?" Marsh chuckled as I continued. "I don't think this is very funny. I was really looking forward to that bowl of soup. What do we do now?" I sighed. "Ask for something else?"

"And risk winding up with another live chicken and snapper," Marsh asked. "Naw. I don't think so! I've lost my appetite, anyway. It flew the coop along with that chicken." Marsh rose, throwing the napkin onto the table. "I don't know about you, Champ, but I wouldn't mind taking a look around this place. Game?"

I nodded, and we soon found ourselves in the basement, entering the pool area. Marsh suggested we take a dip.

"We don't have our trunks."

"That never stopped us before. Or are you too ashamed to show off your skinny ass? If you haven't noticed, bro, no one's around."

"We'll see about that," I replied as I took off my shirt and snapped it at him. Marsh dodged the strike. His foot came down on the edge of the pool and slipped out from under him. I laughed and waited for the splash only to hear a thud and a crack.

I hurried forward in time to watch as Marsh disappeared beneath a layer of ice that shouldn't have been there.

Shock kept me in place long enough for him to sink to the bottom.

"No!" I roared and dove in after him.

He reminded me of a beached whale when I hauled him from the icy depths and pumped the water from his frigid lungs. The water blew from his mouth, bubbling as it ran down his cheek.

Marsh coughed and looked up at me through blood-shot eyes; there was sarcasm in his voice as he asked, "Have I died and gone to heaven?"

I had to laugh. The thought of telling him he had actually gone to hell floated around my head, but, instead, I told him we were still at the manor. "You fell through the ice, and I had to fish you out like a flounder!"

"Who on earth would think of putting ice over a swimming pool?" he demanded as he sat up and tried to collect himself. He looked toward the pool and grimaced. "Who would ever think it possible?"

I just shrugged. "I suppose they wanted an alternative use for it, being winter and all."

He nodded in acknowledgement. "Indoor skating rink. At least it explains how cold it is in here." Marsh shook his head again, exclaiming his dismay. "What kind of hotel wouldn't post a notice that the pool had been converted to an ice rink? For that matter, why wouldn't the concierge have said something about it?"

"I can't answer that," I said. "Let's just go back to the rooms and change. You need to get into some warm clothes."

The remainder of the evening was uneventful, much to my relief. I sat with Marsh in his room for a while and we talked about the freaky events that had occurred.

"It has been a very bizarre weekend," he admitted. "And I'm sorry I doubted you earlier about this place. Maybe you were right."

"Hey, don't even worry about it," I replied. "It's not important, as long as you're all right. Besides, we still have tomorrow and all that fresh powder to look forward to."

"That's right." His voice rose with anticipation. "What's it doing outside? Is it still snowing?"

"Afraid so."

"Excellent!"

Morning couldn't have come soon enough for Marsh. Even though I knew it was out of sheer excitement, I wondered if his tossing and turning in bed were actually memories of being fished out of the pool earlier that evening. Images of him slumped on the tiled floor, stretched out like something in a fish market, haunted my every waking moment. Sleep didn't come soon enough. Even when it did, it wasn't a peaceful, restful slumber. Waking up the next morning to Marsh's endless banging, I felt like I never slept.

"All set to go?"

"Just give me a minute."

"You should be revved after that nap you took before dinner last night!"

He was right. I should have been more awake, but I wasn't. And I didn't want to make him feel bad by telling him he kept me up half the night with his thrashing about. I swore it went on most of the night. The sound of him in bed came through the wall that separated us. I felt I was in the same room, trying to sleep next to him.

In time, I did perk up. A cup of black coffee and donuts helped. Soon after, we were off to the slopes, and, much to our surprise, we were the first to arrive.

"This is odd. With it being a holiday weekend, I thought more people would be out here," I said.

It didn't seem to bother Marsh. "It just means we have the slopes all to ourselves," he said. "And no waiting for the chair lifts!"

It wasn't until we reached the summit and began skiing that we got our first clue of why we were the only skiers. Halfway down the slope, first Marsh's skis and then his boots crumpled. Piece by piece, they fell apart like a snow drift whittled down by the wind.

"What the he...!" he exclaimed as he watched his feet emerge from the boots, still covered by socks.

He had to walk down the mountainside by the time we reached the bottom. "Did you see that? My skis! My boots! They're gone!"

"What did you expect? Henry had them since we were kids; they were bound to fall apart," I said, thinking that our roles were now reversed. He had become the worrywart and I had become the upbeat, not-a-care-in-the world brother. "But the skis, man? What could do that? Acid snow?"

"Very funny, smart ass," he snapped as he stared down at his bootless feet. "No one's ever going to believe this. I know I don't, and I'm the one standing here in my socks!"

"C'mon," I continued. "Let's rent you some new gear and go back up. There's plenty of daylight left and we have skiing to do!"

"Oh! This is so much better," Marsh remarked, as he slipped his feet into a dry pair of socks and ski boots. But even with the new socks and rented shoes, it didn't stop Marsh from venting about our older brother's boots. "He's going to hear about this when we get back!"

"After the weekend we just had, he'll just find it hilarious," I admitted.

We took the lifts back up for our sophomore run, confident what happened before was a fluke. It wasn't.

Midway down the slope, a wave of powder began to fester, bubbling up from the snow-covered earth. Soon, it rose above us. We were stunned by the impossible as the mound raced uphill like a reverse avalanche.

"Oh, my God!" Marsh exclaimed. "What the hell is that?"

Before either one of us could get out of the way, we collided with the mass. Instead of falling backwards, with the brunt of the snow, we continued skiing through it. I felt the frigid snow caressing my cheek, but it was the sound of cutting that drew my attention down to our feet. It was then, and only then, that I saw tiny creatures the color of snow. They were no larger than the sardines they resembled. Their bodies were lined with small, iridescent scales that shimmered in the snow. But their mouths were lines with razor-sharp teeth that devoured both sets of skis and our boots. The only thing that was left was our clothing, socks, and feet! Droplets of blood permeated through, speckling the socks and surrounding snow.

Before my eyes, those too dissolved. The red speckles turned into larger splotches and tiny jabs of pain tingled across my skin. From the way Marsh was hopping, he was feeling the same thing. The sensation was climbing higher. Our pant legs were looking noticeably more ragged.

I thought back to everything that had happened since we arrived. We'd rationalized it all, but was our reasoning wishful thinking? This was all so unbelievable. Were we cracking up, or was it something in the water...the air? The thought terrified me as I met my brother's eyes, unable to voice what I was thinking.

Marshall's thoughts must have mirrored my own. We both looked down at the condition of our legs. We threw aside our poles and flung ourselves down the mountain, half running, half falling the entire way. I continued to feel the sharp little nips climbing higher up my leg. They were already to my knees. Now that they'd tasted flesh they were ignoring my ski pant, which flapped in bloody, tattered strips around my legs. From the corner of my eye, I could see Marsh slapping at his thighs. His face was pale and panicked. I felt on the edge myself.

We'd reached the bottom of the slopes. Before us, to the side, was the resort. Directly in front of us was the heated outdoor pool. I watched the steam rising from its surface and saw our salvation. I grabbed my brother's arm and jerked him toward the shallow end.

"Hey!" was all he managed to get out before I pushed him in, following just seconds later myself. The water burned, but the nipping stopped. All around us, tiny, pink-tinged bodies floated belly-up on the surface. I swatted them away and clamber out of the water.

We departed as fast as we could from the resort. The car keys were in Marsh's pocket, so we never went back to our rooms, leaving behind our bags and other belongings. Marsh refused to return. "They'll just have to mail it back to us. Let's get out of here!"

As we drove through the front gate, I looked out the rear window, watching the manor as it diminished behind a row of iron bars. A worker stood by the front gate, nailing up a sign that read: Pocono Mountain Resort closed for renovations. Skiing prohibited. Coming soon, Poco Loco Chalet, Weekend Resort for the Mentally Insane.

ROBIN M. BUEHLER IS A JOURNALIST IN SOUTHERN NEW JERSEY. SHE HAS had poetry appear in *Taj Mahal Review, New Pegasus, Sigla Magazine, Writers Post Journal, Byline Magazine, Ancient Heart, Poetic Hour*, and *Makata Vol. 6*, to name a few. Her short stories have been in *Gothic Revue, Fantasies: Colection of the World's Greatest Short Stories, Wide Open Spaces,* and *Dark Walls*. The reviews she's written has been in *Sabledrake, Poetic Voices* and *Gothic Revue.* A resident of Mays Landing, she lives with her two Boston Terriers, Buttons and Bows, and her calico, Nana.

THE FOREST OF A THOUSAND LOST SOULS

Danielle Ackley-McPhail

A GOOD GENERAL DOES NOT ALLOW THE ENEMY TO SELECT THE FIELD of battle. I am thought by others to be the best. I should have tried much harder…

I.

It was autumn as my battalions gathered on the field at Asculus, a barren plain wedged between the mountains and the sea. Surrounding valleys bore the bristling signs of successful harvest; our current training ground had seen such spilt blood in its long history as to never be free of the sown salt. In the summer's heat, the scent still rose from the soil, speaking to us rousingly of battle. It was marked for the business of war. For that, we prepared.

The Enemy threatened from the Savage Lands. Our emperor had summoned his forces. We were not the only battalion to so assemble, but we were his chosen. We would lead the fray. Each day, proud young faces filled out the ranks. I did not allow myself to wonder which of them would fall in the battles to come; instead, I dedicated myself to honing them into a lethal force. They must follow my lead without question, for I would see the next harvest, and many more to come; the same could not necessarily be said for them. There was no doubt I would burn more than a third of my forces on assorted pyres before the planted fields were once again ripe, and that was if I were lucky. I expected it would be more.

What melancholy had crept into my heart? I mourned my dead too soon and did not do justice to my men. Yet how could it be otherwise? Lately, in the darkest hours of night, I felt torment at the knowledge that I led so many young men to die. I have been an officer a very long time.

I forced the darkness away. Climbing the wooden dais, I moved to the spot left clear for me, standing shoulder to shoulder with my captains. Silence descended.

"Who are you?" I challenged them, as I have countless troops before.

"General, we are the Emperor's Elite!" their voices rose in precise unison and I allowed myself a moment of pride. These warriors would serve well. The strength in their response flooded me, charging the blood in my veins with added vigor. It gave me confidence we were invincible, my earlier doubts forgotten.

"And how shall you fight?" I continued, keeping my tone outwardly neutral.

"We will fight with His might…. We will fight with His valor…. Our courage is His."

I paused before continuing, allowing them to settle down from their fervor.

"Your emperor has summoned you to war and I am here to see you ready to vanquish the enemy. Your first lesson: Forget the songs you have heard sung of glorious battle. Heroes are not made in war, but created after, by those who have no concept of its horror." The faces lifted up to me were filled with awe. My men marveled at the strength of my words. Little did they know, as much as I spoke to them, I spoke to myself. "Look to the men before and to either side of you...turn and seek the faces of those at your back...these are your brothers, and as they stand beside you, so you stand beside them.

"Do not forget this from now forward: the praise or damnation of those at home holds no true weight, now or ever. What matters is that those who surround you at this moment will share your triumph and horror alike; care for what they think and know that if you respect your oath to them...to me, you will have acted honorably. That is the most each of us can hope for, for in the end, it is the only thing with meaning. They will make you heroes, but you will make yourself worthy." The shadows in my mind taunted me, denying everything I said. I ruthlessly subdued them.

II.

The following weeks were spent in zealous training, my soldiers excelling at every task. I pushed them ever harder, honing their skills beyond proficiency to perfection. I had no choice. The emperor's scouts had brought back messages of movement among the enemy's forces. Soon we would all see battle.

But this was not what chilled my blood and shivered down my spine. Night by night a misty escort accompanied me into sleep, betrayed by a shadow, the muted echo of languidly beating wings, a sudden cackle, a shrilling scream.

New nightmares came to me each time I sought rest. Born by the biting wind off of the sea, they wreathed my slumber in terror and torment and ecstasy. Images of battle...of death...my men spread like dead flies upon the ground. Over and over I watched them, both haunted-eyed soldiers and fresh young faces not yet scarred by battle, all turn their gaze toward foreign shores. Their trust in me was complete. Their trust in me was damning. In the darkness of my own mind, I watched my men die, savaged by a faceless enemy, their entrails strewn about countless battlefields, their lifeless eyes trailing me accusingly while I picked my way over their corpses and waded through mud made black with their blood.

My dream-self ever closed its eyes, but the images could not be shut out. Neither could the screams. It was the torment of souls consumed with terror, agony unleashed in endless shivering waves.

Each morning I woke atremble, my eyes hollow pits and my skin pale beneath its soldier's weathering. More times than I can count, I woke at my own cry, "They are all dead! I have failed them, every one of them is dead!"

Only my aide knows of this, and his dedication keeps him silent.

I struggled to put my unease from me. My troops may be the chosen of the emperor, but their own excellence has kept them here. I had not trained them to die. The dreams were nothing but doubts manifested...unreasonable doubts.

Among the ranks, I marched like a demon possessed, my countenance fierce and my temperament demanding, while inside, my heart died a little more. I pushed my forces to excel at every skill put to them. I watched on, a not-so-silent goad, and even my captains did not know which to fear more: our uncertain future, or me.

"You're overextending, Thalon...Get your stance back in line, find your center and do not stray from it; our foe will not be as forgiving as Ghin here is." My words were stern but encouraging as I addressed my aide. I lingered a moment to watch his next attempt, or so I intended until I spied another among the ranks, his gear an affront to my warrior's sensibilities.

Brief flashes of my nightmares swiftly rising up at the sight, I barked and snapped most ferociously at the man, "Your armor is an outrage, soldier! Whoever taught you such inept care must wish you dead, or you've a wish all your own to gain the other side. I want each plate repaired, in order, and properly assembled before you seek your pallet tonight!"

I ignored the confused and angry flush of half the sergeants surrounding me. I'm sure they wondered what rode me. I wondered myself, but I forced myself not to care. I would do more than score my officers' pride if they did not redouble their efforts to prepare the men as best they could. I would not have even one recruit fall because we failed to train them well.

My blood pulsed, like a caged beast seeking escape, as I continued to tour the ranks. My eyes took on a wild glint and my breathing grew harsh. Everywhere faces confronted me from my dreams. A fleeting image of their dream-deaths cloaked their features in gruesome effigy as I passed each one: Throats slashed to the bone, eyes dangling wetly from their sockets, blood welling from mouths even now calling out the training chants that filled my ears with unfailing precision. The vicious mocking did not end.

I felt cornered. Each step I took, I was followed by haunting whispers, venomous and faint; ghostly screams floated on the breeze, apparently for me alone. My teeth clenched on an answering groan and it was all I could do to keep myself from swirling around in an attempt to spy who taunted me.

Was this madness? Growling, I sought the darkness within my heart. I would wrestle it down and raze it from my being. This would be the battle I fought for my men...my oath demanded it. Shooting a look at my second in command, I left the field to him, and stalked off toward the shore to war with my demons.

III.

The blue-grey sand sparkled like crushed gems in the dying light of day. I had not realized the lateness of the hour. How much better I understood my restlessness. I had lost all desire for sleep, though not the need.

I had managed to work up a lather in pacing my men. At the water's edge, I reached down to scoop up a bit of the incoming wave. Raising it, I stayed my hand mere moments from dousing my head; a shadow crept across the sun, stealing its brilliance, muting its setting glory, and a whispering flutter of leathery wings danced around the edge of my hearing. I trembled without shame.

The seawater was sluggish in my palm and lacked the sharp crispness I had always found so refreshing. A stench unimaginable wafted from the puddle in my hand and the surf at my feet. I was no green recruit; I was a seasoned warrior and I smelt death. But looking down, instead of the blood and offal I expected, I spied a thick green slime coating my hand. Foreboding shot through me.

A gleeful cackle scattered my thoughts as I dashed the sludge away, biting off a curse. Looking wild-eyed at the surf, I nearly cackled myself…madly. The surf was as crisp and clean as the day the gods had wept it. There was nothing in the sand where I had cast my handful. This was madness! With my eyes closed and my jaw and every other muscle clenched, I began my private war.

"These are but dreams!" I roared. "They have no power over me that I do not allow them! You are nothing but unfounded doubt! You are senseless fear! You are nothing but fancy!"

Sweeping out my practice blade, I whirled on the battered, but stout log I'd had my men erect in the sand. Towering over my head, it was my own private practice post and I attacked it with a vengeance. Over and over my blade fell with ruthless force.

"Nothing! No screams! No death! No goddamn fluttering wings! Nothing, do you hear me?"

I descended into obsession, no longer rational enough for words; I punctuated each punishing slash with a formless cry. Rage poured through me and out along my blade.

"Ggrr…ggggrrrr. Augh!"

My muscles burned and my skin felt stretched taut; I dreaded the rumbling swish of the surf, for the little I could distinguish beneath my roars hinted at nasty, triumphant whispers.

"AuuuGGH! Augh…Augh…AauuuggH!"

My heart thudded mercilessly against my breastbone and my breath tripped over itself in its haste. Greyness swarmed my vision and I continued to growl through clenched teeth as I turned to confront the sea. With all my escalating fury I stumbled forward and cast my wooden practice blade like a spear into the depths. As if such a pathetic weapon could pierce the heart of the darkness I sensed writhing there! I would regret the wastefulness later. For now, I watched intently as it lanced through the sky and impaled the ocean smoothly, forcefully. Yet nothing rose up from the depths but a brief splash, and my blade was gone. I fell to my knees and fought against weeping as the waves chuckled at my powerless obsession.

I was too spent to care, too worn by weeks of restless nights, left drained by my futile exertions. I fell forward in the sand, letting the waves wash over me, wanting to scream at their deceptive sweetness. Something was foul here, I thought as unconsciousness claimed me. It was merely well hidden.

IV.

Torn limbs drifted by me on knee-high waves of blood. A body lurked beneath the surface. As I passed, it reached out to me with half a green-glowing hand; there was no head, just splinters of gnawed bone and white cartilage rising from the tattered remains of one of my sergeant's necks.

I should have known him. Even without a face, I should have known him. As things were, it was only his torque—amazingly still in place—that confessed his rank.

As I walked the battlefield, my useless sword dangling from fingers long numb, I could feel the shadow following me. No…they were legion, not just one. Something brushed my back, taunting, and the *shushing* of flexing wings filled the silence left by the carnage. Why did they wait? Why did they not come for me?

"They are all dead! I have failed them!"

Chuckling glee was my only answer, he-he, he-he, he-he…building like a pulse. It was maddening and I could bear the torment no more….

V.

The voices now were deep and rumbling. They did not trouble themselves to hide on the fringes of my thoughts…they didn't bother to tease and taunt…. The voices called me forth from my sleep in words I could not discern.

Gibberish, complete gibberish. But that did not stop my blood from turning to ice. I fought the compulsion to repeat the phrase. To let the words fall off my tongue as they desired to. What did it mean? Relentless…ominous… I could not evade the dread those words evoked in me, regardless of my inability to comprehend them.

When I opened my eyes, some oddity of the moonlight cast a green glow upon the water. It quickly faded as I blinked away the sleep. All save in one spot. Rearing up onto my knees, I stared at the glowing depression in the sand. The moon was not full and did not offer enough light for me to distinguish what rested there.

What I could not see called to me in sibilant whispers, speaking to my soul. Its promises both horrified and tempted, again offering me the terror and torment and ecstasy of my dreams. The darkness in my heart trembled eagerly. The rest of me cringed away.

My sensibilities rebelled as I crouched in the sand. The urge to reach out overwhelmed me. My hand shook as I did battle with it. The dream visions of the weeks past rose again unbidden as I lost my struggle and tentatively reached out, not quite brushing the heavy, gold-swirled statue cradled in the sand before me. The cold intensified before my skin even touched the stygian darkness of the unknown mineral. Revulsion gripped me and my stomach rebelled like a raw recruit's. My soul took one step back from damnation.

Staring up at me, coldly calculating, was a hand-high statuette washed ashore by the treacherous waves. A pair of dark, depthless eyes perched above tentacles that gave the illusion of being poised to lash out at me. A half remembered dream image told me they would be thicker than my well-muscled thigh—my waist even—were this creature to stand before me…or, I should say, over me. For its body would dwarf my own several times over were we face to face. And atop that thick trunk, it head—enormous in proportion—shaped as it was like a familiar sea creature…but so much more sinister than any monster known of within those depths.

It was this thing's reflection that haunted my sleep, the broken bodies of my men scattered like grains of rice at its feet. Its size alone would have made me quail, though it galled me to admit it even to myself...but the sight of the lethal claws, cutting into the rune-covered pedestal it perched upon, left me shaken as my mind calculated their likely length. I could well imagine what a natural complement of weapons such as these could do to my men.

Despite all of this, it was the massive wings folded cloak-like down the creature's back that told me I had spied my demon at last.

The wind sniggered yet again and my fury returned full-force, banishing my doubt. With a swift swoop, I cupped my hand under the wet sand where the idol sat—nothing could bring me to touch the hateful thing directly—and rising, drew back my arm and flung the handful back into the sea.

Only after it disappeared from sight did I notice the fierce dragon prows favored by the Empire's mortal enemy, just now rising from the horizon. The eve of battle was upon us. I knew both thrill and fear.

I could feel the wing-whipped wind howl at my back as I stalked away. My very soul quaked as it encompassed me. I battled horror as my image reflected back at me, until I no longer recognized the man staring back.

VI.

"Rise up!" I bellowed loudly as I entered the camp, my expression grim as I took the sentries by surprise. Quick anger heated my words and my eyes flashed cold, glimmering briefly with a green glow in the dark, if only for a moment. They would pay later for their inattention. For now, dawn was mere hours away, and I intended we would be on the march long before the sun lit the sky. "Fall out and formation in fifteen!"

Officers aligned themselves beside their squads and battalions with precision. Without a word, I stood before them as my aide dressed me in my armor. I forced my eyes not to follow the hulking shadows that darted among the ranks. Ever since my slumber on the beach I had visions to add to my torment. They taunted me as I addressed my men.

"The enemy approaches; no later than noon they will be upon our shore. We will not meet them on a battlefield of their choosing. Gather your gear. We march within the quarter hour and lead them to where we make our stand. The advantage is ours, men, let us press it."

The shadows mocked me, replacing my forces once again with the death-images from my dreams. They played on the doubts I'd struggled to eradicate. Rage filled me, pushing out my fears. They were senseless! They did not exist! Nevertheless, their sniggers grew deeper into all-out, mocking laughter as Thalon handed me my battle blade.

VII.

As we made our way through misty vales, I listened to the *thump-thump-thump-thump* all around me...the horses' hooves...the marching of my men...my quickening

pulse. It was as if we made our way across the inside of a drum, rather than into the fiery red glow of approaching dawn.

We were close. I halted at a rise and waited for my forces to draw up to me. I had always known where I would bring them for this battle that they might draw upon the valor of those who came before. Ahead of me, laid out in that instant for my eyes alone, was the Forest of a Thousand Lost Souls.

No trees materialized from the morning fog. This was a copse of corpses, or what was left of them. A thousand colossal souls found in this place their final rest. Their twisted and broken limbs of aged bone rose like giants, as high as three men, each standing atop the other. Those massive skulls still in place were thrown back upon their neck bones in endless, eternal screams. Side by side with the miles of bones, the armaments of fallen warriors pierced the sky, dwarfing our forces as we stood in their shadow; maces and lances, swords and two-handed axes...every weapon ever imagined planted in the ground reaching heavenward...each one of a size to suit a Titan.

I felt the souls, daring me, measuring my worth on first impressions. My face remained impassive and I stood at the head of my army with justifiable pride. We were worthy to walk among those fallen, to add our legend to theirs...to surpass it, in fact, as I would not...*could* not believe my army would fail.

In the back of my mind, the shadows deepened and surged. My battle lust demanded blood, though I reined it in using the same command I wielded with my men. Behind me, gasps were swallowed in the silence of dawn. I thought I heard faint whispers of 'madness!' at my back, but knew better of my men. I turned to greet my officers as they drew their mounts beside mine. Awe mingled with reverence in their gazes. Glancing beyond them, my eyes trailed across the ranks.

My men did not disappoint. There were flickers of doubt, of unease, but all were quickly quelled. The forces stood ready. Satisfied, I began my descent into the valley. Wending our way through the vast forest of bleached bone and steel that edged the plain was no easy chore, but as I drew closer to my goal, I was overcome by the magnitude of our undertaking. Surely, surrounded by the souls of these valiant dead, we would find our strength amplified tenfold...nay, a hundred fold.

For once the whispers were drowned out. My demons could not overcome the clamoring voices of the dead from a thousand wars. Their screams were rich and strangely savory. The echoes of their ancient battle cries thrummed through my veins. They kept pace with my rapid pulse.

I could sense the foe drawing near, poised and ready to strike, but unfathomably holding back. It was as if I could hear the pounding of their march in my very bones. I could feel a hint of battle lust steal over me like an ever-increasing itch.

...almost time.

VIII.

I barely took note of the furtive looks the soldiers cast in my direction at the continued absence of our foe. I was lost in the ever-shifting parade of ancient dead. I found myself at the center of sifting spirals as the shadows and the legends bound and counter-bound me in their swirling energies.

The glory of past battles flashed before my inner eye. I wanted this for my men: To blood them in triumph, to set them forever above all other fighting men. I would become immortal!

Deep inside me, my soul screamed in outrage at my thoughts, so opposite my usual philosophy. The rest of me was deaf to those cries. Instead, my languid gaze followed as the carrion crows flew by. I relished the sound of flapping wings. They could feel the tension; they could read the signs. They cawed their impatience at our unmoving stance, eager to feast upon the anticipated spoils. My aide flinched when the birds' cries sounded directly above him. At the sight, sudden, inexplicable rage boiled through me, and the conflicting battle between my nature and my actions was finally lost.

Flinched! How dare the man count himself a member of my ranks with so faint a store of courage? He was my chosen, most favored of the common soldiers, personally groomed by myself to one day take his place among my officers. It was a disgrace!

Swiftly I charged, kneeing my stallion to the site of my army's blemish. Weakness could not be tolerated; weakness would drag the whole body down. Retribution was as swift as my mount, and as sharp as my blade.

Crimson stained my view once more as my sword came away bathed in Thalon's blood and I shivered at the cool caress of death. The silence took on the weight of a collective gasp, a quickly quelled cry of outrage.

My blue eyes glimmered green, tremors rippled through me, and surging death cloaked me in ineffable power. The coil drew tighter. Shadows deepened. The thumping pulse quickened. Anticipation was heavy in the air. The whispers rose into a shouted triumph and an eldritch glow crept over the battlefield, encompassing the deadly forest.

No one moved, nor was it likely they were able to. I found myself looking out upon the sky as an unholy light gathered above my head. Something formed in its midst: An engraved amulet suspended from a golden chain. Staring into the glow, the image burnt itself into my scorched mind. It pulsed with power, a power that repulsed me even as I lusted after it. I had to feel its embrace...the splendor it promised. I would be a hero.

No! That wasn't right.... I was not here to be a hero; but still, I reached up my hand. My fingers closed around warm, pulsing metal. I was doomed. As I settled the chain around my neck, the amulet set me glowing in a haze of glory. Nothing was left of the man I'd been.

I looked out and I could see them, the shadows surrounding my army: tangible nightmares rising up in their horrendous magnificence. I grew taut with anticipation. I waited for the dream-images to be fulfilled.

Dark, depthless eyes burned with hunger and tentacles lashed in frenzy. Rank upon rank upon rank of powerful beings stood before me, dwarfing the mortal men. They each resembled my little, cast-away idol.

I heard the screams, indistinguishable from those of my dreams. It relieved me to once again be fully immersed in the jarring auditory assault. I had grown so used to it.

I looked back down at my hand…it burned. I discovered a spiraling void scorched into my flesh. From that void, my nightmare laughed back at me.

My gaze drifted to my soldiers. Looming shadows tore them limb from body and flesh from bone. Numbly I noticed I had underestimated the length of those talons. One pierced the last of my sergeants through his head, and the wicked curve protruded from the man's belly.

It was true then: Every one of them dead….

IX.

The copper-penny stench of blood hung in the air as it dripped from my blade.

I stood in stillness broken only occasionally by squabbling ravens, watching the shadow-creatures sink once again into the cursed soil. As I looked at my men, I struggled to find the dividing line between my nightmares and reality. The ranks were assembled, patiently waiting the arrival of the enemy…the enemy who only now surged along the perimeter of the battleground.

No one moved.

Shocked murmurs shattered the silence and a single voice rose from the approaching horde, "My god! What happened here?"

A solitary scout crept onto the plain, stopping at the edges of my assembly, circling, but going no deeper. His face was paler than the moon as I watched him wheel abruptly and lope away, straight back to his commander.

"They are all dead, sir, slaughtered in their ranks." His voice trembled and I wondered that I could hear him at all, but it didn't matter. My satisfaction grew as I heard mutters of "cursed land" and "ill omens." I knew the thrill of triumph as the enemy forces turned about and marched away with haste. The field was ours; the enemy would not stand against us.

I took my place in the Forest of a Thousand and One Lost Souls, my head thrown back in a cry of ecstasy, my bare bones gleaming in the weak light that occasionally broke through the clouds. I am larger than life…a legend, my mighty sword a monolith beside me, my head thrown back in a cry of terror.

Danielle Ackley-McPhail is the award-nominated author of the fantasy novel, *Yesterday's Dreams*, an urban fantasy based on Celtic mythology. Her other works include *Children of Morpheus* and the upcoming anthology, *No Longer Dreams*, both by Lite Circle Books. She has contributed to *Nth Degree Magazine*, Sabledrake.com, and Darkwalls.com. Her current project, collaborating with Mike McPhail, is *Progenesis*, a military science fiction. You can find out more about her work at www.sidhenadaire.com.

REALITY CHECK

Tee Morris

"ALL RIGHT, I'M HERE," GINA SIGHED, HER BREATH BOUNCING AGAINST THE surface of the The Mirror Room's door. "Now what?"

From 'Homebase,' Jack replied over her radio, "You will now enter The Mirror Room and go to radio silence for thirty minutes. I'm going to read you the website stuff.

"This is The Mirror Room. When conventional treatments for Woodview were not enough to subdue the more unruly patients, they would be confined to The Mirror Room for several days, maybe weeks, depending on the severity of punishment. The longest sentence held was by Samuel Thompson, a total of three months. Official records states that in this room, designed to induce dizziness and loss of equilibrium, he choked on his own vomit. It is said you can catch the reflection of Samuel Thompson lost in the infinity effect of the room, trying to find his way back to this world.

"You will use the Ouija board to communicate with the spirit of Samuel Thompson. We will monitor you on the radio and your surveillance equipment, but you are not allowed to communicate with us. Breaking radio silence will result in disqualification. Your time begins now."

Gina thought to herself, *"Why the hell am I doing this again?"* as she paused for a moment at the open door of The Mirror Room. When she hit their website and applied for the open slot, it sounded like something cool to do. She could still feel the excitement in the sorority house when it was announced that Beta Delta's own Gina Sanders would appear on the Reality TV show, *The Graveyard Shift*. She even got the approval from Beta Delta's national office to wear letters on the show.

Gina was stoked! A shot on the most-watched reality-based television show. A chance to get an adrenaline fix. (A safe one, too, as she knew nothing could *really* happen to her.) And the prize for surviving the weekend: $5,000. *Piece of cake,* she thought. This could be her nest-egg after graduation or that ultimate post-college trip before entering the real world.

Five grand for one weekend in an undisclosed location, and she got to play with ultra-cool techno-toys. It was easy money. A no-brainer, just like the show itself. *The Graveyard Shift* started with five strangers spending a weekend in a place, with no prior knowledge of its location or history, except for one thing: the destinations were classified as "haunted" by world-renowned parapsychologists and legitimate psychics. The challenge of the weekend was to spend the weekend in said haunted location, and at night fulfill a series of simple dares like "Climb into a casket and remain still for thirty minutes" or "Find a grave marker and recite a documented voodoo incantation." She did crazier things during the Phi Kapp house's all-night keggers.

It was a no-brainer, or so she thought.

While she had seen the show before, found its dares asinine, and had a good idea what to expect, Gina didn't expect on answering a questionnaire at her audition. One hundred questions, all of them like this: You are waiting for a cab on the curb. What do you notice? (a) the traffic, (b) the people around you, or (c) the ants around a piece of bread crust. Yeah, okay, whatever.

Looking back on the test, it was some kind of psyche test. The show had designed all of this weekend's challenges to mess with their heads in some way, shape, or form.

Her mind flashed a brief image of Jack. He was a really nice guy, and she found out on their first night that he had a weird phobia of diseases. Last night, his dare was to spend fifteen minutes in "The Rat Trap," a totally light deprived room; the only sound outside of its occupant was of rats above and below him in the tiny cubicle where he had imprisoned himself. What Jack did not know was there was a thin mesh cage above and below him. He was never in any danger, neither by being bitten or catching anything from the rats; but all he heard were the rats, scratching and clawing at one another. He made it five minutes before bailing.

So what if she had signed a release as big as a phone book? If anything happened to her, Gina and her folks would sue the pants off the production company. Prize money or no, she was going to come out ahead.

Gina had already made a complete ass of herself on the first challenge, when she and her "guardian angel" ventured out to a hospital morgue. She remembered screaming at the top of her lungs in one of those classic horror movie screams. Why had Gina screamed? She felt a cobweb lightly tickle the top of her hand when a breeze passed through the abandoned room. That was when she lost her cool and totally wigged out. Her "guardian angel," Stan, had to shout over her decibel-shattering scream. Of course, it was all caught on camera. From Stan's angle. From her angle. And from the night vision cameras located throughout the hospital. Gina was ready to go home then, but she sucked it up and dealt with looking like a wuss on prime time TV.

That was the catch of *The Graveyard Shift*. Fail to fulfill a dare and you are disqualified.

Now Jack was her guardian angel, promising to wait outside, in the cold, out front of The Mirror Room, while she fulfilled this particular dare. Gina gave a half-hearted smile and entered this dilapidated shack with mirrors on the inside of the door, across the floor, and covering the walls, a recessed light in the center of the ceiling mirror her only source of illumination. When Jack closed the door, Gina realized there was just enough room for her to sit cross-legged and for the Ouija board in front of her. *Remember,* she thought to herself, *this is a game, just a weird game for weird kids.*

The thought provided little comfort. The Ouija board's presense seemed only fitting considering her current weekend accommodations. The Woodview Institute for Mental Research supposedly provided miracle cures for insanity before the days of chemical prescriptions, lobotomies, and electroshock therapy. Patients would either come out rehabilitated or would die in the Institute due to complications from their illnesses. At least, that was what the records showed.

Woodview remained extremely tight-lipped about their "radical new approaches" to mental health. In the late fifties, a small team of four investigators, one posing as a doctor, two posing as orderlies, and one posing as a patient, infiltrated Woodview to find out more about their amazing success rate. The investigator posing as a patient never made it out of Woodview alive. One of the orderly impersonators, traumatized by what he saw, was still undergoing therapy to this day. The remaining orderly and the fake doctor continued to tell their stories several times over through books, documentaries, and now in the narrated segments of *The Graveyard Shift.*

Woodview, these two investigators discovered, was a real-life chamber of horrors. The medical staff administered their alternative treatments through satanic rituals and documented Black Magic spells. Some rehabilitation involved psychotropic drugs and bizarre optical illusions that would cause seizures and convulsions. Their theory: the unorthodox treatments were "Fighting Fire with Fire," to push a patient so deep into their insanity that they cured themselves. Overnight, the shining ray of hope for the insane became Doctor Frankenstein's laboratory.

Now, almost fifty years later, the Institute still stood as a warning to the medical field, the grounds surrounded by a chain link fence and barbed wire to keep out the curious and fans of the occult. Gina thought Woodview reminded her of that freaky movie, *House on Haunted Hill.* Gina's boyfriend assured her that they had made up all that stuff about human experiments.

I guess those writers had to get their ideas from somewhere, she thought.

Gina sat in silence, staring at the Ouija board while the voice of Walter Leavinson, the investigator who had posed as an orderly and managed to keep his sanity, recounted on her radio headset his own story behind The Mirror Room. *"Well, I recall just stepping inside it to clean up the filth left behind by someone who had spent four days in there. I had the door open and I still felt this weird feeling of falling, you know, like vertigo? I couldn't keep my balance. Another time I was just cleaning the mirrors and got locked in there by accident for fifteen minutes. I suffered motion sickness for two days."*

She hated these segments. They were piped in over the radio and she was not allowed to retort on account of the radio silence. Gina was convinced that their sole purpose was to mess with contestants' heads during the dares, as opposed to providing background for their benefit.

"I can't imagine anyone spending more than a week in there, let alone a month. How Thompson did it? Personally, I don't think he ever left. There are a lot of cultures that believe cameras steal your soul, you know? What's a camera but a bunch of mirrors, right? So yeah, I believe Thompson is still in there. Somewhere, just looking for a way out."

Gina's breath misted a light fog on the mirror immediately opposite of her, but only for an instant. She was a little surprised that the remaining mirrors were not completely fogged over from her body heat. She knew she was sweating underneath all her winter protection.

After a while, she placed the planchette on the center of the Ouija board and rested her fingertips on it, her memory wandering back to a night after several rounds of Quarters and Ping-Pong Bowling. Gina was convinced her sorority sisters were pushing it around, just to mess with her when she was drunk.

When she thought about the answers that had appeared on the board that night, it made the hair on her arm stand. The answers to the questions started to get personal, then a little creepy. If one or a pair of sisters had moved that thing across the board, their answers were not funny.

Gina suddenly remembered a question from the test: What do you find the most improbable? (a) UFOs and life from other worlds, (b) Mind reading and foretelling the future, or (c) John Edwards and contact with the dead.

There were probably other questions like this on the questionnaire that all eluded to her dislike of Ouija boards.

"Samuel Thompson?" Gina's voice echoed slightly against the glass, giving her a moment's pause. While she was supposed to be on radio silence, this was part of the dare, and therefore allowed. Gina would rather have stayed quiet. Her voice did not sound right in this place. She shifted nervously in her spot and continued, "Samuel, are you here?"

The planchette remained at the center of the board.

Gina could not shake the feeling that this dare was a huge mistake. She heard all the urban legends about this thing: This was how Regan became possessed in *The Exorcist*, people have died when they played alone, and others vomited live frogs and cockroaches. Then again, it was probably just a lot of superstitious hype, like Tarot cards, psychic hotlines, and Miss Cleo.

C'mon, Gina, it's all hype, she thought to herself. *You don't know anyone who has "felt the wrath of a Ouija board," but all youre your friends seem to "know someone who knows someone." Bet you anything these "friends of friends" received friendly warnings from their Muslim neighbors the morning before September 11.*

Just a lot of hype, she reassured herself.

Gina sighed heavily, feeling a little queasy from the infinite effect of the mirrors. Turning off her radio, she huffed in frustration, "How long have I been here?"

The planchette under her fingertips moved to the number "5."

Gina froze. Everything inside her clenched.

"I've been in here for five minutes?" she asked.

The planchette moved in a wide circle across the board, and then again in a little wider of a circle until ending at "Yes."

"Samuel Thompson?"

Repeating its slow encircling of the board's characters, the planchette moved agonizingly to end at "No."

She was not moving this thing. *Okay,* she thought to herself, *this is something subliminal. I'm doing this.*

The planchette moved downward for a moment and returned back to "No."

"You can read my thoughts?"

"Yes," replied the planchette.

Gina shook her head, her heart pounding quickly, "So you're not Samuel Thompson. Were you a patient here?"

"Yes."

"What is your name?"

The planchette circled around the board, pausing over the letters, "H-E-A-T-H-E-R."

"Heather, you know you are not supposed to be here?"

"Yes."

"I want to help you."

"Yes."

"I want you to let go. Just let yourself find peace. It is all right."

The planchette seemed to sit dormant for an eternity until it suddenly moved quickly to "No."

"Don't be afraid, Heather. You should embrace the peace of where you are and where it will lead you."

"No."

"Why?"

The board then replied through the planchette, "E-M-B-R-A-C-E-Y-O-U."

Gina was not going to let this stupid game or this stupid show get the better of her. This stunt had to be rigged. "You're going to escape through me?" Gina scoffed, trying to remember if she mentioned Ouija boards on the questionnaire the show's producers had her fill out to tailor their challenges. "You've been waiting for someone like me to help you escape? Bet you're really pleased with yourself."

The planchette moved to the image of the sun in the top right corner of the board, stopping over the smile the sun made.

"Heather," Gina said, growing real tired of this mind game, "you've watched one horror movie too many."

"Look in the mirror," the voice said clearly.

Gina kept her eyes fixed on the board. She *heard* that voice. She knew she heard that voice, clear and crisp as if she heard it spoken right next to her. There was no echo. *It was in her head,* she assured herself. *It was all in her head.*

"It isn't all in your head. Look in the mirror." The voice continued.

Gina defiantly pressed against the planchette and slid it over to "No."

"Why not?" mocked the voice. *"This is just a game, right? A dare. You knew coming into this room was a stupid thing to do. So come on."* The voice was taking great delight in taunting her, *"This is just a stupid game. A silly dare."*

Gina straightened up and pushed the planchette to "Yes" and then looked up to the mirror in front of her, her own reflection staring back at her.

Her eyes then looked at the other reflections surrounding the single infinite line of Gina's. The unknown cellmate had long blonde hair, matted with time and neglect. She was in a hospital smock, soiled with bits of food, human waste, and what looked like dried blood from her fists. Her knuckles had tiny slivers of glass buried in them, as if this girl had been pounding many panes of glass, looking for a way out.

The unknown face was chillingly void of any compassion or remorse. Heather had been so patient. She had fooled the doctors into thinking she was better, but then Heather was sent to The Mirror Room for driving a fork in an orderly's hand. What the doctors did not know was that Samuel Thompson paid close attention to his alternative treatments. Very close attention. He had found a way to disappear, to hide in the mirrors. There were so many places to hide in here, after all. An infinite number of places. Heather had found her way back when the show's producers wired this little room for sound and video, the cubicle's open door allowing enough sunlight to enter and provide a beacon. It had been a much longer wait for Heather than it was for Samuel, but wait she did. Heather waited for a visitor. For a question. For an opportunity.

Gina learned all this as she looked at the alien reflection moving with her own. She watched herself look down at the board. The tortured girl laughed airily as she moved the planchette to one final message.

"Good bye."

Gina then heard the voice echo over the radio, "Gina, thirty minutes have elapsed. Come on out of there!"

And Gina watched herself get up slowly, unsteadily—as if she had not done this simple thing in a long time—and open the door to the cell to step out in to the cold Pennsylvania night. She pressed her hands against the chilled glass as Gina—the Gina in her world—looked back and waved pleasantly to her as she shut the door.

"Wait..." Gina uttered to herself, and then came the overlapping echo of that single word, causing her to cup her ears at the deafening volume it reached in her glass confinement.

When the din finally subsided, Heather looked around her. An infinite number of reflections all moved with her, looking in every conceivable direction.

Then her world disappeared. The tiny light in The Mirror Room, as it was considered empty, was no longer necessary.

TEE MORRIS' WRITING CAREER BEGAN UNEXPECTEDLY AT THE MARYLAND Renaissance Festival with his portrayal of Rafe Rafton, a character featured in his historical epic fantasy, *MOREVI The Chronicles of Rafe & Askana*, a finalist for EPIC's Best Fantasy of 2003. Tee then appeared in Dragon Moon Press' *The Complete Guide to Writing Fantasy*, a "user-friendly, how-to" guide to writing that earned the distinction of finalist for ForeWord Magazine's Book of the Year, in the Career category.

Tee's latest book, *Billibub Baddings and The Case of The Singing Sword*, spoofs both the Fantasy and Hard-Boiled Detective novel, featuring a tough-talking dwarf detective in 1929 Chicago. At the same time of its release, Tee collaborated with Valerie Griswold-Ford to edit *The Fantasy Writer's Companion*, a sequel (yes, a sequel!) to *The Complete Guide to Writing Fantasy*. The Companion, in its first month as an eBook, went on to become a finalist for EPIC's Best Non-Fiction of 2004. He now descends deeper into geekdom with Evo Terra in the upcoming title, *Podcasting for Dummies*, coming soon from Wiley Press.

Find out more about Tee Morris, his 2005 appearance schedule, and *Legacy of MOREVI* (premiering in July 2005) at www.teemorris.com on the Internet.

THE PAXTON BOYS

Den C. Wilson

"CONSTABLE!" ELLEN BARSTOW CALLED. "THE PAXTON BOYS ARE COMING!"

I pulled myself to my feet with my crutch and hobbled over to the window. Peering down the cobblestone streets, I saw the mob coming towards the jailhouse, with Thomas Boyd in the lead.

Cursing, I fumbled for my keys as I limped towards the cell and unlocked the door. When the lock opened, I flung the door wide and ordered the Indians inside to run.

I tried to make my way to my gun, but my broken leg betrayed me. I fell to the floor just as Boyd and his rabble pushed their way into the jailhouse.

"As constable of the city of Lancaster," I said, my voice creaking in pain. "I order you to return to your homes."

"Die, traitor!" The butt of Thomas Boyd's flintlock struck me on the temple where I lay on the ground. My vision blurred as the smoke burned my eyes.

"Joshua."

I regretted awakening as soon as I opened my eyes. A dozen church bells rang inside my skull. Above me hundreds of barren tree branches spun. My head spun with them as I tried to lift it. I heaved, thankful for an empty stomach. I tried to stand, but fell to my knees. I'd forgotten the splint on my right leg. The limb protested violently against any weight put on upon it.

I heard water flowing nearby.

As I went down, I nearly hit my head on a steamer trunk. I had been lying inside a peddler's wagon.

"Ah, you're awake."

My eyes went immediately from the trunk to the tall figure that had spoken. I blinked in an effort to focus, wincing, as my head pounded in response. I reached up and touched my forehead, finding a thick bandage. I returned to contemplating my nurse. From his long jet black hair, I thought he might have been an Indian, but no. He wore a heavy woolen coat and a broad brimmed hat, both as black as his hair, and carried a long staff. My eyes fixed on his staff. It was carved from oak, with strange symbols, most of which I did not recognize. On the top, two golden serpents were entwined around a bird.

A raven cawed.

He bent over and rested the back of his hand against my brow.

"Your fever has broken."

"Who are you?" I asked.

He smiled. "You don't remember? Well then, you were quite delirious after your wounds became infected. Do you remember the attack?"

I blinked. I remembered both attacks. The first where my horse was shot out from under me and the second. . .

"Where are Mary and Michael?" I gripped the side walls of the wagon to try and pull myself up. "Did they get away?"

"Be still, Joshua. They are fine. They went down to the river for some fishing. Michael has promised us some shad for breakfast this morn."

"We are along the Susquehanna?" I was relieved that the two remaining Conestoga Indians had escaped. I had not completely failed them.

"The Schuylkill," he said. "We shall be in Philadelphia by tomorrow."

"Tomorrow?"

"You have been sick with a fever for several days now, ever since your wounds became infected."

"Who are you?"

"My apologies, friend." My benefactor leaned over me to check my bandages. "Your fever was strong, I had not realized that in you delirium you and I have not had a proper introduction. My name is Toth. Herman Toth."

"Are you a surgeon?"

"No," he said, "just a peddler, but when one travels as much as I, one learns some things about dressing wounds. I'll have a proper doctor look over you once we reach Philadelphia."

I winced at Toth's casual reference. "I failed them, didn't I?" I asked. "The other twelve Conestogas died because I couldn't get their cells open before the mob broke in."

Aye," Toth said, "it was sad day, indeed. I knew the Conestogas well. I've traded with them for -quite a long time- and I know them to be good Moravian Christians, having learned the Bible from the *Deutsch heute*, even taking Christian names."

News of Chief Pontiac leading raids against the English in the west had come to Paxton only weeks before. A small group of Scotch-Irish settlers in the village of Paxton led a drunken assault on the peaceful Conestoga Tribe, killing six. The remaining fourteen Conestoga Indians fled to Lancaster, where the people voted to place the Indians in a jail cell for their protection. My leg throbbed as I remembered the initial skirmish with the "Paxton Boys" and then the final confrontation in the jailhouse.

"Aye, they died, but you did what you could. One man with a broken leg against a mob of over fifty and you managed to get two souls out the back a-fore 'twas too late. You are fortunate that they didn't waste a round on you."

"How did you get me out?"

Toth pulled out a long knife and cut the end of the dressing. "Mary and Michael found my wagon about two miles south of town and told me what happened. I returned to Lancaster to find the rest of their tribe slain and you the only soul who hadn't gone on to meet the Christ."

"And soon the Conestogas will be no more." Michael said, appearing next to Toth.

I gave a start when the Indian spoke. He moved quietly, so I hadn't noticed his approach. Mary stood behind him. Michael's eyes had become harder than I remembered them. I avoided his gaze. Several large fish hung all but forgotten from his spear.

"Michael. Mary. I have not the words to express my sorrow at failing you."

Michael drew his knife and began cleaning the fish on top of an old chest. Mary climbed into the wagon and inspected my dressing. She gave Toth an approving smile as she opened her canteen and held it to my lips. "Mr. Donegal, are you still ill? Mr. Toth has some tonic if the fever still burns."

"No," I said softly. My eyes were drawn to the wooden cross that hung in front of her deerskin leathers. I thought of the senseless slaughter. The Conestogas knew nothing of Pontiac's raids.

Mary shushed me. "Please, Mr. Donegal, you must not get yourself overwrought. The good people of Lancaster County did what they could to protect us."

Michael looked up. "It is a shame that the there were not enough good people in Lancaster County."

"Husband, hush." Mary said. "Mr. Donegal and the others stood by their fellow Christians just as the Bible commands."

"I will not. The Conestogas have always been hated. First by the Five Nations and now by the English."

"Scotch-Irish," Toth said.

"It matters not." Michael pointed at us with the knife as he spoke. "These settlers want more and more land and care not what happens to us. When they hear about Pontiac they become enraged! But Pontiac is far away and we are near. And the 'good people of Lancaster' put us in cages! Then they go to hunt down our killers leaving only a cripple to guard us. But the mob, these 'Paxton Boys,' fooled you, didn't they? They came up from the south while your group was heading west."

"I am sorry." My voice creaked with grief.

Michael jammed the knife into the chest and climbed out of the wagon.

"Where are you going?" Mary asked.

"To see if the Paxton Boys are following us."

Toth said nothing, but placed the cleaned fish into a pan and held them over the fire. I tried to stand again and Mary put her hand on my shoulder.

"Please, Mr. Donegal, you must forgive my husband. He burns with anger yet, but he knows in his heart that hating one's friends is not the will of the Lord."

"And how do you feel about your fellow Christians, Mary?"

"The Paxton Boys are not following Christ's teachings, now are they? You are a good man, Mr. Donegal. Michael and I both know that."

Michael returned an hour later and reported that he saw no sign of the Paxton Boys or any other encampments for miles around. He refused to look at me as he ate his fish. Toth put out the fire and broke camp. Michael said nothing for the rest of the journey.

We arrived at Germantown late in the day. Philadelphia looked like a city under siege. Several men were erecting makeshift barricades and walls around the edge of town. Young boys were hauling wheelbarrows full of black powder or sand to help with the preparations. A middle-aged man with a hooked nose and wearing plain dress looked up from cleaning his flintlock.

"Who art thou, friend?" he asked.

"I am Toth, a peddler, bringing refugees from Lancaster."

The Quaker paused, considering every word. "Toth, aye, I have heard of thee. My name is Edwin Wainwright."

I pulled myself upright in my seat. "Excuse me," I said, "I am Joshua Donegal, constable from Lancaster. I need to speak with the city watch immediately."

"Thee look like thee are not fit for anything but bed rest, but Dr. Franklin is at the Pennsylvania House conferring with Governor Penn."

Toth nodded and tipped his hat to Wainwright. He cracked the reins. Michael and Mary stayed huddled together. Once we were clear of the gate, Toth murmured, "Tis a dark day indeed when Quakers feel they need to take up arms."

Toth took us to an inn within walking distance of the State House. The innkeeper only agreed to rent to us when Toth paid double the normal rent. We spent the rest of winter there as I convalesced under the watchful care of Mary and Toth. I detested being treated as an invalid, but after Toth threatened to tie me to the bed, I agreed to accept their ministration.

I spent that cold December and January all within arm's length of the fire. The other guests of the Inn did their best to wish me holiday cheer, despite my melancholy. Fortunately, I was spared any further infection, thanks I suppose to the salves that Mary put on my head and leg daily. I asked her what it was once, but she would only say that it was "something Mr. Toth had mixed."

Under her care, I felt a growing affection for Mary. She never gave me cause to believe she returned my interest, which only deepened my feelings of shame towards her and Michael.

Of Michael I saw little. He found work as a groom and earned enough to keep him and Mary from being dependent on Mr. Toth's charity. He rarely came to call on me and when he did, it was usually at Mary's insistence. During those infrequent moments, we would sit together in silence; I from my shame and he from his bitterness.

Toth had assured me that Mary and Michael were both safe so long as they remained in the city. Word of the Paxton Boys' uprising had spread. News came that they intended to march into the city and demand more protection from the Governor. Upon hearing this, Toth went over to the State House to express his displeasure.

By February, I felt more ambulatory and was able to hobble short distances with a crutch. On the night of the fourth, Toth invited me to join him for dinner. I had thought it would be just the two of us, or perhaps with Mary and Michael, so my astonishment was understandable when, as I hobbled down the stairs, I saw the Postmaster General waiting for us.

It has been said that the Penn family may be the proprietors of the colony, but it is Benjamin Franklin that is its soul, even if he had been born in Boston. I can attest, having been in his presence, that no finer mind has ever graced the colonies. His years of service to the public had not weighed him and even as he neared the age of sixty, he remained vibrant and alive with life.

"So, this is the brave Master Donegal, the Scotch-Irish lad who stood his ground against the rabble of Paxton with only one leg on which to stand."

I looked to Toth for guidance. He said nothing, but continued to feed crumbs to a pair of ravens that he had somehow acquired over the past few weeks. I stared down at the floor, hoping to find something written on the planks that would help me avoid looking foolish in front of the great man.

"I stood my post, though I failed to save twelve people."

Dr. Franklin frowned and I knew instantly that I should have accepted his praise more graciously. "What matters is that you did what you were able. Two lives saved are still a blessing. But, we are not here to dwell on the past, but discuss what is to be done tomorrow."

"Tomorrow?"

"Aye, son, the rabble that call themselves the 'Paxton Boys' are expected to arrive tomorrow."

"I am certain your defenses will hold against them," Toth said, not taking his eyes off his ravens.

"I still hope that we can reason with them and convince them to peacefully petition the Assembly like civilized men, though perhaps letting them address the Assembly may be more dangerous than battling them on the streets of Germantown."

"Can't the Governor have them arrested?" I asked. "Simply because they live on the frontier does not entitle them to slaughter innocents!"

Dr. Franklin exhaled as he used a poker to turn over the logs in the fire. "Sadly, John Penn is not the man his grandfather was. He wants peace and order above all and is too eager to bargain and trade for it, even if the currency is the lives of innocent men, women, and children. I have done all that I can in the Assembly. My proposals to bring the Paxton Boys to justice have been rejected. Too many in the Assembly sympathize with the frontiersmen. They feel that the Governor should be taking a more aggressive approach to fighting the Indians, and Indians are Indians to these fools, Christian or not."

The bar maid brought in our food and we ate in somber silence. Fatigued, I took my leave. Toth gave me a glass of wine mixed with herbs that he said would help me sleep. He insisted on helping me up the stairs. I did not decline his offer, the pain in my leg getting the better of my pride.

I got/spent the most restful sleep I had had in two months. Before dawn though, I needed to pay a visit to the privy behind the stables, where I saw a figure holding a lantern enter Toth's wagon. Creeping closer, I found Michael rummaging through the trunk. Still unsteady on my feet, I stumbled over a bucket. It skidded across the ground and thudded against the stable wall, betraying my presence.

"What are you doing here?"

"I could ask the same of you. Is that how you repay his aid and hospitality?"

"This is mine." Michael held up a leather sack. "Toth was only guarding it for me."

"Perhaps I should see what Mr. Toth has to say."

Michael crouched down and brought his face inches from my own. "Stay out of my affairs, white eyes, or I'll see that you will be a cripple for the rest of you life."

He turned and strode away from me. I returned to bed.

I awoke an hour later covered in cold sweat, despite the bitter cold of winter. For the first time in months, my leg felt strong enough to walk without the crutch. My head felt clearer as well. Returning to the stables, I found Toth packing his wagon. I told him about my confrontation with Michael the night before. He frowned, but then smiled, as if he was trying to reassure me or perhaps himself.

"Not to worry," he said, "I was holding some personal items of his in my chest."

I pressed him further. "It seems strange that he would need them in the early hours of the morning."

"Joshua." Toth placed his hand on my shoulder. "I must ask you not to inquire further. Michael traveled extensively across the colonies before he and Mary were converted by the Moravians. He spent some time with the Five Nations and learned many of their secrets, some of which may put his life in greater peril than he already faces from the Paxton Boys."

He grasped my head with both of his huge hands. "You won't betray Michael, will you?"

"No, I will not." I stepped out of his grip. "You have my word."

We met the Paxton Boys at Germantown during what I believe without a doubt to have been the coldest February fifth of my life. The air carried a biting cold that stung the flesh like a beast and froze the soul, as if the devil himself had frozen the world when the two factions came together.

On one side of the wall gathered a rabble of Scotch-Irish frontiersman, ill-disciplined and spoiling for another fight. On the other lay a collection of nervous Quakers that the Postmaster General had somehow fused into a militia. The leader of the Paxton Boys, a tall man wearing a heavy black woolen coat and a thick scarf around his head stepped forth. He called himself "Captain Lazarus Stewart", though I never learned if he had ever earned such a commission.

"On behalf of the free men of Paxton, we demand to speak with Governor Penn!"

Dr. Franklin addressed Stewart. "You will speak with no one if you do not disperse this mob. Nothing will be gained by threatening the people of Philadelphia."

Stewart began listing the grievances of the various members of the Paxton Boys, which amounted to accounts of rape and pillaging at the hands of hostile Indians, none of whom were Conestogas, not that this fact meant anything to these filth.

Toth leaned heavily on his walking stick, murmuring softly to himself. My mind drifted away from the conversation as I spied Thomas Boyd in the crowd. His gaze met mine and I could feel his fury at my refusal to die in Lancaster. A shout to storm the barricades drew my attention back to the present. Toth's murmuring grew louder as he stamped his staff into the ground. His two ravens suddenly landed on his shoulders. A dark cloud passed overhead.

Without further warning, the desire to attack fled the Paxton Boys. Captain Stewart agreed to take a few of his men to the State House and petition the Assembly. Dr. Franklin and a few Quakers escorted them through Germantown. I noted that Boyd accompanied Stewart's side as they entered the city.

Toth tugged at my arm. "Come, we must retain to the Inn and collect Michael and Mary."

"What?" I asked. "Why are we leaving? I thought we were here to help with the defenses."

"That part is done. You were brought here to witness what has happened. Now you must help me find Michael before it is too late."

We found Mary in the kitchen of the Inn, but Michael was not in the stables. We searched throughout the square but found no sign of him. Toth grew increasingly agitated and decided that we should head for the State House to find Dr. Franklin. Arriving just as the bell rang to announce the closure of the Assembly, we found Dr. Franklin conferring with several of his supporters. Toth shouted out to him.

"Damn my soul, but I hate the sound of that bell."

"How did the petition go?" I looked around the crowd for signs of Boyd and Stewart.

"As bad as I feared, my boy. The Governor has agreed to increase the bounty on Indian scalps and he declined to press any charges of against the Paxton Boys."

"We must find Michael before it is too late."

"But he was here, in the gallery! He was understandably furious at the Governor's decision and left."

"And what of Boyd and Stewart?"

"They left shortly thereafter."

Toth pounded his staff on the ground.

I tried to follow the conversation. "You don't think Boyd and Stewart would be mad enough to take Michael's scalp, here? Even the Governor would not tolerate that."

"Those fools would do that and more, and find themselves in mortal peril."

Dr. Franklin pulled me over to the hitching post. "Quickly, Joshua Donegal, take my horse. You must scour the city until you find them."

I remembered Toth's strange mutterings and the way the crowd's mood had shifted. "What the devil are you going on about?"

"There's no time!" Toth took a hold of my arm. It felt as if a hundred hot needles past through me.

"What are you?"

"Someone who wants to stop any more bloodshed from happening, now get a move on, lad!"

I found myself obeying Toth without another word of protest. I had looked into his eyes when he grabbed me and I saw something old and terrible as if I had looked into the eyes of the Old Scratch himself. If I had been enjoying *his* hospitality for the past two months, I may have already been damned.

My search for Michael took me the length and breadth of Philadelphia. Michael had made few friendships during his time in this city, but an Indian walking alone in the largest city in the colonies was something many people remembered. I noted that two ravens were circling overhead of me. The newfound strength in my leg had started to wane when fortune smiled and I met an apothecary who said that he had Michael seen heading towards Fair Mount.

I arrived there at nightfall. I had feared that I would find Michael dead or at the mercy of the Paxton Boys. To my surprise, I found Boyd and Stewart trussed up like turkeys next to a massive bonfire. Michael stood before the flames, chanting and swaying as he threw strange powders that caused the fire to explode forth in blues and greens. I dismounted a safe distance away. Michael paid me no heed, his wild gaze fixed on the fire. I reached Boyd and Stewart with as much stealth as I could manage with my leg growing weak again. Both men's heads drooped backward, their tongues lolling to the sides as if they were in an opium stupor.

While I tried to rouse them, a white ball of fire exploded, turning night into day. A hot gust pushed Boyd, Stewart, and me backwards. My injured leg twisted out from under me. The fireball took shape until it held the form of hideous head with two bat-like wings extending? protruding? out of its temples. As its gaping maw opened up, I saw teeth the size of carving knives and smelled a god-forsaken stench. It roared a hideous laugh. I scrambled to my feet as the demon head consumed Boyd in one bite, grinding the poor bastard's bones with a wicked grin.

"Michael! Stop this obscenity!"

Michael stopped chanting at the sound of my voice. The devil's spawn howled with laughter as Michael's face contorted with fear. I knew nothing of what kind of witchcraft he had wrought here, but I could see that he had lost control of beast.

I pulled Stewart to his feet. The sight of the demon head roused him and he screamed like one damned. I pushed him down the hill and tumbled after. Seeing us roll away, the demon turned its attention towards a closer prey: Michael.

"No, I command you, kill them!" Michael pointed at the demonic head.

The demon grinned madly and opened its maw to consume the Conestoga. Ignoring the pain in my leg, I struggled to throw Stewart over the horse's back and climb into the saddle. My horse started to panic as the head turned and started flying towards us.

None too calm myself, I called out in prayer, "Our Father, who art in heaven, hollowed be Thy name..."

Suddenly, two golden snakes, burning like the sun, appeared. They encircled the flying head and then pulled their loops closed. The head vanished with a thunderclap. The serpents crawled back to their master, merged and became the staff of Herman Toth again.

G

"Are you all right, Joshua?"

"Yes. No. I mean, I have injured my leg again."

Toth examined my leg for a moment, then handed me a jar of his salve. "Put this on the area tonight and tomorrow and you shall be fine."

He then touched Stewart on the brow, and the leader of the Paxton Boys fell back into his stupor.

"What was that?" I struggled to find my wits.

"Something the Five Nations had once hidden away that Michael should have known he could never control."

"Toth," I asked, "are you the devil?"

Toth threw his head back and laughed. His hat fell to the ground. I started at his head, surprised at the lack of horns.

"You could call me a trickster. I have had many names: Odin, Hermes, Raven, Thoth, others that would mean nothing to you, but I am not the one you call Satan. He would have left you and Stewart to die."

"Then why did you help us?"

"I have many interests. When you have traveled as far and wide as I have, you develop a fondness for certain groups of people. I had hoped to preserve something of Michael and Mary's people, but Michael was foolish. His desire for revenge outweighed his judgment.

"In any event, I must take my leave of you now. Be a good boy and return Benjamin's horse to him. He has always been a good friend of mine."

"Wait, where are you going? Toth!" I found myself shouting to wind.

The next morning, Stewart, apparently remembering nothing of the night before, took his men back to Paxton and continued to patrol the frontier. For my part, I stayed in Philadelphia and became Dr. Franklin's aide-de-camp. I helped him with his campaigns against the Governor in the Assembly race and his ambassadorship to England to petition the crown to remove the Penn family from direct control of the colony. Mary also traveled with us, as my wife.

DENNIS WILSON ATTENDED PENN STATE UNIVERSITY WHERE HE EARNED his bachelors and masters degrees. "The Paxton Boy" stems from his interest in the history of Central Pennsylvania. He currently lives in Harrisburg, PA with his wife Maria and their dog, Rosie.

TRICK

James Chambers

THE OLD MAN STANDS BY HIS WINDOW, STARING OUT AT the close of day while dusk takes the sleepy neighborhood. Twilight shadows line the dead-end street, and the silhouette of leaf-barren branches lends the concrete the appearance of shattered glass. The dusty scent of autumn rides the air, entering the old man's quiet house through its window screens. It is a scent he knows well and he breathes it deeply into his tired lungs. He has spent his afternoon preparing for visitors. The half-open inner front door beckons. A bowl of colorfully wrapped chocolates gleams on the low table in the foyer. Dying sunlight streams through the murky glass of the storm door. Twice during the day, the doorbell rang, but the old man, unready, ignored it. Now he seats himself in his worn, familiar chair and waits.

Outside, goblin children overrun the darkening block, their wildest energies released in a sugar ecstasy of anonymity and candy-hoarding. Their visages vary wildly—ghost, pirate, princess, witch, pumpkin, hobo, superhero—but their voices sing the same song. Excitement. Anticipation. The thrill of freedom rarely tasted. They flash from house to house, making their way up one side of the road and down the other before moving on to the next block and the next one after, in hope of getting home before supper. The bright colors of their outfits flash, and from behind their masks, their high laughter crackles through the clear fall air.

But the old man sees their true faces; he sees them for what they really are.

Not always did he know their secret. Not in the all long years stretched out behind him when the business of living and earning a living provided suitable distractions from the ugliness. Not even in the few peaceful years he shared with Belle after they retired.

Without thinking, he drops his forearm across the arm of his recliner so that his hand lies palm up on the arm of Belle's chair beside it, ready for the warm grasp that greeted it so many times before, but which does not come tonight and will never come again.

Now the old man makes no mistake. Now he knows their true nature.

And this year he is ready.

It took time to learn the truth, but time he had after Belle went away. More time than he ever cared to spend on his own. Little by little, he cracked their facade, noticed the little oddities in their routines, their comings and goings at strange hours, the way a neighborhood cat disappeared. He spent hours watching and noting, observing their rituals and the faint, strange lights that sometimes burned in the windows of the children's rooms at night. One time, he watched a group of children squirm their way beneath the chain link fence that ran along the train tracks at the end of the road. God knows what hidden lairs they kept in the entangled weeds beyond the barrier. And one afternoon, when a child fell from his bicycle to the hard pavement after bumping into the curb, he sat in the street crying. Unaware of the old man's desperate gaze, he let fall the face he presented to the world and the old man saw the horror that lurked beneath.

Two children run across the edge of his front lawn in their mad door-to door dash to collect goodies. One wears a wizard's cloak and tall speckled hat; the other the delicate fringes and tight leotard of a dancer. He watches them eagerly, but they ignore his weed-cracked front walk and move on to the next house. They have been warned by their parents, he thinks, to stay away from the old man who has seen their secret faces.

Perhaps, he wonders with hope, *they fear me?*

Across the street paper decorations clutter the front window of his neighbor's home. A jaunty white skeleton. A creeping green witch. Foam tombstones dot the front lawn. At the house next door, electric-orange jack o' lantern lights trace the edge of the porch roof and false cobwebbing clings at the corners.

The old man closes his eyes and sees his other neighbors' homes along the road, all similarly attired in this garish manner with icons of mischief and images of the wild spirits rumored to roam free on nights such as this. Every year they accrue these baubles and ornaments and slowly transform the block to suit *their* tastes. Do they think he doesn't know what the signs and symbols mean? Do they think he doesn't see them, their decorations and parties, their fancy candies and disguised children, mocking him and everything his life has meant? Everything Belle's life meant.

They taunt him for what he knows, but their secrets are not safe with him. Let them parade their depravity in public once a year, costumed from the unknowing world in the guise of a child's holiday. Let them raise their terrible monsters in plain sight. Let others walk in ignorance. I will no longer be misled, he reassures himself.

Two boys and a little girl pause before the path to his front door. He observes and waits, listening to their whispers.

"Ronny, if you go there, I'm telling, Mom," says the girl.

"So?" answers Ronny. "Mom didn't say not to go here. It's just Mr. Louis's house, and you're just scared cause of what happened to Mrs. Louis last year!"

How brazen, the old man thinks and then, *Belle, I should have been here, that day.*

"Yeah, Kimmie. Don't be such a baby," interjects the older boy. "Besides, Ronny's too scared to go on his own, aren't you?"

"Shut up, Billy! I am not," blurts Ronny. "I'll prove it, too."

And with that, the young boy's footsteps move toward his house. He slows as he approaches the door. Something inside tells him he should not be here, but he can't turn back now. The old man rises and steps into the foyer, a welcoming grin on his face, warm satisfaction welling in his chest as he recognizes Ronny, the boy who found Belle in this very same foyer. *Perhaps this is what my beloved saw,* he thinks. *Her last vision the sight of an innocent child. Her last impression a lie.*

Ronny climbs the steps, holds forth his orange bag of treats and delivers his line. "Trick or treat."

The old man grabs a handful of candy from the dish and pushes the door open. "Oh, it'll definitely be a treat," he says. "Enjoy!"

The miniature chocolate bars spill from his hands, plunking heavily among the other sweets gathered in Ronny's sack. "Thank you," the boy says.

As the boy returns to the sidewalk, the old man calls. "Make sure you share those with the others. They may be shy...but I know they want some candy, too."

He lingers in the doorway as the trio moves off toward the next house. Ronny hops and bounces, rubbing in his victory before his sister and the older boy. He pulls the chocolates from his bag and splits them up among the others' ready grasps. Together they stop by the next-door driveway while the old man's neighbor, Mrs. Reynolds, backs her car out into the street.

Ronny pulls the wrapper from a piece of chocolate.

Kimmie scolds him, reminding him they'd promised their mother not to eat anything she hadn't checked for them. Ronny razzes her and holds the candy out of reach above her head, teasing her.

Unable to resist such an easy target, Billy moves in from behind and slaps the candy from Ronny's hand, yelling "He shoots! He scores!"

The candy lands under the wheel of Mrs. Reynolds' moving car. The heavy black tire squashes it flat, ejecting its creamy filling from the wrapper. A moment later, air pops like a gunshot, and something hisses a long sigh. The car sags to one side as its tire deflates. Mrs. Reynolds puts it in park and climbs out to examine the wheel, joining the three children already circled around and pointing at the dull metal gleam protruding from the rubber—the back end of a fresh razor blade.

Ronny turns and stares at the old man in the doorway. The little boy's face is pale and tears pour from his eyes. And then the old man realizes his error. He knew them not at all; he underestimated their power. A powerful tightness seizes his chest, and his pulse throbs louder in his head as its beats slow and then weaken. He falls to the foyer floor, landing in blackness.

An hour later the police officer closes the ambulance door and watches it drive off without lights or sirens. Ronny stands nearby with his mother, clinging to her, his face buried in her side. The officer turns. "Funny," he says. "Mr. Louis dying just like his wife did and Ronny the first to find both bodies." His voice comes laced with suspicion not quite strong to make him speak his true thoughts. "Guess it's better this way, though, considering what that old man was up to."

"Yes," Ronny's mother replies. "They never did really fit in on a block with so many young families."

Ronny peers out from behind his mother's shirt, glimpses the officer and then smothers his face again. *If I didn't know better*, thinks the cop, *I'd swear that kid was just smiling.*

JAMES CHAMBERS HAS BEEN PUBLISHED IN THE ANTHOLOGIES THE DEAD *Walk, Sick: An Anthology of Illness, Weird Trails,* and *Warfear*, the chapbook *Mooncat Jack*; the magazine *Inhuman*; and in numerous other venues. His tale "A Wandering Blackness," published in Lin Carter's *Dr. Anton Zarnak, Supernatural Sleuth* received Honorable Mention in The Year's Best Fantasy and Horror, Sixteenth Annual Collection. He can be found online at www.jameschambersonline.com.

THE DOOM THAT CAME TO NECROPOLIS

Steve Johnson

IT IS WITH TREMBLING HAND AND ONLY AFTER LONG DEBATE WITH MYSELF THAT I set down the events that culminated in the fall of Necropolis. There are many reasons, good and solid reasons, that the loathsome details should remain hidden, moldering in the unhallowed dark until the ages pass, and the slow parade of time erases all memory of Necropolis from the minds of men.

But though the telling requires me to remind the world of many dreadful facts which it would sooner forget, still my conscience at last compels me to admit that, without the true account of Necropolis' doom before them, it is all but inevitable that other communities will fall into the same shuddersome errors Necropolis made, and so meet in the end with the same horrific fate.

I remember that it was a particularly gray afternoon in the early part of the winter of 1928 that Daniel Dennison of the Geologic Survey Service came to Necropolis, Connecticut. His Dillinghast motorcycle puttered its two-stroke rhythm against the walls of the abandoned Howard quarry on Innsmouth Road, past the rows of white clapboard houses along Front Street, and up to the peeling, flaking, overgrown Georgian brownstone that served Necropolis as a combination of post office, Federal building, and fire department. A droplet landing in the rain barrel beneath the gutter was the only sound once/after he killed the engine.

Dennison swung one booted, leather-sheathed leg off the cycle. He pulled off his helmet, revealing a shock of unruly black hair above piercing blue eyes. He unbuttoned his leather jacket, draping it casually over the Dillinghast's handlebars, and began unpacking his Special Service equipment from its panniers. He was young for a government man, doubly so for the string of degrees that trailed after his name. He was tall, wide and strong, hard and keen, his face and hands deeply tanned by years of hard work in the sun.

The last thing he removed from the saddlebags was a tie. He knotted it around his neck as he sauntered up the brownstone's steps.

I slipped the book I had been reading under my desk before he could catch the title. It might not have meant anything to him, but I was taking no chances.

"Yes?" I said, as if I had been waiting patiently for him all afternoon.

"I'm Dan Dennison," he said at once. He paused.

"Walter Miller," I replied. His grip was firm without crushing my hand.

"The Survey sent me to take care of a little problem," he said. "Okay if I use your telephone?"

"I—that is, we weren't expecting you till tomorrow, Mr. Dennison."

He chuckled, running a big hand through his hair.

SOUTHERN
RAILROAD
956
RIVER
N
E
G
893
1137
RAILROAD
BELKIVAP-DEREETH

"Yeah, I bet. But this burg is so far off the beaten track, I thought it might take me all day to chase it down, so I came early."

He consulted a complicated-looking chronometer worn wristwatch-wise on a bracelet of sturdy metal.

"Five-oh-four, for the love of Pete!" he crowed. "Just as I figured—if I'd started at dawn, I'd have wasted the whole day. Now, how about that phone, Ace?"

His bluff and hearty manner, so unlike the polite reserve of New England, had thrown me. But I was on familiar ground again.

"Telephone service cuts off at five," I said, spreading my hands.

"You don't say," he said. "Okay, if those are the ground rules, I can run with 'em. I'll be phoning in reports every morning, then," he decided. "If that's okay with you?"

"Oh, yes, certainly. I'm in by nine."

"Nine...well, it can wait till then," he said. "OK."

He spread out a map of Klarkashton County, the same one that hung under glass on the wall. But Dennison's map had curved lines drawn on it in ink, forming a queer extrusion like a hungry pseudopod questing down the Belknap River in search of food.

"Lessee—we're here," he said confidently, though the map showed no town. "That road I took would be right along in here...uh-huh. Thought so. The center of the disturbance must be somewhere between Hill 1137," (his finger touched a triangular mark) "and Hill 893, over here. North of town, then, and probably smack in the Belknap-Derleth watershed. Wet country up there?"

It was the first scientific statement he had made with less than absolute certainty. I confess it took me a moment to realize it was a question.

"Oh, ah, no," I said. "Not that I am aware of. This hill 1137, would it be Ramsey Hill?"

"You're asking me? I just got here, Ace," he said good-naturedly. "It 'ud be west of here, just past the edge of that window."

"Ah? Yes, that would be Ramsey Hill. And Bloch Heights are over here—they would be your Hill 893, although they're really more of a ridge."

"Yeah? These low spots been filled in?" he said, indicating the map.

"Oh, my, yes. Well before the houses were built, I should think."

Dennison snapped his fingers.

"If that don't beat all," he said. "Should have re-surveyed this valley ten years ago, at least. What's got into those boys in Boston?"

"We don't usually have visitors here in Necropolis," I said, trying to be helpful. By the determined look that came into his steely blue eyes, he might have taken it the wrong way.

"'Zat so? Well, Ace, the G-man has arrived. G for geology, that is."

He bent once again to examine the lines on his map.

"Excuse me, Mister Dennison?"

"Eh? Call me Dan, if you want," he said affably. "What's on your mind, Ace?"

"Well...I just have to ask. What do those lines represent on your map? They look so...sinister."

"Sinister?"

"Yes, so queerly repellent in aspect," I said in all sincerity.

Dennison threw back his head and laughed. I felt a sudden chill.

"Sorry," he gasped. "I wasn't laughing at you. But I've been carrying this map around for weeks, looking at it every day, and suddenly it does look sort of like a big amoeba or something, doesn't it? Yep, an amoeba thirty miles long," he said, chuckling to himself.

"You're all right, Ace," he said when he finished. "No, it's not a chart of a huge protozoan taking over the valley. These are magnetic field strengths, recorded by a plane."

"Really?" I hadn't remarked on any aeroplanes passing over the town.

"Yep. We pile these readings up, a little at a time, and draw these lines to connect 'em. Helps when you're navigating a crate in the dark, and all you've got is your compass between you and a dead-reckoning landing."

"Dead reckoning," I echoed. "It sounds so sepulchral."

"Yep, they say if you don't reckon it right, you're dead," he said cheerfully. "'Cept over dry land, there's usually someplace you can put down. Anyway, there's a new mail run that goes right over your county..."

"There is?" I yelped. "They're building a railroad through Klarkashton County?"

"An aeroplane route," he explained patiently. "From Boston to New York. And the Service is supposed to make sure the route's clear of any magnetic anomalies. Things that make you think north is east, west, or upside-down."

"But what unfathomable mysteries could cause such an unnatural deceit? It's almost as if the hand of some nameless horror were intruding into the everyday world of 'planes and compasses. As if the laws of nature weren't laws at all, but mere customs to be overturned by the casual whim of some superior being," I said earnestly. If only I could make him understand that there were things man was not meant to know...

Dennison regarded me quizzically.

"Sometimes it's a vein of iron ore," he said slowly. "Sometimes power lines, if they're big enough."

"Oh," I said, disappointed.

"And there's a hum-dum-dinger of an anomaly here in this county," he continued. "So I'm here to find it and measure it, so we can correct for it on the charts. Lessee...guess I'll start right up here where this contour starts to dip back in, right above Hill 1137. Any roads leading up there?"

"Yes," I said automatically. "But...you don't want to go up there."

"Oh?" he said, interested. "You know something about geomagnetics? Makes sense, you're a native. Well, where should I start, then?"

"It's not that," I said. "But up there is the old Howard place."

He held up a hand.

"You've got to remember I'm from Milwaukee," he said. "The name doesn't mean anything to me. Should it?"

"I suppose not...everyone here knows it's haunted."

Dennison pursed his lips.

"Haunted, huh?"

"Oh, my land, yes," I assured him.

"Scary at night?"

"No one goes near it."

"And in the daytime?"

"Well, once in a while...the road to Hartford goes by there, you know...but never at night."

"Good," he said, rolling up the map. I was relieved he'd seen reason.

"I need a few hours to let the needle steady down, really get a good reading," he said. "A few hours with nobody around."

"Mr. Dennison, are you..."

"I am. Tonight it is!"

He was insane. That was it.

"Care to come along?"

I didn't want to. I had no clear idea what was waiting for us up there, but everyone in Necropolis agreed the Howard place was better shunned than considered. On the other hand, if Dennison went up there and didn't come back, I had no way of knowing whether the government would blame me or not, being the last one to talk to him. Perhaps they might think I should have stopped him?

Either way, I was facing the dread Unknown. And all Unknowns are equally bad. Infinity equals infinity.

However, to stay meant to disagree with Dennison, and although he didn't seem like the type to take that the wrong way, there was always that chance, wasn't there?

I mean, you never *really* know.

So I went, locking the door behind me. Shutters closed in the square as Dennison and I got into the Packard stake-bed we used as a fire truck. I could tell they were watching me—the Peaslees, the Armitages, the Angells and their cousins—but from behind slitted drapes, from darkened rooms.

"Lead on, MacDuff," Dennison said, slamming the door with a clank. We headed up into the hills, leaving Necropolis proper behind.

Soon we were up among the spectacular reds and yellows of the New England autumn, with a corporal's guard of pines keeping the green flame alive till spring returned. The Howard place sat within a house-width of a sheer cliff, dropping eighty feet or more to a bed of gravel. Some of the tombstones in back of the house were slanting, undermined by erosion 'til it seemed they must surely topple into the abyss, perhaps with their mephitic contents preceding them by years or more. I felt a sudden sick dread of looking over that cliff, for fear of what I might behold.

"Hold up, Ace," Dennison instructed. "Here's fine."

I stopped, and he got out, hoisting his equipment cases with ease.

"Are you going to set up here, in the open?" I quailed, for the wind was cold from the east now, and night was falling.

"If I have to," he answered equably. "But unless there are lightning rods all over the frame, that house'll do as well as anyplace." He grinned. "And it'll keep the rain off our heads besides."

I looked about, but saw no clouds.

"Rain?"

"Two hours, the way this blow's shaping up. You won't see the clouds 'til they're almost on top of us," he said offhandedly.

I helped him wrestle his equipment up the narrow, rickety steps. Dennison surveyed the porch with a critical eye.

"Too shaky," he decided, "and not wide enough to keep us dry. Think anyone'll mind if we go on in?"

I paled, but managed to shake my head. The owners of record were long dead, and as for the masters—who knew?

"Swell," he said, and pushed on the door. It gave with a creak and a groan of rusty hinges. Dennison strode into the parlor, stomping his motorcycle boots experimentally along its length. He nodded, apparently satisfied.

"OK, this'll do. Hand me that long case there, will you, Ace?" he said, and commenced to assemble his equipment. Of all the scientific arcana he produced, I confess to recognizing only a roll of lined paper, on which a needle would score marks as the paper unrolled.

"A seismograph?" I hazarded.

"Magnetometer," he said. "Measures the strength of the earth's magnetic field, which varies some over time. We'll take our readings throughout an average day, then see if we can't edit out any interference from local phenomena."

"Such as?"

"Lightning, for one," he said, pointing at the doorway.

The horizon was a solid mass of low, threatening clouds. The promised storm was coming.

Far below, in the valley, darkness lay on the land like a spreading stain.

Dennison wound the spring that powered the paper coil, then watched it unravel while the pen jerked wildly across the page. He flicked a pencil at the edge of the paper, stealing a glance at his chronometer as he did. When enough paper had spilled on the floor, he wrote down the time next to his pencil mark.

"It's really going wild," I observed. Was that good or bad?

"That's just the gimbals," he said. "Ultra-sensitive. We have to give 'em a chance to settle down before the readings will mean anything."

"Which means," he added, turning to me, "that it's time to give 'em some room. Every time we take a step, we set 'em to jiggling again."

"Back to the truck?" I said, dismayed.

"Further into the house," he said. "Better stay on the ground floor, though. Let's see how many rooms we can put between us and the gizmo."

With that, he headed off into the depths of the Howard mansion, leaving me the choice of staying behind in darkness, or following the electric torch he produced from his tool belt. It wasn't much of a choice at all.

We found ourselves in a pantry behind the kitchen, which in turn lay behind the dining room, which in turn lay behind a parlor. There wasn't a back door.

Dennison sat down on his haunches and turned off the torch.

"Saves the batteries," he explained. "And since I located the commode on the way here, I can find it in the dark. Okay with you?"

As intimated before, I was reluctant to disagree with this forceful, possibly dangerous man. I made some noise of assent.

"Great. Now, since we have an hour or so to kill, suppose you tell me about this haunted house story."

I swallowed. That was one of the last things I wanted to discuss, swaddled as we were in Stygian gloom. However, as the alternative appeared to be silence, in which my fears would grow unchecked into what full abysmal blossom I could hardly name, I began at the beginning.

"Old man Howard, the great-grandson of the Howard who built this house, used to own the quarry out on Innsmouth Road. He owned a lot of the houses and employed a lot of the men of this town, as well. But he was never a wealthy man, Mr. Dennison. He loaned out much of what he'd inherited, and over time he never seemed to get back what he'd lent out, much less any interest.

"If you were behind in your payments (and many were) he'd write a letter, perhaps send you a telegram. Telegrams were impressive in those days, oh, my, yes.

"But presently it became known that he'd never take the final step of calling in the law. And after the third or fourth notice, he just forgot about you, or so it seemed at the time."

Dennison shifted his weight.

"I'll bite," he said. "Why didn't he call the sheriff?"

"Because he would have had to come to the courthouse in person. And old Howard never went anywhere during the daylight hours."

"Huh! So he was a vampire?"

"Not exactly. But he acted like one. And when he died ..."

"Yeah? You've got me, now reel me in."

"The people who wouldn't pay their debts just started to disappear. They'd turn up after a day or so, hungry and tired, remembering nothing of the night before," I said.

"Except now they craved the blood of the living?" Dennison said. "Check your sources, Ace. I think I've read this one before."

"No, no, Mr. Dennison! They were and are perfectly normal. Except once they came home, their relatives vanished for a night or so. Then their neighbors, then their neighbors' neighbors. And so on."

"And so one night everyone had disappeared for a day or so ..." Dennison said.

"A *night*," I corrected him.

"A night. And they were just the same, and that's the end of it?"

"I didn't expect you to believe me," I said, stung by the scorn in his voice.

He turned on his torch so I could see his face. He wasn't smiling.

"I haven't said I don't believe you," he assured me. "But what does all that have to do with this house being haunted? The way you tell it, the whole town's equally mixed up in spooky business. Isn't the whole town haunted?"

"Well, naturally *we* don't see it that way..." I began, knowing how pale it sounded.

A sudden crash made us both jump. Dennison crouched, fists balled, eyes alertly scanning the shadowed shelves on all sides of us.

"Lightning," I said to calm myself.

"Nope," he said, already dashing for the front hall. "Something falling against the house!"

I kept the light in sight as best I could. When I caught up with him, Dennison was bent over his instruments, a look of intense concentration on his face.

The pen on his paper spool jittered a crazed tarantella at the very top of its range. Sometimes it jerked off the paper entirely.

"Magnetic flux. High but very unstable," he said to himself. "Hell's bells! That pattern's familiar, for all the tea in China! But where have I seen it before? Think, you mug, think!"

I thought he was referring to me, till I saw him brush a hand over his own brow, urging his brain into action.

"Eureka! No, wait a minute. That doesn't make sense," he said. "Make sense, Hell. There it is. Start doubting the evidence of your senses, without clear and convincing proof of hallucination, and you're for the laughing academy, Dan my boy."

I heard the porch creak ominously, as though burdened by immense, ageless weight.

"Dennison?" I demanded. "What is it? What do you see?"

"Lines on a page, Miller," he shot back. "But they tell me plenty. See, this is like a reading of brain-wave electricity I took once in college. Somehow that pattern's been superimposed on a magnetic field. Queer—it's not like any human brain-waves I ever saw. But it's similar, darn similar, for all the hells in China!"

"But what does it MEAN?" I gibbered.

At that, I heard the doorknob rattle like a serpent's warning. Dennison stood up, brushing dust from his palms.

"Don't know yet," he admitted. Before I could stop him, or utter an agonized cry of fearful warning, he opened the door.

We beheld a trio of manlike shapes, dark and sinister of aspect. They were almost completely black, heads cocked unnaturally to the side, while their posture reeked of unmentionable, unfathomable currents swimming darkly beneath the surface of their intentions. I had the intuition that they were not men at all, but mannikins, manipulated like marionnettes by some unseen, unhallowed, sheerly unbelievable horror from beyond the fields we knew.

"What d'you want?" barked Dennison in a challenging tone.

"You," gurgled one of the half-human wights.

They took a synchronized step forward, as though one single hip joint were swiveling three legs at once. Though it seemed impossible that they could all pass through the door at the same time, each turned in unison like three slats on a window blind, and then they were inside.

Dennison turned his torch full on the intruders. A gasp of startled terror fell from my lips, for they were infinitely more human than I had supposed. They appeared to be three weatherbeaten men, or rather two men and a boy, dressed in checkered wool shirts and tough cotton trousers that tucked into the tops of their thick-soled work boots. I recognized them as the Mallorys, father and sons, who worked the quarry and delivered firewood.

The only thing unusual in their appearance, apart from a certain uniformity of expression, was their eyes. *In each of the six sockets a ball of black fur bristled, as though their orbs had been replaced by oversized, hirsute leeches.*

I fear the sight of them unhinged my reason, but not so much that I cannot remember what happened next. Of my own part I can give no account, for I do not to this day connect the gabbling cries and whining screams that engulfed us with my own brain and voice.

But I know what I saw, and that was this:

One of the men held up a long forked stick like the type used by spiritualists to find underground water. It was as black as his eyes, and possessed of the same furry malignancy. Dennison dropped to one shoulder and rolled aside as the furry black coating of the stick gathered itself, amid a hellish buzzing and rasping, then leapt for his throat.

But fast as it was, Dennison was faster. He snared the magnetometer with one hand, springing to his feet, then with a titanic effort hurled the entire apparatus into the middle of the three men. They produced no sound as they were smashed aside by the machine's weight and bulk, but merely dropped to the ground with hollow thuds.

Dennison seized my arm and guided me through the doorway. I do not believe I would have moved had he not.

But in my paralyzed state I could not cry out (unless I had been doing so all along, insensible), and so I was unable to give any sort of warning when I emerged from that loathsome house of horrors.

For I was facing backward as Dennison pulled me along. And I saw, though he did not, *that the shadows of the pines were moving along the wall.*

Despite the flicker of our electric torch as Dennison pumped his arms, the shadows held still. Then they advanced, extruding themselves in two separate directions, spreading over the front of the house exactly like a pseudopod, some colossal cellular aberration, reaching down the valley to snare two small lives.

I heard the buzzing and rasping resume, much louder, coming from the shadow as it gathered itself on the wall.

Dennison turned, saw the predicament we faced, and flashed his light directly into the shadow.

The shadow refused to yield. Impossibly, incredibly, it maintained its shape and nocturnal blackness against/under the full blaze of the electric torch.

Dennison retreated with me in tow. After a long while that I cannot account for, I sputtered on the cup of hot rum-laden tea he was pouring into my mouth.

"We better not go back there tonight," he said as I swallowed gratefully. I nodded assent.

"No, better we wait till morning, when we can see better," he decided.

I nearly choked on my tea.

"You're going back? Are you mad?"

"We both are. I need you to corroborate my findings, check my data."

"But that house is the abode of powers from Beyond ..." I began, confidently.

"Bunk," Dennison cut me off. "What did we see? Besides a lot of local spook-stories, that is. We saw some guys with black stuff in their eyes and some shadows that don't behave the way shadows should."

"Exactly," I said. He was starting to grasp the scale of what we dared to oppose! "They do not do as they ought—the taint of evil is upon the very shadows that lie in this town—and somewhere behind them the Shadow Princes pull their strings, and men twitch to their urgings ..."

Dennison watched me with a bored expression. I stopped.

"You done? Any more spooks you want to call up?" he said.

I closed my mouth, abashed.

"Okay, then listen. We saw some shadows come after us. By all I know of optics, that shouldn't happen. Right?"

I nodded, afraid to speak.

"Right. So I don't know everything there is to know about optics. That's all it means, Miller. It's just the unknown. Time to shed some light on these shadows and see what makes 'em tick."

"*Just* the unknown? But *anything* could lurk in the unknown," I rebutted firmly. "Don't you see that the deepest and strongest fear is the fear of the unknown, and well it should be so!"

To my surprise, Dennison nodded.

"Mm. Well, that's true enough. You can't fight something you know nothing about. And so far as fear goes, yep, I was scared. Scared white as a sheet with a streak of purest gold down my back, I should hope to shout!"

"Then you see! We mere mortals should admit our helplessness..."

"Hold the phone, Miller!" Dennison barked. "Since when does the universe give two hoots about my emotions? Fear affects my perceptions and *nothing else*. Sure, I was scared. But whatever it was in the dark, it was just the same before I got scared, and the same after. And if we'd never seen it, it woulda *still* been the same!"

He gripped me by the shoulders, swinging me around so his face was in the light.

"You know that, don't you? Whatever chased us, it's either real or it isn't. If it isn't, we're in the clear. But if it is real..."

"It is, it is!" I insisted.

"— then it's got length, width, and height. It's got mass and weight. It takes up volume and occupies a definite interval of time. It has shape, color, temperature, electric charge, and chemical properties like anything else. If it's alive, it's got instincts, unless it's intelligent, in which case it has motives. Whatever it is, we'll dope it out, and then we'll know how to lick it!"

"But we saw it! It was a mass without form, without substance! How can you draw conclusions from nothing?"

"Bunk, I said. "Can you hear radio with your bare ears?"

I blinked. I said no.

"And you can't tell a black thread from white in the dark, either."

"Unless you wait for dawn," I said, recalling the Moslem custom.

Dennison did not—quite—sneer. He did, however, favor me with a pitying look.

"Unless you light a candle, Miller," he said. "Unless you light a candle."

I cannot explain the dire forebodings that twitched through my thoughts all that next endless day. Dennison had called for additional equipment from Boston to replace what was lost at the Howard house, and when it arrived, he spent the afternoon assembling one contrivance after another. The electricity was not sufficient for his machines, but one of them turned out to be an electrical generator fueled by kerosene, which of course we had in plenty.

It was not—precisely—fear of his experiments that gripped me in an agony of lassitude. Nor was it memory of what we had experienced the night before, although that terrible night remained sanity-blasting in my recollection. No, the slithering fear that gripped me was of a wholly different, even alien, complexion. It was as though I were being commanded to fear, compelled in the direction of dread by some influence I could not define, only detect.

I thought of broaching my fears to Dennison, but I thought he might discount them as the fancies of a badly-jarred imagination. Instead, I did what I always did when fear threatened: I sought out the thing in my surroundings which terrified me the most (in this case, the shadow of my phonograph) and stared at it relentlessly as if it became more and more terrifying, till I was completely petrified, unable to speak or move lest I scream at the top of my voice.

As I said, this is what I do when frightened. It has served me all of my life.

The shadows waxed and lengthened as I writhed in terror's ophidian coils. Afternoon was waning and night was coming soon. The shadows were growing, in size and strength, soon to cover all the world as they did every night.

I broke away with an inarticulate cry. This was not the way to avoid fearing the dark!

All at once I was struck with a revelation that seemed perfectly lucid for an instant. The solution to my morbid fears was to strike down Daniel Dennison, with any implement near to hand. A length of pipe, left over from a repair on my leaky radiator, would do perfectly. Because he knew me, he would not suspect until I was within striking reach, and then one swift blow would finish the job. Then the fear would ebb.

I had closed my palm about the pipe's unyielding brass before the absurdity of my plan struck me.

Kill Dennison? How would that lead to anything but madness?

Again I felt the dawn of sudden insight, but it was the same insight as before. Kill Dennison, and the fear would pass.

I had never before been struck with an idea that was an exact restatement of a previous idea. To the best of my layman's knowledge, such a repeat-inspiration did not happen in healthy, normal minds, only in the obsessive dream-world of the neurotic. I feared I might be going mad.

My hand tightened around the pipe as if of its own accord. My hand seemed to know what to do, even if I did not. And that prospect was the most worrisome of all, for what can a *hand* know?

I let go of the pipe with a spasm of revulsion. Or rather, I willed myself to let go. *But the hand refused my orders.*

I saw now that there was nothing I could do to resist the awful command. My very flesh would betray me, already in league with the usurper. Giving in at last to the dread song ringing through my blood, I eased open the door to my foyer.

Dennison was on his knees, his back turned to me, adjusting a bit of ironmongery with a screwdriver. I slipped out of my shoes and tiptoed across the thick pile carpet, my bludgeon poised over my head.

My shadow fell across his back. For a single instant, the veriest edge of shadow peeked over his shoulder and fell on the floor, in front of him.

I swung the pipe down with all of my strength.

Dennison turned, lightning quick, and caught it in his hand.

"Was it something I said?" he said without a trace of a smile.

"Help me, Dennison!" I screeched like a trumpet with a broken reed. "My mind is no longer my own!"

"Yep. You could say that." He seized my other wrist, then steered me into a chair. With a sudden twist, he had the pipe away from me.

"Dennison, what am I to do!? I've become an agent of the Shadow Prince! My will, my very soul, dances to the tune of foreign pipes."

"Brass pipes," he observed. "Still want to give me the conk?"

"No, no," I assured him hastily. "My land, no. I'm no match for you barehanded, I know that."

"Barehanded?" He looked at the pipe in his hand.

"You wouldn't."

"Not if I don't have to," he said. "So you're getting some hoodoo from the spook that roams the hills, huh? Any idea when they plan to break in?"

"Break in?" I wailed.

"Sure," he said coolly. "They know I'm on to them now. They know you didn't bash my skull in. In their place, I'd break in."

"Who are 'they,' Dennison?"

He grinned, cocking an eyebrow at me.

"The Shadow Princes, of course. Just like you said."

I felt the planet sway beneath me. Dennison helped me to a chair.

"Steady, Miller! Sorry to put the skids under you like that," he said. "But y'know, that purple pulp-magazine mouth of yours was right on the money, this time. Shadow Princes is as good a name as any for what we're up against."

I waited, breathless to hear and terrified to know all at the same time. Dennison sat back in my armchair, lighting his pipe. He put out the match on an ashtray on my coffee table, beside an assortment of twigs, leaves, bark, and soil he'd collected over the course of the morning.

"That thing on the wall last night, whatever it was, wasn't no shadow," he began. "But it looked like one; leastways, it was dark and reasonably flat. And it wasn't paint, because it moved sideways in response to light."

"Or our presence," I put in. He nodded.

"Could be. So I asked myself what known phenomena act like that? First place to look, I figure, is mold."

"Mold?"

"Some molds can move, though not very fast. They call 'em slime molds; sort of a weird cross-breed of cat, not really plant nor animal. No known slime mold moves fast enough to see, but like I said, we don't know it all. Bet you'd agree with me there, huh, Ace?"

Now it was my turn to nod, fast and hard.

"Thought so. But you also ought to realize that the part we do know is true. Maybe not universal, maybe not complete, but the truths Galileo and Einstein discovered don't disappear just because we're up against something new."

"So I thought: if this black stuff is a slime mold, or something similar, what properties would it have? Slime molds live on decaying vegetation; no problem finding that in these woods. 'Cept the groundwater around here is brackish, tainted with rust. But you all knew that; you drink rainwater or nothing, right?"

"Yes—the well water tastes metallic, unwholesome."

"I'll say! You don't want heavy metals concentrating in your bloodstream. In fact, this whole area's laced with iron oxides, in the trees, in the rocks. No wonder a compass gets confused around here.

"A slime mold, living off the leaves and bark of trees nourished by groundwater, would pick up a lot of iron along with it. It's not inconceivable that, at least close up, they could affect a compass, too."

I had it, a piece of it.

"And thus distort your instruments, if it were clinging to the wall of the house."

"Kee-rect!" Dennison said. "And don't forget, it was pulsing with an almost human wave-form. Its intelligence might be equal to ours. Which brings me to the question: what was it that was filling up those fellows' eyes? More mold? But mold doesn't grow well on human flesh."

"You said this might be a new sort of mold."

"Could be. If it is, it's learned to inhabit human bodies. That might not kill you, if the mold didn't attack vital organs. But it would make you look pretty darn different inside, I'm betting. That's what this fluoroscope here is for. Would you mind?"

He motioned me over to a camera-like apparatus, connected by rigid members to a dark, thick glass plate. The camera was suspended in such a way as to face the plate. He started his kerosene generator, and the plate warmed to a deep green illuminated color. Pale fumes fogged my parlor.

"Just pass your hand in front of the scope...hold it...good," he said. He slipped a prepared photographic film into a slot behind the plate.

"Now step in front of it. Turn around...let the rays play over every part of your body. Good."

He pulled the plate aside and slid in a fresh.

"Everything looks normal," he decided after a moment. "I'm not an M.D., so I won't try to slice you open..."

"Me?" I gasped.

"Why not? You said the whole town was affected by whatever got old man Howard. You live here; you're part of the town. Whatever it is that makes people act funny in Necropolis, I'd bet money you've got it, too. Q.E.D."

Could that be where my mysterious urge had come? From a slime mold? I felt vastly disappointed, deflated somehow, to know the thing which had nearly caused me to lose my reason was not some cosmic horror with world-girdling occult powers, but the lowest of the lowly inhabitants of the bogs and hollows. I felt low myself, not the abject lowliness of the slave beaten down by almighty masters, but low like an insignificant creature crawling about in the mud, worth no one's attention but its own.

"But see here, Dennison," I said, forgetting courtesy in my despond. "This mold or whatever-it-is—do you truly think it's living inside us, inside me, right at this very moment?"

"Can't say for sure yet, Ace. I'd have to do some more tests. One thing I did think of, though—if it is, I bet it didn't like the fluoroscope much."

"But it didn't hurt when I put my hand in it."

"If you've got a cold, does it hurt when you take aspirin? Unless the stuff's laced into your nervous system, what hurts it won't hurt you. And unless I miss my guess, the reason those guys at the Howard place had gunk over their eyes was the same reason Howard didn't go out in daylight. The mold might be susceptible to light; lots of slime molds like dark places. Remember, they're not really plants; they're more saprophytic, like fungi. Get their energy from decaying matter, not sunlight. And the fluoroscope puts out ionizing radiation that can penetrate opaque surfaces. Like sunshine on your bones."

"So you mean to expose the townspeople to your fluoroscopic light, then," I stated.

"Can't imagine it'll do 'em any harm," he said. "You seem to be all right."

"And if they resist? If they try to expose us to the black mold, as they did last night?" I said.

I heard a clank around the back of the house, where my father's old chain gate hung. Someone was climbing it. At almost the same moment, many feet climbed the steps to my porch, crossed the creaking wood to my front door.

"Any other ways out?" said Dennison, indicating the front and back.

I shook my head, frozen to my seat.

"Better get up, then," he said. "We may have to move fast."

The first blow struck the front door, splintering its panels. Dennison hefted the fluoroscope and aimed it at the door.

A panel jounced from its frame, smashed in. Those outside saw Dennison, but did not stop at his warning. I saw Joe Buell, Charles Pabodie, and the three Carter brothers wielding axes and pry bars. They kept on attacking the door, their eyes abristle with black mold.

Dennison set up the fluoroscope so that the camera was pointed directly at the door, and tugged the glass shield free.

My crystal doorknob, a memento from my father's visit to a predominantly Czech county in upper New York State, sprang loose and shattered on the kitchen floor. I felt a surge of righteous anger.

Seizing a fireplace poker, I stood beside Dennison as the tortured door yielded and my possessed neighbors swarmed inside.

The penetrating rays caught them squarely in their weird phosphorescence. Skin and the whites of socks and shirts glowed an eerie blue in the fluoroscope's ray.

As one, they convulsed, clapping hands to their eyes and contorting their limbs in apparent agony. And yet, they did not cry out, except in wonderment to find themselves thus arrayed on my kitchen floor, like sleepwalkers awaking from a passionate dream.

The back door quaked under a sudden assault.

"Dennison!" I cried, but it was too late.

Sheriff Pitts kicked the flimsy kitchen door aside with his massive, size-thirteen boot. A double-barreled shotgun swung to bear on us.

Dennison tackled me as I stood paralyzed with mortal fear. The gun blasts echoed as one, shattering the fluoroscope to ruin.

Pitts stepped in, reloading jerkily, like an automaton. A fair number of Necropolitans followed him, advancing on us.

Dennison reached under the table and picked up a green duffel bag.

"Is that another fluoroscope?" I gibbered.

"Nope." He slid out an automatic rifle and a Colt pistol, black, heavy, and deadly.

"We'll just have to let light into 'em the old-fashioned way."

I clutched my hands to my ears just in time.

Dennison's rifle sprayed a continuous stabbing flame, dropping the possessed men like tenpins in my foyer. Only when the rifle clicked empty did the last man advance over the threshold; Dennison clubbed him with the rifle butt and slid in a fresh magazine. Throwing a bag of filled magazines over his left shoulder, he avoided the bodies and stepped out on the porch.

"Any man in his right mind, that doesn't want to die, better stay in his house!" he bellowed, his voice carrying to every corner of the small mountain town.

Doors opened on every street. People gathered like iron filings, drawn to the magnet of Dennison's voice.

"This is your last chance! You have two seconds to turn around and go back!"

But it was closer to ten seconds before his weapons exploded in chattering thunder, sweeping the street in steady, metronomic bursts of gunfire.

At his feet, the men who had been bathed in the fluoroscope's rays moaned like lost children.

Those few souls were all that survived of the town of Necropolis, Connecticut that evening. All others were hurled by their inhuman masters into the maw of Dennison's chattering guns, and all of them who opposed him died. Their bodies, when examined, were filled through and through with powdery black motes, like mold infusing a loaf of bread.

The Belknap Valley was sealed off, pending extensive study. Humanity's confrontation, or problematic accommodation, with the slime molds will consume the remainder of this century's energies, if not the history of our race on Earth.

But for the town of Necropolis, Connecticut, the coming of Daniel Dennison was and shall remain

THE END

STEVE JOHNSON IS A CHEMISTRY TEACHER AND AMATEUR WARGAMER LIVING IN Fredericksburg, Virginia. His stories of science and conflict have appeared in *Analog* and *Nth Degree Magazines*. He is a lifelong admirer of both E.E. "Doc" Smith and H. P. Lovecraft and regrets that they never collaborated on a story.

MEAT

by Adam P. Knave

It was break time at the store: my favorite time of the day, next to quitting time. Ever since the outbreaks, sales had been for shit and the place was so quiet you could hear a pin bitch about being dropped even before it hit. I smacked the security bar on the back door with the flat of my hand hard enough for it to sting, and when the door flew open, I drew a deep breath of cool air into my lungs.

Night hovered over the back lot thickly, and a breeze eased along the parking spaces as I lit a smoke. I looked past the flame's dancing shadows into the field behind the store. A squirrel leapt out from under a bush and skittered across the lot toward me, hoping I had some food. I flicked ash at it, which it dutifully inspected before glaring at me and hopping away to try a garbage bin.

The door clanged open, and Jason popped his head out, shaggy dreads flopping across his eyes.

"Hey man, you got a light?" he asked, holding up a smoke and waving it a bit to make it clear why he wanted the use of fire.

"Yeah man, sure," I held my cheap disposable lighter out to him, but kept watching the squirrel. It was digging under the garbage bin, hoping we had dropped something worthwhile. I heard a small noise behind me and spun to see Jason looking like he had just been kicked in the nuts by God.

"Jason, dude, fuck, you okay?" Jason was not okay. It was a stupid thing to ask, but my brain just put it out there on my tongue without stopping to check. He pointed out past me with his half-lit cigarette. I turned to look and saw a few people walking slowly out of the field. I shrugged and turned back to Jason, spotting my lighter on the ground. I bent to pick it up as he screamed, "Zombies!"

The word froze me in place, bent over, my hand curled around the plastic of the lighter. After a second or two, I stood up straight and looked again. Sure enough, they weren't moving right. Living beings didn't move like that. They just ... didn't. I moved toward the door just in time to see Jason vanish behind it. I heard the lock engage. Either the piece of paper we used to keep it from locking behind us had fallen–or Jason had pulled it free. I cursed, slamming my fist into the damned door a few times. They were getting closer. I experienced a moment of panic, a blind moment of time when all thought left me and logic flew the nest like a bird on fire.

But as I looked around, I saw Bud's truck. Good old Bud Rotanski, my stupid-as-hell manager, who used to get so riled up at a mis-shelving of goods that he would threaten to shoot us. "James," Bud would drawl, "I'm gonna go git the shotgun outta my truck and come back here and blow your ass off if this mess ain't fixed."

God bless Bud, I decided as I broke the driver's side window of his truck with one of the rocks from the dividers that marked the end of each parking aisle. There were no keys. I hit my head against the steering wheel and thought about trying to hotwire the truck. I had no idea how to do it, and it would cost me too much time trying. If I couldn't get it going, I would be stuck in a very small place. I hit the steering wheel again, this time with my fist, and looked around the inside of the truck.

I grabbed the shotgun off the rack behind the seat, and opened the door to climb out, wishing all the while that I had acquired a useful skill like hotwiring a vehicle. Then, realizing I'd need more ammunition, I knelt on the seat and rummaged around to find the box of shells I knew he always carried. Thus armed, I scooted around the truck, only to find that the zombies had drawn far too close for comfort. I tried backing away, hoping I could outrun them, play a game of keep-away until the authorities came to deal with the problem. That is, assuming Jason had called them. Not that the cops were known for a good response time when dealing with the undead, but it was better than no plan at all.

I cursed when I saw another group of them coming around from the front of the store. I had to stay calm; they were just zombies. The incursions had been getting worse for years but everyone knew to bug out as fast as possible, and they'd eventually get bored and wander off - unless there were enough people in one spot, then all you could do was hope for assistance. Only I had no safe, secure place near. I took a deep breath and forced myself to calm down and think.

Caught between the two groups, I fired at group in front of me. One of them lurched to the right as I got lucky. My fist pumped in the air and a small shout of joy escaped me before I realized how stupid a move that was. I stopped wasting precious seconds and fired again, aiming for the same zombie I had nicked before, and saw it go down, its head ruined. I fumbled with the ammo to reload. Even as I was snapping the shotgun closed, I realized I knew one of them.

"Boo boo kitty fuck," I said softly, the grin that would normally spread across my face with the words replaced by a grimace. Sheena was my girlfriend, the only person in town I really felt I could connect with, never mind the only other real Kevin Smith fan in our god-forsaken town. And now she was an undead flesh eater.

I lost it around then. I mean, really lost it. The shotgun roared again and again as I fired at everything moving. I stopped thinking, I stopped feeling; I just shot at them as fast as possible, stopping only to reload.

Boom, boom, silence, *boom, boom.*

My entire world diminished to the pattern of noise and light and violence. Sheena went down in a horrible mess of ruined chest and severed neck, but there were still too many of them. When I reached into the box for another set of shells I found I had another problem. The box was empty. Howling with rage, I flung the cardboard box at a zombie and raised the shotgun like a club. The box bounced off its face. The shotgun that followed it didn't, and the thing shook, turning with the off-center and weak blow. A different zombie behind me grabbed the shotgun as I swung it back again and yanked it clean from my hands.

I ran in circles to get back to Bud's pickup. There were all sorts of stuff tossed in the truck bed. I jumped up into it and started tossing things aside, not quite knowing what to grab: a green blanket, a broken hockey stick, a few bottles of oil, one knee pad, a bowling ball, a handful of wrenches, an empty water bottle. Finally, I snatched up the broken stick and the bowling ball. I didn't have a plan; my brain was working on sheer panic.

A zombie got in my way as I tried to jump down, and I swung the hand with the bowling ball on instinct alone. You'd be amazed at how well a bowling ball can work as a weapon against the undead. I know I wasn't prepared for how easily the ball passed through its head. As he went down, I saw that my hand, like the ball, was covered in rotting goo and shards of skull up to my elbow. Uncaring, I pressed on in the only direction open to me, the field and the woods beyond. A few more zombies appeared in front of me. My arms moved without conscious thought: stick stabbing into them, clubbing at them; my bowling ball taking off their heads if they got closer.

The length of my fight was taking its toll, but only on me. There had to be at least forty of them, possibly more in the darkness where I couldn't see. The undead might not move as fast as I could, but they also didn't tire like I did. They just pressed on. The bowling ball felt heavier with each swing; the hockey stick was harder and harder to raise another time. My adrenaline was wearing off, and I knew I couldn't hold them off like this much longer. Looking around, I finally recognized the part of the woods I was in. I had played in them as a child. Once I had my bearings, I remembered a cave less than a mile away. I knew I had to make it. Just that far and I would have someplace that would allow me to defend myself more easily, someplace where they couldn't surround me, a place with a single point of entry to watch over. My only hope was that eventually they would go off in search of less active food. I hefted the stick, now slippery with zombie innards, and took off as fast as I could manage.

The zombies' lack of speed didn't matter a lot in a close to pitch-black wood when the person they were chasing was so tired that he could hardly stand upright. My feet struggled to find footing, half-tripping over twigs and the occasional beer can in the dark. I used the stick to swat at branches in my path, just trying to escape, to make my goal.

Only when I got closer to the cave, relieved to see it where I thought it was, did I stop to think about what could be inside it. For all I knew, it could be filled with more zombies. Hell, there might be a bear in the cave napping, or snakes, or any number of things that fell on the "Detriment To Life" side of the chart. Realizing I was devoid of any real semblance of choice, I stopped making lists of what might be and ran into the cave as fast as I could, stick held out in front of me.

It was empty, blissfully and simply empty. The zombies were less than fifteen feet behind me, so I fished out the lighter I'd retrieved in the parking lot. I kicked as much detritus together as I could near the mouth of the cave and lit myself a nice bonfire—positioned, thankfully, so the smoke drifted outside the mouth of the cave and not in to choke me. The fire blossomed quickly, stopping the zombies in their tracks, some of them even taking slight shuffles backward. Even they dimly knew that zombies catch fire like toilet paper under most conditions. Maybe it was the rags they wore like they were Armani, or maybe their Jell-O-like guts were

2005

extra flammable. A lot of them left after a few minutes, but some of the heartier ones stayed. We all knew the fire wouldn't hold out forever.

I sat down in the cave to push the slime off my arms. I wanted to just go to sleep right there, lean back and pass out and to hell with it all, but I didn't fight my way clear of all that carnage just to die in my sleep. I kept scraping the zombie sludge off myself and flexing the fingers of my right hand, the bowling ball on the ground nearby, just in case. After all that swinging, my fingers had cramped something fierce; they felt like they might never move again. Really, they felt like the rest of my body: inert. The zombies were at the mouth of the cave, keeping their distance, but only just. The fire was still going, but I didn't see much more I could add to it to keep it going once it started to die out. I considered my hockey stick but set it back down, determined to go out fighting.

That was around the same time I saw the wound on my arm. It wasn't large and it wasn't too deep, but I didn't remember getting it. I decided that either the raw end of the hockey stick had cut into me while I was swinging it about so wildly or a branch had caught me while I was running through the woods. I wouldn't have noticed because my attention had been on other things while racing to the cave, and the adrenaline would have dulled the pain.

My throat itched and my eyes stung. The cave mouth still looked mostly clear, but smoke was occasionally drifting into my area, so I tore off part of my shirt and wrapped it around my nose and mouth, hoping to block out the worst of it. The last thing I needed was to be too busy coughing to fight for my own life.

I stood slowly and stretched, trying to force some life back into my body. I felt stiffer than ever with every passing moment. My knees fought against the squats I was doing to limber up, and my back complained with each bend. The fire started to die down a bit. I pushed my body a bit harder, preparing myself for the fight ahead. Only a few zombies still remained outside the cave, but it wouldn't take more than one to finish me off. I hefted my stick quickly at a sound and saw a small animal dart past the zombies and the fire into the cave, looking for shelter, too. As I watched it move, it eyed me carefully. I put my stick down. It was just a squirrel, I realized, and wondered inanely if it was a relative of the squirrel in the parking lot. When the smoke blew to one side, I could see that the moon was high, which meant the night was still young, so dawn wasn't even close. I closed my eyes just for a second and heard a sound. A thin bass drum beat somewhere nearby, constant and distracting. Clearly, I was losing it, wondering about squirrel families and hearing distant drums much less caring about them in the middle of a zombie attack.

No, I really could hear a drumming sound. I opened my eyes and looked around, trying to place it. The squirrel looked back, and slowly I realized that what I heard was the little rodent's heart. I shook my head and peered closer at the furry little thing. It took a step back. My hand shot out and grabbed it, pulling it toward my mouth. I bit its head off with a satisfying crunch and enjoyed the sensation of a squirt of hot copper blood. As I swallowed and started to go back for another bite, I realized that I couldn't normally hear the beat of a squirrel's heart. My stomach lurched and I felt ill, but I told myself that it was nothing that another bite of squirrel couldn't fix.

I stood up, grabbing my stick and bowling ball as I did, and looked out of the cave's mouth. The zombies that stood there, three in number, were looking at me differently. I dimly realized I could hear noises from them: a calling, a breath of friendship, of brotherhood, that didn't need words. I was one of them now, and they accepted me. I beat at the fire with my stick, my thoughts starting to grow as sluggish as my knees, and walked right up to one of them. The zombie ignored me, content to have me right next to it. I nodded and started to walk off and they followed me. The woodlands looked alive to me in ways they hadn't before. I could hear the beating hearts of animals all over and the silent calls of zombies close by. I could see differently too, a mixture of heat and normal vision that made no sense at first in the once dark night. I kept blinking, trying to clear my vision, but instead slowly grew used to it. It must be how things were supposed to look. I glanced back at the zombies following me and nodded at them. They just kept following.

We entered the field beyond the woods together and saw some of the other zombies still clawing at the back door to the store. I grinned a sick grin and joined in. Together we beat at door, but it wouldn't give. I waved my little zombie crew back and we all stood there, sensing our brethren at the front of the store trying the same thing. I also knew a few of them were holding back a cop car somewhere close by. Someone had called the authorities. I moved forward, waving the others back, and tried to speak, but all that came out was a worthless croak, not words. I coughed and spat; a squirrel ear landed wetly at my feet. I tried again.

"Jason? They're gone. Let me in." I said slowly but urgently. I felt a ripple of confusion from my companions. They didn't have the ability to speak; they communicated through feelings instead of words. They pulled aside further, giving me room. I repeated my painstaking sentence. Jason had been a self-serving prick, locking me out in the first place and causing this, but I had confidence that a wave of guilt, combined with a sense of security, would change his mind. The lock on the door turned with a soft click and it opened a fraction. Jason stuck his head out, and the other zombies who'd stepped back as I spoke helped me by grabbing the door and swinging it wide open. I looked at Jason and *tsk'd,* shaking my head slowly. He screamed as a zombie lunged for him.

I could hear them, for they were my family. The zombies were friends. We all went to bat for the same team. Jason, though, he was a friend too, once. My brain fought itself and neither side seemed to be gaining control. I was stuck in a no-man's land of being. Both sides of the fence tugged at me, trying to gain final control of my mind. I shook my head and pushed aside the zombie trying to bite Jason.

"My bowling ball will work pretty damned well on you, too." I spat at Jason, "Meat," and drew back my arm. The other zombies pushed into the store, leaving me to my kill. Jason whimpered as a zombie brushed past him, and I swung my arm forward. Right into and through that zombie's head. The other zombies stopped in their tracks, again confused. If I were one of them, and something told them I was, why would I attack them? The undead ate living flesh—they didn't stop and attack each other.

Something wasn't right about me. I was definitely undead, but I still had my presence of mind, even if it was a bit slower than it used to me. Mom always said I would never get through college, so the loss of brain power didn't bother me too much. My mind was made up. As they stood there confused, I hefted my stick and ball with newfound determination and waded into them.

The undead fell before me easily. I was as strong as they were, and I was faster than most of them too; just not as nimble as a living human. I was somewhere between the ends of the spectrum. I couldn't work out why. That wound I saw on my arm in the cave was not obviously a bite, but people got bitten and they all just turned into normal zombies. This scratch must've been from one of their nails, or maybe a zombie had drooled into it as well. It certainly wasn't your normal zombie chomp. Something about me, or the nature of the wound or ... there was some unknown quantity involved. Then again, maybe this happened from time to time, a bad transition. A half-breed, someone trapped, like me, between both worlds. I decided to puzzle over it later, if at all, and concentrated on clearing the doorway.

Finally, I had destroyed enough of them that Jason and I got the door closed again. I left him staring at me from the back of the store, puzzling at me, as I shambled around to the front. Seven zombies stood outside around a cop on the ground with his face a few feet away, his head half eaten and discarded. The zombies were struggling with the locked doors and safety glass. I opened the door enough to slip out, walked right up to them, and started swinging. They stood no chance. A few of them bit me, but what did I care? They couldn't infect me again. I lost a finger, my left pinky, but I didn't need that to swing the hockey stick. I'd care later, when I tried to pick my nose.

I could see Jason looking out through the glass doors. The kid was cheering me on. He was whooping it up from safety while I did all the work. He could've grabbed something and come help, but no. It looked easy enough from in there anyway, and truthfully, it wasn't too hard. They were slow and were still wrapping their senses around one of their own turning on them. I swung and decapitated another one, but then the one behind him seemed to catch on. It lunged for me as I recovered from the swing. This one was going to be a problem.

He tackled me, forcing me down, and landed with his elbow jabbing my wrist hard enough to jolt my hand open, making the bowling ball roll free of my grip. I tried to swing the hockey stick but the zombie shifted. My weak swing missed, allowing him to wrench the weapon from my grasp. I slammed my forehead into his face as hard as I could and felt his nose break, but he didn't care any more than I would've. He shook his head slightly, a spray of thick slime splattering my face, and sunk his teeth deep into my shoulder.

I pushed at him but to no avail: he was sunk in and I couldn't dislodge him quickly. He worried at my shoulder, trying to bite my arm clean off. I grabbed at his face with my free hand and clawed his eyes out. Slowly. His grip on my shoulder slacked off just enough for me to push him off. He laid there, groping around for me, while I kicked his head in. Grabbing up my stick and bowling ball again I backed up to the front door, sweeping the area with a level gaze and sensing no other undead nearby. The attack was over. I had sent them packing. Me, James Reed, a lowly stock boy in a third rate store, had defeated a pack of zombies. Jason unlocked the door as I got to it and then suddenly braced against it, so the door would only open an inch.

"You aren't going to kill me, right man? I mean you're just... you're, you know... on our side?" He was white as a sheet, his heart beating loudly in my ears, the noise forcing me to replay what I heard before I could answer.

"Yeah, Jason. I don't know why but I'm still me. I mean, yeah," the words came out sluggish and low, "I'm one of them, but I'm one of you, too." He sighed in relief and pushed the door fully open to let me in. Most everyone else who'd been in the store made a break for it, not even thanking me, just edging away from me as they ran. Bud ran by and I called out, "Sorry about your window," as he fled. I don't think he heard me. It was just Jason and me, and I could tell he wanted to leave, but was afraid of me still. Too afraid to just bolt. I shuffled to a bench and sat down, patting a spot next to me. Like a nervous deer, Jason sat down as far away as he could manage.

"So it's all good, right, man? Now you can be like some great force, right? I mean, you can take them out yourself, maybe turn the tide for everyone somehow, right?" His voice was on the verge of breaking with each sentence and I just laughed.

"I suppose, sure. I could be a force to be reckoned with huh, Jason? I could be famous even."

"You could, man, you could. Do talk shows in between fighting the undead and shit. You'd be a national hero. No, no, a global hero even." He started to relax by degrees.

"I would, wouldn't I?" I grinned at him and stood up, shaking the bowling ball I still held. "Kids will want toy replicas of my mighty weapons, huh?" Jason laughed at that, nodding. I grinned down at him and hefted the ball.

"They will! You'll be rich and famous, man. Just think of it." Jason stood and grinned at me, comfortable now in my presence.

"Do you want to see it? See the weapon that defeated hordes?" I boasted and lowered my arm a bit. Jason nodded with a smile and bent down to get a closer look at the ball. I swung it back as he bent over and crashed it into his head with a loud crunch that sent him fully to the floor, unconscious.

"The thing is, Jason" I told his unmoving, but still live and tasty body, "I'm not one of you. Or them. I'm on my own side. Meat."

Not long after, I strolled out of the store as best I could manage a stroll, chewing on Jason's left leg as I went. In the distance, I could sense some zombies. They could sense me in return. I tossed the rest of my snack into the road and went to introduce a few more zombies to my bowling ball.

Adam P. Knave has writes for TwoHeadedCat.com and Too Much *Coffee* Magazine. He has also published fiction, most recently for Die Monster Die! books. In his spare time he enjoys time with his wife and three cats. He can be reached at adampknave@gmail.com.

TINY DOLL-FACE

Mattie Brahen

THE HOUSE LOOMED BEFORE HER, COLD AND SEPULCHRAL. "SO I'M finally, formally, invited to visit with your mother. Remarkable, the power of a small gemstone." She waved her ring finger in the sunlight; the diamond's facets flashed.

"She's still not happy about it, Doll-Face."

Sarah ignored his favorite sexist endearment. "It's high time you stopped letting your mother run your life," she said as he led her to the parlor.

The gaunt woman in the wingback chair surveyed her with an uncertain but dignified scrutiny. Her hair, dyed black, was pulled back into a twist, her face thin, but her eyes dark and sharp. Sarah smiled at her, determined to be pleasant. "Hello, Gertrude. How are you?"

"Not well, but managing. Wally knows my back can be sore. Just sitting for more than half an hour is a challenge."

More likely stiff, *that back of hers,* Sarah thought, *from that rigid attitude.* She stared around the room, noticing all of the dolls. "What a stunning collection."

"Some of them are quite rare," Gertrude informed her. "Take that small Egyptian doll. A grave doll, done in the image of a servant who would serve the deceased in the afterlife. And the tiny crude figure beside it is a voodoo doll, made in the likeness of a victim, whom the magician wishes to control or kill."

Sarah swallowed and sat closer to Wallace on the sofa. "I prefer the modern dolls."

"No doubt you played with those fashion floozy dolls as a child."

"Uh, no. I never owned one of those. I liked paper dolls." She changed the subject. "Wallace has told you we've set the date."

Gertrude nodded, as an older man came in, wheeling a tea trolley. "We'll have tea now. Alexander, please pour. This is Wally's Uncle Alexander. He lives here as well."

Alexander bent over the trolley and fixed them each a brimming cup. It was fragrant and warm, and Sarah sipped it, taking the edge off the chill in the room.

"Yes," Gertrude said, "Wally has told me of your wedding plans. I personally can't imagine his moving from home and hearth, but he seems bent on having you, and I know of only one way to please his desire. More tea?"

Sarah held her cup out. "Then you'll give your blessing to the marriage."

"Sarah," Wallace cut in. "That is my place to ask."

"Then you ask," she returned, quickening anger making her stomach queasy.

"Mother, will you accept Sarah into the household?"

"Yes, dear. But, of course, there's no need for you to leave home to do so."

"Wait," Sarah piped, surprised and disgruntled that the word had come out in a tinny squeak. "We're not living here. He's a grown man. We need a place of our own, Gertrude."

Gertrude shook her head, a crafty smile playing on her lips. "But he belongs here. And done our way, my dear, not even death will part you from him." And then she mumbled, a string of guttural sounds, nonsense words.

"You're impossible," Sarah said. "Wallace, let's leave. I've sorry, but my patience is exhausted." She started to rise. She heard Wallace reciting his own hodge-podge of gibberish, as a dizzy spell hit her. She sank back into the chair, seeming to fall into it.

She had no memory of blacking out, but when she awoke, her limbs felt stiff and she was laying naked on a bed, in a darkened room. Wallace was beside her, fondling her. His hands seemed much larger than usual, and she wondered if she was sick with fever, imagining it.

He reached over her and turned on the bedside light. Sarah gazed up at him in horror. He had doubled in height and the shock caused a scream to rise in her throat. But her mouth would not open.

"Mother knows best, tiny doll-face," he cooed at her and kissed her lips, forever frozen in a fetching pout.

MARILYN "MATTIE" BRAHEN IS THE AUTHOR OF THE WELL-RECEIVED novel *Claiming Her*, plus stories published in *Scheherazade, Marion Zimmer Bradley's Fantasy Magazine, Fantastic, Dreams of Decadence, Crafty Cat Crimes,* and Marvin Kaye's *Ultimate Halloween*.

FANTASY

AUTUMN OF IMMORTALITY

Jeff Lyman

Aurora and I danced again,
a last sad waltz, rememberance,
upon our courtyard of stone.
We have not danced this way in years,
my wife, my love, in elegance.
But on this night we shone
beneath the rising moon.

Look away, Aurora,
from the past that dissolves.
Turn away from a thousand generations.
The hour is late, and maybe
it is time for us to go.
Come, take my hand
and walk into the night.

Our boys are all asleep again
with gluttony and decadence
winding through skeletal dreams.
I'm losing control of them,
fighting my irrelevance.
Our mighty and shrouded family
burns and melts away.

Sing to me, Aurora,
of a time that is gone,
when we laughed at the glow of the horizon.
Sing of thrones
and of cities, and of friends that are lost
Then we'll dance,
and waste away the night.

The young ones cannot understand
the wars we fought to stay alive.
They are their own breed and not mine.
They hunt the night and crave the sport
and lack the will to even try
to build and empire of time
against the passing years.

Look East, Aurora,
Do you see the darkness fade?
Now I think that the nightsky will be blooming.
The dawn will come, Aurora
and it's time for us to go.
But first, my love,
sit and rest a while.

I was the king who drank the cup;
you were the queen who urged me on.
We swore in the new moon's haze
that we would fill each other up
and hold us through the seething night
until we assaulted the day.
And watched the rising sun.

Await the sun, Aurora
as the moon, it descends.
Look away from the brightening horizon.
So the sun, Aurora,
it is time for us to go.
My wife, my light,
dance with me tonight.

THE KINDRED

John C. Wright

THE MISTS PARTED. A TALL GREY CLIFF OVERGROWN WITH VINES AND creepers rose above the trees. Perched atop the cliff, surrounded by mossy boulders, was the strange house. It wore a narrow, high-peaked roof of slate above walls of wet grey stone. A door of oak inscribed with circular designs opened out sheer into the gulf of air above the cliff.

Two streams fell down from the ferns to either side of the high house, turning into rainbows and mists as they plummeted down the cliffside. Even had there been a ledge below the door, one would have had to wade one or the other of the waterfalls to reach it.

The waterfalls fell into a little bubbling pool overshadowed by green trees. On the rocks near the pool stood a ragged man, shivering, craning his neck, looking upward.

"There must be another door." he said to himself. "On the landward side. But how to reach it? The witch must have some path she comes down."

Clouds pushed down against the cliffside. The house was lost again behind the fog.

The man narrowly searched the ground at the base of the cliff, and looked among the angular columns of rock that climbed the cliffside. "Perhaps she comes down some hidden way," he murmured to himself. "But why would she have hidden it?"

Behind him, a young lady dressed in green stepped out from the brush nearby, making no more noise than a ghost. Her cloak and kirtle were the color of the leaves crisscrossed with cunning patterns of dark or tawny threads and beads, confusing to the eye. She wore a shawl woven with designs of herbs and flowers. In the shadow of the shawl, her face was fair, and her eyes were quiet, wise and grave.

"The way is clear for all who have eyes to see," she said.

Her voice was cool and soft, like rippling water.

The man jerked and turned. He stood amazed a moment, eyes wide, mouth slack, panting. She saw he was a well-muscled young man, clean-shaven, wearing a dirty brown smock. Dirt and twigs dangled from his close-cropped hair. His face was scratched and bruised. Rags tied with cord protected his feet.

He saw a woman, slender and beautiful, with eyes as green as glass. From beneath her shawl a lock of hair as gold as corn-silk curled along her cheek.

She said, "Yet those wise enough to see it, might not take that path. The wise would see that house is meant for solitude."

The man dropped to one knee. "My lady! I did not—I meant no harm. We know you live alone. I told them not to trouble you! But they sent me, you see, because they knew you had helped Garnock when he came. I am of his blood..."

She glided forward. Grass-stems rippled against the hem of her long cloak, leaving tiny droplets. "Fear not. Stand. I deem it ill to have any man kneel."

But he put his head to the ground.

"Please help us. The horse-riders who conquered us rule us cruelly. The lord Scarapant is a tyrant who taxes us to destruction. He has levied an aid against us to promote the wars with the Northmen. But the crops were ruined by vermin this year, and there is nothing to pay. Yet those who do not pay are impaled or burnt or exposed in cages. The whole county seethes with rebellion. Even his own men hate him...."

"What has this to do with me?"

He looked up. "But you are the witch…? Your magic power..."

"My name is Nimlos. There is no witchcraft, no power, only knowledge. My Art consists only of listening to beast and bird, of paying heed to Nature. I listen, I watch, I learn. There is no mystery in this. I tried to teach this to your father Garnock."

"He was my grandfather's father," the man said, slowly rising. "The stories say you seemed young then, too."

Nimlos smiled. "A tortoise a thousand years old told me once the secret of how never to grow old."

"And you say you have no power?"

"Over men, I do not. They do not think as beasts do, and I cannot reach their thoughts."

The man was silent a moment. Looking angrily at the ground, he said, "Lord Scarapant lives in fear of you. His men will come for you as they have come for us. Till he is overthrown, your solitude is not secure."

"Let me see your hands." She took his large hands in her small, firm grip. Her shawled head bowed, she ran one finger along the lines of his palm.

"You speak the truth," she said. "Your lord will interrupt the labor of my study 'til he knows it is no threat to him. Yet there must be another hand at work..."

She straightened. "I will come."

They were on the path leading to the castle, when seven men with drawn swords came out of the bushes before them. The men wore jackets of boiled leather, and caps of leather and iron. Nimlos turned her head. Eight other men came out onto the path behind.

The leader was on horseback, a spear at rest in his stirrup. He wore a jacket of iron rings, as did his steed. The barding of the steed and the surcoat of the man bore the heraldry of the horse-lords. His hair was streaked with gray. He wore a coronet of iron coated with hammered gold. The man's arms were bare, except for several bracelets of gold about his wrist.

The leader took off one of these arm rings and threw it to the young man who had been leading Nimlos. The young man caught it eagerly, and bowed, and turned toward Nimlos with a frightened, angry look. He backed away.

"I forgive you," she said. "You did not deceive me. Not only are you shaven with a razor, but the calluses on your hand show you work with a sword, not with a plowshare." She turned toward the leader. "I have come to speak with you."

The horseman laughed. "I am Lord Scarapant. You are the prisoner of my lance. I arrest you in the name of the king."

"Why?" Her voice was cool and remote.

Scarapant's gaze was flinty and hard. "For conspiring to aid the rebels against me. By following my man here you showed your true colors. The sentence is death."

Nimlos smiled. "Had you merely wished me not to trouble you, you would have left me to my studies. But you have made me curious. What do you dream to compel from me with your threats? Who put your hand to this?"

Along the path there came then another mounted man, riding without bit or bridle or saddle. He was dark-eyed and dark-haired, with harsh and handsome features. His tunic and long mantle were of unadorned black silk. On his shoulder, restrained by no jesses, was an unhooded hawk. At the feet of his steed there trotted two red-eyed boars. The boars were plated with iron armor; their tusks were capped with sharpened steel.

She regarded the dark newcomer. "You do not carry a sword."

Sir Scarapant spoke. "He is my servant, my wise man and advisor. Servants are not permitted arms. He is not the lord here."

Nimlos did not turn her eyes toward Scarapant. "You mean he wishes not to appear so."

For a moment, the man in black sat looking at her. Then he hissed and raised his hand. The boars plunged toward Nimlos, snorting, terrible tusks bent forward to impale her. Yet, somehow, when they reached where she was, they nuzzled at her feet, grunting happily as she stroked their ears and eyes.

The man in black hissed again. The two boars trotted back toward him. The soldiers were now in a wide circle, far from where the boars had rushed, weapons trembling in their hands.

"You are Nimlos, I presume? I am Radsvid. I would bid you a good day, my dear, but, I fear, none will be forthcoming. You have a proud and willful look to you. It may take some pain to drive that pride away." To Scarapant he said; "She is one of my Kindred, my lord, though I do not recognize her. I had not known any of the Kindred were yellow-haired. No beast will harm her; most would obey her. Were I not here, your own steed perhaps would throw and trample you."

Nimlos said, "I will wish you good day, Radsvid, for I wish harm to none. Why do you seek my death?"

He smiled. "My pets would have gored you if you had been a human being, it's true. But had you been no more than other mortals, we could have gotten no use out of you. The penalties for not being useful, you see, are quite high. You should remember this when you visit our torture dungeon; those who are not useful in other ways, there learn to entertain us with their pleas and screamings."

Scarapant raised his hand. "Magician, do not be so uncouth. We are governed by King's law." To Nimlos, he said, "You are condemned a rebel. Law allows me to commute the sentence for any rebels who aid our flag. My magician tells me you know secrets unknown to others of the Kindred. Teach him. I will consider this sufficient aid to our flag, for as long as you continue, to hold off the penalties of justice.

Otherwise, the law permits me to deliver you to torment and to execution. How do you choose?"

"With endless patience, toil, and diligence have I gathered the fruits of my learning, and paid heed to many wild things. I did not do all this for you. What do you offer me to reward me for my labor?"

"Your life," said Scarapant. "If you obey me in all things."

"You will allow me live if I devote my life to you? You will be taking the very thing you say you will be giving. No. I have no interest in this. Leave me."

"Woman, do you not believe that I will kill you if you do not obey me? Do you not believe me?" shouted Scarapant.

"Once I spoke with a caterpillar both before and after she became a butterfly. From her I learned that there is nothing of what you call death. Our bodies will be cast aside like old cloaks, and we shall receive new bodies, more glorious than these. No, my lord, it is not that I do not believe in you; it is that I do not believe in dying."

Scarapant made an impatient gesture to his men. "Seize the witch and bind her."

"Do not." said Nimlos, staring at a soldier who had stepped forward. "The first of you who touches me shall surely die, I promise you. What? Are none of you willing to perish for your lord's pleasure?"

There was a nervous stir among the men. None came forward.

"Radsvid! Take her!" shouted Scarapant. Radsvid smiled and gestured with his hand. "After you, my lord."

Scarapant dismounted. When he stepped forward, his men came nervously after him. "Fools!" he said. "She is but an unarmed girl." And he seized her by both wrists.

She bowed and put her lips to the back of his hand. He shouted in pain and slapped her to the ground. Her shawl fell away. She lay fallen on the path, her hair spread out in golden ripples, her cloak flung wide like wings. Before she could rise, four men had pinned her down. In a moment, her arms were bound behind her with tight cords.

Scarapant stood rubbing his hand, staring with distaste at the two puncture wounds swelling behind his thumb.

That night, a guard brought her up a narrow flight of stairs, up from the stench of the bloodstained cages in the dungeon, to a high room in the tower, scented with pomanders, and lit with candles burning before tall mirrors.

The head of the narrow stair was hidden behind a tapestry. The guard shoved Nimlos forward into the chamber. Her hands were bound behind her back.

She saw Scarapant, limbs blue and swollen, sweating on his couch. His eyes were rolled up in his head. On a small table to one side stood a jar of water-leaches, a phial of oil, some linen bandages, and a scalpel. Before the wide, tall windows, looking out on the gallows in the courtyard, stood Radsvid, draped all in black.

The red light leaping against the roof showed there was a fire in the courtyard; the sound of someone screaming rose into the air. "Poor fellow." murmured Radsvid mildly, dropping the curtains, and turned toward Nimlos. There was no one else in the chamber, except a hound, which laid his head on Scarapant's lap, and whined.

Radsvid turned. "She's still dressed. She's still in her traveling cloak. Don't the torturers molest young women any more? Did you search her to see if she's carrying poisoned knives? She's not even bleeding anywhere."

Nimlos said, "They were afraid to touch me."

The guard said, "We had no orders, your eminence. The inquisitor showed her the instruments, but we had not been told to apply them. We could not proceed further without my lord's order."

"Well, now," said Radsvid. "My lord is giving no further orders tonight, I deem. Tie the young lady to that chair, and make certain that the knots are tight. If she gets too comfortable, she might nod off."

"You are a fool, Radsvid," said Nimlos.

"Why, thank you, my dear. What makes you think so?"

"That you had me brought here secretly. You expect me to cure your lord, and say later that you had done the healing."

"Well, yes, certainly."

"And you dare to think my creative power, my learning, skill, and art can be taken from me, compelled by violence?" Her green eyes flashed; her gaze was haughty. "What do you imagine will stay my hand if you put your lord under my scalpel, or bid him drink a brew my art concocts?"

"We shall see," said Radsvid. "First, tell me where you threw the poisoned needle you scratched my lord with. Blackfang here," he pointed to the hound, "tells me he can smell the poison in the wound, but he does not recognize it."

"Do you think that I, who listen so carefully to all that creatures tell me, would overlook to listen to the subtlest of beasts? I learned the serpent's art."

Radsvid waved the guard to stand on the far side of the chamber. He leaned over the chair where Nimlos was bound, and spoke softly.

"All of the Kindred can speak to beasts; it is our only art. Yet none ever have I heard can spit poison from their teeth, or see in the dark, or walk as silent as a cat, or do the other things the humans here say you do."

"You waste your art," she said. "I have seen your boars, trained for battle, and your hawks and hounds and horses, given only to aid the wars and hunts of men. You command nature. But have you ever stopped to listen?"

"Waste? Waste, you say? You offend my pride, sweet Nimlos. A handful of the Kindred secretly rule all this land, for we have given the rulers here horses and the art of cavalry. Their mounted spearmen can defeat all enemies afoot, and we ensure all enemies a-horse are thrown."

"And is your art insufficient to stop the plague of vermin they say ruined the crops this year? It was by your doing, I think."

"A political necessity, my dear. The local lords were reluctant to go to war; but no one is tempted by the promise of plunder more than a hungry man."

"And no army more swiftly defeated than a starving one. You wish your own people to lose. Why so?"

Radsvid bared his teeth. "They are not my people! Once, the Kindred ruled mankind, before they learned the use of fire, when they were like other beasts, and vulnerable to our command. Even afterwards, when they hunted in the forests, we were worshipped and obeyed, for we were their only source of game. Now they are grown too civilized for the Kindred to rule openly; we are forgotten and despised. To men who live in cities, we must dissemble all our works, and appear to men only as counselors, or wise men. *Pfaugh!* Many long years of our effort it took to see their empire crumble away; now, a thousand petty barons squabble in its place, easier prey for us. But it is not enough. The Kindred in the east have succeeded admirably. A savage and nomadic people have overrun that land. They are utterly dependant on the herds of kine they follow. And thus, you see, more vulnerable to our power. And the people of this land grow ever weaker as we stir up wars among them, and more and more flee to the woods to live as men did at the dawn of time. The nomads of the east shall rule here soon and we shall rule through them. Our old glory shall be restored to us!"

"You call this glory? You would destroy all cities, art, craft, and learning. It is a vermin glory."

"Better to be king of a pack of barbarians, than merely equal to a civilized man." he smiled. "And if we can drive the nomads back to deeper savagery, we may one day be revered as gods again."

"There is a flaw in your schemes."

"Do you really think so?" Radsvid straightened.

She squirmed in the ropes. "Destruction is your goal and ignorance your ally. Ignorance can never overcome knowledge. You under-guess the knowledge of mankind, how much they can learn."

"Oh? I see no humans rushing here to aid you."

"I am human, Radsvid. I am not one of the Kindred. I learned your art."

He stepped away from her, blinking. "You lie."

"I have learned your art better than you yourselves."

Radsvid sneered. "Why? How much did you learn from talking to your butterfly?"

She stood up and the ropes fell away from her. "All butterflies know how to escape from being bound up in cocoons." She turned and flung her hand out toward the guard. His hand clutched at his face as he fell back, screaming. A tiny knife, no longer than a woman's little finger, quivered in the socket of his eye. Radsvid scrambled backward.

"You have thought to bind me," she said, standing tall, one hand raised high. "I cannot be bound. You thought to terrify me. I cannot be made afraid. You thought to win my art from me. I cannot be compelled."

When she threw her second knife, the hound, Blackfang, leaped up in front of Radsvid to protect him. The little blade struck the dog in the chest.

Radsvid danced backward in a flurry of black silk. He seized the small table, spilling the medical equipment, and held it before him as a shield. Nimlos circled, her hand still raised. The couch with Scarapant was between them.

"They say porcupines can throw their quills with great skill," panted Radsvid, also circling. "Did you learn your knife-throwing from them? You do not answer. I think perhaps your hand is empty now."

"You did not see the knife before," she said calmly.

"Perhaps I should rush you," he suggested.

The dog, meanwhile, had crawled into the lap of Scarapant, where it lay, trembling and whining. Scarapant was cold and stiff.

Nimlos now had her back to the window. "Poor Blackfang. You used your control of him to kill him. You treat all mankind the same. No need to attack me any further, Radsvid, you have won your goal. I will teach my art."

"This is a trick, I think." He had backed up near to where the guard had fallen.

"No." she said. "You have convinced me. For too long I have devoted myself to my art. Now, I see, I cannot serve my art but that I also serve mankind. Once everyone knows what I have learned, once I have taught it in seminaries and universities all across this land, I am certain you will find someone willing to teach it to you. Then, of course, there will be no need to bar you from learning it, since the Kindred will have no power all other men do not have."

Radsvid screamed. "You will not! Ours secrets are ours alone!" Now he bent and swiftly picked up the guard's sword. He spoke more calmly. "Your knowledge is not so great as to allow you to leave this room alive, is it, my dear? Talking to cute little butterflies does not help you to fight, does it?"

In the moment when he stooped for the sword, she had cast open the windows behind her. "She taught me one other art she knew," said Nimlos, throwing wide her cloak. "And by this, I knew that knowledge has no limit to its power."

The silk inner lining of the cloak of Nimlos was woven with designs of majestic colors, patterned and shining like the wings of the butterfly. She stepped back out through the window and silently sailed up and away into the night.

Radsvid, staring dumbly, allowed the helpless sword to slide from his weak grip. A moment later he saw her shining high above, as the night winds blew her across the face of the moon. Exalting, weightless, free, her head thrown back, her arms flung wide, she flew. Nothing he knew could hinder her.

On she soared.

JOHN C. WRIGHT IS A RETIRED ATTORNEY, NEWSPAPERMAN AND NEWSPAPER editor, who was only once on the lam and forced to hide from the police who did not admire his newspaper.

He presently works (successfully) as a writer in Virginia, where he lives in fairy-tale-like happiness with his wife, the authoress L. Jagi Lamplighter, and their three children: Orville, Wilbur, and Just Wright.

His novels include: *The Golden Age, The Phoenix Exultant, The Golden Transcendence, Last Guardians of Everness*, and the forthcoming *Mists of Everness.*

TO THE BEAST

C.J. Henderson

ANDRA MOVED FORWARD CAUTIOUSLY THROUGH THE TREES. COVERED HEAD to toe by her cloak, she continued on, shielding her pale, northland skin from the sun. The cloak's hood hid her thick blonde hair, as well as shading her thinly angular face and crystal blue eyes, two other features which marked her as a Lomonian.

As a witch.

Skirting through the endless brush, she watched and listened for any sign of the gargor. Their duel was well into its second day, but she had yet to find a trace of him. Nearing a gradual incline of moss-greened stone, she stopped to examine the ground. What could possibly have been the remains of a footprint stared up at her from the edge of the gradually sloping shale.

Kneeling next to the rocks Andra placed her hand on the track, closing her eyes—concentrating—asking when the print had been made. In her mind's eye, she saw the sun cross the sky backwards over and over.

Old, she thought. Too old to be of any help to me, even if that thing *did* leave it.

Perhaps the gargor had come to the valley early to scout for ambush sites, hiding places, whathaveyou. It was possible, she knew. But, whatever the case, the print was old and useless to her now. Frustrated, the young witch broke off her concentration. She lay back wearily against the rocks, giving up her search temporarily for the first time since their duel had begun. Quite simply, she needed rest. At midnight the day preceding she had entered the Northern end of the valley; the gargor had entered from the south. They now had to remain until one of them surrendered or was slain by the other.

Andra closed her eyes, aching to both rest and think. She had gambled that the gargor would march straight into the interior, wanting to begin fighting immediately. She had gone straight to meet him. She had lost.

"Filthy, rotten lizard," she grumbled. "Most likely still asleep, curled up in a tree somewhere a dozen miles from here. Now he's fresh and rested and ready for battle, and I'm exhausted. Out there laughing at me, aren't you? Miserable gargor."

Andra, She Who Would Be, Daughter to the Mother to All, held back a sniffle. Admitting she had made a mistake, she decided to correct it before anymore time was lost. Stretching out in the nearby brush, she curled into a comfortable position, whispering to the ground as she did so. At her command, vines untangled, grass grew quickly, and the sweeping plants above her lowered their leaves, all helping to hide her small form while she slept. She fell asleep without fear, knowing the plants would awaken her if the gargor came near.

Round one had gone to the beast.

The afternoon sun warmed Grakar's scales. He had been awake for several hours. Patiently he sat cross-legged, watching for movement. The witch, he knew, would be expecting Grakar to hunt her.

To the Shade with her, he thought. Damn Lomonians think they know us; think to stop us—hold us back as they would the humans. Well, gargors are not so easily outguessed, little princess. Nor are we easily killed.

The powerful reptilian flexed his shoulder muscles slightly, stretching their skin tight across his back. Again his mind reviewed his plan. He would let the witch come to him. He would not leave his ledge until he spotted her. He would do no hunting, build no fire, make no sounds—these were things that would help the Lomonian.

He would not do them.

For over four hundred years each successive Gargor clan had hoped to recover Hotor's talisman. As a bauble it was worthless, nothing but blue quartz and badly worked lead. As a political totem, however, it held great power. The gargor nation had been splintered thousands of years in the past by the Lomonians. One of the concessions given to the witches by Hotor, the gargor king, was his medallion of state. Over the centuries many clans had tried to regain the talisman. Thieves had been sent to Lomonia. Renegade witches had been bribed; clans had gathered together into armies. None had ever returned from the north.

But Grakar would not fail. Heskar, his father, had planned too well. As the gargor thought on his father's manipulations, a fat dragonfly flitted past his eyes. Although his mouth moistened instantly, eager to betray his hunger, he held back his tongue. Instead the massive lizard reached for the sack next to him from which he pulled forth a strip of dried beef.

"Chew it," he ordered himself. "Chew it slow; wet it with your own juices. Save your water; conserve. Conserve rations; conserve strength, conserve nerves. You've set your traps. You will lure the witch. She will come to you eventually, and then she will die. Hotor's Talisman shall come to the Kar clan."

The dragonfly landed on the gargor's snout. Yellow eyes stared at the insect until it satisfied itself that there was nothing for it there. As it flew away, Grakar smiled.

"You will be proud of me, father."

Round two had gone to the beast.

Sleeping beneath the protection of her plants, Andra dreamed of the last meeting between her mother and the head of the Kar clan. She found herself back again in the massive meeting chamber of the Lomonians. High in the frozen northlands, still mostly unexplored by gargor or human, her race dwelled quietly, ignoring the gelid cold and the winds which carried it. She remembered Heskar, his sneering address to her mother. It had bordered on insult, but only slightly. No comment had been made; it was not the time.

"Great Charri, Mother to All," he had mocked, "You Who Are, Charri of Lomonia, all Gargoria bids you long life."

"You are far from home, Heskar. Why have you come to the North to all this cold which you do not enjoy?"

The gargor had stood granite still, quietly staring at the Queen Mother of the witches. Nearly seven feet tall, the lizard had then bent its powerful frame in an impossibly graceful bow. Andra shuddered slightly at the memory. Heskar was nothing more than tight muscles and heavy bone covered in scales and bristles and menace. His pale green eyes stared out from below the hood he wore. Wrapped in cured animal skins, he stank of death, a towering pillar of living destruction, waiting to explode.

"I am here," he had answered calmly, "for what is mine."

"The talisman is not yours. It is Hotor's."

"Hotor is dead," smiled Heskar.

"He gave it to us," countered Charri.

"He gave it to the dead. You, nor any here, was born then. Lomonia has held our soul long enough. It shall be returned."

The gargor's words curled slightly into a snarl. Andra stood by her mother, taking in the debate that followed. Decades earlier the gargor's demands would not be taken seriously. Any one or two clans attacking Lomonia would have posed a tiny threat, but times had changed. Heskar had planned for years, playing on Gargoria's national pride, manipulating clan after clan into joining the outcry for the talisman's return.

"We wish no quarrel with your people, Heskar." *You are not so easily beaten now through direct combat. We would look for easier ways to maneuver you.*

"Nor we with you, Mother to All." *I am power now—I can mobilize all Gargoria. Even if you would stop us all, your losses would be staggering.*

"Surely there must be some way this matter can be resolved between us as civilized peoples. We are not humans after all."

There was an almost imperceptible wince in the room. The human race was Lomonia's fault, an off-branching of the witches many thousands of years in the past. Magicks were almost unknown to them now. On this point Heskar had thrown them into a discussion without implying insult. Charri had smiled; the gargor had grinned. Andra simply watched, fascinated.

Their debate had continued throughout the day; planned approaches had been used, reviewed, and discarded. Tradition demanded such actions, but it had been apparent to both Charri and Heskar in the first hour of their talk what would be agreed to—a duel was unavoidable. By the second hour, Andra realized it also. After that, she had merely waited for the combatants to be named.

The announcement came long after the princess's patience had run out. She had long since removed herself to a corner of the great hall, annoyed at the lengthy court procedure. Finally, however, all was agreed upon. Which valley, which day, which hour, all the rules—all of it. The combatants could take any weapons with them, use anything they found. They could take in supplies or live off the valley. It was a contest to the death, or surrender.

"And who will our combatants be, Heskar?"

"Two of equal rank. Two with reason to fight. Two bound to try their best. Two who have most to lose." *I would name you and I, but that's what you want, isn't it? I shall let you name them. We both know who will be named.*

"There are many of equal rank amongst our peoples," Charri started. *But only two will be named. Of course it will be the children. It is always the children.* "But outside of ourselves who could we name to fit all of your qualities? I could suggest, for instance, your Heskar and my Andra, but it would be so ridiculous ..."

"Agreed. My warrior son against your child? Not a fair contest at all. She is too young, too undisciplined, too arrogant..." *Disagree with me, witch. Give me the girl.*

"Andra? My daughter...?" *Do you mean it, Heskar? Are you trying to draw me in, or truly exclude her? Do you know as much as I think you do, or not?*

Or more?

Suddenly the dream ended. Andra awoke, but did not move. Clearing her senses, she sent tendrils of awareness out in every direction, touching the grass and shrubs and every animal around her for fifty paces. She could feel no other presence. Rising slowly, she disengaged herself from the plants that had shielded her with great care. Then, satisfied that nothing large was moving in the area around her, the young witch proceeded further south into the valley.

Night had already fallen, meaning she had slept for many hours. Now that it was dark, cooler, the gargor would be seeking shelter. He would not stay out in the colder night air. She cast questions ahead of herself as she walked. Allowing herself to seep into the surrounding terrain, Andra joined almost completely with it, searching for her opponent. She had no luck. He had rested against none of the trees she could reach, trod on none of the grass, been seen by no beast. The witch combed the air for the death screams of victims. Hundreds had died in the valley that afternoon, but none of them at Grakar's hands.

A sudden thought abruptly changed Andra's direction. She drifted noiselessly through the brush, coming to a stream that fed the valley. She stepped into it, ignoring its freezing chill—an easy task for any Lomonian. Standing still, eyes closed, she hunted for miles down the silent water for those interruptions in its flow where something or someone had stolen from it that day. Fox, bird, trellig, bear, racker, mole, badger—animals of every sort she had ever known had dipped the river that day, but no gargors.

Dismayed, Andra crossed the stream with strong, easy strokes. She grabbed playfully at a passing trout, her mind drifting for the moment backward to childhood games. She stopped suddenly, however, her abruptness startling the fish.

"Undisciplined am I? Arrogant? I'll show..." Andra forced herself to stop. Turning back to her original destination, she continued on toward the opposite shore.

"I *am* disciplined. The gargor is only a warrior, a killer of flesh. In many ways he is no better than a human. And yet, he is out there, waiting for me... winning."

Perhaps I *have* been arrogant, she thought. Maybe it isn't so impossible for a "mere" gargor to give a Lomonian trouble. Even a princess of the line.

Pulling herself up on the opposite bank, Andra began to put together the facts she had, including those she had resisted.

It was always to be a duel, she told herself. They knew it. Mother knew it. Grakar knew he would be chosen. Did mother know I would be her choice? Did she know it would be Grakar and I in this valley from the beginning? Did Heskar?

Andra was reluctant to think the gargorian could manipulate her mother. But, if Charri had not been manipulated, had known about the duel, that Andra would go, then why was she not prepared? Charri had known for months Heskar was going to force the issue of Hotor's Talisman, which meant either the Queen Ruler of Lomonia, Charri, She Who Is, had been used, out-manuvered by a gargor, or she had sent her own daughter into a fight for her life unprepared.

Am I supposed to lose, the girl wondered. Are the gargors supposed to recover their foul totem?

"Doesn't anyone care what happens to me?"

No sound came that could answer her question. If the gargors were meant to have their talisman back, it could have simply been handed to them—could it not? No, something was happening which Andra did not understand. She realized, however, that her present situation was no time to find her way through the past. Only the future held any validity for her at that point—a future in which she had to defeat a cunning warrior, or die herself.

"I am sitting next to a stream to which I can talk which tells me nothing. I have sat long enough for my dress to dry, for all of me to dry. My opponent is waiting. To keep him waiting longer would be rude."

With new resolve, Andra rose and began to make her way through the forest which began scarcely three feet from the river bank.

Round three went to the witch.

Several hours before the next dawn Andra found herself another resting place. She napped there until the sun broke over the mountains to wake her. She came awake quickly, fully alert almost instantly. Immediately, she began sniffing the air around her for a trace of her foe. Still there was nothing. She contemplated taking animal form, but decided against it. Fish could be speared; birds brought down with an arrow. No animal she could transform into could best a gargor in combat. Better to allow real birds to be her eyes, and to scout for real beasts to be her strength. She had been keeping track of several large animals in the valley.

There was a racker, one of the great northern cats, nearby; she had kept track of its whereabouts. She had also been gently herding both a wolf pack and a bear in a Southerly direction. If she needed them, they would come to her aid. The problem of keeping track of them while searching for Heskar was a difficult one, but Andra felt more comfortable knowing she had allies, even if they themselves were not yet aware of their alliance.

What made her less comfortable were the growing clouds above. A storm would change the air, curtailing her ability to stay in contact with her surroundings until she could readjust. Storms were difficult things for young witches to control. Nature's more violent secrets were the last to be revealed. Andra had little knowledge of the rhythms of rain or lightning, sleet or thunder, as of yet.

Gargor shamans can predict the weather, she reminded herself. Could they have picked this time as part of their plan?

"They might," she whispered. "Being able to control the weather, we have never cared to predict it. Did you plan *this* well, Heskar?"

Andra frowned, trying to unweave the pattern of political machinations which had brought her to the valley. Her major stumbling block lay in one question: of what use was Hotor's Talisman to Heskar? Even if the trinket could unite all the tribes of Gargoria, still he could not challenge Lomonia. There might be a great conflict, and many witches would die. But in the end, Lomonia would continue, and Gargoria would not.

It made no sense she could fathom.

Suddenly, however, Andra's attention was stolen by a piercing scream. It was the pitiful cry of a rabbit, somewhere up ahead. She moved toward it cautiously, although to do so tore at her soul. The faint cries only one such as herself could hear were heart rending. She could feel the creature's rapid heart beat, hear the blood pounding in its ears. Calling to it, she received strange impressions. The rabbit was caught, trapped, pinned down, but there was no enemy. No creature either menaced it or even seemed to be aware of it.

Andra continued to move quietly—cautiously. Parting the last brush between herself and a clearing, she saw the rabbit dangling by one of its hind legs caught in a hand-made grass rope. The creature strained, jerking and kicking, tumbling and gyrating in every direction, but could not free itself. The princess bit at her lip. There was nothing she could do.

The trap is Grakar's. He wants me to reveal myself.

She dared not move forward. The gargor might return before she could release the animal. If he knew his trap had been sprung, he might already be on his way. She had to leave; the snared animal was doomed. But, something had to be done.

Scream little hopper, thought Grakar, watching the swinging beast from his ledge. Call the child out of the wood. Bring her to me. Patience is not my brightest cloak and I would see an end to all this waiting.

The gargor scanned the clearing, searching the trees beyond, waiting.

"Come, little witch...Hotor would join his people and I would drain a frosted mug of..." Grakar's words broke off abruptly as he watched a wolf suddenly dive from the trees and clamp its jaws around the helpless rabbit. The hunter swung with his prey for a brief moment, then fell to the ground as the grass rope broke, the already dead bait still tight in its jaws.

The gargor scanned the area. He spotted no trace of Andra. His eyes narrowed as his balled fist struck against the rock ledge upon which he was perched. Other wolves approached the clearing as well, but the one Andra had called snarled them all away, sharing his prize with only his mate.

Round four went to the witch.

Grakar stared upward into the darkening sky as the first drops of rain began to fall. Extending his hand, he felt at the drizzle, gauging exactly what type of storm was to follow.

Warm, he thought, but not so much that it will stay such. This one will grow cold. This one will mire the valley.

Thunder rumbled overhead in agreement, slamming its way through the premature darkness. Jagged tines of lightning pronged their way across the sky, some few slashing downward, flaming trees out on the far plain.

Grakar turned from the storm, retreating into a small recess in the cliff wall behind him. His cloak already drenched, he removed it quickly, trading it for a water-repellent wrap stored with his other supplies. Once again, the wisdom of his father's plan unfolded for him. It did not matter that he had brought hundreds of pounds of supplies with him; he had not traveled long enough for it to be a burden. No, he had entered the valley and made his way only a few miles to the spot his father's scouts had picked. There he had set up camp, and there he had waited. Now, however, it was time to begin the hunt.

"This weather will not befriend our princess," he chuckled as he buckled his sword to his side. "For the time of the storm few of her powers will help her."

Looking over his other weapons, the gargor ignored his bow, knowing the limitations this heavy a storm would pose to arrows. Stooping, he picked his daggers instead. The first blade he secured inside his left boot, the second in his belt, humming as he did so. Grakar found the rain's tapping comforting—invigorating. He knew as long as it held, the witch's main defensive abilities would be useless. Standing straight, the gargor took his pike from its place against the recessed wall and headed out into the storm.

"I know you're out there somewhere, little witch. Somewhere close. If I am wrong, of course, the storm will muddy my passing and you will still not be able to find me. But if I am correct..." Grakar savored the thought for a moment, thin lips curling at the thought of Andra's lifeless body, "then this shall all soon be over."

The gargor moved down the cliffside with slow, sure motions. He was not worried over being spotted by his opponent. The sky had inked over completely. No moon was showing, and the lightning had moved far to the west. Coming near the foot of the cliff, Grakar leapt forward holding his pike over his head with both hands. He landed with a short, heavy thud. Instinctively he headed for the forest, knowing his foe would seek shelter within its pines. Nothing so tall it would draw lightning, but still fresh smelling and dry underneath.

"If she's nearby, and I'm certain she is, then she'll be in the grove near the slate falls."

Grakar headed in that direction, his grin widening. Ignoring the trickles inching their way beneath his collar, he rotated his pike once, twice, thrice in his hands and enjoyed the feel of it.

Round five had gone to the beast.

Andra sat beneath a large pine listening to the rain. The trees grew so close together where she had sought shelter that hardly any rain could squeeze through the tightly locked branches. All about her rested the pack of Bloodsmile. Only females, of course, rested near the young witch, the males having stationed themselves at defensive points throughout the grove. Out of the darkness, Bloodsmile approached Andra. He pawed the ground in patterns, adding appropriate growls from time to time, letting the Lomonian know that none of his pack had seen the gargor.

"Bloodsmile is my friend; I thank him for his kind protection."

It was not what she said, but what she made understood through sound and gesture. The wolf nodded its head low to the ground, and then dropped its mouth open in canine good humor. It was a pure moment, and Andra enjoyed it.

The ancient pacts between witch and beast still held. Dogs man had stolen, but the wolves were Lomonian forever.

The princess lifted her hand to say more, when her gesture was halted by a howl that pierced the grove over the drowning force of the storm. It was Mauler, the Scarmaker, brother to Bloodsmile. All the wolves strained to the sound. A similar barking came, then once more, followed by a silence sudden and horrible.

Bloodsmile moved forward three paces, ears up, lip curled, eyes closed. The great ears strained, all concentration thrown into understanding what the pack's outermost scout was telling them.

That was a challenge.

What's he found?

The next howl told them all. The snarls and barks and every other noise they heard after that was combat. Andra pushed her senses through the grove, line-of-sight moving from bird to mouse to dragonfly, racing to reach Mauler, to join with him, enter his mind, see through his eyes. All around her, the great wolf's threats and curses vibrated through the trees telling of a combat impressive but cruelly one-sided. The barks were replied to only with the pound of the storm—and silence.

And of a sudden, the silence was shattered along with time as hearts broke and souls wept. Great Mauler, the Scarmaker, disappeared from the night sounds, suddenly and completely. That he was dead was fact—Andra could feel the hole in the forest the size of the old warrior's spirit.

We have found your enemy

He has found us

Bloodsmile reflected for a moment, then made her to understand, *No matter. Go with Nightrunner—he can lead you safely further back beneath the trees. We shall deal with the lizard*

Andra growled in acknowledgement. Bloodsmile was already gone. Listening to, feeling, watching the pack move off, the witch departed in the other direction with the cub, Nightrunner. Settling back far into the grove, the pair listened to the struggle in the distance. Something moved through the wolves with speed, thrashing, spearing, breaking them by ones and twos. Andra held the cub tightly to keep it from shaking.

Then suddenly, all was quiet save for the patter of the constant rain. Both Andra and Nightrunner strained their hearing, but all that came to them was the sound of water trickling through the tightly packed branches. Finally, however, a faint scraping revealed itself to them. Nightrunner began to growl, but Andra wrapped her fingers around the cub's muzzle as she began making her way further back through the trees.

The princess knew it was Grakar approaching. She moved softly, leaping from one bare patch to the next. She had only gone a few hundred yards, however, when a shadow-hidden pool of rainwater sent her crashing to the floor of the grove. The gargor knew her position instantly. As the young witch struggled to her feet, she realized Nightrunner was gone. Before she could call to him, pitiful pup-growls came from the distance.

Andra heard the chuckle, then the thud.

The witch screamed and ran away into the darkness.

Round six had gone to the beast.

Although the gargor had picked up Andra's trail relatively quickly, the witch was steadily outdistancing him. His battle with the pack had gifted him with a number of wounds—several painful—one serious. Moving in a limping run, Grakar cursed;

"Come back, filth. Face me. Fight me!"

Andra continued to run. Something in the gargor's voice did not ring true. Yes, the creature did want her to face him, was confident she could not stand against it in combat. But, there was something more.

It's not that it simply wants me to turn and face it, she realized. There's something about the direction in which I'm traveling it does not like.

The thought gave the witch renewed energy. Looking forward just as a shaft of lightning broke the sky, she saw a cliff wall that gave her ideas. She knew Grakar was injured. If he were not, he would have surely caught up to her by then. Injured, he would not be able to climb. If she could but reach one of the ledges, she told herself, she would certainly be able to find some kind of advantage.

Andra felt broken branches and sharp stones slicing her feet open through her water-logged boots, but she did not care. The princess made her way wildly across the expanse, desperate to reach the cliffs. A roaring shriek from behind her let her know Grakar had seen her, that he shared her notions on the advantages of height. Smiling, she threw herself against the rock cliff and begged it to reveal its handholds to her.

As she crawled up the face of the granite wall, Andra gave off calling for the bear and the racker she knew were in the area. They had not responded and she needed all her concentration focused on reaching the ledge ahead of her. Behind her she could hear the gargor just beginning his ascent. Eyes closed, hope flooding her mind, the young witch strained her left arm to its utmost, stretching her muscles, pushing, grasping—

The ledge!

The thought fired her mind as her fingers found the hold she was looking for. With an agonizing swell she flooded her body with a rush of energy, putting all her reserves into pulling herself up onto the outcropping. As she did, she discovered the reason for the gargor's incessant cursing. She had found his hiding place—his supplies.

His extra weapons. Two hunting knives. A sturdy length of quite strong rope. A bow with a full compliment of arrows.

A giddiness she could not control flooded the girl. The bow she understood. Had used such a thing. It had range. She could attack from a distance. Safety.

"Surrender, witch," Grakar screamed from below. "All you need do is return to us Hotor's Talisman. Take back your life. You have no right to anything else. *Surrender!*"

And then, the racker appeared. Stepping down silently from the topmost reaches of the ledge, the massive forest cat growled with menace at Andra's enemy. The gargor had lost his sword to the wolves, but he still had his pike. He brought it up as the racker leapt. Thick oak rang against the cat's skull. The racker tumbled aside, hitting the ground hard.

"Surrender," Grakar called again. Then, suddenly, the cat was on him, dragging him back down to the base of the cliff. Above them, not willing to leave her fate to the racker's ability, Andra struggled with the gargor's bow in the rain. The weight of the great weapon defied her, refusing to bend as she tried again and again to loop the second end of its string. Skin tore from her fingers, blood dribbled down her hands, feeding the weapon.

"Great mother of all," the girl screamed, "give me this one thing!" The bow string's loop slipped into place just as the death cry of the racker echoed upward through the rain.

"Nice try." Grakar let his broken pike slip from his grasp. "But not nice enough."

Panting, bleeding from a dozen spots, the gargor started back toward the cliff. Hand over hand, he forced his way upward, ignoring the pain of his various gashes. His blood was flowing, but with just a bit more effort he could reach the witch and end their contest.

Healing can wait, he mused.

Then, all thought fled Grakar's mind as Andra appeared on the ledge above, his bow in her hands. Before he could react she began to bend the bow back, her arrow aimed directly at his chest. Unable to retreat, unable to reach any protective cover before she could fire, he chose instead to pull his last remaining dagger from his boot. Andra's bloodied fingers, unable to hold the powerful bow string any longer, released their missile. She peered through the darkness and the rain, watched the arrow strike, stick in her enemy's chest. She watched Grakar's hand falter, almost dropping his last weapon. Almost.

Hurriedly she grabbed up another arrow. With more skill than she would have believed she possessed, she notched it and began to pull back the mighty bow once more. The effort tore at the muscles in both her arms, her shoulders. The gargor raised its arm, poised to throw. Thunder crashed as he hurled his blade, even as the girl released her arrow. What effect his dagger might have had, however, he did not get to see. He had begun tumbling back down the sopping cliffside even as the dagger left his fingers.

Round seven went to the witch.

"How?" Andra awoke slowly—groggily—confused at first. "How did I get home?"

Images flashed in her mind: the racker, the ledge, firing the arrows, Grakar's blade in the air, striking her. The princess's hand instinctively went to her side, but she found a bandage instead of a wound.

"Daughter, you must be calm." Queen Charri sat in an over-sized chair near her daughter's bed.

"But, I don't remember any...how, how did I get home?"

"Grakar brought you."

"What? But I slew him."

"No," the Queen smiled politely. "You did not. Your shafts barely pierced his armor. He fell because he slipped on the rocks. He climbed back to the ledge where you were, removed his blade from your side, stemmed the flow of blood."

Andra fell back into her pillows as her mother explained how the gargor had cleaned her wounds and bound them, then his own. How he had cared for her while the rains continued, and when they were finished, how he had brought her home.

He had not killed her. The princess absorbed the notion that she had not been worth the killing. The gargor had won. Hotor's Talisman was on its way back to Gargoria. Andra apologized for her failure, her sorrow immeasurable. Her mother's attempts to console her were futile. The princess knew she had doomed Lomonia. Once the gargor clans had been united, they would swarm north and all would be lost. Her heart filled with a rare pity, the queen whispered;

"No, they will not." When Andra's blinking eyes signalled a lack of comprehension, the queen continued. Heskar needed Hotor's bauble to unite his people. This will take years. When he is done, however, it is not us upon whom his intentions will be turned. There would be no profit which one such as Heskar could understand in that."

And then, Andra understood everything. Lomonians did not prize gold or gems. The witches were powerful enemies and made poor slaves. Heskar would not lead his legions against the witches. No, he would lead them against those who had what he wanted—those Lomonia feared far more than they did the gargors—

"The humans. You want the gargors and the humans to fight, to destroy one another."

"Of course, my child," cooed Charri. "If we could have just handed the gargors their toy, we would have. But that would have been an insult to them, 'take your toy, we do not fear you.' They might have begun a hideous war just out of pride. If we did not return it, they might have begun the same war."

The queen looked down at her daughter, seeming so fragile in her bandages, so pale from loss of blood. It would have been so, so inconvenient if the girl had died. It was true she had been a tool. And, as Heskar and Charri had imagined, one that played her part as they needed it to be played. Grakar had shown great political savvy himself, not slaying the princess.

Andra turned away from her mother, staring at the far wall. The queen assumed she understood. Such a thought, that one had been used, that they were not in control of their destiny, was always hard to entertain. Charri left quietly to give her daughter time to reflect.

She did not first dry the girl's tears. Indeed, the notion that there might be tears to dry did not even cross her mind. Instead her thoughts turned to other matters of state that needed her attention. The final round had gone to the beast.

But she had won the war.

It was all that mattered.

AUTHOR C.J. HENDERSON IS AN ORIGINS AWARD WINNER WHO, IN HIS TIME, has earned his keep as everything from a movie house manager and blackjack dealer to a roadie, card shark and stand-up comic. He is the creator of two series characters known around the world, private eye Jack Hagee and supernatural investigator Teddy London. Over the past quarter century he has written over thirty books as well as hundreds of short stories and comics. His work has been seen in numerous anthologies, as well as such magazines as *Cemetery Dance, Dragon, Espionage, Startling Science Stories, Crypt of Cthulhu, Different Worlds, Tales of Lovecraftian Horror, Fantasy Gamer* and scores of others. As for his comics work, he has written for both DC and Marvel, as well as such wide-ranging companies as Archie and Penthouse. As a gamer, he has been around the block a few times as well. He has rolled the dice in Lake Geneva, WI, back in the days when it was still the home of TSR, and he has sat across the table from such notables as sci fi painter James Warhola, Lovecraft scholar Dr. Robert M. Price and everyone's favorite cartoonist, Gahan Wilson. He was also Larping over twenty years ago, back, as he says, "before it had a name."

Sweet Liam Roanes

Danielle Ackley-McPhail

You left behind a trail
...footprints in the sands
...ripples through the waves
...blissful agony etched upon my heart
Leading me to the precipice.

Your calls were a siren song
...drifting on the wind,
...rising from the surf
...echoing in my cries,
Tempting me at the cliff's edge

Lost in the memory of your skin
...like cream silk against my lips
...like slick grey velvet beneath my fingertips
...like salty sweetness tipping my tongue
Drawing me into your madness.

Why did I not notice
The melancholy edge to your laughter
...the sorrow underlying the joy
in your endless eyes?

Blessed of the divine children,
Cursed immortal soul,
Call down a storm upon this shore
That nature may cry my tears—

For I have lost my heart to a selkie,
And I've lost my selkie to the sea.

THE GIFT

Melanie Florence

I COULDN'T HAVE PICKED OUT THAT OLD WOMAN AGAIN ON A CROWDED STREET. I never even got her name. At first appearance, she fit in with all those other nondescript senior women: short, bespectacled, somewhat overweight and dressed in a drab, polyester pant suit. At our parting, however, her appearance was something else altogether.

We met when she asked to share my table in the dining car. I thought she must be a widow, like me, traveling alone. But then the watery, pale blue eyes burned into me with such intensity that I found my miserable life story gushing out. She, in turn, described sorrows much deeper than mine. She had lost a country, siblings, and a pregnant daughter.

For the first time in years, I felt like reaching out for advice, guidance. "Please, tell me how you carried on after losing so much."

"I was chosen," she said succinctly. "And through it, I developed a passion and a purpose. I found meaning."

"But what were you chosen for?"

"To create beauty."

"What beauty? Paintings? Tapestries? Sculptures? Music?"

She smiled, revealing worn, gray teeth. "All of those things."

My body stirred with desire. "Please, I'd like to know more."

She smiled again. "You came to me just in time. I have a design for you, but with this gift comes responsibility." She nodded. "Yes, you must always be responsible." She folded her gnarled hands on the table. "My body's wearing out," she said. "I've known it was time to give my pleasure, my pain, to someone like you for quite some time now." She bowed to me. "And I will, if you choose to accept it."

I glanced at her tired, haggard face. Her bottom eyelids sagged and her wrinkled cheeks fell down into jowls. Her short, white hair stuck out in thin dry wisps and veins protruded from the backs of her liver-spotted hands. I must have misjudged her age earlier because she now appeared to be very, very old.

Anticipation rose in my breast. "Are you saying that you'll teach me your craft?"

She shook her head vigorously. "No, no, no. I can only give it to you. As you must give it to someone else when it is your time."

What did she have to give me? I wondered. I sat silently for a moment while the train gently rocked us back and forth. My seat faced forward, into the future, and the old woman, with a full life behind her, sat across from me, facing where we had just been. As it was now, my life was a meaningless, dark tunnel. How could taking this woman's gift make it any worse? Nodding, I held out my hand. "I'll accept your gift."

She stretched out crippled fingers and touched the back of my hand. A surge of vibrating energy climbed up my arm, my neck, my face, and dove through my eyeballs into my brain. It was over in a split second. Confused, I turned to ask the old woman what had happened. But as I opened my mouth to speak, the woman changed. Her faded-blue eyes framed by sagging eyelids, wrinkles, and jowls transformed into deep blue orbs over smooth cheeks blossoming pink. Her thin gray hair turned thick and blonde, and feathered around her face, reaching the shoulders of her now peach-colored pantsuit.

I shook my head. This couldn't be real. I looked at my fifty-year-old hands, the wedding band I still wore. Same trim nails, same knobby knuckles. I raised my gaze to the youthful face across the table from me. Had I hallucinated the old woman?

She smiled, showing white, straight teeth. "I see that you've already started. But I must warn you. Once you begin creating beauty, you'll think you can control it. But you can't; it will control you."

The train's brakes shrieked and the train slowed. She rose from the table and looked down at me. "Now you'll have an adventure," she said, smiling. "But remember, it's best to remain anonymous." She turned quickly and left the dining car with an energetic stride.

I jumped up to follow her, but she had vanished. Bewildered, I clutched a doorway to brace myself for the train's stop. A few minutes later, as I shakily descended down the narrow steps, every sensory detail stood out like it never had before. The cold heavy suitcases tingled in my hands and Denver's dry January chill caused my eyes to smart. Steam from the hissing train swept around me, turning the scenery gray and white, while a meandering chorus of greeting voices pricked at my ears. A mixture of cigarette smoke and car exhaust invaded my nostrils. It seemed like the numb shell muffling my senses had cracked, allowing a stream of sensitivity to flow in.

My baby brother Sam wove through the throng to greet me. "Hey, Sis," he said, his words hanging in a cloud. He pulled me toward him and a thousand points in my cheek itched against his rough wool coat. Releasing me, he asked, "How was your trip?"

"Fine," I answered. But in reality, my mind was skipping like a scratched record. Was the old woman real? Or was I going crazy? I tried to shake off these thoughts, but my mind kept jumping back onto that same track over and over again.

"Let me take your suitcases, Sara," Sam said, reaching out. As his soothing baritone voice resonated inside my head, I heard it like never before. It was lovely.

I followed Sam to his battered orange pickup. He threw my heavy bags into the bed and turned to me again, his eyes shining under a distant light. "Are you sure you're doing okay?"

He circled his large, gentle hands around my upper arms and I felt the two bands of pressure through my heavy coat.

I looked away from his glowing eyes. "I'm...I'm just tired."

"Well, you'll have a bed soon enough." He unlocked my door and I hitched myself up into the truck. He walked around to the driver's side and climbed in. "We haven't had snow in a few weeks so it's pretty dry and dusty," he said, turning the key.

I watched the dark, familiar streets and businesses whiz by. But wait. Why were flowers blossoming in January? And why were the neon lights splashing like fireworks against the dark sky?

Sam pulled up in front of a dingy duplex and turned off the motor. He sat for a moment with his head bowed, his hands in his lap. "I'm sorry. It's kind of rundown, not much to offer "

I interrupted, "It's more than enough, Sam. You're giving me a place to stay."

Sam showed me my room.

As I lay on my bed, I pondered the old woman and the infusion of sensation into my once dismal world. Maybe she gave me the ability to *perceive* beauty again, I thought before I drifted off to sleep.

The next thing I knew, the light was on and Sam was standing in my bedroom doorway wearing worn, paint-spattered overalls. "Why don't you go to work with me today?"

"What time is it?" I asked, groggily.

"Early," he said, laughing. "Well?"

I threw back the covers, glad for this chance to start over. "Sure. Might as well do something useful."

"Good. Put on some old clothes."

Sam buzzed with energy and enthusiasm as he drove to a dilapidated two-story brick house and parked in front. "This my favorite HUD house. It's one of four that I'm currently fixing up and reselling."

"So you like this new job of yours?" I asked.

He nodded. "Very much."

Sam led the way up the cracked sidewalk and stood before a solid wood front door streaked with peeling varnish. "It's fun. Every house has its own personality. You'll see." He flung the door open and walked through the doorway.

I surveyed the empty living room. Black marks marred its off-white walls, stains discolored its shag carpet, and the acrid smell of cat urine hung thick in the cold air. This house's personality doesn't appeal to me, I thought. I sighed with relief. Everything was bleak again; I must be back to normal.

He beckoned. "Come on in. I'll show you around."

We began with the attic above the second floor. Flipping on bare light bulbs, he pointed out defects and explained how he was going to fix them. I, in turn, wrinkled my nose at peeling wallpaper, stained carpets, cigarette burns on window ledges, cracked drafty windows, leaky pipes, and chipped porcelain. But something told me that this house was not really that disagreeable at all; it was crying.

By the time we reached the first floor again, a man and a woman were waiting for us at the base of the stairs. Sam's hand glided through the stale air as he introduced us. "Danny, Tina, this is my sister, Sara. She's going to be helping us until she figures out what she wants to do with her life."

Danny was fifty or so with a pot belly stretching a dirty, torn tee-shirt and an odor of beer, sweat, and cigarette smoke. "Glad to meet you," he said, shaking my hand.

Tina's diminutive body was topped with bleached yellow hair and a leathery face. She was dressed in washed-out, holey jeans and a Denver University sweatshirt much too big for her.

"Hiya," she said in a soft voice.

Sam pointed his thumb at Danny, who was already walking off through the archway between the living room and kitchen. "Danny's fixing up the kitchen." Sam turned back to the living room. "And this is my project." He bent over and lifted an edge of the carpet and swiveled his head up to look at me. "Look. It's a parquet wood floor. It's nasty now but I think it'll look great after it's refinished."

I nodded, visualizing it shiny and smooth, peeking out from under an oriental rug.

Straightening up, he said, "Now I'll show you what Danny and Tina are doing."

I followed him through the archway. A new stainless steel kitchen sink rested on the counter amidst pieces of PVC pipe, rags, and tools. Danny was on his back, grunting as he wrenched at pipes underneath the old sink. As I grimaced at the worn linoleum floor, the scarred counter top, and the chipped paint on the cupboard doors, a mental picture overlaid it all with a new blue counter top, oak cupboards and brown tile floors.

We walked back through the living room, down a hallway, and to the bathroom. As Sam rested his large body against the door frame, I had to hunch under his arm to see Tina crouching over a hole in the floor where the toilet had been. The old, rust-stained toilet rested at a tilt in the bathtub and the dirty sink was filled with tools.

"Well Tina, is the floor rotten after all?"

She nodded without looking up.

"Go ahead and start taking it out then. New floorboards are in the garage." As she nodded again and reached for a tool, my mind projected the competed bathroom over this torn up one: a crisp white tile floor, a claw-footed tub, a standing sink, gold fixtures, and a new toilet.

We edged out of the doorway and walked into the family room, a long add-on at the back of the house. "And this is your room to work on," Sam said with a wave of his hand.

My stomach lurched. This room was nauseating. The floor was painted a yellow-green and decades of cigarette smoke had tinged the pale wood paneling a dull brown. The low stucco ceiling made me feel claustrophobic.

"Why don't you start with the floor," Sam said, walking to the corner of the room. He bent over a pile of rags and tools and walked back with a scraper in his hand. Squatting, he knocked on the floor with a knuckle. "Feels hard, like tile." He scraped the floor once and a few chips of paint came up. "And the paint seems loose. If it's tile, we might be able to use paint remover. But if its linoleum, we'll probably have to tear it up." He stood up and handed me the scraper. "See what you can do with scraping first, okay?"

He grinned down at me and I was comforted by the spark in his dark brown eyes.

"Have fun," he said, patting my shoulder. "I'll be back in a bit to see how you're doing."

After he left, I turned around slowly and studied the horrible room. Not only was it suffocating but it reverberated with a low humming or whispering sound. My skin tingled. Was the noise coming from outside? I walked to sliding glass doors on the back wall. As I scanned the yard, searching for a power line or transformer or other sound source, the steel gray sky turned blue. The stark, naked cottonwood trees came into an interlacing outline as the tangled mess of shrubs next to the fence sprouted bright orange fruit. Tiny juncos, finches, and meadowlarks flew up out of the unmowed weeds, landing on the shrubs. A gray squirrel ran across greening grass and the air he pushed stirred a breeze that moved its way up grass, shrubs, and tree trunks, to the tops of the cottonwoods. The swaying large branches left a shimmery trail of broad arcs across the sky.

I closed my eyes tight and opened them. Blue sky, glittery trail, birds; they were still there. My eyes must be playing tricks on me, I thought, turning away.

I walked across the bare room with my hands over my ears to block out the humming.

But each solitary step echoed and thumped into my head. Hot tears slid down my cheeks and I crumpled to the floor. What was happening to me? Why was my husband taken away and then my sanity? I pictured his eyes, into which I had spent years gazing, his strong Roman nose, his thick dark hair, his full soft mouth, his purposeful, determined walk. As I spilled each tear, a drop of depression seeped out, and as I inhaled each breath, my heart had lifted a notch higher. I looked up. So had the ceiling. It had risen and changed into a stamped tin ceiling of squares within squares.

Giving into the pull of the room, I knelt on the hard floor to scrape the paint. The scraper slid smoothly over the surface from grout line to grout line, pushing crumbling paint ahead of it. I saw now that the floor consisted of tiles impregnated with splotches of color. I pressed down harder and the splotches refined themselves into fine brush strokes. I scraped faster and thin slivers of paint peeled off. I blew them away. With both hands now, I pressed down and scraped and blew. Pressed, scraped, blew. Pressed, scraped, blew.

"Hey, that's very unusual," Sam said from behind me.

I was so engrossed that I jumped at his words.

He chuckled. "Sorry I scared you." Then he looked down and rubbed his whiskery chin. "I'd like to get at the whole picture, but now I'm afraid to use paint remover. Might ruin the tiles, take the color off. Hmm, I think I'll call my ceramic expert."

While he punched in some numbers on his cell phone, I thought about what Sam just said. Sam saw the picture; that meant I hadn't been seeing things that weren't there.

He left a message, pocketed the phone and turned back to me. "Keep scraping for now, okay? I'll get back to you after I talk to Steve."

After he left, I stood up and stretched. Then I walked to the sliding glass doors with the intention of putting outside light to my back so that I could better contemplate the floor. I squinted. Faint impressions hovered just beneath the yellow-green veneer, a pattern just out of reach. I unfocused my eyes and refocused them, as if I was looking at a Magic Eye picture and finding the 3-D picture within it. An image was there; I knew it.

As I stared, the yellow-green color gradually dissolved. Bit by bit, the floor became an impressionistic bouquet in pastel colors, emanating from the middle of the room. I circled the room. At each degree around the circle, the flowers on the opposite side were upside down and the flowers facing me were right-side up. Before my eyes, hazy flowers became detailed and then identifiable: roses, daisies, carnations, baby's breath, forget-me-nots, all tied up in a shiny red ribbon in the center of the room. A sweet scent permeated the air.

I blinked, but the pattern remained. I blinked again. It was still there. I bent down, sniffed a rose and breathed in its spicy fragrance. This was too real. "Sam! Sam, come here!" I screamed.

His rapid footsteps grew louder and stopped in the doorway. "Wha…t?" Scratching his head, he glanced at me with a puzzled look on his face. "How'd you do that? It's beautiful."

"So you see it, too?"

Danny and Tina piled up behind Sam.

Danny eyed me warily. "There's no way you could scrape all that paint this quickly. And...the ceiling's different."

"I, I..." I looked down at the scraper in a shaking hand that didn't seem like it was mine, then up at the high, shiny ceiling.

Danny backed out of the doorway. "This is giving me the creeps," he said, already around the corner.

Sam responded in a daze, "Danny, I'll be with you in a moment."

But Tina ran to me and clutched my arm. "Sara, if you can fix this room...can you fix people, too?"

Staring into Tina's bloodshot eyes, I thought back to how the old woman changed on the train and shuddered. Did I really make her grow younger? If so, how? And how did I change this room? How could I fix something again if I didn't understand what I did? "I don't know if I can, Tina. I really don't."

Sam gently pried her hand off my arm. "Could you leave us alone for a few minutes, Tina?"

She ducked her head. "Sure, boss." But on her way out of the room, she paused in the doorway. "When you figure it out, could you try it on me? Don't forget about me, okay?"

Shrouded in turmoil, I pressed my hand to my forehead. "Sam, could you take me back to your house?"

"Of course." His strong arms shook slightly as he supported me to the truck.

Throughout the afternoon, I sat on Sam's living room couch, trying to figure this out.

Until Sam, Tina, and Danny saw the floor, I thought I had either changed my outlook in some weird way or was developing mental problems. But now I had proof of the old woman's gift: she gave me the ability to create beauty. She said I wouldn't be able to control it, that it would control me. And already, I knew she was right.

Sam came home in early evening with a take-out pizza. He flicked on the lamp and smiled uncertainly at me, a shattered woman frozen to the couch.

By then, I had figured it out. If I glanced at something, I visualized its improvement, but if I stared at it long enough, I caused it to change. But what it would change into was, so far, beyond my control. I knew that from now on, I would have to be very careful.

I watched him set the pizza on the coffee table and walk into the kitchen. I heard the refrigerator open and shut again. He came back with a beer in each hand. "Want one?"

Keeping my eyes on my hands, I shook my head.

He set the extra can on the coffee table and plopped down on the other end of the couch. Facing me, he asked, "How'd you take the paint off?"

I shrugged.

His baritone rose reverently, "What you've uncovered is a work of art. I've never seen anything like it before. I can't sell that house now; I have to keep it for myself."

I glanced at his oriental rug and nodded. It was the same rug I had pictured earlier over the parquet living room floor.

He gulped down the beer and crushed the can with one hand. Reaching for the other one, he said, "But maybe you'd better not come back to the house. Danny's all freaked out and I don't want to lose him. He's one of my best workers."

I nodded, now understanding why the old woman said it was best to remain anonymous.

"Don't worry, I won't."

He frowned under furrowed brows. "Don't get me wrong, Sis; you're welcome to stay with me as long as you want. You can help at one of the other houses, or not help at all, if that's what you want to do."

"Thanks, Sam, but I just realized what I need to do. You see, I haven't mastered this new gift yet. But even now I see that if people know who's responsible for it, it'll spin out of control.

So I think I should travel for a while." I leaned forward and gazed beauty into his troubled eyes.

"Don't worry, Sam. This is a good thing. For the first time in a long time, I see a whole new world ahead of me, and a future full of possibilities."

Melanie Florence was raised in Colorado and has an M.A. in biology. She has lived in six western states before moving to Fairfax, Virginia. She's had jobs in everything from banking to outdoor botanical work and right now feels like she's found her niche in writing short stories and mystery novels.

HOLLOW GROUND

Danielle Ackley-McPhail

A CRACKLING HISS FILLED HER EARS, LIKE SAND SCOURING CANVAS WALLS. It was impossible to tell where the sound came from, with it echoing off the thick, inky blackness that shrouded the chamber. The dark intruded on her personal space as no physical being could; every move was an invasion, an uninvited intimate caress, and retreat bought no distance.

R'hona—thrice blessed among the Desert Dancers—was not used to such an assault. She wanted to lash out, to flex her claws and see what color the night bled, if at all.

If at all...that was the sticking point. She allowed her jaw to relax, drawing in a slow, silent breath and rolling it around her mouth. Musty with age, damp with the season, a faint wisp of green things growing—a scent no doubt carried in upon her person. This deep vault had no vents to the surface world. Despite the dankness, there was a hint of bone-dry dust. Nothing else was betrayed on the currents of the air.

The situation made her uneasy; not only because it took her far from her home, but because she'd been forced to this city to deal with an imposter...some hell-spawn perpetuating acts that blackened the honor of her sect. R'hona would restore that honor, if it kept her from her beloved desert, Kylo'By, forever.

Dropping to a crouch, she rested her head against the coolness of the wall. Every nerve she possessed strained to pinpoint her opponent. Her jaw clenched. An abomination bested her. The thought tore through her and left her weak.

In silence, R'hona shook herself sternly. Self-doubt was not a trait a Desert Dancer should ever know. To doubt was to taste a little from Death's cup...to taste was to taint the purity of her warrior's oath.

Her unease stemmed from this city and its cold, heavy stones. Foundations cutting off the earth and roofs keeping out the light. One could not stretch out on soft sands that still held the warmth of the noonday sun. One could not roll aside timber and slate to savor the gentle rays of the dawn or allow the mild brush of the morning breeze. No, here in the midst of so-called civilization, people huddled under mounds of blankets with heated rocks surrounding their feet. And they hardly, if ever, truly saw the sun.

So many layers between men and the essence of the world; no wonder they could not sense the evil among them. R'hona herself felt cut off, muffled in humanity. It had cost her much just to sample the air, more than it should have. She must do what she came here to do quickly. Only then could she return to the shifting sands of the Kylo'By.

"Za'ha'bitu, show yourself." The words snapped from her like the angry click of a sand turtle's jaw. She called out to the Dust Child lurking in the darkness. Another crackling hiss was her answer, more mocking than ever.

"Bitu'a'bax"—Spawn of a broken oath—"You possess something that belongs to the Desert Dancers. I will not allow you to continue to corrupt our name."

As she spoke, the focusing chants trained into her from childhood pulsed through her mind. She matched her heartbeat to their rhythm and, still crouching, she circled the room. Falling silent, like the desert wind rippling the still waters of an oasis, she drew her blade. Sifting the darkness for any trace of movement, any hint of sound that would betray her prey, she pushed her senses past the point most others considered impossible.

This was worse than a game of sand spider-and-scorpion. Her adversary was not merely waiting her out. The Dust Child mirrored her motion, gliding in the darkness as if they truly danced. Step mirrored step until R'hona raged at it. Her efforts brought them no closer to engaging battle.

"By'al's Teeth!" R'hona growled the oath. "You will not make mockery of this! Do you fear my blade so?" she taunted, using the moment of stillness to gauge how near the other had drawn to the door. A deadly hint of a smile briefly touched her lips. The abomination was not fleet enough to escape before R'hona intercepted. "You are right to do so...I am known as By's Scorpion for both its deadly swiftness and its sting."

Darkness moved against darkness, and by some unfathomable means, R'hona could sense her quarry trying to slink by. There was no way she would let it gain its freedom. She countered the creature's maneuver. It was difficult. The dead, long-hewn rock of the chamber floor felt slick and unyielding beneath her feet, so used was she to dry, burning sands, firm, but shifting. Even so, she moved with the fluid grace of a warrior.

She snarled as she taunted the Za'ha'bitu further. "Perhaps your maker crafted you of toe nail clippings, for all you seem to be good at is running away."

All went still. Completely still. Like the desert before a sand storm hit. And now, just as then, a whisper of movement on the air was all the warning she received that a mighty force coiled nearby, ready to strike.

R'hona moved swiftly, with smooth, flowing motions, and, above all, in silence. It was not wise to remain where her voice had marked her. Despite her outward contempt, she was quite convinced the one she faced would match her skill for skill. They were not exact, but near enough that neither held advantage for long.

Her nerves spiked in a determined effort to get her attention. Without giving any thought to why, she dove away from the wall. Behind her, metal rang on stone. A controlled roll carried her away from the attack. She threw her sword arm up, blade toward the direction from which she had come. Sparks flew as unfriendly steel drew down on her.

R'hona ground her teeth. Her arm tingled from the hit. Her blade still rang. She forced the other's weapon away with an upward sweep of her own. In a single, flowing motion, she continued down and around into a thrust. She heard a sound like metal scraping sun-hardened brick, followed by a sharply drawn breath. A faint tingle burned across R'hona's ribs. She ignored the odd sensation. She was unmarked.

She must keep it that way. Again she rolled as steel sliced the air where she had been. She scrambled to gain her feet before that unseen blade made another strike. The door was at her back. It would stay that way. R'hona half-crouched, her weapon ready and her stance balanced. A shushing came to her ears, as if someone walked through a thin scattering of sand. Locking in on the sound, R'hona gave the battle cry of her people and lunged. Her blade sliced the air with a deadly whistle. Low…more felt than heard.

Her aim was true; her luck was not. Even as she felt her blade bite, a ribbon of fire sliced through her own sword arm. She gasped and whirled aside in an evasion more instinct than thought. The Dance Master taught her well, but somehow she had not done justice to his teaching. Rage filled her. Shame engulfed her. She would not go home triumphant. She would return to be judged, an unfit blade, her flaws revealed in battle. No Desert Dancer marred by scars retained the honor of that calling.

So be it. She might be dead in all ways that mattered, but she would take the Za'ha'bitu with her.

Folding her injured arm tight against her body, R'hona adjusted her stance to restore balance. She switched her blade to her left hand and praised By' that she had not lost the weapon altogether.

There was a dry chuckle in the darkness. She tensed and tracked it. The creature had moved away. It sought to wear her down. Instead it had given her a reason not to hold back. Though she still drew breath, she was dead; now all that remain for her was to ensure the creature joined her in the grave. R'hona went on the offensive. Again, the battle cry, and she unleashed her wrath. She slashed. She thrust. Fluid lunges and dance-like whirls. When the enemy withdrew, already R'hona was there waiting. The chamber echoed with screams of rage and the ring of well-tempered steel.

She was mad with fury and channeled that into her strikes. Her eyes by now had adjusted to the shadowland of darkness, where shape and movement defined all in the near absence of light and color. In the abyss, she could see her foe's death. Overextended, the fool could not come back around to block R'hona's blade. Poised in vibrating stillness, a contradiction she shared with the desert viper, she drew back her machete and whipped it around to that unguarded space where her adversary's shoulder and neck met.

In the seconds before steel sliced skin, light flooded the chamber. R'hona cried out to her gods. Reflexively, she jerked back. Her heart pounded. Her mind screamed in denial. And yet she was committed to her strike. Pulling back could not avert what she'd set in motion.

She watched in shock while her own face grinned maliciously back at her. The barest edge of her blade scratched the neck she'd aimed for and her own felt the sting. A gash opened to reveal emptiness beneath, from which no blood flowed. Her eyes scanned the creature and saw evidence of other bloodless wounds. R'hona could feel the projection of their pain on her own flesh. Bile filled her throat and her sword arm trembled. She nearly dropped the weapon, except training prevailed and she was spared that one disgrace.

Dark brown eyes locked with empty pits that held too much intelligence for R'hona's sanity. The features were hers: the dark, swirling tattoos that framed her face at the hairline, the nose slightly crooked from a training encounter she would never forget, the bow of the lips quirked in just such a way meant to unsettle an opponent.

R'hona stared at herself in horror. The abomination she looked upon was a perfect reflection, but one thing was off: it was a solid shade of rusted-iron red, like she would have been, were she caught in a sand storm. The creature was the color of the desert. How ironic. Save for the coloring, and the emptiness inside, that was her image before her. This was a Dust Child, created from the sloughed off matter of R'hona's body.

The startled servant who'd opened the door screamed and the Abomination laughed silently. It had no words, no breath to make them, no tongue to form them. It was hollow inside. Empty of matter and without initiative, it focused completely on the purpose for which it was made. It had no thought but for whatever poison was whispered in its ear at creation. Clearly that had been to blacken the honor of the Desert Dancers.

As she watched, it raised its blade, but not toward her.

Its mouth formed silent words. She read them off its lips.

"Once one, always one, even in death."

R'hona could not move quickly enough. Horrified, she watched the blade's descent. It sliced through that dusty breast smooth and slow, the surface crumbling in the blade's wake. The weapon fell from the creature's fingers. It clattered on the stone amidst a growing pile of sand.

It took a moment for the shock to wear off. It was replaced with agony as R'hona felt the death-wound blossom in her own chest. Stunned, she looked down, noting numbly, as the dying do, the minute details of her being, as contradictory as they were: The absence of blood, the unmarred skin, the trembling sob she must have voiced, though it was muffled to her ears.

None of that mattered.

Darkness once again drew intimately close, as she felt life leave her.

DANIELLE ACKLEY-MCPHAIL IS THE AWARD-NOMINATED AUTHOR OF the fantasy novel, *Yesterday's Dreams*, an urban fantasy based on Celtic mythology. Her other works include *Children of Morpheus* and the upcoming anthology, *No Longer Dreams*, both by Lite Circle Books. She has contributed to *Nth Degree Magazine,* Sabledrake.com, and Darkwalls.com. Her current project, collaborating with Mike McPhail, is *Progenesis*, a military science fiction. You can find out more about her work at www.sidhenadaire.com.

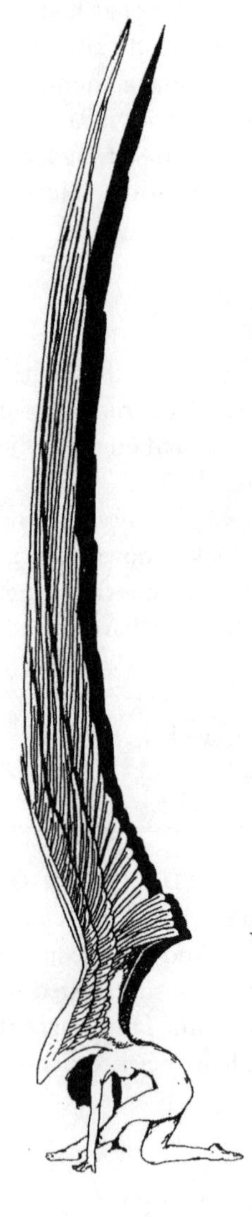

WHERE EAGLES CRY

Patti Kinlock

Silently, where eagles cry
by harvest moonlight golden-white
she dances in the autumn night
bare arms uplifted to the sky.

Woman-goddess, child of earth
limned in heaven's brilliant fire
culmination of desire
creation marveled at your birth.

The stars are circles set ablaze
congealed to white lines as she spins
a universe contained within
kaleidoscoping in her gaze.

Then black as midnight's final hour
her hair falls forward on her breast
as on her knees she falls to rest
before the wellspring of her power.

Pale, ghostly as aurora's flame
the moonface shimmers on the stream
where darklight shadows jump and gleam
and none but wind shall call her name.

None shall pass but bird and fox
and nature gives no reason
but the changing of the season
upon the eve of equinox.

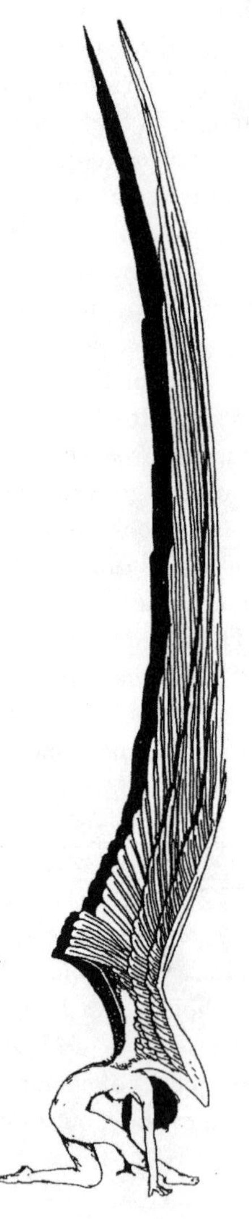

THE POPPET

L. Jagi Lamplighter

My poppet lay upon the ground trampled beneath the horse's hooves and scarred by the wheels of the carriage. I was too old to cry with all my cousins looking on. I turned away as if it did not hurt. My Uncle Albert saw me, through. There was pity in his eyes.

Devastated, I returned home and sat in the winter parlor. My poppet was gone, her fragile head caved in. I did not remember how I had felt when my mother died. However, I was sure that at the age of four, I could not have suffered as I suffered now. Surely, no one could suffer such pain and survive.

It was thus, staring into the flame that my Uncle Albert found me. He held his hands behind his back, and he was smiling.

"Come, Kitty, m'love," he said. "I've brought you a present. Here's a brand new poppet!"

I wanted no new poppet, but Uncle Albert was so kind that I could not bear to disappoint him. Uncle Albert was a guard at London Tower. Father said that he led a dismal life. So, I looked up and attempted to smile.

"Thank you, Uncle Albert," I said meekly.

Uncle Albert came close to me, adjusting his breeches, so that he could crouch beside me.

"Can you keep a secret?" he asked conspiratorially. I nodded, solemn in my sorrow.

He brought a small blue figure from behind his back, about a third bigger than his hand.

"This is no ordinary poppet," he whispered, his eyes gleaming merrily in the firelight. "But the favorite poppet of the wrongly accused Queen Anne Boleyn, dead these seven days by the condemnation of her royal husband, our good King Henry VIII. I found it in her prison chamber. She was a kind and gentle woman. Not a word of what she's been accused of is true."

I leaned forward, amazed despite my sorrow. Hesitatingly, I touched its tattered dress, worse for its stay in the Tower. It was a sweet-faced doll, and delicately made.

"The Queen's very poppet?" I asked.

"Her very poppet," my uncle answered. "Now as you have lost a poppet, and this poppet, she has lost a girl, perhaps the two of you can comfort each other."

He placed the poppet gently in my lap, then winked at me and strode from the parlour.

Queen Anne Boleyn's poppet was light in my hands. Her dark locks were soft as real hair. A scent of candle tallow issued from her, along with another familiar smell, sweet yet salty.

Her smock was of bits of blue cloth. Around her waist was knotted a pretty velvet ribbon, of black and midnight blue. She was quiet different from my lost poppet, who had been a robust and cheery doll, but I took pity on her. I brought her upstairs and set her on the trunk by my side of the bed.

That night, I had many dreams, all murky and troubled. In the morning, there was only one that I remembered. I dreamed an archer came to my door and aimed his arrow at my heart. The arrow's feathers were blue and jet. Afeared, I held up Queen Anne's poppet and cried that its face was not my own. The archer went away, but his laughter remained, hoarse like the cry of wolves or ravens. When I awoke, my stepmother's baby was yowling.

By the morning of the royal wedding of King Henry and Lady Jane Seymour, three weeks later, Anne's poppet and I had become good friends. I brought her along to her usurper's wedding, tucked in a carry purse. She was too delicate, and too scruffy, to travel beneath my arm.

The crowd was ecstatic and the streets were packed. All around, people praised the Lady Jane and denounced Anne Boleyn: 'adulteress' and 'witch'. I petted Anne's poppet and whispered that we knew the truth, she and I. We were an island of sensibility amidst the raucous throes of ignorance. In the crowd were one or two other solemn figures. I wondered if their secret was the same as ours.

The royal couple rode from the cathedral in a gilded and bejeweled carriage. King Henry stood, hands upon his hips, his wide grin visible for all to see. Often, he stooped and kissed his new bride. I strained to see her, this seductress who stole Anne's husband and her life. Jane had been Anne's maid-of-honor, before she betrayed her. I imagined her as dark and sly. To my delight, Henry finally moved away, and I caught a glimpse of Jane's face. What I saw gave me two shocks.

The first was that Queen Jane Seymour looked to be a sweet-faced and shy girl. The second was that her face was the face of Anne's poppet.

That night my dreams were wrought with horrors. Twice, I woke screaming. The first dream had been of the black-cloaked archer. I dreamed that he ripped Queen Jane's wedding bodice. His hand came away soaked in blood.

In the second, Anne Boleyn herself came to stand by my bed. Only, in my bed, her daughter, the tiny Princess Elizabeth lay. When Anne tried to reach for her, a wind blew Anne away. Without Anne, Elizabeth broke apart, as my poppet had beneath the wheels of the carriage.

I was out of breath when I reached London Tower. My rapid flight must have disturbed the resident ravens. They wheeled and cawed above.

"What troubles you, Kitty, m'love?" my uncle asked when I found him.

"It's very important, Uncle Albert!" I cried. Then I whispered. "It's about the poppet."

Solemnly, Uncle Albert led me to a quiet corner in the gate house. He sat me on a wooden trunk, and then squatted down before me.

"Uncle Albert," I began. "Do you think it's true that Anne Boleyn was a witch?"

Uncle Albert was taken back.

"I think not," he said. "If she were a witch, why would she have let her husband kill her?"

"Uncle Albert," I asked softly, "Is it true that you can kill a person by making a poppet of them and hurting the poppet?"

Uncle Albert's eyes widened. His face lost some of its ruddy color. "You'd better tell me all about it, Kitty-love." He said slowly.

With shaking hands, I drew the poppet from my bag.

"Today," I said, "I finished a new bodice and skirt for the poppet. When I cut away the poppet's old dress—it was starting to smell bad—I found this."

Carefully, I lay the poppet on the trunk beside me, and pulled away her tattered smock. The little poppet was made all of candle tallow. She had a full bosom, a navel, and other womanly parts. The wax of her chest had a rosy hue, as if there was actually a heart beneath her little bosom.

"By God's head!" my uncle swore.

"Look! At her chest!" I whispered, my voice catching in my throat.

Over the rosy spot on the chest was scratched the words *Sagitta fari hic*. Uncle Albert looked at it, frowning.

It came to me that Uncle Albert could not read Latin. Sorrow and pity welled up in me. I wondered if Uncle Albert could read at all. I said. "It reads, 'Arrow strike here.' And I keep dreaming of an archer whose arrows are the same color as this velvet tie." I held up the poppet's black and midnight blue ribbon. "What does it mean, Uncle Albert?"

It had never occurred to me that adults could be scared. My uncle's face was very white. He swallowed three times before he spoke.

"I think we have a problem, Kitty," he said. He didn't even call me 'm'love'. "If we harm the poppet, it may hurt Queen Jane, who is a decent girl. However, often the ghosts of those who are wrongly accused are trapped here in the world, forced to wander in torment until Judgment Day, unless they are avenged. From your dreams, I gather Anne Boleyn is such a one. Not a happy fate for any soul, much less an innocent one. No, I think our only course is to bring the poppet to a priest and have Anne's unhappy ghost laid to rest."

I spoke in a very small voice. "Uncle Albert, isn't that a Papist ritual? I don't think that the king's new religion allows exorcism."

Uncle Albert was silent for much longer than I wanted to wait. The wind howled outside the window boards. I heard the ravens. I kicked my feet against the trunk. Finally he spoke again.

"Wisely or foolishly, we have taken the poppet into our keeping. Perhaps it is God's will that we judge its fate."

"Us?" I squeaked. "Oh no! Uncle, not us! Why, if we chose wrongly, our very souls would be eternally damned. Can't we get someone else? A Priest? Another little girl? Let her solve the problem."

"The poppet has come to us," he said, and he laid his large and weather-beaten hand on top of mine. "It is our responsibility. If we passed it on and the new owner chose wrongly, the sin would still be on our heads, for we could have prevented it. Better to go to Hell for our own lack of judgment, than for someone else's."

"But, the Bible says, 'Judge not lest ye be judged.'" I said.

"Solomon was a judge," my uncle said, "and the Bible called him wise."

From then on, as I walked, kicking stones, or sat, poking at my needlework, I thought about life, and justice, and Solomon, and death. 'Judge not,' The Lord Jesus said. Yet, Solomon was wise. I puzzled at it, reading ancient Latin texts and studying the Bible with my father's chaplain.

In my most private moments, Anne Boleyn pursued me. She dwelt in my thoughts by day and hounded my dreams by night. I saw her standing above Princess Elizabeth, staring longingly, or kneeling in prayer in her prison chamber, weeping. In my mind's image, she wore a simple black mourning gown, like I had seen my Aunt Mary wear to her husband's funeral, and a velvet choker of the blue-black ribbon her poppet wore. Her face was always solemn and sad.

At first, Anne's poppet sat in a place of honor upon my birchwood trunk. Several times, I determined never to harm her. Yet, so touching were the pleading looks Anne gave me from my dreams, that once or twice I awoke and lifted my comb to rent the doll, before I realized what I was about.

So, I locked the poppet in the trunk and hid the key downstairs, beneath the loose flagstone in the winter parlor. Once or twice, I thought of choosing once and for all, but the fear of eternal damnation, should I chose wrongly, paralyzed and tormented me.

However, on the day that King Henry issued the royal proclamation announcing that Queen Jane now carried the crown's heir, the nature of Anne's visits changed. That night, I dreamed she came before me and stared with stern and accusing eyes. With one hand she removed the blue-black choker, revealing an angry red line across her neck. Her head then tumbled sideways, falling from her body. Only it was my head. On the ground lay the shattered Princess Elizabeth. There was a hoofprint in her chest and the bloody indentation of a carriage wheel formed a crown across her brow.

With each announcement of the health of Queen Jane and the child to be, these nightly visitations grew more horrible. Now, I was doubly glad that I had locked away the poppet. In the dim-lit early hours, when I awoke to haunting images of disembodied heads and ghostly memories of worms devouring my innards, it was hard to remember I had wanted to make a wise decision. Once, I actually padded to the door of the winter parlor and stood with my bare feet on the cold stone, staring at the spot on the floor that covered the key. However, I turned away and went back to bed.

For it occurred to me that there was no assurance that damning my eternal soul would take the nightmare away. What if Queen Jane were to haunt me?

Then one night, I awoke to see a lone figure hovering at the foot of my cot, lit by a glow like early morning, only it was still dark without. The figure wore a dark gown, through which the tapestries on the far wall could be seen. The rustling of the leaves outside seemed to take on a rhythm, like a voice whispering words.

"Kitty," it seemed to whisper. "Why do you hold me here?"

"I fear for my eternal soul." I said aloud, and then felt ashamed. How foolish I was speaking into the empty night! Again I heard words, as if whispers in the wind.

"Do you believe that you will escape the burden of my suffering, drawn on these many months by the hardness of your heart?"

"Surely," I said aloud. "God could not burden my soul both with Anne's suffering and with Jane's fate. That would not be just." I sat up and hugged my knees in the dark. The figure remained, and the unearthly glow.

"Just?" "Do you still believe God is just? Ahh, the innocence of childhood. Not so long ago, I was a new bride, with beloved child and doting husband. Now I am dead. My husband sleeps with my chambermaid, while my headless body rots. My little daughter is no longer allowed the title Princess. They call her 'bastard' and 'Little Whore.' Is that just?"

"Perhaps Anne...you...brought this fate upon yourself," I said, eager for some other soul to take the blame.

"What if I did?" continued the whispered rustle of a reply. "My little Elizabeth surely did not. She is but a babe."

"How does this touch on Elizabeth?" I asked.

"Ah, little one, you know so little of the world. Once, Elizabeth was the hope of the realm. What future does she have once Jane's babe is born? She will be a discarded heir, fated to become the pawn of every petty noble whose wine-inspired whims tempts him to lust for the throne."

"So you want Jane to die before her child is born?" I whispered, suddenly understanding.

The figure's head nodded once.

"What of Jane's child?" I asked. "Jane's unborn babe is as innocent as your Elizabeth."

"It is you who believe that God is fair, my child, not I," the whisper replied. "Each moment I remain here burns my soul as hotly as might the fires of Damnation. Yet I am constrained to stay until Jane's death." The whisper grew silent, and then rose again. "Even until the last, I did not believe Henry would kill me. He loved me once. He told me so—so many times."

I lay quietly in the dark and closed my eyes. Sympathy for Anne welled up in me, and yet I kept seeing before me my stepmother's babe with its chubby hands and wide blue eyes. I imagined Jane's child would be like that, a tiny bundle with the poppet's sweet face.

"What would Solomon do?" I wondered. "He would wait until Queen Jane's babe was born and then stab the poppet. That way both women would be dead, and for the same crime. You stole Henry from his first wife, and Jane stole him from you. Yet both women would leave behind a child."

"So be it," said the rustling voice. I opened my eyes to protest, but I found myself alone.

I grew ill, so great was my fear. The words 'So be it' echoed in my delirious mind. I feared both Anne and Jane. My uncle came to soothe me, but his visit brought no resolution. I could not bear it. Even Heaven was not worth this pain.

"I'll do it!" I cried aloud, "Let me be damned by choice, at least, rather than by omission."

The day that the birth of Queen Jane's son, Prince Edward, was announced to the realm, I took the key from beneath the flagstones and unlocked the trunk. Anne's little poppet lay atop my hope chest quilt. I lifted her out and stripped her of the pretty garments I had fashioned her. There she lay, naked in the candlelight. I held her closer to the flame and read again the words upon her chest. *'Sagitta Fari Hic.' Arrow Strike Here.* Carefully, I took up my embroidery needle and thrust it through the rosy spot upon her bosom.

I expected some resistance. Instead, the chest cavity caved in and thick red blood gushed out, covering my fingers. I screamed, staring transfixed at my bloody hands. The room grew misty, then dark. I sensed motion.

Rising from darkness, I beheld winged men rushing by, astride demon horses. Midnight wolves howled and yapped at the feet of the steeds. All followed the black archer with the blue-black arrows, whose trumpet blares were like the howls of the wind. The smooth wall against my cheek...wall?...floor!

I was on the floor. Blood was on my hands. Blood splattered all about. My shoulder hurt. My head felt light. When I could see clearly, I stumbled to the chamber pot, bent over it, and vomited. Then I went out to the well and drew water to wash my hands.

To my surprise, all the blood washed away.

When I heard the news, I ran all the way to London Tower. My uncle was in an empty chamber, clearing out the remaining possessions of the former occupant.

"Uncle Albert!" I cried. "Am I going to Hell?"

"So, she is dead then," he said. Then for a long time, he was silent.

I waited, wondering if those as unclean as I should treat with other men. Might my sins stain them as leprosy stains those who touch a leper? I felt infinitely apart from him, as if I could never again be what I had been.

Then, my uncle took me in his arms and held me. And I was again just a little girl.

"Ah there, Kitty m'love, ah there," he said.

I told him what I had done. He listened. His thin legs and gnarled hands trembled, though he tried to hide it from me. Nevertheless, I saw relief in his eyes, relief that it was finally over. He stepped away and looked at me with new respect, as if I were a noble woman instead of just his niece. I repeated my question.

"Do you think I will go to Hell?" I said.

"I don't rightly know about such mysteries," he answered after a time. "None of us can know the Will of God. But if I were you, I would figure that you were not going to Hell, rather than otherwise."

"Why is that?" I asked, surprised.

"Think of it this way, Kitty Love," he said. "If you believe that you are damned, you will be likely to take other bad actions in your life. Hope of Heaven will no longer urge you to do good. Then, your later deeds will lead you to Hell, whether you are damned now or no. However, if you believe there is a chance and always do your best, you may still win your way to Heaven."

This made some sense to me, but I was not satisfied.

"This act alone, however?" I asked. "Do you think it is enough to send a soul to hell? If I died today, for instance?"

"I am not a priest or even a cunning man, Kitty m'love," my uncle said. "Such mysteries have not been revealed to me."

"But could God still love me, a murderess and a witch?" I cried.

"Ah now, Kitty darling," he smiled sadly. "I'll not say what you want to hear. I won't tell you that you did wrong and watch the Devil strangle you on your own guilt and self-pity. You did the best a girl could do. The best a girl could do. Maybe a saint could do better, but the King's new religion does not allow for saints. So we must be satisfied with the mere best of men and girls."

"I tried to be fair," I wept, burying my head in his wool vest.

"Even Solomon could not have done better," Uncle Albert said. "Do you think God is less fair than Solomon?"

L. JAGI LAMPLIGHTER WORKS BUSILY AT TRANSLATING A MANUSCRIPT FROM another dimension that appeared one day on her doorstep. In the meantime, she is writing her second novel and, from time to time, produces a short story. She has had stories appear several anthologies and has written numerous articles on Japanese animation. When not writing, she switches to her secret identity as wife and stay-home mom. She lives in Centreville, VA with her dashing husband, author John C. Wright, and their three darling boys, Orville, Roland Wilbur, and Justinian Oberon.

PREMONITIONS

Dan Foley

MY NAME IS JOSH HAIDER. I'M AN AVERAGE 22 YEAR-OLD IN EVERY WAY, except that I know who my soul mate is. (I also know how I'm going to die but that's for later.)

Well, I don't know *exactly* who she is. I mean, I don't know her name, but I know a lot of other things about her. I know she's about my age, has short blond hair, and stands about five-foot six. She wears an Irish Claddagh ring on the pinky finger of her right hand with the crown turned inwards. That tells me her heart is not yet taken. She's fairly attractive by anyone's standards, but to me, she's beautiful. I especially love the small scar that runs through her left eyebrow. It gives her face a hint of mystery. To be completely honest though, the only things I'm really sure about are her face and the ring. Over the years I've built a picture in my mind's eye of what I think the rest of her is like. It's more than that, though; somehow I just know things about her.

I first saw her in a dream when I was fourteen. It wasn't a wet dream like so many of them were back then. It was just a normal dream. Her face, silhouetted against a sky so blue it took my breath away, was all I saw. Her features had been slightly blurred. They had rippled, as if I were seeing her through a veil moved by a gentle breeze. As silly as it seems, I fell in love with her the first time I saw her. It was completely unreasonable, but true. She was obviously old, at least twenty, but that didn't matter to me. With the certainty of youth, I knew that she was my destiny.

It was six months before I dreamt of her again, but I had imagined her every day since that first night. Once again she appeared in my dream with no preamble. Suddenly she was just there, but this time, her image was clearer. Her features still rippled but only slightly. And again, all I saw was her face, framed by the impossibly blue sky. That was the first time I had noticed the scar.

Usually, I don't remember my dreams. A flicker of memory upon awakening, or a jolt if I have a nightmare, but I hardly ever remember details. If I do retain any specifics, they're usually gone in a matter of minutes. I have too much to deal with in the real world to concern myself with dreams. But she was different. She stayed with me always, never more than an idle thought away, haunting my imagination.

After that second time, Sarah (that's what I decided to call her) appeared in my dreams every four or five months or so. In each dream I learned, or sensed, something new about her. That's how I found out about the Claddagh. I saw it on her hand as clearly as I usually saw her face. I had no idea what it was at the time, but eventually I saw its mate in an Irish craft store. I now wear it on my right hand, but I wear it with the crown turned outwards. Worn like that it means my heart is taken.

It got to where I looked forward to seeing her. I would go to sleep willing her to appear and awake disappointed when she didn't. Worse, she was starting to affect my life. At fifteen, I only looked at older women and I foolishly compared all the girls I met to her—or rather, to my ideal of her. And, not surprisingly, not one of them measured up. As a result, as far as girls were concerned, I grew up a loner.

When I was sixteen I found my first true passion other than Sarah. It was hiking. I loved to get out in the woods near my home in New Jersey. I would spend hours by myself, exploring the hills and valleys of the Ramapo Mountains. They weren't high, or majestic; they were comfortable. Mountains like the Rockies dare you to climb them. The mountains in the east welcome you. Their stark naked beauty in winter, the promise of rebirth in spring, summer's celebration of life, and fall's flaming foliage drew me in like a lover's embrace. I was always more comfortable in the woods than anywhere else. I could easily walk up to fifteen miles a day if I wanted to, but most of my trips were shorter than that. Occasionally I would hike for distance, but most days I just went in search of solitude.

When I was eighteen, I finally met a girl who moved Sarah to the back of my mind. She didn't supplant her of course, but she definitely got my interest. Her name was Carol, she had dark hair, was a petite five-foot two, and was as different from my idea of what Sarah was as the Rockies were from my Appalachians. Luckily for me, she made the first move in our relationship; otherwise I might still be saving myself for a girl I might never meet. A girl who might not even exist, for all that I thought I knew about her.

I met Carol during the summer between high school and college. I had a job working for my uncle delivering appliances. One of my deliveries was to Carol's house and, since both her parents worked, she was the one who had to stay home to accept the delivery.

I arrived at her house with a new washing machine just before lunch. "Hi Josh," she greeted me when she opened the door. She was a year behind me in school and I had seen her around, but I didn't know her name. Obviously she knew mine though, and it made me self-conscious.

"Uh—hi," I stammered. "I've got your new washing machine on the truck. Where should I put it?"

"In the garage. My Dad will hook it up when he gets home."

"OK," I responded, still racking my brain for her name. Then, as if in answer to a prayer, a gift from the gods appeared. Looking over her head into her kitchen I could see a note board on the wall. On it, in red marker, was the message: "Carol, don't forget! Washing machine today!"

Armed with a name I didn't feel quite so awkward. When I rolled the new washing machine into the garage I was even relaxed enough to comment on the trail bike hanging from the back wall.

"Nice bike. Whose is it?" I asked.

"Mine," she responded, with obvious pride. "Do you ride?"

"No, I walk," I answered. "Well, I mean I hike," I added.

"Where?" she responded, actually sounding interested.

"Just in the woods, nowhere special."

"How far do you go?"

"I don't know; depends on how I feel. I usually go for most of the day and just see where it takes me."

"Really? Would you like some company some time?"

I couldn't answer her right away because I was too surprised. When I did respond, all I managed to croak out was, "Are you serious? Why would you want to hike with me?"

"Because it might be fun. And I sure can't go hiking through the woods alone, can I?"

Carol was new, exciting, and a challenge. Not to mention that at eighteen I was horny as hell. Dream girls are fine but they do nothing for a guy's physical needs. On our first hike I was nervous and uncertain around her but we got through that. Boy, did we. I never knew a walk in the woods could be so much fun.

Carol and I had a great summer together, but when summer was over, so was the romance. I left for college in Tennessee and she started into her senior year of high school. Both of us found more convenient partners to spend our time with. The most memorable thing about Carol was she brought me out of my shell. After her I had a fairly normal social life, girls included.

It was in my sophomore year at the University of Tennessee that I got my first glimpse of how I was going to die. Initially I didn't recognize it for what it was, but eventually I did. Like Sarah, it came to me in a dream. Another dream that stayed with me after I awoke. It was a vivid vision of a mountain stream. In the dream I was looking downstream from very near the level of the water. Directly in front of me was a small pool. At the end of the pool the water spilled out into a narrow channel that ran through a series of large stones before it dropped out of sight. The bank was undercut on both sides. It was a typical mountain stream that floods in spring and then dries to a trickle in the fall. I've seen dozens like it on my hikes.

It wasn't until the third time I had the dream that I realized there was an unmistakable feeling of wrongness about it. I would wake up in a cold sweat and be unable to get back to sleep. Unlike my dreams of Sarah, this dream filled me with dread. After a year, I felt with certainty that the dream was a premonition of my death.

At first it freaked me out pretty badly, and for the next year I avoided the mountains like a bat shuns daylight. But I was miserable doing it, I felt lost without my hikes. I had never realized just how essential they were to my mental well being. They were therapeutic. In the solitude, the mechanical process of one step after the other, and the absence of the myriad demands of life, I seemed to have access to my soul. The trails and woods were where I solved my problems, made my plans, and plotted my future. I couldn't live without them, even if it meant dying in them.

I made my first trip back to the mountains after exams were over in my junior year. It was a weekend hike on the Appalachian Trail, or simply the AT. It was in early June and, thankfully, I had the trail mostly to myself. I did meet one couple who were through-hiking to Mt. Katahdin, in Maine.

The thought of hiking the entire trail, all two thousand one hundred sixty-eight miles of it from Mt. Katahdin to Springer Mountain in Georgia, was intoxicating to me. The more I thought about it, the more I was determined to do it. I would start the hike after graduation. It would be a transition point in my life, providing closure to my school years and an interlude before the decades of professional life that lay ahead.

I planned the hike throughout my senior year. Unlike most hikers, I planned to walk from Maine to Georgia because the hike would take at least five months and I couldn't leave until after graduation in June. I thought of asking a friend to go with me, but knew having someone else along would lessen my experience and deprive me of the solitude I craved. I needed that solitude to figure out what I was going to do with the rest of my life.

The other thing that happened in my senior year is that my dreams of Sarah and the stream started to occur more frequently. By April I was having one or the other at least once a week. I guess any normal person would have cancelled the hike because of the premonition about the stream, but I refused to let it control my life. And, if it was a true premonition, I didn't think there was anything I could do about it anyway.

My hike officially started on the summit of Mt. Katahdin, at sunrise, on June 13. For that one day in my life I was the first thing the sun touched when it rose over the United States. Then, after that brief moment of anticipation, and armed with a copy of *The Appalachian Trail Thru-Hikers-Companion*, I embarked on what would probably be the longest hike of my life. A hike that would provide countless stories to bore generations of unborn Haiders.

As pumped as I was, the first day on the trail was still fairly relaxing. I hiked at a reasonable pace and easily reached the first of many shelters that I would sleep in on my journey. The shelters were spaced about a day's hike apart all along the trail. The plank floors weren't very comfortable, but they provided some shelter from the elements. I slept in a lightweight, one-man tent when I could, but camping on the trail was only allowed in designated campsites so most nights were spent in the shelters. Happily, the first night I had one to myself.

As tired as I was after a full day of hiking, I still had a hard time falling asleep that first night. I lay in the lean-to staring out at the night sky and thinking about the hike ahead of me. Sometime during my musings I must have fallen asleep because suddenly I was gazing into Sarah's face. And then, just as suddenly, I was staring at the stream. I awoke with a start and, despite the warmth of my sleeping bag, found myself shivering. Unnerved, I didn't sleep well the rest of the night. It was not the start I had expected for the trip.

My hike continued like that throughout Maine. Great hiking during the day followed by vivid dreams of Sarah or the stream at night. On nights I dreamt only of Sarah I spent the next day on an emotional high. I walked lightly and even the most difficult parts of the trail were a joy. If I dreamt only of the stream, the following day was filled with dread and the trail was formidable, challenging me at every step. I would stumble over the slightest obstacle and cursed myself for not bringing a companion. It was only my resolve not to let the dreams control my life that kept me on the trail. By the time I reached New Hampshire, I felt like I was hiking a frayed, high-tension wire instead of the AT.

During my second night in New Hampshire, my dreams attained an intensity I had never experienced. Sarah and the stream were there together, flickering back and forth in front of my eyes like images in an old-time silent movie. This time though, when I woke up, the visions of Sarah and the stream remained with me. It was as if they had been burned into my consciousness. And, there was a frightening urgency about them. Any chance I had of sleeping that night evaporated along with my resolve to finish the hike. *That's it,* I thought. *I'm out of here as soon as it's light enough to walk!*

The morning that greeted me when the sun finally rose was the exact opposite of my mood. The sky was a vivid blue dotted with spotless, billowy clouds that hung motionless above the soaring peaks of the Presidential Range. The air was cool and dry with a promise of warmth but not heat. If ever a day was designed for postcard photographs, this was it. It was a perfect day for hiking and it seemed as if old Mother Nature herself was trying to lure me into finishing the hike. Fat chance, Mom! As soon as I decided to keep on going, the damn clouds would turn black, the sun would disappear like the last beer at a frat party, and rains of epic proportions would make my life miserable! So, with a mood only slightly brighter than a burned out light bulb, I hit the trail on what I hoped would be my last day in the mountains.

Four hours later the day was more beautiful than it had been at sunrise. My mood was no better though, because I had been haunted by visions of the stream every step of the way.

I heard the stream before I saw it. I was walking through a section of the trail that cut through a stand of white pines when I was greeted by the unmistakable splash of water over rocks. I knew what it was immediately, and the goose bumps that prickled my skin had nothing to do with the drop in temperature in the glen. When I actually reached the stream it was almost anticlimactic.

A log bridge spanned the water where it crossed the trail. As I stood on the bridge I knew that I was very near the point of origin of my visions. I physically cringed as something inside urged me to follow the flowing water down the mountain. I considered ignoring the feeling but I couldn't do it. So, acting like the fool in a horror movie who just has to look behind the creaking door, I set off downstream. The only thing that really bothered me was that I wasn't going to get to meet Sarah after all.

The trek down the streambed was precarious, but it was impossible to walk alongside of it because of the heavy brush that lined its banks. The rocks in the streambed were dry and inviting, but many were not stable. Every once in a while one would wobble when I stepped on it. Twice I almost fell. Walking in the stream was no better because underwater the rocks were coated with a thin slime that made stepping on them treacherous.

About a hundred yards from the trail, the stream dropped out of sight over a narrow ledge. Somehow, I knew that just past that ledge was the spot I had been visiting in my dreams for all these years. *Last chance. Just walk away,* I told myself as I approached the edge. It was like telling a moth not to approach a flame. I knew death awaited me just a few feet away, yet I could not resist moving forward to meet it. I only regretted I had found death before I had found Sarah.

As I approached the ledge, the stream started to reappear. On each side I saw the familiar undercut banks. Roots from the surrounding trees poked out of them, looking like oversized, curious worms or menacing fingers from earth-dwelling trolls. Another step and I could see the large stones at the end of the pool with the water flowing between them.

As I moved closer to the ledge, the pool I knew was there started to come into view. And then I saw a girl. Her back was towards me and she was lying face down in the water. Her arms were spread out in front of her holding her head above the surface. I was so surprised it took me a minute to realize what I was seeing. It was Sarah!

After that I just reacted. I jumped the three feet from the ledge to the pool, landing in water as cold as a winter morning. The gravel and sand at the bottom shifted under my weight and I fell headlong into the chilling water myself. When I lifted my head from the pool an exact replica of my vision greeted my eyes and fear gripped my heart. Not caring, I scrambled around to Sarah. She looked at me with uncomprehending eyes, obviously in shock. Immediately I could see why. Her left leg was wedged between two stones and it was obviously broken. The water below her head was about two feet deep and she was straining to hold her face above its surface.

Moving as quickly as I could, I stripped off my backpack and wedged it between her chest and the bottom of the pool. Then I set to work freeing her leg. Sarah was conscious throughout the whole process, but barely. If I hadn't come when I did, she wouldn't have lasted much longer. It took me about a half an hour to free her. I had to dig out one of the stones trapping her leg to get her loose. When I had her free, I laid her on the bank and got my first good look at her.

She was everything I had seen in my dreams. Short blond hair. The scar I loved running through her...right eyebrow? It should be the left eyebrow. Then I noticed her entire face looked backwards. Her hair was parted on the wrong side, her face tilted wrong. It was like looking into a mirror...or a reflection in a pool!

Suddenly everything snapped into place. My dreams had come from Sarah. For years I had been seeing what she saw trapped there above the water. Her reflection in the pool, rippling with the water's surface—the perfect blue of the sky behind her-her hands held in front of her to keep her head out of the water. Everything had come from Sarah. Somehow, she had called me. Across time and distance, she had called me. And I had come.

DAN FOLEY LIVES IN CONNECTICUT WITH HIS WIFE TERE. DAN HAS WORN many hats in professional life, including Sailor, Licensed Senior Reactor Operator, Nuclear Operations Consultant, and more recently, an Insurance Agent. Dan started writing late in life, publishing his first short story at the age of fifty-seven.

Dan has three daughters, all of whom enjoy a good horror tale. His four grandchildren are not old enough to read his stories yet.

Desert Night

Patti Kinlock

These desert sands I've roamed afar,
And walked beneath the glowing stars
More bright than any I have found—
So close I longed to pluck one down.
Through twilight haze of purple-blue
The stars are bloodflame's deepest hue,
Their constellations random-tossed
Like rubies strewn on jeweler's cloth.

Silver moonlight streaks my face
Through silence deep as endless space—
It seems that I have found at last
The place where present meets the past.
Atop this dune, 'twixt Earth and sky
The windsong's plaintive, mournful sigh
Still echoes down the vault of time
To eons past, and warriors' cries.

Such simple beauty, stark, unmarred,
Is touched by naught but wind and stars.
These virgin sands stretch on for miles
And I, mere mortal, but an isle
Surrounded by infinity
Adrift on swirling sandy sea
Of dunes receding out of sight—
The shifting tides of desert night.

FRANKIE'S WISH

M. J. Harris

On December 7, 1988, a devastating earthquake struck Armenia, registering 6.9 on the Richter scale, with an aftershock minutes later registering 5.8. As a result, nearly 70% of the buildings were destroyed with 100,000 people dead. More than half a million people were left homeless. The city of Gyumri was severely affected. To this day the City of Gyumri lies in shambles.

NATALIA ROLLED ONTO HER BACK ON THE LUMPY MATTRESS. A WIRY SPRING poked her and she winced. The sunlight poured in from the slit in the patterned sheet-curtains and temporarily blinded her. She rubbed her green eyes and yawned a yawn of fatigue and weariness. Another day.

When she was a child, she had been eager for each new day and would rise early, leap from bed, and go to school with a lively spring to her step — an inborn confidence due to hope for the future. But not now. Now, she secretly wished there would be no new days, that she would fall asleep at night and never wake up. Now the only "spring" was the one poking her back.

So many times she tried to remember what normal life was like. What did she used to enjoy? What filled her with excitement? Sewing was something she loved to do. She and her grandmother would sit for hours knitting shawls or designing curtains. A warm sense of love filled Natalia as she recalled those days of her youth. It seemed all she had to cling to were those wonderful memories. There was no time to sew now, and no needles or thread. Her days centered around going to nurse check-ups, waiting in food voucher lines, or pulling vegetables from the forgotten fields just so they could have dinner.

Rimtak, her husband, grumbled beside her and tugged the wool blanket closer about his body. He faced her through squinted eyes. "Happy Anniversary," he said. He smiled, pursing his lips and she leaned over and kissed him though his breath was stale. He stretched and rose quickly.

Natalia took longer to rise, but finally stood, carefully stepping over her 10-year-old son Frank's sleeping body on the mattress next to theirs. She pulled on a thin cloth skirt and sweater and slipped into her loafers. She tiptoed out the front door of the domik to light a fire on the small wood stove.

How grateful she was for this stove! It was donated by a relief agency two years ago when it was discovered she and her displaced neighbors had been missing hot meals and barely surviving after the quake.

Natalia shivered at the coldness outside, but soon the kindling was ablaze and she leaned forward and warmed her calloused hands. The crumpling of newspapers and snapping of twigs caused little Frank to stir and he stretched and yawned too. His father helped him to stand and, once he was dressed, adjusted Frank's leg brace and gave him the last millimeter of his medicine on a spoon. 'Natalia, we need more medicine," Rimtak called.

"I know. I plan to go to the nurse's station today." Her tired voice cracked and she cleared her throat. She dared not tell him about her plans to search for a small boutique near the nursing station where she could get her hair cut. He wouldn't be too happy to discover her desire to spend their little money on something so vain.

Natalia forced a smile when Frankie stepped out of the small domik they called home and sat on the stoop in front of the door.

The domik was a metal shipping container donated by a relief agency to all of her neighbors. They were meant to be temporary shelters, but unfortunately had turned into permanent residences when the government failed to come through with funds to pay for three hundred new homes as planned.

But today was an important day. Not only was it their anniversary, but it was the day Rimtak and Natalia were due to hear from the regional administrative offices. They had waited patiently for over a year to be issued a housing certificate, which they could use to legally move into an apartment in the center of town. One of her neighbors had already moved. They had invited Natalia and her family over for dinner, after settling in, and enjoyed a warm meal around a cozy dining room table.

Frankie's skinny physique cast a long thin shadow over Natalia as the morning sun peeped from behind the far mountains. "Cold," he said.

"I know. I'll have oatmeal ready in no time."

Natalia worked swiftly at filling up a half gallon of water from the community tank into her black iron pot and set it atop the stove, the fire now roaring. She wondered if this would be the last time she cooked on the outdoor stove, if this would be the last time she awoke to a cold morning without proper heat. This time tomorrow, maybe they would be living in a new home with a full kitchen and a stove.

"Come, stand here. Warm your hands."

Frankie slowly stood and limped down to the warm fire. "Warm," he grunted. Natalia smiled but she ached inside, wishing for the day he would speak clearly again. Ever since The Quake he refused to speak. Only within the last month, with help from a counselor at the nurse's station, had he begun to break out of his silent shell, but only speaking one-word phrases.

"Well, I am off," Rimtak announced as he swung open the domik door and stepped down toward the stove. He pulled on his torn jacket and leaned over to kiss his wife. Their quick kiss was louder than expected and echoed against the domiks.

Rimtak suddenly pulled her close and swung her around. "Remember, today is the day we hear from the marzpetaran," he announced. "We'll finally get our housing certificate in the mail."

Natalia smiled and held him closer.

"No more will my wife have to cook outside," he continued. "And no more going next door to use the restroom." He sighed deeply.

Natalia smiled but pushed him away. "Get going. You'll be late." He zipped his jacket and hurried toward downtown where he would work until noon at the bakery. Then he would head back home for lunch and off to the church. The destroyed, fallen church.

Natalia crossed her arms and eyed her husband as he walked past the neighboring domiks, the vacant weed-filled lot, and then old St. Gregory Church. She noticed him pause momentarily at the church—what was left of it, now a pile of rubble.

Unaware that she watched, Rimtak stood motionless and held his head down. Perhaps he was praying. Feeling as if she was somehow violating a sacred moment, Natalia quickly turned back to the stove and worked at stirring the oatmeal.

She wondered how long Rimtak would insist on rebuilding that old ghost of a church. It had fallen in the Quake, along with the rest of Gyumri. Why did he care? No one else was interested in rebuilding it. Hadn't he known God had forgotten them? Why couldn't he accept the fact that even God's great eyes were not big enough to watch over the people of Gyumri?

"Morning to you." Roza, their neighbor, suddenly appeared at the wood stove and began warming her wrinkled hands. "It's a cold one today."

"Mm hm," Natalia mumbled. She was in no mood to talk to Roza and hear once again how strange Rimtak was for attempting to rebuild the church. But Roza wasn't the only one who stated it was foolish—many of the locals would come out in the evenings and stand and watch Rimtak clearing away debris, stacking stones, sweeping broken glass, and complain about how silly he was. Even Natalia questioned her husband's objective, but she loved him and supported him.

She quickly spooned oatmeal into two tin cups, one for her and one for Frankie. She hurried to the door of her domik and she and Frankie went inside and let the door swing shut before Roza could say any more. "Come on, eat up. We need to get to the nurse's station this morning," she instructed him.

They sat on the mattresses to eat. Furniture was something they had little of. Just the two queen-sized mattresses they had excitedly pulled from a deserted building a few days after the Quake, and a worn card table in one corner. There was a shelf on the far wall that held their two cups, four plates, and a bag of plastic utensils they got from the nurse's station. There was also a Bible and a few other books Frankie had saved, and a neat pile of clean clothes on the second, larger shelf.

Natalia's favorite part of the home, though, was a cup of flowers that stood proudly and colorfully in the center of the card table. Rimtak made it a point to pick fresh flowers every day after work. Yesterday's pick was a mismatched purple and red and green that brought brightness and a sweet scent into the otherwise drab domik.

Despite the fact that four years earlier most of the city of Gyumri had fallen, the flowers and plants and trees outside continued to grow unscathed and beautiful. In contrast to the rubble and twisted metal found throughout the streets of the city, the surrounding fields were a-bloom with tall sweeping grass, colorful flowers, trees of apples, pears, mazzards, pomegranates, and an incredible variety of grapes. Natalia was often amazed how Mother Nature continued to thrive without help from anyone, while the people of the city were beat down and seemingly staying that way.

But the quake was not something they discussed. Her neighbors would rather converse about their latest hardships or frustrations or lack of government assistance. No one dared utter a word about the friends they had lost in the quake, or the parent or spouse or newborn baby they had lost in the tragedy. No one dared recount how they found their dead husband or mother smashed flat beneath a fallen roof, how they had to crawl over their dead child to escape the shattered wreckage of what was once called home. Nobody wanted to reminisce about what they were doing at that moment when the world shook and their lives changed forever. No one wanted to talk about the painful memories that lingered in their minds and hearts every waking moment of every day, the memories from which they would never be freed.

Natalia had been home cooking khengali that cold morning in December. Shousie, her baby girl, slept peacefully in the crib beside her. Rimtak was in bed. He stayed home because he was feeling ill that day. Frankie was in school taking a spelling exam. He was one of the only people in the entire school that survived, perhaps because he immediately hid under his strong desk when the walls began to tremble.

Their family had lived in a small but comfortable apartment then. Rimtak worked many years at a textile factory. His office was plowed to the ground by another building that fell right on top of it. His entire work crew and boss were killed.

Natalia remembered the roof of her apartment falling in on her and the ceiling and curtains catching fire from the stove. She lay buried beneath rubble for a few still moments before Rimtak was able to carefully but quickly drag her body up and out of the building. She had been too stunned to walk. Her head and back had been severely injured and soon she passed out. When she awoke later, Rimtak was holding her in his arms; the entire town around them in shambles. The only sounds were wailing and groans of despair. Their baby girl did not survive.

Little Frankie's left leg was severely damaged and his foot had to be amputated. He also lost two fingers on his left hand. He never spoke a word about what he witnessed, but through one of several drawings he had made at the nurse's station, at the urging of a trained counselor, Natalia was able to piece together what he had seen. There was a sketch of a frightened stick-figure boy huddled under a square desk, five disfigured children scattered about him.

Natalia and Frankie finished up the last of their oatmeal, and, while Frankie concentrated on a chapter book he was reading, Natalia swung a dry towel over her shoulder and walked outside to wash out the tin cups in the water tank.

Roza was now cooking something at the wood stove. "I will put the fire out when I'm done here," Roza muttered.

"Okay," Natalia said. "Good."

"Is Rimtak working on the church tonight?" Roza asked, taking a step toward Natalia, apparently taking her few words as an invitation to chat.

"I don't know." Natalia shrugged.

Roza crossed her arms and clicked her tongue. "It's really a worthless cause. What is the point?"

Natalia didn't have the energy to defend herself or her husband and so quickly headed into her domik without another word. She counted her coins, but it didn't take long. She had five. Every week when Rimtak brought home his earnings, as little as it was, she stashed away a few coins.

Today was their wedding anniversary and she wanted to look nice. No matter how often Rimtak complimented her, it didn't make up for how un-feminine she felt. Bathing only twice a week and going without makeup for over two years, her thick blonde hair twisted up everyday into a tight bun, Natalia simply felt ugly. She persuaded herself that getting her hair done would be a gift to Rimtak also. He would be delighted to see his wife beautiful again.

After she and Frank combed their hair and splashed their faces with cold water from the water tank, the two of them set off on the long trek to the nurse's station. They paused to admire the beautiful shiny gold cross in the shop window next to their domik community. Despite its price, it was something Rimtak always boasted he would purchase once the church restoration was complete. Frank pressed his hands longingly on the glass of the shop window and stuttered, "Papa's—cross."

Natalia put her arm around her son. "I know. It's beautiful, isn't it?"

As they walked on slowly, passing rubble and partly-rebuilt homes and banks, memories of her first days in Gyumri filled her mind. It had been a joyous time. She fell in love with Rimtak very young and they were soon married and having children.

To this day she didn't know what she would do without Rimtak and his strength. He had a fighter's spirit. He would not allow the Quake to destroy him. It had destroyed his family, his home, his city. But it would not destroy him. He chose instead to focus on what they still had—each other, their future. Somehow the loss of their baby daughter, Frankie's innocence, and their home, made everything but faith unimportant.

Initially, the town was set for reconstruction. Russian workers came to assist and new hope revived the hearts of the people. Unfortunately, most of the work came to a halt with the fall of the Soviet Union, and the temporary workers went back home. There were half-completed buildings everywhere. Natalia shook her head at the fragile buildings she passed. The clock in the town square still stood eerily frozen in time at exactly 11:41.

They passed the destroyed apartment complex they had called home years before. It was now a pile of rubble and broken glass. Three small children ran about the rubble, playing hide-and-go-seek.

Natalia felt her heart sink. It was hard to maintain a sense of hope and faith with signs of destruction everywhere. She found herself praying as she walked. She had all but lost faith in God, but now she quietly called out to him. "Lord, I need some good news today. I need a miracle. Even a small one. Please...let just one good thing happen today."

Soon they arrived at the nurse's station and Frankie went into a back office to meet with his counselor. How grateful Natalia was for this station and for the supplies and friendships the American workers provided! She found herself looking forward to her nurse appointments, even if it was just to get a refill on toiletries and medicine for Frankie.

"So good to see you again," the head nurse, a short, heavy-set woman named Margaret, called out when she saw Natalia coming through the door. "You doing okay?" she asked in broken Russian. She handed Natalia a small plastic bag of toiletries and gave her a tight hug.

Natalia smiled. "I am. I am." Then she straightened and asked nervously, "Do you know a good place I can get my hair fixed?"

Margaret smiled and flipped her hand as if swatting at a fly. "I know a thing or two about hair. What do you want done?"

Natalia twisted a strand of dangling hair around her finger. "Just a trim—or—something."

Without another word, the nurse led Natalia to a metal chair. She untied Natalia's hair band. She fluffed out her blonde tresses and grabbed a new comb from the stack of toiletry supplies and began gently combing. "You have beautiful hair," she commented.

Within moments Natalia's hair was neatly cropped and she admired it in a small mirror.

"Would you like a little lipstick?" the nurse asked gently. "You have a beautiful face."

Natalia shyly nodded, still admiring her haircut in the mirror. She looked alive again. A tear came to her eyes as Margaret softly applied dark red lipstick to her pouty lips. Natalia cleared her throat to regain her composure. Rimtak would be so delighted when he saw her. "Thank you so much. What do I owe you?"

The nurse waived her hand again and grinned. "You don't owe me anything. It's what I am here for."

Natalia shook her head. "I insist." she reached into her purse and pulled out the five coins. She refused to let this hair trimming be another act of charity, of which she had been a constant recipient. This was something she had saved money for, something she had looked forward to for so long, and she refused to get it for free. Finally, Margaret accepted all but one coin.

When Frank was finished with his counseling session and Natalia had been issued some additional medicine for him, the two headed home, Natalia feeling a bit lighter on her feet.

There was a deserted fountain down a short path off the main street and they took a moment to rest against it in the shade. She and Frank leaned against the fountain and snacked on apricots she brought along from home.

There was a little puddle of water left in the once-elegant fountain from the prior week's rain, though the fountain itself was cracked and a big chunk of concrete was missing. The centerpiece, whatever design it had been, was now nonexistent.

Feeling a bit liberated after her haircut, she pulled her last coin from her purse and held it out to Frank. "Go ahead. Make a wish." Frankie reluctantly took the coin. He held his hands to his chest and squeezed his eyes shut as though his world depended on it. Natalia was curious what he was wishing for, but didn't ask. Finally, the young boy tossed the coin into the fountain. Together they watched as the lone coin whirled in rapid circles and then dropped down into the wet gutter drain and out of sight. Natalia bent over and peered into the drain, wondering where the coin had gone, but it was too dark to see inside.

"Mum," Frankie said, pointing past her.

She looked to where he was pointing and noticed a small gutter that led to a trench with weeds growing about it. Something shiny was glistening in the sun. She stepped toward the trench and then got down on her knees to climb under a thick bush, her knees becoming wet and green from the moss. She gasped at what she found. Dozens of coins, some Russian, some American, piled in a heap. They must have been all the coins drained from the broken fountain since the quake.

At that moment, Natalia felt like God had leaned down from Heaven and lovingly caressed her shoulders. Was it just a coincidence or was the sun glowing especially strong on her face? Perhaps God was shining his love on her. Natalia put her hands into the coins and looked up at the sky. "Thank you, Lord," she whimpered. "Thank you."

She arose, a new hope in her spirit, and quickly packed the coins, every last one, into her large satchel. Frankie helped as best he could. The two of them could hardly wait to get home and show Rimtak.

For the first time in what seemed an eternity, Natalia felt a sense of hope. Not so much because of the money and the fact she now could purchase an anniversary gift for Rimtak, and some new shoes for Frank, and perhaps some supplies for their new home, but because for the first time in a long time she knew for certain God was watching over them.

Oh, what Rimtak would say. He would be delighted. Lately, they grasped at any good news: warm temperatures in the forecast, clean water for the water tank. It was about time for something unusual and great to happen.

It was a long walk home, Frankie trying hard to walk as quickly as possible despite his awkward limp, and Natalia struggling with the weight of the coins jingling in her purse. Rimtak's words filled her mind as they walked. "Belief in my God is based on faith, not sight," he often said. She thought of her husband working wearily each night on the church, just like Noah building the famed ark in the middle of the desert. She realized for the first time that he was working on the church not because of some obsessive hobby but because of his strong faith that things would get better.

When they finally arrived home, it was dusk. Natalia was surprised to find Rimtak sitting on the porch of the domik, his head defeatedly in his hands. Usually at this time of evening he was busy working on the church.

"Here, take this," she whispered to little Frank, carefully handing him the purse full of coins. The weight nearly pulled him over and he struggled to stand up straight.

She approached her weary husband. "Rimtak, are you all right?"

Rimtak looked up at her, his eyes beet red. "You were right. There is no God."

"What are you talking about?"

"I got the letter from the marzpetaran," he explained, his Russian accent always stronger when he was upset. "They denied our housing certificate." He stood, his fists clenched. "Did you hear me? They denied our housing certificate!"

Roza peeked her head out her domik door. Another neighbor, curious, appeared.

"We have lived here all these years, through the Quake, through the turmoil, working for a living, and it means nothing!" Rimtak glared, red fury coloring his face. He headed for the abandoned church in strident steps.

Natalia covered her mouth in worry. She had never seen her husband this way. He always wore a brave face. If he lost his self-control, she didn't know how she would maintain hers. "Rimtak!"

He ignored his wife, muttering under his breath. He approached the church across the street and stood, his fists on his hips, staring into the work he had completed. A few piles of rubble had been cleared. One wall had been erected. All with his own hands.

Natalia glanced around. Frankie was not in sight. Where had he gone?

She hurried over to Rimtak, and grabbed his arm, but Rimtak jerked away from her and began to rip down the single church wall. He pulled at the wood and tossed it to the ground. He kicked the fallen lumber and picked up a large concrete slab and with all his strength, lunged it far away from him. It hit the ground and crumbled to pieces.

Rimtak too fell to the ground, as shattered as the pieces of crumbled concrete. Natalia dropped down beside him and put her arms around him. "It is okay, it is okay."

By now the usual neighborhood crowd had emerged, but this time they were not watching Rimtak work on rebuilding the church. They instead watched, speechless, as Rimtak and Natalia embraced in the rubble, rocking back and forth. Somehow Natalia had the strength to stay calm, to not panic. Somehow, she had strength she never knew she possessed. "It's a good day today," she whispered to her husband. "It's our anniversary, remember? And I have a wonderful surprise."

Rimtak, now humbly sniffling, looked up at her and drew one of her blonde tresses away from her cheek. "You cut your hair," he said, half smiling, half crying.

"Yes but that's not the only surprise," she began softly, trying to carefully form her words. "You know, I believe God is trying to speak to you, Rimtak. He wants you to build this church. He wants us, needs us, to have a temple right here in the center of our city —."

"Nobody wants the church rebuilt," he interrupted. "Name one person that does."

"God does." Natalia answered. "Your faith in God is what has kept me, what has kept this whole community, going. I don't think we could survive without that."

Suddenly Frankie appeared beside them, pushing a small rusty shopping cart. It held a large box. "Papa," he said in his weak voice.

Natalia was taken by surprise. She did not know what was inside the box but she was relieved her son had reappeared. She figured he had transferred all of the coins into the box.

Rimtak slowly stood, sniffling, and unfolded the lid of the box. Carefully, gently, he pulled out the golden cross they had seen in the store window. It weighed about ten pounds and was approximately three feet high. "Son." he began, but stopped, unable to continue.

"Frankie, how on earth—?" Natalia stood. Then she bit her lip. The cross had a steep price tag of 50 Rubles. It was probably equal to the amount of coins they had found.

"Rimtak, I want to talk to you," a deep male voice said. Natalia and Rimtak spun around to see their neighbor, Gwishen, standing beside them. Now it was time to hear a long speech about how useless it was to work on the church. They had heard it for so long, but it would hurt especially hard today.

"I have some good tools," Gwishen announced, clearing his throat. He held an old hammer in one hand, a bag of tools in the other.

"And I have some supplies," another man said, standing beside Gwishen.

Natalia shuddered as she looked about at several of her neighbors, all holding what few tools they possessed.

"You're going to be living here a while," Gwishen said. "We might as well get to work on the church."

Speechless, Rimtak nodded.

Rimtak, Natalia, and Frankie pushed the shopping cart toward their domik and Rimtak retrieved his tool chest. All types of decorating ideas filled Natalia's mind. They could paint the church white and the inside would have red carpet and red wooden pews. She could see it now. She and Roza would sew colorful curtains for the nursery windows. And yes, Rimtak would form a tall steeple on the roof of the church and post the gold cross at the very peak.

MONICA "MJ" HARRIS HAS BEEN WRITING SHORT FICTION FOR 15 YEARS. She first read about the terrible Armenian earthquake in an issue of *World Vision* magazine and, after researching the subject, wrote "Frankie's Wish" as an ode to the survivors who still live in the destroyed city of Gyumri. Monica is currently working on her first novel *A Weekend in April.* Monica resides in Southern California with her husband Marcus, and children Vincent, Jessica, and Samantha.

SCIENCE FICTION

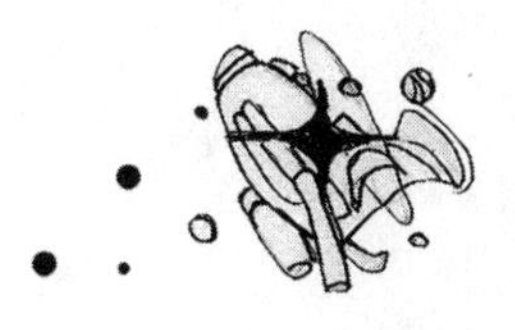

SELF-REFLECTION

Danielle Ackley-McPhail

I watch myself
stride confidently by,
splendid with youthful vigor,
graceful, beautiful, miraculous
a tribute to the wonder,
the horror,
the folly
of modern science.

As if what society needs
is another excuse
for divisiveness.

With a whole new spin
on self-loathing,
I call him monkey-me
as he runs the maze of humanity
to the scientists' bell.

We may share
the same genetic code,
but he is two percent less me,
and two inches shorter...
before my age bent me.

I call him monkey-me
and rue the day
I offered up my cells,
desperately grasping
at the hope for immortality.

Father's Monument

John C. Wright

Jason Caidron sat in the shade of the trees at the edge of the cliff, watching the leaves fall slowly, whirling, blowing, dancing down through the air, eventually to fall into the sea. His face was careworn, sad. He neither stirred nor spoke, but sat staring downward, forever down.

The time was autumn, and the trees were rich which many colors: gold, scarlet, copper. The sea below was black and green, criss-crossed with restless lines of pure white froth. The air was brisk and smelled of salt.

Jason's wife, Muriel, had come up the green, grassy path from the odd, little, old-fashioned house, and walked into the stand of trees where Jason was. Leaves rustled under her footsteps. Her eyes were red with recent tears.

Jason spoke without looking up. "Is he any better?"

She folded her hands tightly around each other. "He asked about the time travelers again. He said..."

"I don't care what he said..."

"Well, he's your father, Jason! Not mine! At least you could have come to the hospital with me!"

"I don't care about what he said about the time travelers. I want to know what the hospital administrator said about the operation."

"They can't do anything... they won't do anything without some assurance of being paid. The government money won't cover an operation like this."

They were both silent for a time.

After a while, he said softly, "I've been sitting here watching the leaves fall down into the sea. The first moment they get free of the tree, some of them swirl up. Look. Almost looks like they're dancing, doesn't it? Going round and round. When the wind is coming right up the cliff, they can stay up, oh, I don't know, maybe ten minutes. Maybe longer. They look like they'll never come down. But gravity always wins out in the end. They turn into brown wet slop once they hit the water. And they all go down...."

More silence. Muriel sat down beside her husband.

She said, "Did the lawyers ever call back about having the contract set aside? Can we back all the money your father paid out to that metallurgical firm? Any of it?"

"No. They said no. There are no psychiatric records, no evidence that Dad was unfit or incompetent when he mortgaged the house, when he sold his assets. I'm the only one who knows he believes in the Time Travelers."

"So that's it? There's no way to raise the money?"

Jason said angrily, "The metals and the other material for the monument are bought and paid for; the company president said he had to develop special furnaces to mold and shape this alloy; Dad paid for it. We can't get the money back."

"Can't we sell that damn metal?" There were tears again in Muriel's eyes.

"Who would want it? Who in the hell would want it?" And he picked up a handful of the brightly colored leaves lying on the grass beside them and flung them out over the brink.

Muriel said, "He asked about you again today."

Jason said nothing. His face was stubborn, sullen. Muriel said angrily, "You've got to go see him! He's your father! If you don't... how do you think you will feel ten years from now? Twenty? What if our kids didn't come visit you when you were sick, if you ever needed help..."

"I'll go," he muttered angrily.

"What if it was you laying there with those machines and things stuck in your arm..."

"I said, *I'll go!* All right?!"

"I'm sorry I shouted," she said softly.

"You never understood what it was like between me and my father."

Muriel picked up a leaf and toyed with it. She said softly, "Is that my fault? You never explained it."

"You know he's crazy."

"I think he's sweet. At least he believes in something."

Jason said in a cold voice, "And I don't? I believe you shouldn't believe in things you can't see. It offends reason. All the scientific achievements of Western civilization are based on..."

"Are you going to go see your father? That's what I find offensive. That you would let him sit there in that smelly hospital bed and..."

"I already told you I was going!"

Later that day, Jason was at the hospital, getting permission to see his father. It was outside of normal visiting hours, but the head nurse gave him permission nonetheless. He talked with the doctor briefly beforehand.

As the nurse was walking him toward the room, she asked in a bright, cheerful voice, "He's doing much better today; he made a joke."

"What did he say?" Jason asked dubiously.

"Oh, I was asking him about his name. 'What kind of name is Nadreck Caidron?' I asked him. 'It's from the Forty-Eighth Century,' he says, just like that. And he smiled so. There was a twinkle in his eye."

"Yeah. Yeah. He's a great kidder."

She let him in to the room. The man in the other bed was asleep, and Jason drew the shabby plastic curtain between the two halves of the shared room.

His father was propped up in the mechanism of the bed. Tubes ran into his arm; a clear plastic tent was erected around the head of the bed; two oscilloscopes on a rack next to the bed kept up a steady beeping. The smell of medical disinfectant permeated the room.

They had shaved his hair, making the white tufts of his eyebrows seem all the furrier and larger, like the phony eyebrows on a store-front Santa.

Apparently, Nadreck Caidron had been watching television. His eyes were open, and the television on a stand above the door was quietly talking to itself. But Jason's father did not speak or move when Jason entered.

Jason stood there for a long, horrid, moment. "Oh, god..." he whispered. He thought: *and I never had a chance to say I was sorry. I never had a chance. Oh, God, please don't let him be dead.*

Nadreck blinked, his eyes focused. "I am not dead yet, Jason. I had entered a secondary level of consciousness, to allow my mental probes to explore the alternate temporal chronoverses congruent to this reality. There is a probability distortion in this timeline, only a few hours or days away. It may be the shockwave of the approaching time-ship. However, my powers cannot detect whether it is simultaneous with this time-stream, or entering an alternate probability line. There are additional steps we must take to raise the probability manifold to the threshold energy levels."

Jason was surprised at how deep and vibrant his father's voice sounded. He felt a moment of vast relief when he heard his father speaking. Jason sat down quickly in the chair next to the bed, his knees weak. Then he heard what his father was saying.

For a moment, an unreasoning anger took hold of him. Slowly he forced the tension to sink out away from his muscles. He made himself nod and look understanding.

"I've decided to finish building your latest monument for you, Father."

Nadreck merely looked at his son silently, no expression on his face.

Jason shifted uncomfortably in the chair. "I mean... you've told me so many times why you build them. So the archeologists in the far future can discover them, and get the message, and send back a rescue ship... right? Well, I've decided to help you. They're going to get the message now. They're coming. Well? I'm... I'm trying to help you. Why don't you say something?"

"The specialized nerve-ganglia our race uses to probe probability effluvia can sometimes detect the particular time-space reactions created whenever someone lies, Jason. A lie creates, if only for a moment, a false reality structure. It is an attempt to alter reality..."

"What the hell do you know about reality! No, I'm sorry, I'm sorry, I didn't mean that..."

"I know that, in this reality, the doctor told you to tell me whatever you thought would instill in me the will to live. That doctor amuses me. Does he think his primitive brain is a match for the special nerve-consciousness training of a chrononaut from the Forty-Eighth century? He need not worry about my will to live. I expect to be rescued from this primitive era...."

"You shouldn't have told the nurse you were from the future."

"I did not sense that it would create any paradoxes or discontinuities. Her destiny will continue along its maximal energy path."

"They're going to lock you up in a nuthouse."

"You disappoint me, son, if your prognosticative neurons are so ill-trained that they cannot distinguish likely from unlikely futures. I'm sorry I was never able to complete your training."

"I don't have any super-powers, Dad," said Jason heavily. "No one does."

"What about the time when you were coming home on the school bus..."

"Will you stop talking about that already!"

"How do you explain..."

"It was a coincidence."

"And I've told you what coincidences really are. When the Time Lords meld an alternate line back into the main time-stem, those events and chains of cause and effect which have no explanation in the revised timeline have to be soldered together by probabilistic manipulation."

Jason sat there and listened, his hands folded in his lap, a sinking feeling in his stomach. He thought: *Am I going to spend my last time with my father going over this same dumb argument? Over and over again?*

"Father," he said slowly, "I want to ask you something. This is not easy. But you know how sick you are. I don't know how to ask you nicely..."

"Just say it, my son."

"I'd like to talk to our relatives. Can you tell me what your real name was before you changed it? Who my grandfather and grandmother were? They might want to know, if I have to invite them..."

"I was born Nadreck Caidron. Your grandparents will not be born for twenty seven centuries."

Jason sighed. He sat very still and quiet in his chair, feeling deflated and defeated. "I'm... I'm sorry, Father."

"For what, son?"

"I don't know. For everything, I guess. For us never getting along. For me never believing you. I'd like to believe in your time travelers, really I would."

"Have you ever tried to believe?"

"Now, don't start that again!"

Feebly, Nadreck reached out with his hand and squeezed his son's hand. The strength in his voice was absent from his fingers; his grip was weaker than a child's.

"We've always gotten along," Nadreck said.

"We always argue."

"Well, son. Some people get along at a louder volume than others."

Jason laughed. He was surprised at how good he felt to hear his father speak a normal sounding sentence; a sentence that didn't have any words starting with "chrono-" in them.

Jason wondered, not for the first time, what his father had actually been like as a child. Obviously he had read science fiction. Obviously he had been hurt, perhaps very badly, or attacked by some problem he couldn't face. And so he had escaped into the glossy colored pictures of his favorite pulp magazines, into the world of bullet-shaped rocket ships, of beautiful women in metal brassieres, of tall, neon-colored towers reaching up from the fields of futuristic utopias towards the conquered stars. A perfect, simple world.

Jason shook his head. He could not bring himself to forgive his father. Other people had daydreams, wishful fantasies. Other people didn't abandon their sanity to cling to their dreams. Brave people faced their problems.

Nadreck's voice gently interrupted Jason's brooding thoughts. "Where you in earnest, when you spoke?"

"What? What did I say?"

"That you wanted to believe. Are you willing to try?"

"Dad..."

"I suppose not, then."

"It's not that," Jason said. "People can't believe things by wanting to believe them. Not honest people, anyway. You have to believe what the evidence proves."

"Time Travelers can't leave any evidence of their existence. It would create an anomaly. An anachronism. You know that."

"How convenient," said Jason. It came out sarcastic. Immediately he was sorry. Couldn't he be polite to his own father?

"Son. Think about it logically. At some point in the future, time travel will eventually be invented."

"What if it is impossible?"

"If it is impossible in this timeline, it will be possible in another. And if the Time Travelers ever will exist, then they always exist, in any period, forever. Anything that happens in history happens because it is part of their grand design. It has to be. And no one need ever die. Why would the Time Travelers ever let anyone die? At the final moment, just before death, they can come and perform a rescue. We don't see them because they freeze time, and accomplish all their work in an instant. The dead bodies we see, what we bury and cremate, those aren't the real people. The Time Travelers enter the time-stream, take a small tissue cell sample, and construct a clone body. The real people are replaced with unliving clones at the last moment, and taken away to the far future. It's a beautiful life there, Jason. I cannot leave until the probability has been created that you will be coming after. I am in pain, and I don't wish to wait further. Please try."

"Why does it matter what I believe? A thing is either true or its not. My belief doesn't change the matter." Jason hated himself for continuing to argue. He wondered why he couldn't help it.

"It is simple quantum chronodynamics. If a Time Traveler shows himself to someone who doesn't believe in time travel, the shock will change that person's life forever, perhaps in some unexpected way. This could have disastrous repercussions along the resultant time stream. But someone who believes already, for them, a time or place could be found where the revelation would have no changes on belief, and hence no changes to history."

"But, if I build this monument ten years from now, or if my grandchild builds it, according to you, the time travelers will find it eventually anyway, and they would have already come back to save you."

"Until it is done, there is a probability that it might not be done. They would be unwise to attempt a manifestation into the timestream prior to the point of greatest certainty. So I must lie here, in pain, with these primitive doctors and their backward medical theories treating me, while you drive the point of certainty further into the future every moment you delay."

Jason was silent.

Nadreck closed his eyes. He parted his lips, and spoke softly: "The towers of Metachronopolis, our city we have established at time's far end, lift their museums and gardens high above a world-ocean that has swallowed all the continents of this era. Suspended in the fluid of those waters are the molecule-engines that can rejuvenate my body at a cellular level. I long to see once more the golden towers shine, their crowns higher than the atmosphere. I yearn to bathe in the waters of the Living Ocean."

Jason sat there sadly, unable to think of a thing to say.

For a time, Nadreck was silent.

Then he said in a frightened voice, "They haven't come to rescue me before this because I've been doing something wrong. The previous monuments were not made of durable enough materials. I have great hopes for this new alloy. But they are not allowed to come save me till the monument is complete. If they bring me out of this time-stream at a point before I complete my monument, then there will be no monument for them to find, and so they cannot come back to bring me out. You understand? The future version of me who has already been rescued will not be allowed to help me unless the law of cause and effect is satisfied. A paradox could destroy the universe. Everything would devolve into null probability...There would be nothing left. Nothing left."

Jason had never, never in his life before, had never seen his father frightened. The sight shook him. He knelt down by the bed. He wanted to take the old man in his arms, but was afraid to disturb the medical apparatus, the tubes and wires.

"Father, I swear I will complete the monument for you. I'll finish it. I'll make sure they find it."

Very gently, Nadreck laid his thin hand on the crown of his son's bowed head. "Yes. I see that you will."

"It's not that I believe you, now. It's just that—it doesn't really matter to me whether I believe you or not. I'll do it for your sake."

"Have you ever wondered why you get so angry about this, my son? Why this is the one topic you can never let rest? No? Well, go home and think about it."

"If I don't see you again... I love you, Father."

"I am proud and well content with you, my son, and I return your good love. Go now; when you hear that I have died, believe no such report. In truth, I will not have died. Do not sorrow. We shall meet again in the lawns and gardens beneath the golden towers of Metachronopolis, the City Beyond Time."

"Good-bye, Father."

"For now. Only for now."

Back at the house, Jason found his wife on the porch, fussing with some crates which were piled there, next to the porch swing. She had pried some of the boards of one crate away with a crowbar. Beneath the packing-stuff, Jason caught a glimpse of a slab of pale amber metal.

"It's the monument," Muriel explained. "A van from the lab people brought it while you were out."

"It's opened." Jason said, coming close.

"I know we talked about trying to send it back... but...Well, I had to see what it looked like. That alloy. I've never seen anything like it. It's beautiful. And what's all that flowing doodles and curlicues? Those lines and diagrams?"

Jason leaned closer in spite of himself, and drew some of the plastic packing material aside. The crate held a number of alloy slabs. The metal glistened and gleamed in the sunlight, like silver water rippling across gold sand. The effect was breathtaking.

Each plate contained the curlicues and swirls inscribed into its surface. Between the swirls were line diagrams showing starpositions, perhaps to indicate dates.

"Father has some dog-eared notebooks hidden in the attic filled with this swirl-writing. It's supposed to be the futuristic language of the Time Travelers. Looks like one of those ciphers school kids make up, doesn't it? He probably made it when he was a kid."

"I think it's nice-looking."

Jason ran his fingers across the burnished surface. The metal was hard, obdurate. The stuff of his father's dream. It had cost his father his life's saving to buy, so that there was no money left to pay for surgery...

"I hate it," Jason whispered. "This thing is going to kill my father."

Muriel looked at him, her eyes sad, saying nothing.

Jason said, "I promised my dad today I would finish his damned monument. Now I don't know."

"What's wrong?"

Jason wouldn't answer.

Muriel said, "I know what's wrong. You're so proud of the fact that you don't believe him. You think helping him build his monument would be like admitting defeat. And you can't stand to do that, not after all these years. Not even when it's his dying wish..."

"Muriel! For God's sake!"

"Am I wrong?"

"What a terrible thing to say. How could you say that about me?"

"Am I wrong?"

"Of course you're wrong. You're so stupid sometimes I can't believe it! Do you actually think...You think I would..." Jason found himself shouting. He turned his back to his wife, arms folded, clutching his elbows with his hands.

The anger drained out of him. He sighed. "Yes, you're right. At least, you're partly right. I always thought that someday, one day, he would admit that he was wrong, that he was making it all up. I thought now would be a good time. But he can't admit it."

"So why does that make you so angry? He believes one thing. You believe something else. Why can't you just let it rest at that?"

"I get angry because..."

"Because what?"

Jason shook his head. "When I was a kid, just a little kid, dad would tell me stories about this golden city at the end of time. It had wide parks and fountains growing at the base of golden towers made of invulnerable energy-metal. Towers taller than any towers in our world. So tall the upper floors were pressurized. The sidewalks were made of crystal, and glowed with light at night. All the people were young and healthy. Starships were launched from the tower-tops, and rode on beams of energy, like searchlights, up out into space....

"I wanted it to be true," Jason said, "And when I got older, and found out my father wasn't telling the truth, I felt betrayed. Lying to a child."

"Get over it," she said.

"What? What did you say?"

"Some parents tell their kids about Santa Claus or the tooth-fairy. They grow up. They get over it. You're grown up. Get over it."

"But he still believes in the damn tooth-fairy! The goddamned Time Traveling tooth-fairies and their chrono-ships! If he didn't believe in them, he would have saved his money and been able to pay for the operation, and he wouldn't be... he wouldn't be... he wouldn't be about to die." Jason drove his fist down on the packing crate.

When his hand struck the metal of the monument, it gave out a loud, clear, ringing tone, like a bell. The note was so clear and pure that Jason stared at his hand in utter surprise, and listened, unmoving, while the echoes hummed and died around him.

Muriel said only, "He doesn't want an operation. He wants this instead. You don't have to agree with him. Just help him. Not the way you and I think he needs help. The way he wants it." She pointed at the monument. "He wants this."

Jason was silent, staring down at the crate.

"OK," he said. "Help me drag it out to the site where he wants it put up. Dad picked this spot, up the hill and back from the sea. Hired a geologist to predict what would still be above sea level twenty seven centuries from now. Another waste of money. But that's the spot."

At about midnight, after working all afternoon without a break for dinner, Muriel gave up and walked down the hill to find her house and her bed. Jason, tools in hand, kept right on working and working, eyes aching blearily, back throbbing, arms leaden. He worked by the light of his portable gas lantern. He would not stop.

Jason heard birds chirping. Not long after that, the horizon grew pink. The sun came up in a welter of indigo clouds. Jason's head swam with a strange clarity. He had passed beyond fatigue to a sort of disorienting tranquility of mind.

It was less than an hour past dawn when he finished, and the dew was still thick on the grass, the air still sweet with early morning chill.

Jason walked slowly backwards to examine his handiwork. The monument was shaped like an obelisk, a slim, straight fang of gold-white metal, glinting in the cherry light of the newborn sun like an icicle. On every face of the monument, were swirled and curvilinear glyphs, surrounding simple diagrams of circles and lines.

A sudden stabbing pressure went through Jason's head, a sense of tension and release.

Jason thought, "The special cells in my brain must be detecting the shockwave of the time-ship. They have entered this phase of reality..." Then he laughed and lightly slapped himself on the cheek. He rubbed his eyes. "You never get over what your parents tell you, do you?"

Jason's cellphone had a camera built in. He took a snapshot of the monument, thinking to show his father what he had done. Then, since the phone was in his hand, he decided to call the hospital room and share the news.

His fear grew during the moments that the phone rang with no answer. The front desk picked up the call. His fear was given more time to grow when the front desk transferred the call to the station nurse. The nurse was a young man who explained in calm, sympathetic tones, that Mr. Caidron was in the ER. His condition was very serious, and the doctors were doing everything possible....

Jason did not remember at what point he slipped the phone back into his pocket. Perhaps he had started running before the nurse had finished speaking. But the path led down the hill, and curved along the sea-cliffs, where the larch and spinet and tall, slim beach were dropping their colored leaves into the waters.

There was a man in white standing on the path.

Jason's footsteps slowed. The man looked familiar, but Jason did not recognize him. His eyes were large and dark, his head was bald, and the white garment, some sort of metallic fabric, fell from shoulderboards in smooth drapes, leaving the man's arms and legs free.

The man spoke. "The one you seek is not dead."

Jason said in a voice of hope and wonder: "Father...?"

His father looked so young, so new. He shined with vitality. In a choking voice, Jason whispered: "But, I thought, in order to see the evidence of time ... I had to believe ..."

"You believed enough to complete the monument."

"And that was enough?"

"That was a seed. In the first projection of these events, you will find my old notebooks in the attic, translate the inscription on the monument, and discover I knew the exact hour and minute of my death. That, in turn, will convince you to study the notebooks and complete your childhood training: you will develop your probability-energy control to a point where skepticism was no longer feasible. Your belief will be complete then, and a visitation then would have no time-effect. This meeting, while premature, is merely a short-cut, and hence will not change the recorded future."

"Father, thank you for being so ... so patient with me."

"Once you are accustomed to knowing the outcome of events, you will find the virtue an easy one to practice."

"What happens now?"

"Life! You will live out your span as history reports, without change, except that now you will know, rather than suppose, that the end of life is not as it seems. And, yes, before you ask, my daughter-in-law, my grandchildren, and all of us together shall enter the shining city beyond the reach of time and death. I leave you only for a time."

The man in white was gone. The moment he vanished, there was a gush of wind, as if a sudden vacuum had appeared in the spot where he stood, and this gush of wind carried some of the colored leaves dancing in the air up away from the sea, up the cliff, over the edge and onto the path.

There was one leaf, a long, slender thing of pale gold color, that flowed up from where it had been falling into the dark sea, and landed gently at Jason's feet.

Jason picked up that one leaf and saved it.

Later, after the funeral, Jason tried to explain to his wife why the grief was not so painful.

To his infinite surprise, she believed him.

JOHN C. WRIGHT IS A RETIRED ATTORNEY, NEWSPAPERMAN AND NEWSPAPER editor, who was only once on the lam and forced to hide from the police who did not admire his newspaper.

He presently works (successfully) as a writer in Virginia, where he lives in fairy-tale-like happiness with his wife, the authoress L. Jagi Lamplighter, and their three children: Orville, Wilbur, and Just Wright.

His novels include: *The Golden Age, The Phoenix Exultant, The Golden Transcendence, Last Guardians of Everness*, and the forthcoming *Mists of Everness.*

CHIMERA

ALLIANCE ARCHIVES ™, CIRCA 2042

Mike McPhail

IT WAS, AS ALWAYS, A DARK, MOONLESS NIGHT; TAU CETI THREE–DEMETER–HAD no natural satellite to lighten its nighttime sky, yet to its human colonists, this new world had proven a kindred spirit to their old home. Tonight things alien moved about the old growth forest: strange creatures that brought with them the ancient need for war.

It stood among the tall wind-blown grass at the edge of the forest, at about one foot at its shoulder. Its appearance was that of something man-made, but it moved with a grace and certainty that could only come of a born hunter, a cat. Clad in contoured armor plating affixed over a heavy mesh suit, one might assume that this was some soulless machine of war, rather than a creature of flesh and blood. Both descriptions had merit. The creature was a Parr, a by-product of the mind-machine interface experiments conducted by Dr. Jonathan Parr. Equipped with the end result—a synaptic interface—they had become the covert eyes and ears of the Alliance military.

"Don't go too far up range," psicommed a voice in scout Ma'Rou's head, *"with your transponder off, it's hard to keep track of you."*

Ma'Rou stopped, casually turning to look back in the direction of his teammates. On his display were three florescent green triangles superimposed over the scenery; each one had a slightly different internal marking and was capped by a three-letter reference code designed to mimic the name of its user. The icon MKC was the closest. The other two were back behind it and proportionally smaller to help denote their relative distance.

"Suit Mode, range to nearest icon," he thought; a branch appeared from the icon linking it to a line of data; TRP MKC SCT 021. Ma'Rou shifted his attention to the compass displayed at the bottom of his helmet's visor; it read 284 once he lined it up with the icon.

After some quick math, *"I'm at twenty-one meters, bearing one-oh-four,"* he thought; in a fraction of a second, the suit's onboard computer interpreted his message and transmitted it via the Psicom.

"Acknowledged," Trooper MacKencey, his handler and friend, responded. *"Do you have anything?"*

Ma'Rou turned to look across the grass-filled clearing before answering, *"I thought had something on the EM scan, but its signal was intermittent."* Then as if on cue, small rhythmic pulses peaked along the green line of the electromagnetic graph. *"Stand by,"* he added. He tried to localize the direction by moving his head from side to side. Suddenly, the EM peaks grew rapidly in strength.

More out of instinct than training, Ma'Rou crouched down as low as possible on all fours and used the grass for cover; with his armored belly touching the ground, he realized that he could feel the vibrations of something approaching, and approaching fast.

With his fur puffing up under his armor and the primal part of his mind screaming *"Run!"* he held his ground and tried to get a bearing on whatever was heading his way.

"MacKencey!" He mentally yelled over the Psicom; without waiting for an acknowledgment he added, *"Something big;* grrrrrrowl."

That was all he managed before whatever it was ran past him. He tried to get a good look at it, but couldn't. Even through his suit's night-imaging scopes, it was just a dark silhouette against the background of the night. The thought filled him with primitive terror.

"Ma'Rou, say again," psicommed MacKencey as he rushed to take up a kneeling position next to one of massive tree trucks. He surveyed in the last known direction of the Parr.

In light-amp mode, his helmet's imaging scopes could pick up and amplify enough ambient light to turn the dark world around him into a pseudo color day; but still, nothing around him looked out of place.

"Troy, report," inquired the voice of Sergeant Thompson over the trooper's com.

"Standby: something may have happened to the Parr," he commed. Taking a deep breath, he shifted his weapon up into the ready position, making sure to keep the helmet-displayed targeting reticle aimed high, for there was no way of knowing where Ma'Rou was.

"Ma'Rou from MacKencey..." he psicommed then strained to listen to his mind's outer thoughts, *"...can you hear me?"*

Unlike the conventional com system, the Psicom had no click or beep to announce the beginning or end of a message, and in personal contact, all one was supposed to receive was the voice of the sender, nothing else; but as the message started to form in his mind, an overwhelming sense of imminent danger surged through his body.

"It's coming your way!" screamed Ma'Rou into MacKencey's brain, seemingly willing him to get up and run from some unseen horror.

It felt like he'd stuck his finger into a powered light socket; MacKencey fought to regain control over his body and suppress the false sense of terror. Disengaging the Psicom and getting a handle on his emotions would have been the smart thing to do, but that would have left Ma'Rou out on his own, and that wasn't going to happen. With the sound of his own heart pumping in his ears, MacKencey forced himself to slow down his breathing and get his mind back on the business at hand, namely looking for whatever was moving up on him.

"Sergeant, Ma'Rou reports that something is moving up on us, but I still have nothing on light-amp," he commed. "Suit mode, thermal imaging," he instructed his suit's Pacscomp. As his display shifted into shades of cool blues and warm reds, something leaped into his field of view, at the very edge of his peripheral vision.

He heard the beginning of a response from Sergeant Thompson when whatever was out there landed with a heavy thump just behind him. It struck like an explosion. There was a blur of motion and MacKencey's consciousness faded out.

It was like falling upward from the bottom of a deep well. As he approached the opening, reality came back into focus; all the while, a disembodied voice called to him from the darkness.

"By Jonathan! This is no time to be dead, monkeyboy." It was the all too-familiar feline voice of Ma'Rou. He bounced up and down on MacKencey's back as he growled at him; no doubt in and effort to bring him around, or at least work out his frustration at his demise.

"Okay…enough, I'm still here," MacKencey groaned. A burning pain in his temples flared at the sound of his own voice. "God, I'd hate to be dead and feel like this," he added as the Parr jumped from his back.

Carefully, he attempted to move each part of his body that he could remember owning. When he sat up, a wave of nausea hit him. He grabbed for the helmet's release claps. If he threw up before he got it off, he could choke on his own vomit.

With both hands, he attempted to grab hold of his helmet's side-mounted scope housing. He had to get his hands into the finger depressions on top. He felt for the wrap-around traction pad. If he could get his hands in place, his thumbs would automatically line up the clasps on the underside of the helmet. Or at least, that's how it was supposed to work.

His right hand found its mark; the left one came up empty. The scope was gone. Panic welled up; the pain in MacKencey's forehead was almost blinding; "Remember your training," he said to himself, practically hearing the voice of his instructor. "Focus on what you need to do to survive." Concentrating, he forced himself to calm down. His breathing slowed. As it did, the pain and nausea lifted slightly. His head still throbbed, and his throat was raw and burning, but he regained control.

He looked down at Ma'Rou, who was now sitting in front of him with his head slightly tilted to one side. When he moved his head from side to side, the image distorted with the motion. McKencey realized that there was something wrong with his helmet's display. He hoped that the problem was with the suit and not him.

"Can you see anything?" Ma'Rou psicommed. Without waiting for an answer, he continued, *"Your helmet's torn open in the back and it looks like your Pacscomp's had it, too; the housing's gone and all that's left is the interface connections and one of the high-density antennas."*

McKencey lowered his hands form his helmet, "If my Pacscomp is gone, then how are we communicating?" he inquired.

"Maybe I'm putting out enough energy at this range that your remaining antenna is picking me up?" psicommed Ma'Rou.

"Not likely," stated MacKencey, still managing to think clearly through the pain. "You still need the Pacscomp to interpret and translate the incoming signals, let alone transfer them to your synaptic interface."

"Well, then, you have two choices," responded Ma'Rou with a level of amusement in his voice. *"Either you're somehow picking me up on your remaining antenna, or we are communicating directly mind to mind."*

MacKencey's brain ached at the prospect. "Let's go with the antenna pick-up theory. I'm not up to having a religious moment just now."

"Works for me," psicommed the Parr.

Although the pain was subsiding, it was still hard to organize his thoughts. "What happened?" asked MacKencey.

A feeling of guilt preceded the Parr's response. *"Whatever it was ran past me on all fours; its arms and legs were skinny, and kind of reminded me of the way a giraffe moved."*

"A giraffe," said MacKencey as he started to look around for his weapon.

"If you're looking for your rifle, don't bother. It's in pieces over there." MaRou stood up and pointed with his body.

Then suddenly the obvious dawned, and he turned to look back in the direction of his teammates; no icons were visible. *"Thompson from MacKencey,"* he commed. No response. *"Williams, do you read me?"*

"Save it, Troy," psicommed Ma'Rou, *"After it killed you..."* he paused and walked a few feet in the direction where the rest of the team lay, *"...it ambushed the others."* For a moment he stared into the distance, trying hard not to look at the two time-stamped florescent red icons blinking on his display. *"Over there at about twenty meters."* He turned and walked back to MacKencey and settled again at his feet. *"I confirmed that they were both dead."*

For both of them, the feeling of loss was intense.

"Damn it," said MacKencey, knowing all too well that now was not the time to mourn for his fallen comrades, not unless he planned to join them. He didn't. Reaching around to his right hip, he released the safety catch that held his sidearm secure inside its form-fitting shell. With a practiced hand, he drew the pistol and brought it up for inspection.

"Where'd the little bastard go?" he asked as he worked the side of his pistol; the weapon was now loaded and ready to fire.

"The beastie ran off toward our landing site," Ma'Rou circled in careful, stiff-legged steps. In contrast, the tip of his tail twitched back and forth with rapid jerks. *"I don't know if it thought there were more of us, or if it was trying to cut off our line of retreat,"* he speculated.

MacKencey held the pistol out in front of him and pointed it at a nearby tree. He then depressed the leading edge of the pistol's handgrip, releasing and cocking the firing pin. A pull of the trigger would now discharge the weapon; it should have also signaled the suit to generate a targeting reticle, which it didn't.

"Oh, like I wasn't expecting tha,." he said to himself.

Ma'Rou turned in response to his statement. *"Trouble?"*

MacKencey rolled onto his knees. "Yeah, my targeting is out," he said as he pressed his free hand into the tree to steady himself. "I'll have to take off my helmet

ALLIED

to shoot with any accuracy." The very thought filled him with apprehension. Without his helmet, he would be blind against the night.

"You're in no shape to take this thing on, and with your Pacscomp gone we have no way of contacting the others; we need to get away from here." The Parr headed away from the last known direction of the attacker. He stopped after a few feet and turned back to see if his friend followed.

MacKencey just stood there, leaning against the tree, to consider his next course of action. It could take hours to climb down to the road, let alone walk into town while trying to avoid being detected by the locals. Besides, time was not on his side; in less than an hour, the team would be overdue, and with no contact, his comrades would eventually deploy another squad to investigate. Most likely to suffer the same fate as we did, he thought to himself.

Now standing, the pain only seemed to grow with his efforts. "No drugs," he said to himself; despite all of the lovely military pharmacopoeia at his disposal, without the suit's Pacscomp A.I. to make an empirical diagnosis of his injuries, he could very well incapacitate or even kill himself.

Pushing off from the tree, he took a step toward the Parr, "Scout Ma'Rou," he said in as firm a military manner as he could.

In response, the Parr turned and sat upright facing him. *"Sir,"* he psicommed.

"What shape was either Sergeant Thompson or Trooper William in?" he asked, not really wanting to know the details.

A sense of dread and horror pushed at MacKencey's emotions. *"What that thing did was unimaginable."* psicommed Ma'Rou as he walked back. *"It literally bent and twisted their extremities until they snapped under the torque; it was as if it was trying to kill the men without damaging the armor."*

MacKencey tried to force the image from his mind and took a deep breath, "Right," he said, then took another deep breath. "Their Pacscomps self-destructed when they died, but Sergeant Thompson was carrying an external long-range com; if the beastie didn't mess with it, we have a shot at calling home."

He pointed roughly in the direction that the Parr had indicated earlier; Ma'Rou understood and led the way to their fallen comrades.

Walking over the uneven, root-covered ground would have been tricky under normal conditions; with a faulty imaging system, his head pounding, and ears ringing, it was proving even more difficult, but not impossible.

"Ma'Rou," he said.

"Yes?" replied the Parr.

"If that beastie shows up, I want you to make a run for it; it's vital someone survive to report this." MacKencey looked around as if just speaking of it would summon the creature.

Concern mixed with stress flavored the Parr's response. *"You know that Chean would never let me back in the house if I left you out here."*

That was another thought that Mac was trying to suppress. "You have my instruction; otherwise this was all for nothing."

"Acknowledged," psicommed Ma'Rou, who now exuded nervous tension at the thought of being out there all alone.

As they approached, MacKencey could make out a shape in the low grass. An armored boot rested on a massive root that protruded from the ground; the boot belonged to an Allied trooper.

They were less than five yards away from the body. Ma'Rou stopped, suddenly tense and alert. He turned and looked off to the side, then ran for higher ground. As the Parr leaped up onto a nearby rock, MacKencey's heart almost blew out of his chest at the possibility of his attacker's return. "Report," he demanded.

"Stand by," the Parr murmured, as he moved his head slowly from one side to the other. *"We have company, and it's not the beastie."* MacKencey moved towards the rock and took up a position behind the Parr; through his scope, he could make out three pairs of small, infrared spot lights, like the kind found on light-amp goggles; the sight dispelled his fears and helped focus his mind.

"That makes sense," said MacKencey. He quickly turned and surveyed the surrounding area. "This way," he said, then took off at a quick jog.

Ma'Rou jumped from the rock and ran to catch up. *"What makes sense?"* he psicommed; the Parr's question went unanswered as MacKencey jogged on.

The sight of the dead trooper was bad enough, but in some ways it didn't live up to the horrors that MacKencey had imaged. The trooper was sprawled there on his back with his arms flung out to his sides; one leg was up on the protruding tree root, while the other was folded back underneath his body at a seemingly impossible angle. His head was angled back and to one side; the ground around it was smooth and almost mirror bright, looking almost like hot tar in the false-color images from MacKencey's night vision scope.

MacKencey just stood there looking down at the trooper and cursing himself. Lying before him was a man he considered not just a comrade-in-arms, but a friend—and without his identification icon, he wouldn't have been able to tell if this were Sergeant Thompson or Trooper Williams.

"Troy, hurry up," called the Parr, a sense of urgency and the need for flight underlining his message.

"Acknowledged," replied MacKencey, who was still looking around for the trooper's weapon. "Where's his gauss rifle?"

"I didn't see it last time I was here," psicommed Ma'Rou, who was on the verge of making a run for it. *"Troy, take cover!"* he demanded and darted off for a nearby tree.

MacKencey stopped and looked in the direction of the strangers; through his helmet's directional pickup mic, he could hear their approach over the sounds of the night. Crouching low, he moved quickly and quietly towards Ma'Rou's position.

Even over the ringing in his ears MacKencey could hear the approaching men. They were anything but stealthy as they moved through the forest's undergrowth and deadfall; in fact, at least two of them were talking, as if this were just a late-night walk in the park. In the meantime, Ma'Rou had moved to a vantage point among the tree roots to watch their approach.

"They're over here somewhere," one of them said to his companions. "Chimera indicated that it took down three targets."

"Chimera," thought MacKencey, "a mythological monster. How appropriate."

"Over there!" said another, almost shouting with excitement. "I can see a boot sticking up."

In response, MacKencey tighten his grip on the pistol, which he held with both hands at the ready, near the side of his head. "What do we have?" he psicommed over the pounding in his ears.

"We have three men in heavy mesh body armor; two are armed with bulky looking, drum-fed assault weapons; the third is unarmed and holding a data pad," Ma'Rou psicommed back.

MacKencey held position as the Parr continued to report. The two armed men moved up, their helmet-mounted, infrared spotlights lighting up the body of the fallen trooper; they kept the body at gunpoint as they kicked at it. Satisfied that he was either dead or immobilized from his injuries, they lowered their weapons. They called over the third man. Without waiting, one of the armed men slung his weapon and knelt down next to the trooper. He searched the body as the second gunman eagerly looked on. Ma'Rou subvocalized a growl. A matching rumble echoed in MacKencey's chest. *"Troy, they're searching Sergeant Thompson,"* he psicommed; hatred underlined his words. When the third man drew closer, Ma'Rou noticed that all of them had a dark-colored plastic tag hanging from the front of their armor.

MacKencey's stomach tied itself into a knot. "Ma'Rou can you access the sergeant's base computer?"

"Stand by," replied the Parr; time clicked by in heartbeats. *"Affirmative."*

"Okay, when I give you the word, activate his helmet's spotlights; full spectrum and at maximum diffusion," he instructed.

"Acknowledged," A strange feeling of both excitment and mischief played down the link between them to echo on MacKencey's emotions. I'm never going to get a handle on how they think, he admitted to himself.

After sliding his pistol back into its holster, MacKencey carefully reached up and grabbed hold of his helmet. His right hand gripped its all too familiar guide points; his left had to probe along the damaged underside to find its mark. After a few moments of searching, his thumb finally slipped into the clamp's opening. With both thumbs, he pressed forward against them. The neck seal gave with a faint snap as it separated from the base of the helmet.

A rush of crisp air slipped past the gap in his suit. His attention was captured by the diverse green smells of the forest. For a moment, all he wanted to do was sit there and let the cool night ease his burning head and calm his stressed nerves. The sound drew the Parr scout's attention. Ma'Rou turned and watched as MacKencey finished removing his helmet, revealing a dark gray, astronaut-style comhood; his helmet was still connected to the armor by two extendable cables. Carefully, he lowered it down behind his head on top of the suit's armored backpack, where it promptly locked itself into place.

MacKencey's eyes blinked hard, then went wide, dilating against the darkness. They created an eerie, mirror-like shine as seen through Ma'Rou's scopes; he looked like a man who had gone blind from cataracts.

Drawing his sidearm, he once again brought it up to the ready position next to his head. After a few deep breaths, he looked blindly in Ma'Rou's direction. "Ready," he said quietly.

"Ready," psicommed Ma'Rou as he returned his attention back to the strangers.

MacKencey gently shifted his weight from his knees back onto his feet. He slowly stood up, using the tree for cover. "Now," he ordered and pushed himself around the side of the tree. His mind raced when the ancient fight-or-flight response kicked in on a wave of hormones and adrenaline; the world around him shifted into sharp focus and time itself slowed down.

He knew that ballistic mesh body armor was no match for the five-millimeter, armor-piercing spitzers now chambered in his sidearm; only a strike against a steel or ceramic trauma plate might deter the projectile from fulfilling its unholy purpose.

In the blink of an eye, the fallen trooper's helmet lights flared; the delicate electronics of the strangers' night-vision goggles overloaded, setting off the failsafe to prevent them from burning out; with the power cut, the strangers were plunged into a technologically-induced world of darkness.

The men swore, their hands grabbing for their goggles. MacKencey leveled his weapon, squinting against the glare. His training took over as he subconsciously aimed and fired at any potential threat.

In rapid succession, MacKencey fired two rounds into the head of the man standing at Sergeant Thompson's feet; the sound of the impacts was like a hammer smacking against concrete. Before the body even hit the ground, MacKencey shifted his aim to the second man, who had already raised his goggles and had his forearm up to shield his eyes.

Shots echoed through the woods as the first round punched through the stranger's arm and tore though his face. With the dampened recoil of the weapon, the second round landed just above the first, striking him at an upward angle in the forehead. The stranger's life ended as abruptly as his comrade's.

By the time the second body rolled over, MacKencey already had the third stranger in his sights. Only the terror in the man's expression prevented MacKencey from firing.

"Don't move!" he yelled as he started towards the man. In response, the stranger opened his hands and spread out his fingers to show he was unarmed; he had dropped the datapad when the first shots were fired.

"Cover me, but stay here," ordered MacKencey to his unseen companion.

"Yes sir," responded Ma'Rou via his suit's external speakers; the flat monotone voice was deceptive, to say the least; one would never have expected to find that it belonged to a twenty-pound house cat.

With his pistol held at eye level in a two-handed grip, MacKencey carefully stepped over the body of his fallen comrade. "Okay, you know the drill," he said sarcastically while still moving slowly towards him, "helmet off; hands on head, fingers interlocking."

The stranger's hands shook as he slowly undid the chin strap on his helmet and then lifted it from his head.

"Drop it behind you," instructed MacKencey.

He let it go with a thump and put his hands on top of his head, as directed. The helmet thumped as it landed behind him. MacKencey stepped up and pushed the muzzle brake of his pistol in to the stranger's neck; reaching around with his left hand, he opened the stranger's holster and withdrew his pistol; which he threw off into the undergrowth somewhere behind them.

Ma'Rou once again spied the plastic tag hanging from the stranger's vest. *"Troy,"* psicommed Ma'Rou, *"I think they're wearing some form of electronic tag."*

MacKencey stepped back and surveyed the stranger. He reached up and grabbed the two by four inch piece of black plastic, "What's this? A lift ticket?" he said, then pulled at the object.I It came away with a snap.

"No!" gasped the stranger.

"Tick, tick, tick," sounded in Ma'Rou's helmet; a series of corresponding small sharp peaks appeared on the electromagnetic grid at the bottom of his display.

The Parr's horror once again pushed at MacKencey's emotions, but this time he was expecting it. "Acknowledged," he said softly into his comhood's pickup mics before Ma'Rou started to psicom. "Remember my order," he added.

Ma'Rou reluctantly responded, *"Acknowledged."* He moved off into the high grass to watch.

The stranger could only hear part of the conversation, but it was enough. His eyes went wide with fear.

MacKencey backed toward one of the men he had killed. "Throw me his tag!" pleaded the stranger who took his hands off his head and started to move forward.

"Don't!" growled MacKencey as he knelt down next to the gunman's body; the stranger stopped, clearly on the verge of panic.

MacKencey eyed the gunman's bulky assault weapon. It had better be full of M142s or I'm so boned, he thought to himself as he dropped his pistol and made a grab for the weapon.

The stranger did not hesitate to turn and make a run for it, but he didn't get very far; the machine appeared like an animated shadow, seeming to separate itself from the surrounding night.

With a smack, an unseen blow struck the stranger. His last screams of horror were forever trapped inside a smashed larynx and collapsed trachea. Even before he could react, a second blow had struck him about the left side of his head. Like a hangman's noose, the force snapped several vertebrae in his neck; he was dead before his body hit the ground.

Still kneeling next to the other gunman, MacKencey had unslung the weapon and had it in his hands when he heard the attack. In the brief time that it took to look up, the stranger's body was already tumbling over like a rag doll.

His killer just stood there watching. Waiting. Even with the illumination from the fallen trooper's helmet spotlights, the thing was barely visible. Under such circumstances, the mind tended to invent shapes rather than perceiving them, and right now, MacKencey's imagination was working over time.

So far the creature hadn't attacked, which strengthened MacKencey's hope that these were the beastie's handlers...and that the plastic tag he now held was some form of electronic identification. The question now was: could the thing visually identify friend from foe?

Forcing his eyes down, MacKencey rolled the gunman's weapon onto its side and checked its fire selector. The toggle was pointing at a small green crossed out rectangle. A press of his thumb moved the toggle onto a line of red markers.

When he looked up, his blood ran cold. The beastie had moved closer. It was now less than three meters away. A combination of fear and curiosity ran through him now that he could see it.

It was an anthropomorphic machine that stood almost two meters tall; the head was connected directly to the torso like a fixed turret, yet there were two covered eye-slits that started in the front and ran halfway around both sides. Its barrel-like torso was smooth, almost as if it had been cast in one piece. The color was light-dampening matte gray. The extremities were long, slender, and tapering, they strongly resembled heavier versions of conventional medical prosthetics: designed to mimic, but not appear to be, living flesh.

Now be a nice monster and just stand there while I kill you, thought MacKencey as he shifted his weight to help resist the weapon's recoil. Firing accurately from the hip—even at close range—was risky, but he felt he had no choice; if the beastie had some level of built-in self-preservation, it may not attack a handler, but it might very well run away at the sight of a weapon being leveled at it.

It just stood there watching the trooper—that is if something without eyes could convey such an impression– like a guard dog awaiting instructions to strike. MacKencey was still sizing up the problem when he noticed that the beastie was in fact not standing still, but slowly shifted its weight back and forth from one leg to another while its hands anxiously fanned opened and closed.

MacKencey's curiosity didn't stop him from depressing and holding down the trigger. In rapid succession, three rounds burst from the muzzle of the automatic shotgun. Against the pounding recoil and mechanical action, the angle of the weapon climbed, placing the first round into what might have been the beast's abdomen.

On contact, the miniature grenade detonated. Its small, shape-charge warhead erupted into a directed jet of superheated gas. In an instant, a tongue of flame vaporized a hole in the outer armor. The surrounding material melted and splattered about in molten droplets.

With a pop and a bright flash, the second round found its mark high on the beast's chest; the third passed over its shoulder and detonated somewhere off in the distance. MacKencey released the trigger and watched as the beastie stood there for a moment, wisps of smoke drifting away from the concentric strike points of the grenades. As if suddenly seized by gravity, its torso collapsed downward onto its hips and its arms dragged through the air to land with a smack against the ground.

Standing up, MacKencey brought his weapon up to his shoulder and kept it at the ready. Cautiously, he walked towards the toppled machine. It looked dead No, not dead, he thought. Destroyed.

MacKencey lowered his weapon and much to his surprise found the Parr standing next to him, reaching out his front paw to bat the leg of the beast. *"Can we go home now?"* he psicommed.

The sight of Ma'Rou pawing curiously at the machine, as if it was a just something new he had found in the yard to play with, broke the tension like a hammer blow. MacKencey laughed. "Okay, I'll go call us a ride," he said and headed back toward the body of his comrade.

While MacKencey rummaged around in the fallen trooper's side pouch, the Parr climbed up onto the machine's chest to have a better look. Moving up toward the head, he crouched down to nose at something viscous that seeped out of a blown seam along the thing's side.

"Troy, you need to see this," psicommed Ma'Rou; concern and confusion accented the message.

"Acknowledged," he replied, now holding up the long range com unit.

MacKencey walked over and knelt down by the Parr. He stared at the dark liquid oozing out onto the ground. He tried to dismiss what he saw as some form of hydraulic fluid, but in the back of his mind, a new horror formed.

Reaching over, he touched the dark liquid. It was warm. He could feel through the suit's contact pads that the liquid was thick, almost oily to the touch. It was an all too familiar sensation...blood.

BORN INTO A MILITARY FAMILY, Mike McPhail's lifelong dream was to join NASA. To that end, he attended the Academy of Aeronautics in New York, majoring in aeronautical design. At the same time, he enlisted in the Air National Guard.

While working towards his goal, a sudden illness brought a halt to his dreams. After recovering, he had to come to grips with his new reality, so he chose to put his hard-earned technical skills and imagination to use as a writer.

Today he works as a graphic designer and digital photographer for Sidhe na Daire Multimedia ™, his work has been seen internationally. Among his projects are a number of stories based upon the upcoming *Alliance Archives ™ Martial Role-Playing Game* ™ series, a manual-based, military-science fiction that realistically portrays the consequences of warfare.

WEZLESKI TO THE RESCUE

C.J. Henderson

PHILIP...T-THAT CAN'T BE WHAT I THINK IT IS..."

The shape stirred at the sound of voices. Its watermelon-sized head swaying back and forth, it sucked down great lungsful of air, snorting away its confusion.

"Can it?"

Remarkably, considering what had just transpired—its forced trip from home, blink-of-an-eye, *wham*, bye-bye semi-tropical forest/welcome to America—the leathery, gray thing had adapted to the science-shattering moment in which it had just participated quite quickly. Actually, far more quickly than the two presumably more-intelligent men staring at it were managing.

"Around here, Maxie, I think it could be."

"You don't mean ...."

Already adjusted to its new surroundings, unaware of the uniqueness of its situation, the thing shook itself, casting away the momentary hesitation the newness of sixty-five million years of progress should inspire in a being from the zero end of the equation. No longer concerned with the electric lights, tiled floors, and plastered walls which had replaced the soggy field in which it had been feasting, its head split along a sharp line, displaying several rows of ivory spikes, many still festooned with strips of fatty muscle.

"I think I do mean it, Max. I think I mean that very thing."

Having cut through the overpowering pungents assailing its nostrils, the shape filtered through the smells of ammonia and paint, ozone and perfume, dust, coffee, and the other uninteresting aromas on the air, zeroing in on the essential odor of the men before it. Bellowing its delight at finally identifying smells in its new world as coming from the tasty column, the thing rose to its full height and began striding forward, the very picture of joyful determination. The pair of men acted with suitable consternation.

"It's a goddamned dinosaur, Phil!"

"Jesus Christ! Wezleski's done it again."

The gentleman was correct. Oh, a complete and hungry saurian was a variation on the usual tune of chaos heard in the halls of the Pelgimbly Center for Advanced Sciences, to be sure, but the melody was far too recognizable. For sadly, the postulate would have to be immediately agreed upon by all in the know, from janitor Swenson to Director Aikana, herself, if there were a dinosaur loose, *anywhere,* anywhere at all in the entire world—which, as everyone knows, has not seen claw nor scale of any living dinosaurs for a long, long time—at the bottom of it all had to be Dr. Wendel Q. Wezleski, Ph.D.

"Run, Philip!"

Actually, Professor Philip Morvently was already around the far corner, urging his colleague, the more excitable Dr. Maxim Ginderhoff, to try and keep pace with him. Behind them both, but closing the gap with little difficulty, came the great gray beast, which, some thirteen minutes into the future, would come to be know as Fluffkins, but not before a great deal of blood and slaughter and the violent breaking of things which had not been seen outside the venerable halls of the Pelgimbly Center for Advanced Sciences since the last great foreign war, or inside those halls since Thursday previous.

"It's catching up to us," announced Phil.

"Quite aware, professor. In fact," Max ran the figures in his head, glancing over his shoulder one last time to give his equation a final check before presenting it as a hypothesis, "the way it's managing to out-pace us, I'm thinking its line of trajectory is going to intersect ours in less than eleven seconds."

Agreeing whole-heartedly, Phil shouted back to his colleague;

"Remsley, pages 72 through 75."

Puzzled, Max almost slowed his pace. Certainly the professor was referring to Otto Remsley, or more specifically, his seminal 1984 text, *Living with Fear*. But, pages 72 through 75—what that reference could mean he had no idea. Sensing the doctor's confusion, Phil clarified;

"The paperback, not the hardback."

Suddenly everything was made clear. But, of course, *Chapter Seven, Agreements Made in Fear*. The point in the book where Remsley quipped so eloquently on the humor in danger when it caught groups by surprise, and the pacts that could be made under such pressures. Max started to chuckle at such wit from his esteemed colleague. Then, his split-second of jolly reverie past, he flashed-back to their current shared reality, remembering exactly *what* they had been agreeing to, reminded by a snort of white-meat scented moisture on the back of his neck. Grabbing his companion's sleeve, the doctor tugged with urgency, shouting;

"In here!"

Max and Phil managed to execute a quite dramatic left turn into the second-level biology lab just as the brute thing snapped at one or the other of them. Skidding helplessly on janitor Swenson's immaculate tiles, the great beast slid past the doorway, one massive leg raised upward, swooshing onward to the end of the hall where it collided rather firmly with the far wall, knocking loose two fire extinguishers and the Center's cherished picture of L.D. Goodhue holding up two fingers behind Johannes Croning's head at the dinner held the day after the latter had announced his new shell-molding process.

"Bar the door."

Max needed no encouragement from his erstwhile colleague. Indeed, he had already started to slide forward several lab stools and a half full box of Blakely & Son's Bunsen burners.

"Something heavier, old boy," Phil chided his partner in amateur survival. "Equal mass. Distribution of force, that sort of thing—yes?"

Max nearly blushed. Even mind-numbing panic of a sort never actually experienced by any living human being was still no excuse for a scientist forgetting his fundamental principles of dynamics.

But, ohhhhhhhhhhhhhhhhhh, he thought, grabbing for something that might stiffen the barrier the pair of researchers were hoping to build between themselves and the slavering thing in the hall, *that Wezleski!*

There simply wouldn't be a need for such enthusiasms at all if it weren't for that darned Wezleski.

Oh, how the name made Max flush with a rage not compatible with his elevated blood pressure. Come to work and find eighty-seven of the eighty-nine windows of the western wing not only shattered, but the resultant shards pincushioning a low flying plane brought to ruin by the shattering, and only one name could be attached as the cause—Wezleski. Break for lunch and hear the arrival of scores of firefighting volunteers, along with their hooks, ladders, and hoses, all eager to have away at the volcanic eruption transforming the formerly immaculate south lawn into something from a Ray Harryhausen film, and there would be only a single Center member whose reputation might come to mind—Wezleski. Reach for the last jelly doughnut, and find that not only is it missing, but replaced by a spiny creature the length of a standard spatula, the width of a generous dinner plate, with the eyes of a collie and the disposition of an Orthodox Jew at an all-you-can-munch bacon-breakfast and certainly, but one signature could you see on the dotted line...

"Wezleski."

"Less muttering, more stacking," encouraged Phil. Oh, to be certain, the professor was not trying to change his companion's disposition toward their absent brethren, merely his immediate fixation upon him for, outside in the hall, the gray thing had made its way back to the biology laboratory. Already it had begun to pit its tiny, fairly one-dimensional intellect against the awesomely complex three-dimensional concept of the swinging door. And, since it had already shown itself to be somewhat of a Paleozoic genius, it was doubtful Max and Phil had much time left.

The thing stared and stared at the spot where its prey had effectively vanished. It had followed them to the exact spot where it now stood. It knew it was correct in this, for their odor still hung in the air. Indeed, it was strong and juicy and growing stronger, filled with the delicious drippings of desperate fright in which the horror's growling belly simply delighted. In fact, it could smell them, could hear their squeaking noises, it could practically taste them in the air. It just could not see them. Still, it had not lived to the ripe old age of many passings of the sun by not learning a thing or one thing and another thing. The beast knew that if it could smell something, it was there. So, trusting its nose, it began moving forward toward the wall.

Its snout touching the door, the thing was taken with the fact that this flat gray nothing seemed somehow different than the flat gray nothing into which it had slammed several minutes earlier. Whereas its forceful encounter with that flat gray nothing had been rather painful, it losing the lop-sided battle quite completely, this flat grayness was different. It was not stationary. It moved.

"It's pushing the door!"

"Well then do join me in pushing it back."

The scientists resisted with the strength they would use to oppose the theory of a flat earth, or the rights of cinema stars to proselytize for scientific causes. The memory of Susan Sarandon and Wynona Ryder lecturing the General Assembly on the dangers of conservative Christians being allowed to clone mad armies for Jesus still burned into his mind, Max strove valiantly to hold the breach by himself as he shouted;

"Phil, release all the animals."

"What?"

"Just do it!"

No Wezleski, of course, Dr. Maxim Ginderhoff was still an intellect with which to be reckoned. All throughout the biology room, cages adorned the walls and floor filled with all manner of experimental fish, fowl, and furbearer. As Phil threw open latch after latch, allowing escape for the various chickens, cats, white mice, and so on, Max began kicking away bits and pieces of their barrier, even as the thing in the hall started increasing its efforts to reach the delicious sounds it heard multiplying inside the lab. Reaching the monkey cages, Phil asked;

"Even Brodsky's chimps?"

"Everything."

"He'll be awfully cross; he's very keen on how close he is with his cancer research."

"Open the cages."

"Max, he's got them up to two packs a day."

"Philip! Unfasten the bolts or I shall stroll over there, unfasten the deltoids of your left shoulder from the area of the trapezius, grasp the resultant dislocated appendage firmly at the intersection of ulna and carpals and *beat you to death with it!*"

Sensing the seriousness in Max's tone, Phil complied, releasing Dr. Brodsky's prize chimps into the melee, all eight of which immediately began an insane search for cigarettes, seven for the cool, fresh taste of Marlboros, only one determined to uncover the coveted pack of Winterfresh Menthol Lites the doctor saved for those of their octet who performed exceptionally well, ringing the right bell in response to the proper colored light series or managing to get at least an act or two of Hamlet typed up from memory before coughing up a nicotine-flavored lu'gee into their IBM Selectric.

Finally, with hamsters, ducks, rabbits, and everything else filling the air with fur, feathers, and consternation, Phil rejoined Max at the door. Adding his delicate but willing shoulder to the barricade, he both informed Max that all the test subjects had been released and inquired as to just why the hell such a thing had been done. The doctor explained.

"I'm willing to wager that our friend out there, eager as it is to acquaint itself with the best scientific minds of our day, is not all that erudite itself."

"Points conceded," Phil granted as the door continued to push inward. "Go on."

"I'm thinking," answered Max, just catching his balance as the beast pulled away for a moment, causing the door to rush back toward the hallway once more, "that if one side of a swinging door confused our new best friend, that similar results might be achieved by the opposite side as well."

"Acceptable premise," agreed Phil as the beast came at the door again, expending much more force than it had previously. Digging in his J.C. Penny loafers, he asked, "have you given much thought to testing it?"

"Indeed. If you note, our friend has fallen into a pattern of pressing against the door, pulling back, and then coming forward with more force. Delightfully predictable. I propose when next it relents, we back away, and then, when it comes forward again, we allow it to enter the laboratory while we exit. Once inside ..."

"With all the animals on the menu ..."

"He will forget about us ..."

"And we can trap him in the lab!"

"Precisely."

The great beast stopped for a moment, vibrations it had never felt before stunning its external radar.

"He's slowing ..."

"Now or never ..."

The thing was shocked. The spark that raw human consciousness could generate had actually touched it through the door, not harmed it, no—not a physical touching ...

"He's still there—you can feel him."

But, pressed against the moving gray nothing, the mindless thing almost *awakened*, almost noticed something beyond the few senses it knew and trusted so well. But then, the first of the new aromas caught hold—

Inside, Max rapidly waved the notes he was carrying, a rather insightful symposium lecture he was to deliver at 2:30 on the social significance of the fact that Monty's Python's "Always Look on the Bright Side of Life" was the most requested song at funerals around the world, blowing the rising smell of the lab animals under the door.

"Come on, big fella, we do chicken right."

Suddenly the air was alive with a thousand new pure fats and bloods that were so overpowering as to intoxicate. The beast wavered on its feet, giddy with wonder at what treasure might be inside the vast gray nothing.

"He's going to move soon, yes ...?"

"I'd say in three ..."

His foot on the side of his body which was not the other side of his body dug into the treacherous floor. His eyes hooded, shoulders flattened—

"And two ..."

Deep breath, rush of blood, brain exploding with oxygen, order given—*forward!*

"One."

Max and Phil fell to the floor with the grace quickly learned by all those whose permanent place of employment was the Pelgimbly Center for Advanced Sciences, falling back with the perfect rhythm all truly rational souls gain in times of stress. Two-stepping as the door swung open, violently propelled as it was by the blood-fever rush of the only dinosaur to know the sweet dream of feasting on domesticated lives, the esteemed doctor of thermodynamic physics bounced back toward the hall with the much-valued professor of non-linear philosophy sliding out quietly behind him.

Allowing the door to swing shut, they locked it quickly with Morvently's official key as a Dean of Sciences, and then slid down the wall opposite, laughing and cursing, ignoring the hideous screaming, screaming, screaming coming from the other side of the door as they tried to answer the questions of the many flocking to find out what all the previous commotion had been about. There were, of course, a goodly faction who were also quite curious about the screaming, screaming, screaming, as well.

In only a few minutes Dr. Ginderhoff and Professor Morvently were able to give a fairly detailed account of what had happened to them, specifying their suspicions of grievous blame and to which of Dr. Wezleski's addresses to forward them to in their footnotes, despite the constant questions from those in the crowd, especially janitor Swenson, although it was apparent he was mostly concerned with how his tiles had gotten so streaked, and who was going to have to clean up "... der stinkin' piles of dinosaur crap," and of course, the screaming, screaming, screaming, when suddenly, the constant din of the country dinner being served tartar in the main dining room of the biology laboratory ... stopped.

No more screams.

None at all.

For a very long moment ...

And then ...

"Who in Hell took my Luckies?"

"Wezleski?" asked Phil.

"Wezleski," snarled Max, diabolical loathing closing one of his eyes, curling his delicately sensitive instrument-like hands into fists. "Wezleski!" snapped Max, envy and humiliation raging against the indifference he knew the crazed Wezleski would feel toward everything that had happened in his wake.

As the crowd moved toward the swinging door of the biology lab, they all gasped involuntarily as the door suddenly swung out toward them.

"Hey, some kind of mess in there, huh?"

Dr. Ginderhoff moved forward, moustache twitching, open eye bulging, face crimsoning over like Russian wheat at sunset, his hands clutching and opening, clutching and squeezing, only to find himself blocked by the venerable Director Aikana. Knowing her staff all too well, the good Director thwarted the promised blood-letting with a bit of tact, deflecting the doctor's misplaced rage into a weapon for truth.

"Dr. Wezleski," she snapped with authority. "What was that thing? Why did you bring it to the Center? Explain yourself before those horrid people from UPN force their way in here again."

"Oh, you must mean Fluffkins," answered the somewhat dazed looking scientist. "I noticed him leaving through the field as I returned."

"What?" The innocent single word was actually voiced by a number of the crowd. Indeed, there were a great many exclamations, but this one is quite representative and thus should suffice.

"I thought I'd finally cracked the problem with inter-dimensional travel. Trouble is, I only back-doored my way into time travel again."

"Groan..." Once more, not a complete tally of reactions.

Wezleski opened the door behind him and invited everyone to move into biology lab 5A, or as it would be affectionately remembered for years after, ye olde slaughterhouse, as if ushering them into Fluffkins dining hall would somehow endear them to his tale. But, unbelievably, after but a few fairly incomprehensible moments of explanation, the eye-popping reaction to which can only be compared to the first ever audience to experience Willis O'Brien's King Kong; the sensation of seeing the Earth as only the astronauts have—floating in space, back in the womb, snaggled to a life-giving umbilical, viewing a motherfigure the size of everything and the width of it squared; or that wonderful moment in 1905 when a brave new world was created at the moment when elastic rubber replaced the traditional whalebone and lacing used in women's foundation garments, the Director said;

"You're telling us, that when you went through the time stream you displaced an equal mass to yourself and what you took inside with you. It could have been two hundred and fifty three pounds of sea water, or coal, or riverbottom that came to us, but no, precisely, it was a dinosaur of a vary nasty, snapping, unbehaved type we had to contend with while you dallied elsewhere."

"Yeah, I think so," admitted Wezleski, puzzling to remember if he had meant anything else.

"And before I assess the damage you have done to our esteemed Center, yet again, Dr. Wezleski, I want to know something...why did you call that beast 'Fluffkins?' as if you knew it?"

"Because I did know it."

Now, remarkably, at this point, having lived through so many purely wezleskian moments as that shard of time they were all sharing with the only M.I.T./Yale/Cambridge alumni to have ever taken The Most Dangerous Man in Science Nomination twenty-six times in only eleven years (the duplications caused by his common, multiple category nominations within the same year, usually creating a split vote that would allow some other knucklehead to walk away with the trophy), you would have thought at least someone would have begun edging toward the door.

"You see," he explained, with that unknowing way he had of luring the foolish to their doom, "geared as I was for intra-dimensional travel through inter-dimensional means, when I hit the damn time stream again, my ratial-mass threw an anchor out to pull me back—Fluffkins. But, since I was on an extended trip, I was actually there before, during and after his ..."

"Its."

"Excuse me, Dr. Ginderhoff?" asked Wezleski.

"It's not a 'him,' it's an 'it.'"

"Hey, I was with *him* long enough to assign enough anthropomorphic characteristics to allow the pattern to establish itself. Comprende?"

Ginderhoff hated Wezleski's embracing of popular culture means to explain his sloppier descriptive characteristics. Then again, he hated Wezleski's favorite lunch, any tune he might chance to whistle, and even the tie given him by the Women's Alliance for Runaway Decency. Honestly, he just plain hated Wezleski. But, with his vision blurring and the pain in his arm turning to numbness, he decided he had more important things to think about at that moment.

"Anyway," Wezleski continued, "I disappeared from where I was twice, Fluffkins, three times. That means I was able to study him after he ate all the bio critters."

"Hold on sixty seconds," snapped Professor Morvently. "How could you have been around this creature any length of time? It obviously considers the human smell the dinner bell..."

"You have to rub yourself with fruit juice and not give off any signs of fear. All right?"

Morvently rolled his eyes. The crowd stared. Aikana wondered about this research Wezleski had mentioned. Her need to find dollars in any situation, the Director steered the conversation back to the doctor's studies.

"Oh, yeah...anyway, I ran tests on ol' Fluffkins when he got back. It's a complete study of the effects of modern life on prehistoric cultures. Fluffkins chowed down on mega overdoses of nicotine and perfume extracts and carcinogens—everything that was in biology. I've got it all stretched—the numbers ring. Someone out there should be happy."

Aikana smiled. Her mad bomber of scientific research had done it again. No matter which outcome the research favored, she already knew to whom she could sell it. Her soul lifted as the tally she could see for damages and lost loveable furry things was far outstripped by the minimum bids she could already hear jangling in the Center's deepening pockets. Pleased beyond reason, she spoke without thinking.

"Well done, doctor," she cooed, meaning it. Loving him once more. "Do give me your notes."

"Sure," answered Wezleski without hesitation, always happy to follow the dictates of the Director, "One minute. I left them on the other side."

Turning on his heel, he reached out and grabbed an arm.

"C'mon Swenson, help me look for those notes."

And the two men stepped through the time portal to retrieve the asked-for papers. Sending not two hundred and fifty three pounds over to the other side, but some five hundred and eighteen pounds, instead. Of course, it might have displaced some five hundred and eighteen pounds of sea water, or coal, or even of riverbottom. But no, none of those were precisely what was returned.

What anchored their trip was something smaller than the last time. Tiny in comparison—but still remained the rows of ivory spikes and unruly disposition.

Smaller, indeed, just more of them. Two hundred and fifty-three more of them, to be exact. All of whom, upon arrival in ye olde slaughterhouse, heard one massive sound voiced from thirty-two some various throats:

"Wezleski!"

AUTHOR C.J. HENDERSON IS AN ORIGINS AWARD WINNER WHO, IN HIS TIME, has earned his keep as everything from a movie house manager and blackjack dealer to a roadie, card shark and stand-up comic. He is the creator of two series characters known around the world, private eye Jack Hagee and supernatural investigator Teddy London. Over the past quarter century he has written over thirty books as well as hundreds of short stories and comics. His work has been seen in numerous anthologies, as well as such magazines as *Cemetery Dance, Dragon, Espionage, Startling Science Stories, Crypt of Cthulhu, Different Worlds, Tales of Lovecraftian Horror, Fantasy Gamer* and scores of others. As for his comics work, he has written for both DC and Marvel, as well as such wide-ranging companies as Archie and Penthouse. As a gamer, he has been around the block a few times as well. He has rolled the dice in Lake Geneva, WI, back in the days when it was still the home of TSR, and he has sat across the table from such notables as sci fi painter James Warhola, Lovecraft scholar Dr. Robert M. Price and everyone's favorite cartoonist, Gahan Wilson. He was also Larping over twenty years ago, back, as he says, "before it had a name."

ADRIFT IN THE MAELSTROM

Will McDermott

15.12.2400 ESD | 16:30 HOURS | ETS MIRUBOOTO (SCOUT CLASS) | DAMAGE REPORT | ACTING CHIEF ENGINEER GRANT AUSTIN

IT HAS BEEN TEN STANDARD HOURS SINCE OUR ESCAPE FROM THE SZYLUZAN MARAUDER SHIPS. THE LAST SALVO THOSE BLOODY SNAKES HURLED AT US SHATTERED THE COMMAND DOME AND DESTROYED TWO MAIN STRUTS JUST AS WE PASSED THE HYPERSPACE THRESHOLD.

CAPTAIN WILSON AND MOST OF THE BRIDGE CREW ARE DEAD; SPACED WHEN THE DOME CRACKED. ONLY ENSIGN ANTHYRUS SURVIVED. I GUESS PLANTS...ER...BOCHTS DON'T SUFFER EXPLOSIVE DECOMPRESSION. IT SCUTTLED INTO ENGINEERING ON ITS FRONDS SEVERAL HOURS AGO. ACCORDING TO ANTHYRUS, NONE OF THE UPPER DECKS SURVIVED THAT LAST HIT. WE'RE ALONE.

ENGINEERING SUFFERED MAJOR DAMAGE AND CASUALTIES AS WELL. WE LOST CHIEF ENGINEER DUNN, LIEUTENANT MAAS, AND SEVEN OTHER CREWMEN WHEN STRUT NUMBER TWO FAILED, CAUSING AN EXPLOSIVE FEEDBACK THROUGHOUT THE MAIN POWER SYSTEMS. ONLY EIGHT OF US REMAIN. MYSELF AND THREE OTHER HUMANS—MIDSHIPMEN 1ST CLASS BRADLEY WEITZ AND HALIM BAKAR, AND MIDSHIPMAN 3RD CLASS AMI SOTO—LEAD THE REPAIRS. ENSIGN ANTHYRUS, THE PLANT...BOCHT...PILOT, TWO HORSEBUGS...ER...SHLOAG YEOMEN NAMED MOOG AND GORM, AND THE BIRD-BRAIN...DAMN...V'T'DANGA...TRANSLATOR, ENSIGN KUCZKU, ALSO SURVIVED, FOR ALL THE GOOD THAT'LL DO US.

WITH ONLY FOUR STRUTS REMAINING, WE'RE LUCKY THE SUBSTRUCTURE DIDN'T COLLAPSE INTO THE SINGULARITY DRIVE. AS IT IS, WE'VE LOST ATTITUDE CONTROL AND HAVE BEEN SPINNING THROUGH THE MAELSTROM FOR THE LAST TEN HOURS, WITH NO WAY TO MONITOR OR CORRECT OUR COURSE.

WE'VE COMPLETED REPAIRS, AND CAN ACCESS SHIP'S SYSTEMS FROM ENGINEERING, NOW, BUT THE NEWS IS WORSE THAN EXPECTED. BOTH DAMAGED STRUTS ARE A COMPLETE LOSS, AND THE REMAINING STRUTS CAN'T HANDLE THE EXTRA POWER LOAD, SO WE'RE EFFECTIVELY AT TWO-THIRDS POWER; NOT NEARLY ENOUGH TO GENERATE A STABLE HYPERSPACE THRESHOLD.

WE CAN MANEUVER, BUT THERE'S NO TELLING WHERE WE ARE WITHIN THE MAELSTROM, AND NO WAY TO DETERMINE OUR POSITION WITHOUT CREATING A THRESHOLD. WE ARE LOST....

Lieutenant Austin replaced the voicedat recorder on its clip and ran his fingers through his thinning hair. As he scanned the report, he realized that he should probably clean up the language. 'Alien slang terms have no place in an official report,' Dunn would have said; at least that's what he'd listed on the latest official reprimand. But what did it matter now?

'Lieutenant?"

The voice came directly into his head. Austin would never get used to that, but it was a reality of the modern space force, so he had to live with it. The birdbrains had made it possible to communicate with the other races, which had been hailed as a huge step forward in alien relations. Whatever! But without his translator, he wouldn't be able to "speak" to most of the crew, such as they were.

Kuczku stood before him, her leathery wings folded like two fins behind her. Her odd, double-jointed legs always made it look like she was sitting on an invisible chair. And Grant would never get used to that reptilian bird face with those bulbous eyes poking out from either side of her long, hooked beak, nor the pointed peak on her head, which turned back and forth like a rudder as her head swiveled to keep her eyes on the subject of her study.

"Lieutenant," the voice came again into his head. "Anthyrus reports another ship on the sensors."

'Another ship?" asked Grant. He pushed past the translator and marched through the ruins of the large circular room toward the pilot. Engineering was at the base of the substructure connected directly to the struts, which passed through the room like six massive pillars, forming a perfect hexagon.

All the workstations surrounding struts two and five had been destroyed by the power feedback. They were now little more than piles of molten slag, still smoking, hissing, and popping ten hours after the attack. The bodies of the dead had been stacked in one of the lifts. But death hung in the air, and the emergency lights lent the chamber an awful green glow, leaving much of the deck in looming shadows.

A clicking sound over to one side drew Austin's attention. Soto, Weitz, and Bakar were loading the last of the larger debris—struts and wall panels that had collapsed in the explosion onto the back of Moog—or Gorm—all of the horsebugs looked alike to Austin.

They had three bulbous body segments, plus a head; the effect looked sort of like an ant, but with an extra segment. Each segment had a pair of legs, but the bugs often walked around on just four of their legs, using their front limbs for grasping and lifting. They were as big as a small horse and covered with thick, short fur. One of the yeomen was black, while the other was mostly brown. Austin could never remember which was which.

The shloag being loaded was clicking its mandibles while the antenna on its head waved around wildly. Kuczku stepped over toward the group. "What's he saying?" asked Soto.

Kuczku looked at the shloag, apparently reading its thoughts as the words clicked and buzzed through its mandible. The translator then looked back to Soto. She cocked her head as the translation was beamed into her brain. Soto turned to the shloag and said, "Sorry, Moog. We'll be more careful." Soto pulled several pieces of debris from the shloag's back, lightening the load.

Austin shook his head and picked his way toward the pilot. Kuczku hurried to catch up. Anthyrus, the bocht pilot, sat at a workstation attached to strut one, looking like a large potted fern that somebody had left on a chair, except without the pot. The leafy tendrils of a dozen stalks waved and weaved over the control panel, tapping out commands on the controls in a blur.

That's why they made such good pilots, thought Grant as he sucked in his stomach and then tucked his shirt tail back into his pants. *Hard to keep up with a multi-limbed creature. Not that it did them much good in the human-bocht wars.*

The workstation screen showed two blips; one in the center and the other at the extreme edge. Two of the pilot's fronds raised up from the back of the plant and began making intricate patterns in the air in front of Grant. Kuczku translated the bocht sign language inside the lieutenant's head.

"It's at the extreme edge of our sensors, sir, but I am attempting to focus the field to get more information."

A moment later, the blip at the edge of the screen moved toward the center and expanded into a triangular outline. The hairs on the back of Austin's neck stood up, sending a tingle down his spine. He didn't need the computer to tell him what that triangle meant.

"Szyzulan!" he said.

The plant's speaking fronds waved again as the triangle resolved further into the familiar batwing shape of a szyzulan ship. The translation came through a moment later. "You are correct, sir. It looks to be Szyzulan—Raider class. But sir…?"

"What? What is it?" snapped Austin. He glared at the plant, futilely. If it had normal, human eyes, it would have withered under his scrutiny.

"It appears to be dead in space."

15.12.2400 ESD | 18:45 HOURS | ETS MIRUBOOTO | STATUS REPORT | ENGINEER GRANT AUSTIN

WE ARE PREPARING TO BOARD THE SZYZULAN RAIDER. BIO SENSORS SHOW SOME ODD READINGS, BUT NO SIGNIFICANT LIFE SIGNS. WHATEVER LEFT THEIR SHIP ADRIFT IN THE MAELSTROM SEEMS TO HAVE KILLED THE CREW AS WELL. THIS IS AN AMAZING OPPORTUNITY! WE WILL BE THE FIRST EARTH TRANSGLOBAL CITIZENS EVER TO BOARD A SZYZULAN SHIP.

ANY REPORT ON THE TECHNOLOGY CONTAINED WITHIN WILL BE WORTH A HOUSE RANSOM IN BONUS PAY. IF WE'RE LUCKY ENOUGH TO UNCOVER THE SECRET BEHIND THEIR MASS DRIVERS OR THE ALMOST MAGICAL ABILITY THEIR SHIPS HAVE OF BANKING AND TURNING IN THE VACUUM OF SPACE LIKE A HYPERJET IN AN ATMOSPHERE, WE COULD ALL BE MILLIONAIRES...ASSUMING WE EVER GET HOME.

MORE IMPORTANTLY, THE POWER READINGS FROM THE ALIEN SHIP SEEM NEAR-NORMAL. WE MAY BE ABLE TO SIPHON OFF ENOUGH POWER FROM THE RAIDER TO OPEN A HYPERSPACE THRESHOLD. THEN WE CAN GET OUT OF THE MAELSTROM, FIND OUR BEARINGS, AND LIMP HOME WITH OUR PRIZE....

Austin floated in the void between the two ships, tethered to the mooring cable. The red, blue, and purple swirling maelstrom surrounded him, nagging at his senses. Swirls seemed to lick at the edges of the ice-cream-cone-shaped *Miruboota* behind him, as if the maelstrom was slowly devouring his ship. Prolonged exposure to the maelstrom was said to cause hallucinations and even insanity. Best that they get inside the raider as quickly as possible.

But Austin couldn't keep his eyes off *Mirubooto*. The damage had been even more devastating than he had imagined. It looked as if the entire top of the ice cream cone had been scooped off, and even now, plasma leaked from both shattered struts. They would have to find a way to shut that down when they got back.

A tug on the cable pulled Austin around to face the raider again. Moog and Gorn had reached the alien ship and locked on several magnetic footholds. One of the bugs tinkered inside an access panel next to the airlock while the other helped Kuczku detach from the cable and hook her boots in the holds. Austin was next, with Soto, Bakar, and Weitz bringing up the rear. He'd left Anthyrus on board because he really couldn't risk losing their pilot, even if it was just a plant.

The raider looked like a black stain growing in the multi-colored swirls. Its long wings swept back from the midpoint of the oblong fuselage. At the rear of the ship, he could just see a flat, fanlike tail section. For a moment, Austin thought he saw the tail flutter, but he decided it must have just been a trick of the swirling plasma.

"We need to get out of this infernal maelstrom!" he called through his space suit's intercom. "Moog! Gorn! Hurry it up. Rip open that hatch if you have to!"

He heard the clicking reply through his earpiece followed by Kuczku's translation in his head. 'I think I almost got it!" said the shloag at the panel.

The other bug grabbed at Austin to help him hook on, but he pulled away and fumbled his way over to the clamp himself. When he looked back, the bug had set several more clamps on the other side of the door and was helping Soto.

"Now would be good," Austin said, indicating the door.

The clicking response was translated: "I think I need midshipman Soto's help, sir."

I should have known, thought Austin. "Fine! Soto, help the bug. But Moog and Gorm, you enter the raider first and secure the airlock." Bugs first, that had always been Austin's motto.

Soto took the tool in her gloved hand and worked at the controls for a moment. The hatch slid open and the two shloags pulled themselves inside. A moment later, they reappeared and helped the rest of the crew into the airlock. It was a tight fit with two bugs, a bird, and four humans once the hatch slid closed. Austin tapped his foot waiting for the shloag to open the inner hatch. There was no way Soto could move forward to help this time, so they were at the mercy of the stupid bug. Precious seconds passed before the hiss of air signaled the opening of the hatch.

Kuczku screamed in Austin's mind and the outer hatch blew off.

Wind rushed past Austin, pushing him toward the opening. Weitz and Bakar yelled for help. Austin flailed at the side of the airlock, trying to find something to grab onto. Then he felt his body lift off the floor. He looked up into the helmeted face of a bug. One of the shloags had grabbed him and Kuczku. With two legs wrapped around the edge of the inner hatch, the bug heaved its way through the opening.

Austin tried to look back to see about his other crewmembers. But all he could see was the other shloag, buffeted by wind and debris, inching its way through the opening. Weitz and Bakar continued to cry for help. Austin was sure they had been sucked back out into the maelstrom. But Soto was oddly silent. He called out, "Weitz! Bakar! Soto! Report! Are you okay?"

He couldn't hear anything but screams over the roar of the wind. After a terrifying minute, the world went silent again and Austin was lowered to the ground. He scanned the crew. The two shloags had made it inside along with Kuczku and himself. Soto walked out from behind the other bug, saluted, and said: "We lost Weitz and Bakar, sir."

"What the hell happened?" he yelled. "Moog, Gorm, what did you do?"

The bugs chittered and clicked in protest. Austin hardly needed the translation. "We didn't do anything!" and "We weren't even touching the controls, sir!"

Austin pushed his way past the bugs and looked out the hatchway. The outer hatch was just gone. He could see the cable floating loose in the maelstrom. The hatch must have ripped it off the side of the ship when it went. He couldn't see Weitz or Bakar in the swirling colors. "Weitz, Bakar!" he called again through the intercom. "Report."

Nothing. The screams had stopped. "Anthyrus?" he called. "Can you see Weitz and Bakar?"

"Sir?" came an immediate response in his mind.

"What?" growled Austin.

"I cannot reach Ensign Anthyrus's mind from here, sir. I'm sorry. I cannot translate your orders at this time."

"Dammit!"

Austin continued to stare at the swirls for several minutes. He had never felt so helpless. There was absolutely nothing he could do to help Bakar and Weitz. Vertigo eventually set in, and he had to turn away or risk throwing up in his helmet. He looked at the remains of his crew. The shloags stood at attention.

Austin wanted to be furious with the bugs. He wanted to blame them for the loss of Weitz and Bakar. Somebody…some traitor…had cost him two men—real men—and Austin wanted nothing more than to punish those responsible. But the bugs were right. Neither of them had been anywhere near the controls when the hatch exploded. And they had saved everyone they could reach. He came to attention in front of Moog and Gorm, and saluted them. "Good job, men," he said. "Without your quick thinking and strong…um…limbs, we all would have been lost."

Soto and Kuczku slumped against the wall on either side of the hatch. He could read the despair in Soto's face even though most of her angular features were hidden beneath the helmet. The bird was harder to read, but…something jarred Austin's memory. "Ensign Kuczku!" he yelled.

"Sir?"

"You screamed in my head right before the hatch blew." Austin felt he had found his traitor, and stared the v't'Danga down. "How did you know what was going to happen?"

Kuczku's head weaved back and forth as it tried to get both eyes on his commander's eyes. "I did not know, sir," came the mental reply at last. The bird slumped back against the wall again. "I felt…something…invade my mind…it stabbed at my thoughts with an intense, almost fanatical hatred. I…I think there's something…alive…inside this ship, sir!"

"Alive?" Austin asked. "But fern, I mean Ensign Anthyrus stated there were no significant life signs. What could be—"

'A ghost." said Soto. Her almond-shaped eyes had gone wide and her olive skin paled.

Austin shook his head, thinking that Soto's ancestry was showing itself a little too thickly. Her people might believe in ghosts, but this was the 25th century, by God. "Don't be ridicu…" he started.

But, the bugs clicking, chittering, and buzzing stopped him in mid-sentence. He waited for the translation. "We know next to nothing about the szyzulan, sir! They may have the ability to manifest after death."

Manifest? That must have been Kuczku's word, thought Austin. "Poppycock!" he said out loud.

"They do seem to have some mystical powers, sir" added Soto. "The way their ships fly through space as if they were in an atmosphere has dumbfounded us for years."

'There is a presence aboard, sir," added Kuczku mentally. "Beyond that I care not to hypothesize. We should be careful."

"The Ensign is right," said Austin. He snapped back to attention. The crew did the same. "We came here with a mission. We will take all due precautions, but we must find a way punch our way back into normal space, and this ship is our only hope. We'll stick together and head toward engineering. It will most likely be at the back of the ship. Kuczku, you and I are up front. Moog and Gorm, guard the rear. Soto, keep an eye out for…anything unusual."

The mood of the crew was subdued, and they moved through the empty ship in silence for some time. Austin was struck by the odd structure of the ship. The main compartment was basically an oblong cigar, and the wings curved gracefully toward the back of the ship. But there were no curved lines inside the ship. The corridors were triangular and ran in straight lines, intersecting in star patterns in what he guessed was the middle of the ship. But there was no central corridor that ran the length of the raider, so they found themselves meandering from the center to the very edge and back again.

They checked each chamber they came across, but had not found Engineering yet, and their air supply was nearing half-full. They also had found no szyluzan, nor had Kruczka felt the presence of their "ghost" since leaving the airlock.

"Where's the crew?" asked Soto after they opened the hatch to another empty chamber.

Inside were bunks and cabinets stocked with odd-looking personal items, including something that Austin thought looked like a rotary polisher, which he had seen in several other rooms. It was all the same, each time.

"I don't know," Austin replied as he closed the hatch. "I guess the ghost got them all." His tone was only partly sarcastic. The dead, silent raider was starting to get to his nerves as well. "But if we don't find engineering soon, we'll have to turn back. We still need to find another airlock and then set up a new cable, and our air is getting low."

Moog chattered and buzzed. Austin recognized the slightly deeper timber of its clicks. Kuczku translated: "The air in here is breathable, sir. A little thin, but we should be fine if we're careful."

"Let me check, first," said Austin. He snapped off his helmet and took a tentative breath. The air was stale, and it did feel a little like mountain air. Strangely, there was no stench of decay. Perhaps the crew had abandoned the ship? "It seems fine. But if there is someone on this raider who can control the airlocks, we still need to be cautious. We'll remove helmets in shifts to conserve our oxygen. Moog, you, me, and Kuczku first, and then in ten minutes, we'll shift. That should about double our remaining air. Save at least twenty minutes in your tank for the return trip through the maelstrom."

They moved on down the corridor again with their helmets snapped to their belts. But as they entered the next star-shaped intersection, Kuczku screamed, "Duck!" into all of their minds. The crew dove to the floor. Austin heard a sharp crack beside him. Something warm and wet sprayed onto his cheek.

He turned his head and saw Moog lying dead on the floor next to him. The shloag's tear-drop-shaped head had been caved in by what appeared to be a large chunk of cut stone. The stone was a jet black octahedron roughly two feet from point to point, and over a foot wide in the middle. It was a huge, black diamond, steaming in the growing puddle of Moog's yellow blood!

"That's…" began Soto, who lay on the other side of the dead shloag.

"I know,' cut in Austin. He pushed away from the pool of blood and knelt with his back up against one corner of the five-way intersection. He scanned the corridors, but saw nothing at all down any of them. "It's the exact shape as the boulders they hurl at our ships with their damn mass drivers. Where the hell did it come from?"

Gorm chattered and buzzed as he crawled to another corner. Kuczku translated. "From the angle of the impact and where the object ended up, I would guess it came from this corridor."

"Right," said Austin. "You heard the man. We go that way." He pointed down the corridor Gorm had indicated. "Somebody or something doesn't want us here. But Transglobal forces don't back down. Right men?"

A chorus of voices and translations all said, "Yes, sir!"

"Helmets back on and weapons out," he continued, pulling out his pulse pistol. "Gorm, get Moog's air tank. We'll come back for his body later."

Soto and Kuczku helped Gorm attach the extra tank on his back, and then they inched their way down the corridor, with Austin in the lead. Two more massive diamonds flew at them. Austin could have sworn he saw one appear in midair before it raced down the hallway. Perhaps it was a ghost. But he wasn't yet ready to share that thought with anyone else.

Kuczku warned of another diamond missile, but Austin didn't see anything. He dove to the floor as a pulse weapon fired behind him. "Got it!" yelled Soto. "That one came from behind us,' he said. "I never even saw it until Kuczku's warning."

"We're close," said Austin. "I can feel it."

"So can I," said Kuczku in his mind. "The entity is nearby. And it's not fanatical hatred I've been feeling. I…I think it's insane!"

The triangular corridor dead-ended not far past the last attack. A hatch separated them from what Austin was now sure must be engineering. He could feel the thrum of power in his bones just as surely as Kuczku could feel the presence of their ghost. The markings next to the hatch were also very different from those they had seen on the crew quarters.

"This is it, men…and ladies," he added, looking at Soto and Kuczku.

Gorm clicked and chittered. "I am also female, Lieutenant."

Austin had to smile. He'd never known. For that matter, before today, he probably wouldn't have cared. "I'm terribly sorry, Gorm. I…I meant no offense."

Chitter, chitter click: "None taken, sir."

Austin took a moment to survey his crew. They weren't such a bad bunch. "Are you…ladies ready?" he asked. "After what we've seen so far, there's no telling what might lie inside."

All three crewmen came to attention and saluted. Austin opened the hatch, thinking that if he were about to die, at least he would go surrounded by women.

The scene before them was eerie even by the standards of this bizarre day. The room was shaped much like the black diamonds that had been hurled at them, like they had stepped inside one of the octahedrons. The chamber was all strange angles and pointed corners. Even the ceiling rose to a point above their heads.

They had entered in the middle of one of the sides. Metal grate flooring provided a flat surface that stretched across the four-pointed chamber. The only problem was that the grating was littered with corpses—-szyzulan corpses.

The snakes looked no less menacing in death. They were easily eight feet tall and completely covered in overlapping scales, much like the exterior of the raider. Their inhumanly long arms and legs still bulged from underlying muscles, even in death. Their elongated, curving necks seemed to simply end in a wide, toothy grin, while at the other end, their tube-shaped bodies lengthened into thick tails that stretched out well past their clawed feet. They truly looked like snakes, even with those powerful limbs.

But, as far as Austin could tell, the bodies were the only thing in the room. It was completely empty, other than about two dozen dead snakes. If this was engineering, it was damned strange.

Gorm must have had similar thoughts. The shloag clicked and buzzed, followed by Kuczku's translation in his mind. "Where are the controls? The workstations? Where are the engines?"

"I wish I knew," Austin replied. "I was sure this would be engineering. Can't you feel the power of the place?"

The others nodded. Austin was about to close the hatch, but he noticed a faint glow coming from one of the corners to their right just as Kuczku said, "It's here," and then fell to the floor in a heap.

Austin and Soto knelt down next to the translator. Soto lifted Kuczku's helmet and rested it on her knee. "Are you all right?" asked the midshipman.

Kuczku's bulbous eyes were closed, but Austin could tell that they were moving rapidly under the leathery eyelids. Her body quivered as if she were cold or frightened. "Ensign!" he called to her. "Kuczku! Wake up!"

A weak reply entered his brain. "It's…fighting…me. Can't… So much…pain!"

Austin looked at Soto. "Whatever's fighting her is in that room. Stay with the ensign. I'm going in." He stood and checked his pulse pistol. "Gorm! You're with me. Stay sharp!"

There was no reply. Damn, with the translator out, he was as good as alone. Austin patted Gorm on the back and tried using standard military hand signals to indicate what he needed. He was mildly impressed when the yeoman nodded. That skill was only required of officers and marines. He gave her a thumbs-up.

Gorm, holding a pulse rifle in her two front limbs, scuttled into the chamber ahead of Austin. He quickly moved in and took the lead. "Follow me," he signed as he picked his way through the dead bodies toward the glow in the corner. "Watch out for projectiles."

Their boots clanked on the metal floor and the echoes came back to them in odd patterns as the sound bounced around the diamond-shaped room. Gorm chittered and fired her pulse rifle behind Austin. He turned, expecting to see another flying, black diamond. Instead, he faced two hulking snakes coming toward them.

"My God!" cried Austin. "They're alive." But it was almost immediately obvious that the szyluzans were not alive. Their narrow heads lolled off to the side and their beady eyes were closed. Plus, they lurched unsteadily across the chamber, their outstretched arms flailing like zombies in a bad holovid.

Austin fired three quick blasts of charged plasma at the snake closest to Gorm, shattering several layers of the zombie-snake's protective scales, but doing no real harm. Gorm fired again, this time aiming for the creature's knee, which nearly buckled from the rifle blast. Austin concentrated his shots on the same knee, finally cutting through the beast's armored skin and ripping the leg off at the knee.

The dead snake fell to its remaining knee, twitched a few times, and tried to crawl towards them, but then dropped to the metal flooring and lay still. Gorm and Austin looked at each other, then as one, turned their weapons on the second zombie. After several shots from each weapon, they cut through its leg as well.

Austin gave his crewman another thumbs-up and turned back toward the glowing corner, certain that it was their destination. The closer they got to it, the more the ship seemed to throw at them. As if the thought were prophetic, he turned right into the flailing arms of two more snake zombies. Where the hell did they come from? Didn't I just leave this party? One of the snakes knocked the pulse pistol from his hand while the other clawed at his space suit, ripping a huge gash in the side of the steel-enforced fabric.

As he grappled with the huge snakes, Austin heard Soto's voice over the intercom. "Whatever you're going to do…hurry, Lieutenant!" he cried. "Oh my Go—"

The transmission went dead. Austin tried to pull free from the zombie snakes, but they swarmed all over him. It was all he could do to stay standing under the onslaught. "Shoot, Gorm!" he called over the radio. "Blast us all if you have to. We must get to that corner!"

But Gorm didn't shoot. He could hear the shloag's clicking and buzzing voice in his earpiece, but without the translation, it meant nothing to the lieutenant. Then, all of a sudden, he was loose. Austin fell to the floor and rolled away from the zombies.

He looked back and saw Gorm, reared up on just her hind legs, towering over the two zombie snakes. She held them off the ground in either hand, while her middle legs pummeled their scaly bodies. But the snake's claws had ripped through Gorm's suit and Austin could see yellow blood oozing from several wounds in the shloag's body.

Gorm clicked once in his ear and shrugged her head toward the corner. Austin jumped to his feet and ran toward the glow, jumping over snakes who clawed at his feet. For some reason none of them rose to stop him, but he almost fell several times as their scaly arms tried to trip him.

Austin reached the corner and stood, dumbfounded for a moment. Set in a niche cut into the corner hung a wrinkled mass of organic flesh. It seemed to glow with some inner light that pulsed in an erratic, or perhaps impossibly intricate, pattern. It was held in the air within the niche by tubes that connected to the wrinkled, bluish mass at the top and bottom, and on both sides.

Austin heard a thud behind him and turned to see Gorm lying on the floor beneath the still forms of the two snakes she'd been battling. Two more snakes twitched and pushed themselves off the floor next to Austin. No time to think, so Austin acted on gut instinct.

He grabbed what could only be called a brain and yanked hard. The tubes held onto the brain for a moment, but the soft flesh finally gave, ripping at the connections as he pulled it from the small alcove. Austin felt more than heard a scream of pain inside his mind as he pulled the brain free from its housing. Gray ooze spilled from the holes in the wrinkled flesh.

Austin turned back toward the newest zombie. They faltered for a moment, and then lurched forward again. When the first one struck at him with its claws, Austin thrust the brain forward, impaling it on the snake's claws. Another scream echoed in his head, and then both snake zombies dropped to the floor without even a twitch. The glow from inside the brain faded…and the lights in the raider all went black.

The lieutenant clicked on the flashlight attached to his wrist and picked his way back across the room. Gorm was alive, but badly injured, and her space suit was torn to shreds. Austin pulled the shloag's helmet off so she could breathe.

"I'll be back," he said, and then rushed out to check on Soto and Kuczku. The translator was back on her feet, but Soto was dead, her helmet and head smashed in by a damned black diamond.

He clapped Kuczku on the shoulder. "Too many dead heroes today," he said. "But we have to help the living ones. I'll need Soto's space suit and air supply. Can you retrieve Moog's suit? Gorm will need it if she has any chance."

27.02.2401 ESD | 19:00 HOURS | ETS MIRUBOOTO | SHIP'S REPORT | CHIEF ENGINEER GRANT AUSTIN

IT HAS BEEN OVER TWO MONTHS SINCE OUR ILL-FATED EVA INTO THE RAIDER SHIP, AND I'M STILL UNSURE WHAT HAPPENED. IT SEEMS OBVIOUS THAT THE BRAIN HAD SOME IMPRESSIVE MENTAL POWERS, INCLUDING TELEKINESIS AND SOME SORT OF MENTAL ATTACK THAT IT USED ON ENSIGN KUCZCU. BUT EVEN NOW, THAT THOUGHT SEEMS LUDICROUS TO ME, EVEN THOUGH KUCZKU'S RACE, THE D'T'DANGA, OBVIOUSLY HAVE MENTAL POWERS OF THEIR OWN.

WHAT SEEMS MORE AMAZING IS THAT THE BRAIN SEEMED TO BE POWERING THE ENTIRE SHIP. ALL OF THE RAIDER'S SYSTEMS WENT DEAD THE MOMENT THE BRAIN CEASED FUNCTIONING. OUR SUBSEQUENT SEARCH OF THE "ENGINE ROOM" FOUND THREE MORE BRAINS—ONE IN EACH CORNER—AND ALL INERT.

I DON'T THINK WE'LL EVER KNOW WHAT HAPPENED TO THE SHIP AND ITS CREW, BUT KUCZKU SEEMS TO BELIEVE THAT THE LAST BRAIN WENT INSANE AND KILLED THE OTHER THREE, PERHAPS OUT OF PARANOIA, AND THEN PROCEEDED TO KILL THE CREW AS WELL. SOUNDS PLAUSIBLE ENOUGH, BUT ONLY AFTER SEEING EVERYTHING I HAVE SEEN. UNFORTUNATELY, WE HAVE NO PROOF.

BUT WE ARE BACK IN NORMAL SPACE, AND LIMPING TOWARD A NEARBY STAR SYSTEM. WE HAVE MIDSHIPMAN GORM TO THANK FOR THAT. IT WAS HER BRAINSTORM THAT SAVED US FROM A SLOW DEATH IN THE MAELSTROM, AND I THANK THE GODS OF ALL OUR RACES THAT SHE SURVIVED THE ATTACK IN THE RAIDER ENGINE ROOM.

OVER THE LAST TWO MONTHS, WE WERE ABLE TO ATTACH THE HULL OF THE RAIDER TO THE BROKEN ENDS OF STRUT NUMBER ONE. GORM REASONED THAT THE ODD, CRISSCROSSING HALLWAYS OF THE ALIEN SHIP, ONCE FILLED WITH PLASMA, WOULD CONDUCT POWER BETWEEN THE SINGULARITY DRIVE AND THE SUBSTRUCTURE OF *MIRUBOOTO*.

IT WORKED PERFECTLY AND WE WERE ABLE TO GENERATE ENOUGH POWER ON FIVE STRUTS TO OPEN A HYPERSPACE THRESHOLD. THE STRAIN MUST HAVE BEEN TOO MUCH ON THE RAIDER, THOUGH, AS IT DISINTEGRATED SHORTLY BEFORE WE ENTERED NORMAL SPACE, TAKING WITH IT ALL PROOF OF THE BRAIN-OPERATED SHIP.

IT SHOULD BE NOTED THAT MIDSHIPMEN BAKAR AND WEITZ DIED IN THE SERVICE OF THE TRANSGLOBAL ALLIANCE. ALSO LET IT BE KNOWN THAT MIDSHIPMAN SOTO AND YEOMAN MOOG GAVE THEIR LIVES IN THE HEROIC DEFENSE OF THEIR SHIPMATES AND SHOULD BE AWARDED THE GOLD SHIELD POSTHUMOUSLY. MIDSHIPMAN GORM AND ENSIGN KUCZKU SHOULD ALSO RECEIVE THE GOLD SHIELD FOR THEIR HEROIC DEEDS ABOARD THE SZYLUZAN RAIDER. IT HAS BEEN AN HONOR TO SERVE WITH ALL OF THESE CITIZENS....

Austin replaced the voicedat recorder in its slot on the panel and scanned the report. Then, just as he had a dozen times in the last two months, he reached out and pressed delete, saving only the last paragraph. Even with proof, nobody would ever believe the report as written. And he'd had enough reprimands in his career. His file didn't need a psych notation as well. Austin picked up the voicedat recorder and began again.

WILL MCDERMOTT NORMALLY PLAYS IN OTHER PEOPLE'S WORLDS. HE has written two novels (*Judgment* and *The Moons of Mirrodin*) and six short stories in the *Magic: The Gathering* Universe, two short stories in Monte Cook's *Diamond Throne* role-playing setting, and most recently finished a *Necromunda* novel for Games Workshop. This is Will's first foray into his own universe, a galaxy-spanning future of exploration, conquest, and racial tension. Will lives in Hamburg, New York, with his wife, three children, and one large, insane dog.

THE LAW OF THE KUZZI

James Chambers

THE BOYS HUNKERED LOW ON THE SHEET-METAL PLATFORM AND WAITED for the next chromatic eruption to illuminate the night. They were not supposed to be there, high up on the narrow catwalk that topped one tower of the New Dodge dew wells. The fragile array of thermal reactive sheeting, strung on hinges between several makeshift framework structures, captured condensation and funneled it into low, squat tanks in the valley below. The settlers had salvaged the sheeting from the *Triumphant*'s massive cooling system, yet durable as it was, its reactive coating eventually grew stale with wear. After more than four decades on Byanntia, they had little left unused in storage. Bad enough it was dangerous for the boys climbing around on the lightweight structures untended in the dark, but lately, the dew wells had proven barely adequate to bolster the water supply of the community. Damage to even one tower could jeopardize lives.

Such thoughts, though, were as far from the boys' minds as Byanntia was from Earth. Tonight was a celebration, and the trio had been anticipating the promised fireworks through months of hard toil and rigorous schooling—ever since Thom Horton and Mick Busco had announced finding the necessary raw materials to make explosives. In each boy's pocket nestled a rare cigar, pilfered with care from the storehouse where they had spent the past several decades in nulltemp storage, doled out in miserly fashion to celebrate new births and other momentous occasions. Despite some of the farmers' efforts to cultivate tobacco crops, the addictive weed would not take root in the Byanntian soil. Thus, they could only obtain fresh smoking supplies on the periodic trade vessels from Earth. The next ship, due in two weeks, would replenish the humidor. The boys hoped the new stock would cover the three missing stogies. It was a calculated risk, but then, so was everything on Byanntia.

Although they knew the importance of the dew well arrays, the boys felt confident that they could come and go without harming them. Not only did the tower offer a secret place where the three friends could savor their booty free of adult interference, but it provided the best unobstructed vantage point for the pyrotechnics. Up here, the boys were eye-level with the fireworks.

A screaming whistle sheared the dry air, then went silent while sparks of gold fire scintillated across the black sky. They blotted out the endless twinkling stars above and left afterimages floating in the boy's eyes.

The next rocket shrieked upward, producing a palpable concussion and a rainbow of shimmering, metallic flickers.

The third turned the world crimson and tangerine and illuminated the landscape like a miniature red sun.

That's when Frank Duncan spotted the long, dark shape trundling over the eastern hills. "Hey," he said, jamming his elbow into Colt Bukowski's ribcage. "You see that?"

"See what?" asked Colt. "Fireworks are damn near burning out my retinas."

"Man, quit griping, already, will you?" snapped Grant Drasinovich. "It's always something with you."

"Well, we're not even supposed to be up here," nagged Colt. "We get caught, and you know we're spending the next month digging trenches for the irrigation system overhaul."

"No one's going to find us," Grant grumbled.

Three rockets erupted with a rhythmic crackling, their green and amber light painting the air.

"There it is again," said Frank, pointing. "Way out there. Up in the hills."

"I don't see anything," Colt answered.

"Wait," interjected Grant. "I see it. Up on the ridge near that willow sapling, right? Looks like some stray kison calves—oh, damn, I just lost them."

"No, not there. Lower," Frank said. He palmed the back of Grant's head and turned it.

"Oh. Coming down the eastern trail. Yeah, I see it. Looks like a Crawler," Grant said. "Is that smoke coming out of it?"

Frank squinted and shielded his eyes with his hand as an electric, champagne burst brightened the shadows and thrust the damaged Crawler into stark view. It was headed toward New Dodge. A column of dark smoke wafted from its rear section. The gentle burbling of its motor reached across the plain.

"Who could be out there? Everyone's in the town square for the party," said Colt, now seeing the vehicle. "We better tell your Dad about this, Frank."

"Yeah, you're right," Frank agreed. "Let's go."

"But what about the fireworks? And the cigars?" pleaded Grant. "It's probably just someone coming in late from Verdi's Plain. Geddy McCarthur herds his kison out that way sometimes, and you know he's always late for town events."

"No way, man. I saw Geddy dipping into the punch with old man Matson before we left." Frank raised an eyebrow and pitched an impatient glare his friend's way. "Besides, that Crawler look like any model you've ever seen before?"

The Crawler was larger than any of those in New Dodge: heavier, with stronger treads, and reinforced siding. The boys had seen that much in the tide of light coming from the steady bombardment of cheerful explosions. Grant shook his head and grunted his concession. "No."

A moment later, the boys were scrambling down the latticework toward the dusty earth. They leapt the final four feet to the ground, each rolling to his knees for an instant, before they raced off toward the lights and voices of New Dodge.

In the foothills, the Crawler continued its slow progress toward the settlement. Behind it, tall, slender figures crested the ridge, topping the lone, young willow there by several feet. They stood in silent appraisal of what filled the once-empty valley: the building and lights of New Dodge, all of it as alien and unwanted as the short, baldish creatures that dwelled there. They were disturbing, these beings who draped their bodies in patches of cloth and fiber, who worked the land in strange ways, grappling and struggling with it, forcing it to their own ends, rather than living in accord with the natural rhythms. Even the cycle of the Gr'nar, among the most powerful natural forces on Byanntia, had not been enough to cow the obstinacy of these brash and defiant beings called "men" and "women." Tonight would be different. So it had been decided in the hearts and minds of the stealthy watchers. On this night, the frail human parasites would glimpse the real soul of Byanntia, and then their true measure would be taken.

Far from the darkness of the hills, picnic tables cluttered the town square. The people of New Dodge feasted on fresh kison, whole grain breads, young stinger leaves, and cakes and pies baked with the meager surplus of sugar, cream, and dried fruit donated by the surrounding ranches and farms. From the walls of the school, the medical center, and the administration building, which most people called "Town Hall," hung strings of cold, glowing lanterns dripping soft light onto the festivities. A makeshift band of fiddle, guitar, horns, and drums played a fast-paced song that set many party-goers to dancing.

The entire day had been spent this way, given over to the arduous effort of eating, drinking, relaxing, and laughing. It was a rare occasion in the hardworking community, one that delivered an invigorating break from work and routine. It was a true holiday, a fête of distinctly Byanntian nature, different from those times small groups of settlers paid their respects to their origins by observing the holidays they had carried with them from Earth. This day, this observance, could only be celebrated on Byanntia and only by the people of New Dodge.

Back on Earth, before the settlers left, before even the *Triumphant* had been built and their equipment gathered, their journey charted and planned, their lives uprooted and cast upon a new course, scientists and researchers had issued an analysis of their chances for survival. It came in the form of a one-hundred gigabyte document that contained instructions, guidelines, and databases designed to increase their chances of founding a permanent settlement in thirty-seven different environments. Among all that information, a single statistic imprinted itself on the minds of the settlers: the scientifically derived fact that their chances of success rose from 22.7 percent to 64.3 percent if they lasted for eighteenth Byanntian months.

Today marked the forty-first anniversary of the first Turning Point, that historic first day of the settler's nineteenth month on Byanntia, which had marked a new phase of hope and optimism that carried them through many of the bleak times that had followed in the ensuing decades.

Even the dour Stuart Duncan felt the high spirits electrifying the crowd tonight. At a table near the edge of the square, he craned his neck upward to take in the pyrotechnics display and considered the hardships the people of New Dodge had overcome—the missteps and the close calls, the friends and family members lost and put to rest in the semi-arid soil of their adopted home. He thought, too, of the many laid in the ground for whom this planet was the land of their birth, for only those who had come on the *Triumphant*—the First—could rightly call this place adopted, and when they lost one from among the second or third generations, the tragedy always seemed somehow greater than losing a member of the First. Still, they carried on.

Each of the settlers shouldered part of the burden, but Stuart felt its pressure more than most in his post as sheriff. He knew these were good people who surrounded him, every one of them, but disagreements were inevitable. Differences of opinion were as common here as they had been on Earth. Such things could poison a place like New Dodge, a town barely past its infancy for all its years on the ground, and now, finally, taking its first steps toward a greater permanence. Duncan and the town leaders did their best and so far it had sufficed. They had guided the town to another Turning Point. But with one weight lifted from his shoulders, Stuart knew that others waited in the days ahead.

Sharon Duncan hooked her arm through the crook of her husband's elbow and twined her fingers around his, rubbing their deep calluses. She leaned toward him and whispered, "Lighten up, Stu. Relax. It's a party, remember?"

"I am relaxed," he claimed with a broad smile.

"Uh-uh. I know that look. It's one hundred percent pensive. There's not a slack muscle in your body. So, you listen to me. If there's anyone here who has earned a night off, it's you. It's the Turning Point, and you got us here through another year. Now, enjoy it for a couple of hours, because tomorrow, it's back to business as usual for everyone," Sharon said.

Duncan scooped the back of his wife's head with his broad, thick-knuckled hand, and pressed her lips to his, holding her there for a long moment while the warm breeze passed between them. Breaking away, he said, "You're right, you know."

"Of course I am, darling," Sharon purred. "When was the last time I was wrong?"

Stuart knew the best answer to that question, but the teasing reply dissipated at the sound of a familiar voice calling to him—Frankie, hollering from the far edge of town. He turned and saw his son racing across the outskirts of the buildings, his two best friends hard on his heels, all of them pounding their legs like the Gr'nar was breathing down their necks. Stuart shifted around on the picnic bench and waited.

"Bet I know where they've been," he said to Sharon, his expression hardening.

"That boy," Sharon muttered as she felt her husband's shoulders draw tight. "Don't let him ruin your night, Stu."

"It's not my night about be ruined," he replied.

"Dad!" Frankie yelled again. He stumbled to a stop, skidding to one knee in the dirt, and knelt there panting, trying to speak. "Dad," he repeated.

Grant and Cole pattered up behind him, the two boys bending over and sucking air. The run into town had lasted just over a mile, but the boys had covered the distance like a sprint, bounding and leaping over rocks and gullies, pumping their legs to maximum speed, ignoring the blood pounding behind their eyes.

"Dad!" Frank belted out between gasps. "We got company! Someone's driving a Crawler down the east trail. We've never seen it before. It's on fire or something."

"What are you talking about, Frankie?"

"We saw it, Dad, coming this way. A strange Crawler. Smoke coming out of it," Frank huffed. "Coming down the east trail."

"So, you three were up in the well towers?" Duncan barked. "No other way you could see the east trail at night."

Frank grimaced. "Yeah, Dad, yeah, we were. I know we're not supposed to be messing around up there. We just wanted to see the fireworks. But listen, that Crawler we saw will be here soon. You can count on that. It's already inside the shield perimeter."

Frank's quick admission snapped Duncan into focus. Under other circumstances, the boy would have hemmed and hawed, searching for a way to avoid the punishment he knew he was due for disobeying his father and breaking the law. That Frank had owned up without skipping a beat made it clear how alarmed he was by what he had seen and that he was doing his best to warn the town. Duncan respected that. It was the kind of behavior he'd tried to teach his son, the kind of thinking it would take for New Dodge to survive over the long haul.

"All right, I believe you, Frankie. You did the right thing by telling me," Duncan said. "Don't get it into your heads that any of you three are off the hook for being up in the towers, but I appreciate what you've done. Now, listen, I got a job for you. Whoever is coming into town, it's probably best if we go out and meet them halfway, and until we know what we're dealing with, we don't need any diversions. So, I need you three to get down to the south clearing fast as you can and tell Thom and Mick to cut the fireworks short until they hear from me. Got it?"

All three serious-faced boys nodded.

"Then get going!" Duncan barked.

The trio took off at a dead run toward the town square and the meadow on the far side of New Dodge.

Duncan walked to a neighboring picnic table where the Matsons and the Hughes sat. Jacob Matson and Garris Hughes had broken off talk with their wives, distracted by Duncan's conversation with his son. The last few weeks had been nerve-wracking, for New Dodge suffered through its third drought this year, and the two men had watched the arrival of Frank and his friends with worry. The town had been teetering on a knife's edge of survival, and the settlers had come to despise unwanted intrusions. Bad enough the skirmishes with the Kuzzi they had weathered a few months back. Up until that bloody episode with the Gr'nar, the Kuzzi had more or less ignored them for years. But after Jacob Matson had single-handedly just about killed the legendary, invisible beast that came out of hibernation only every 68 years, the creatures had deposed their leader, the moderate Chief Bollatu, and tensions had flared. The conflict had settled down to a workable coexistence for the time being, but it was a long way from a permanent solution, barely enough to hold the lid on if nothing upset the balance.

Sheriff Duncan watched Jacob Matson rise, and he felt a pang about asking the man to exert himself. The lawman and the rancher were both well on in years, but Jacob had recently been diagnosed with a terminal illness and was already living and breathing three or four months beyond Doc Lieber's best expectations. And Jacob had lost his son Chad about fourteen months back, one of the first human victims of the Gr'nar. Chad had been meant to take over running Twin Feathers, the Matson's ranch, but that responsibility had now fallen to his brother Joseph. Duncan told the two men and their wives what Frank had reported.

"So, I need you fellows to raise the Guard. Figure our better halves can spread word to the crowd to keep it low key while we set up a blockade out on the east trail. I don't want that Crawler rolling in here until we know who's driving it and why. Bad enough the damn thing already made it inside shield range," Duncan said.

"Smart thinking, Stu," Matson agreed. "I'll go over to Town Hall, open the weapons vault, and prep some repellers. Want me to sound the alarm?"

"No," said Duncan. "Let's see if we can do this quietly. If it turns out to be nothing, I want folks to have a shot at getting back to the party."

"In that case, I'll round up the men, and we'll meet you on the trail," said Hughes.

Frank nodded and loped off toward the eastern end of town.

Elsewhere, the three boys elbowed their way through the crowd, jostling settlers and stepping on toes. They carved a pathway of surprised yelps and scolding shouts until they broke free on the other side. They flew downhill, letting the incline carry them until each step was almost a bound, covering far more ground than the boys' natural strides. They yelled and waved their arms the whole way. Thom and Mick paused at the sight of the trio, then lit a fresh rocket that blasted overhead, where it unleashed a ring of blue sparks. Mick pointed his lighter toward the fuse of the next round, but Grant plowed into him at full speed, knocking them both into a tumble on grass.

"Grant!" shouted Mick when they stopped rolling. "What the hell is your problem, boy? You trying to kill me?"

Frank filled them in on the situation while Thom helped his partner back to his feet. The two men set aside the next firework shell and squinted into the eastern blackness. Thom raised a pair of field glasses from their strap around his neck and peered through them toward the east.

"Don't like this," Thom commented. "Running a Crawler at night without lights is a good way to pitch yourself into a ditch. Must have a good reason for wanting to keep a low profile."

"More likely, it's a bad reason," said Mick. "I told you I saw someone over the ridge past Verdi's plain the other day. And there's no call for anyone to be out there this time of year."

"And I told you it must have been Kuzzi," Thom retorted.

"I know the difference between an eight-foot tall striped monster and a man," snapped Mick.

"Well, whatever it is, I can't say I'm ready to roll out a hearty welcome. Guess we better grab our repellers and hustle our rumps up there with the rest of the Guard," Thom decided.

"You fellas stay here and keep watch on the works," Mick said to the boys. "Not a good idea to leave them unattended. But don't even think about playing around with them. Need to be a trained professional to do it safely."

"No, you don't. It's easy," chided Grant. "Just hold the damn lighter to the fuse then duck. Hell, you can do it, I can do it."

Mick slapped Grant in the back of the head. "Don't even think about it. Mess with my fireworks, and I will make it my personal obsession to see you on waste reclamation duty for the rest of your pathetic childhood. I do not need to hear it from your father for the next ten years if you blow yourself to smithereens."

Thom doffed his field glasses and handed them to Frank. "Here, you can hold onto these, too. Was using them to spot our aim. They got night vision."

"Cool, thanks," Frank said.

With that, Thom and Mick dashed up the hill toward the town center.

Already, three men were marching to the eastern edge of town, armed with repellers and bolt throwers. The boys watched their silhouettes cross the steady glow from the lights at the power plant. A larger group of men trailed them, carrying picnic tables, which they turned over on their sides and set in the dirt to form a crude roadblock across the path, about fifty yards outside of town. Next came Garris Hughes and Richard Finch, shuffling along with shoulders bowed under the weight of a heavy *noonlight* that had once been part of *Triumphant*'s signal array. They planted it beside the tables. Finch swiveled the light's drum around and activated it.

Icy illumination painted the trail, turning it to afternoon for more than a hundred yards. As far away as they were, the sudden light still hit the boys with a sharp, harsh glare. The rumble of the Crawler drew closer while their eyes adjusted, and by the time they could stare straight on toward the arc of the noonlight, they could see the Crawler rolling across the edge of the shadow and nosing to a stop just inside the range of the light. Black smoke, coarse and oily in the brightness, drifted from the back engine compartment.

"Man, talk about timing," said Colt.

For a cold minute, nothing happened.

Stuart Duncan, Garris Hughes, and the Joseph Matson stood thirty or forty feet out in front of the makeshift checkpoint, repeller rifles hanging loose and ready in their hands. The Crawler idled, its engine gurgling and belching forth occasional bulbs of black soot that smelled of burning engine fluid. In the town square, the people of New Dodge grew silent and the band set down their instruments. The eyes of every settler turned toward the east, where spillover from the noonlight bounced and rippled on the flapping thermal sheeting of the distant dew wells. A stray wind caught some dust from the trail between the men and the Crawler, lifted it, spun it in a miniature cyclone that held for a moment, and then dropped it back to the ground.

With a mighty creak, the forward hatch of the Crawler swung outward and a man emerged, one hand cupped across his brow to take the edge off the artificial brightness. He took three steps down the trail and then stopped. One hand fumbled inside his coat until it emerged with a pair of desert sungoggles that he donned to protect his eyes.

He cleared his throat, and the sound carried through the silence.

"Well, Hiya," he called. "See you brought out the welcoming committee. Not necessary, but much appreciated. My name's Barnes Mungelson. My crew and I apologize for dropping in unannounced, but we could sure use some help."

Mungelson wore loose-fitting clothing of the kind favored by rangers and desert researchers for its comfort and protection from the sudden, swirling sandstorms that plagued the Junsuka. Several days' growth of beard spotted his jaw line. He looked tired and his left arm shook.

"Always happy to lend a hand to a neighbor," responded Duncan. "It's just that, well, pretty much every human who lives here on Byanntia happens to be down in the town square tonight. So, I think you can understand our intense *interest* in a new face. What business brings you our way?"

"Well, there's damn few humans on this ball of dirt and even less civilized living, that's no lie you're telling. I guess this must be the famous town of New Dodge," said Mungelson.

Duncan's eyes narrowed and he tightened his grip around the stock of his repeller. "Mr. Mungelson, I asked you a question," he stated.

Mungelson bristled.

"So you did, so you did," he muttered. He stuck one hand behind his back and waved two fingers toward the Crawler. "Doing research out in the damn desert brings me to Byanntia. Collecting samples, monitoring weather patterns, looking for signs of new and interesting life brings me to Byanntia. And given our current situation, I'd just as soon I had never set foot here. We hit a sinkhole coming across some dunes and slid into some submerged rocks. Banged up the Crawler real good. Our pickup isn't scheduled for another week, but we caught a bead on your satellite beacon and figured you were close enough for us to pull in to make some repairs."

"What outfit you with?" asked Duncan.

"LunaTech," said Mungelson. "Got all our papers and permits in the Crawler. Be happy to show them to you, though I have to say, I wouldn't mind knowing your name first."

"I'm Sheriff Stuart Duncan," he said. "I expect we'll be able to help you fix that Crawler. We got some spare parts and half-a-dozen crack mechanics. But I'll take you up on that offer, I think. So, let's see those papers, meet your crew, and have a look at your cargo."

"Sure, sure, Sheriff," Mungelson said. He rotated, waving for Duncan to follow him. "Come on with me, and I'll introduce you to my guys. One of them is injured. Sprained his ankle digging the Crawler free. He'll be all right, but I suppose he wouldn't mind some painkillers if you have a doctor in town."

"We do," said Duncan. "We'll see to his injuries as soon as we take care of business."

"All right, then," replied Mungelson. He reached up to the hatch and pulled himself back into the Crawler.

Duncan looked over his shoulder at Garris Hughes, and whispered, "You catch that signal he flashed back to the Crawler?"

"I noticed it," Hughes said.

"All right, then," said Duncan. "Keep us covered. I'm not back in a reasonable amount of time, pull everyone into the square and get ready to blast this bunch to dust and debris if they cross the town line."

Hughes nodded.

Through the field glasses, Frank saw his father's subtle wave, hand at his side, in silent signal to Joseph Matson and Richard Finch. The two men broke off from the group, outside of the range of the noonlight, and disappeared into the night. Frank tried to track them, switching the glasses back to night vision, but the plume of smoke flooding out of the Crawler obscured his view.

"I don't believe it!" blurted Colt. "Your dad is going into the Crawler."

"Yeah," Frank said, dangling the field glasses from his neck. "Guess he wants to make sure everything is all right before he lets these people into town."

"You think that's a good idea?" asked Colt. "Going in alone?"

"What do you think they're going to do, Colt? Kidnap him and run? Where would they go? They obviously need our help. It'll be fine. You know my Dad. Has to have everything signed on the dotted line before he so much as takes a leak. He's just being careful."

"That Crawler has seen better days, I'll tell you," observed Grant. He took the field glasses from Frank and scanned the vehicle. "Look at those scratches and gouges. Must have been some pretty sharp, hard rock to take chunks of metal like that out of it. Back tracks are off alignment. Probably leaking fluids under there, too."

"Well, I figure we can get it fixed for them," Frank said. "As long as we got Choi and Tomlinson around, there's not much mechanical work we can't do."

"You think your dad is going to have our hides for being up in the dew towers?" wondered Grant. "That was pretty damn stupid, I guess. Not that we hurt anything."

Frank shrugged. "He won't let us off, you know that."

"Look, he's coming out!" blurted Colt.

Duncan emerged from the cabin of the Crawler, and the boys fell silent, captivated by the ongoing exchange on the edge of town. The stranger followed. The two men shook hands in the vehicle's shadow.

Duncan returned to the checkpoint. "They back, yet?" he asked Hughes.

"Nope," Hughes said. "So, what do you make of these guys?"

"Everything seems to be in order. Got the papers from LunaTech, just like he said, notarized by a duly appointed representative of the United Rim. And he showed me a few bins of samples they got stored. Still, something doesn't feel right," Duncan explained. "That Crawler has taken a beating, something more than just tipping over on some sandy rock, I'd say. And there's a strange smell in there. Faint. Can't place it, but I know I've smelled it before."

"Papers can be forged. Samples can be faked," Hughes noted.

"Sure can," acknowledged Duncan. "And I'm no soil scientist to say whether their rocks and dirt are the genuine article or not."

"Want me to send Pete Dawson to fetch Professor Ridley? He'll tell you in a second if the stuff is genuine," suggested Hughes.

"Already thought of that," Duncan said. "And I see it this way—if they're on the up and up, no problem. If they're not, the sooner they think we're onto them, the sooner this could turn ugly. I think we should get them under control, separate them from that Crawler, and then we can get down to the nut of this on our terms."

"Why don't we just send them packing?" said Hughes.

"Broken down and injured? They need a place to go. Can't be sure they'll leave if we tell them to. They could just linger around out in the foothills and make trouble for us. Or worse, they might find their way into the squatter camp and rile that bunch up. More trouble we don't need. Better to keep them where we can see them," Duncan said. "And, Hell, who knows—maybe they're just who they say they are."

"I kind of doubt it, but all right; we'll clear the trail another sixty yards or so to the vehicle shed. That Crawler ought to be able to make it. I can post fifteen, twenty men to block the path toward the square," Hughes said.

"Do it," said Duncan.

The sheriff approached the Crawler and waited for Mungelson. He surveyed the odd damage to the vehicle, the scratches and dents left as if something had raked across the hard shell and tried to pound its way into the interior. A hairline crack ran through the windshield, and Duncan pondered a dozen scenarios that could have broken glass made to withstand an avalanche. He felt satisfied by none of them.

Mungelson ambled out of the Crawler and met Duncan at the center of the trail.

"Have your guys follow my men to the garage. Then we'll get you squared away and see about some food and sleeping quarters for the night," Duncan said.

"That sounds better than fine, Sheriff. I'm grateful to you, my new friend," replied Mungelson, a toothy smile creasing his broad face.

"Now, just hold off on all that," clipped a clear, stern voice from the darkness beyond the edge of the trail. Joseph Matson and Finch emerged into the light, their repellers up and cocked, one aimed at Mungelson and the other at the Crawler. Something coarse and wet dangled from the crook of Matson's arm and flapped in the half-hearted wind. The men's expressions lit an anxious fire in Duncan's gut.

"Whatever line of bull this scum has been feeding you, Stu, forget it. Him and his men are dirty poachers and liars. There's blood all over the back tracks of this Crawler, and we found this in a broken storage compartment back there," Matson said. "Thing is full of them."

He hurled the fresh skin to the ground.

It fluttered in the tepid breeze and unfurled, its blue, black, and gray striping unmistakable, as were the dark red patches of blood spotting it. A caustic odor rose from the dead flesh, the same scent Duncan had sensed in the Crawler, but stronger, an odor he now recalled from when men had fought and killed for the right to keep this stretch of ground they called home.

"Kuzzi hide," uttered Duncan.

Cold dread filled him then melted away to searing rage.

Duncan swung once, the blow so unexpected and fast that Mungelson took it flat in the center of his face without quite knowing what had hit him. He doped it out seconds later after he had dropped to the ground, rolled once, and came to rest on his back. Duncan lurched over him with his repeller aimed at the poacher's heart. His knuckles were numb, but he felt confident his fingers could still squeeze the trigger.

Back in the clearing, Grant, still watching through the field glasses, cried out, "No way! Your dad just decked the guy, Frankie."

"Give!" Frank ordered, seizing the field glasses, raising them to his eyes. "Oh, man, that's a Kuzzi skin on the ground. These guys are hunters!"

"Outlaws," Colt said. "Then that means they're armed."

Looking down at the wounded man, Duncan brimmed with venom. "Give me one good reason not to blast a hole in every single one of you sleazy sons of bitches," he growled.

The vengeful edge in his voice shocked his friends as much as it did Mungelson. Hunting Kuzzi was illegal, punishable on Earth by life in psychiatric rehab, but that had not stopped a black market for the creature's hides and organs from springing up. People who measured their souls in wealth and power had proven more than willing to spend small fortunes for the pride of owning secret items made of genuine Kuzzi hide, or for the pleasure of consuming the tiny clusters of glands in their chests that contained a rare chemical that was hallucinogenic in humans. There was more than enough money in it to tempt men like Mungelson, ample lucre to pay for their ships, bribe officials, and purchase the equipment needed to land in the wilderness. A week's hunt could garner a hundred hides for clever, stealthy hunting parties, though the Kuzzi often proved dangerous prey. Career poachers were a rare breed. One who survived more than four hunts earned the tag of veteran, and those few who lasted six often earned enough to retire for the balance of their lives and live like kings. Not many did, though.

Everyone waited for Mungelson's answer, their attention fixed to the steady black hole at the end of Duncan's repeller.

Mungelson wiped his blood on his sleeve and cleared his throat. "They're jes' animals," he slurred. "Not human."

"They're intelligent," Duncan retorted.

"By whose standards?" burbled Mungelson. "They're savages! Wild beasts! Dirty creatures roaming the hills with no more sense of social structure than a pride of lions. Sophisticated, yeah, but not like men. Way I heard it, the whole lot of them have just been biding their time waiting to see you killed by the Gr'nar. And yet, here you are, defending them?"

"This is their world, not yours," Duncan said. "They're not supposed to be like men. It doesn't mean we're free to murder them."

Mungelson laughed. "It ain't murder, and I really don't care what you have to say. I thought we might work out an arrangement like reasonable, worldly men, Sheriff, but I'm just as happy to do this the hard and unpleasant way. Now, throw that repeller over here or I'll have my men lob a *blisterbomb* into your happy little gathering down the road there."

The top hatch of the Crawler clanked open and a dirt-matted figure popped up, a broad launch tube poised on his shoulder. The glow of its targeting display colored his face a pale green. He pointed the weapon upward, indicating the arc that would carry its projectile into the town square. Duncan recognized the gun and knew its range, knew what it meant for the settlers.

The missile would cover the distance in less than two seconds, then explode twenty or so feet overhead, dispersing a liquid sheet of death that would drench anyone below it, burning through clothing to coat their body with thick, caustic oil. Within seconds, the settlers' skin would turn bright red and erupt with plump pustules and heavy blisters. The fumes would travel into their lungs and the same process would begin internally. Within a minute they would be lying on the ground, writhing, unable to move, barely able to breathe, and then the inflammations and lesions would swell and burst, carrying flesh away in great swaths shed like a snake's skin. In less than three minutes, all those caught in the blast spray would be dead and reduced to bone and molten meat. Duncan played it out in his head. He thought of Sharon, pictured her body decomposing inside and out while he stood by helpless to save her.

"I got a bead on this prick, Stu," said Finch, steadying his repeller on the man atop the Crawler. "Let me take him out, and end this right here."

Finch was a top marksman, but if he missed or failed to kill the poacher in one shot, it could mean a painful death for many of the settlers. "Just hold off there for now, Rich," Duncan said. "Now that we have the truth, I want to hear what Mr. Mungelson really wants."

The satisfied smirk on Mungelson's face burned Duncan, but he saw no option other than to stall until an opportunity presented itself. He activated the safety on his repeller and threw it to the ground. The poacher stood and brushed dirt from his clothes. He sniffled, produced a stained handkerchief, and pressed it to his face, shivering as pain shot through his head and down his neck.

"One hell of a punch you got there, Stu," he snarled as he groped around for the repeller and found it. "Impressive for an old fart. Any harder and I'd be breathing out the back of my neck."

"Let's hear it, Mungelson. What do you want?" Duncan demanded.

The poacher shook his head. "Damn fool you are. You and all your friends here. Trying to find a way to live with those foul beasts out there while Earth stews in its own filth, suckling at the meager teat of clean meat and produce you send back. Men could take this world, make it our own, and live like we were meant to—free! Instead you choose to scrape and sweat, spill your blood into the soil so it can drink it up in a heartbeat like it never even existed. You make me sick, *Stu*."

Mungelson pulled the handkerchief aside, opened his mouth and stuck two fingers in while he mimed gagging and choking.

"Just tell me what you want," blasted Duncan.

"Fine," said Mungelson. He drew himself up inches away from the sheriff and leaned in close to his face. "We want protection and shelter until our ship comes to take us away. And then we want use of your landing facilities. Those miserable Kuzzi are getting smarter. They caught wind of us early this time and they were waiting. Came at us in a horde while we were stowing our take from one of their hunting parties. Got some new, heavy weapon, battering ram kind of thing, like a redwood trunk. Nearly broke their way into our Crawler, except the thing is built like a tank.

We limped away from them, but they've been following us for two days. Thing is, we can't spend another week exposed in the wild and we can't risk them interfering when our ride comes. So, you and the rest of New Dodge are going to put us up until then, fix our Crawler, feed us, hide us from the Kuzzi, and then help us lift off. Got it?"

"If the Kuzzi have been tracking you, Mungelson, then they know you're here," Duncan said. "You're asking me to put New Dodge at risk."

"Understand something, here, Sheriff—New Dodge is already at risk. We used a fair number of blisterbombs fighting off the Kuzzi, but we got more than enough left to deal with your little shithole town here. So, I'm not asking you for anything, Stu. I'm telling you," Mungelson said.

"Think it through, Sheriff," Joseph Matson warned. "Even if we cover these animals for a week and then let them leave, the Kuzzi will know we helped our own kind get away with slaughtering their kind. They'll never trust us after that. Won't matter a bit that it was under duress."

"I know that, Joseph," Duncan said. "But what choice have we got?"

"Just take a minute to give it some thought, Sheriff. That's all I'm trying to say," Matson continued, and Duncan picked up on the young man's unspoken message—*buy some time.* Something had been set in motion. Duncan did not know what to expect, but he had faith in his friends.

"Go on and let me take the shot, Stu," pleaded Finch. "I'm telling you, I got this bastard dead to rights."

"Yeah, maybe you should," Duncan said, putting on a show of ambivalence. "Figure we don't take our chance now, we're just delaying the inevitable. We either fight this ragtag pile of kison turds or thousands and thousands of Kuzzi. Maybe we'll get lucky with these losers."

"Uh-uh," Mungelson said. "You listen to me before you do anything rash, Stu, because my associate atop the Crawler is but one member of my crew, armed with the firepower necessary to cripple your little tin-walled happyland here at the push of a button. Go ahead and kill him. Kill me if you think you're fast enough. You'll be signing death warrants for a lot of people and your own at the same time. Well, you got the facts. Rest is up to you, Sheriff."

"You're putting me in one hell of a spot here, Mungelson," Duncan said.

"Quit stalling. I ain't got time for shooting the breeze," the poacher spat back.

Duncan began to reply, but the blazing report of a bolt thrower cut him short.

The shot had come from the rear of the Crawler, the portion still cloaked in night, and the flash had pointed toward town. The poachers had a sniper mounted back there, out of sight, equipped with an infrared viewer and a long range weapon. Duncan cursed his stupidity for not anticipating such a maneuver as he whirled around and looked for the gunner's mark. A second shot fired. Through the narrow spaces between buildings, the sheriff saw Mick Busco and Thom Horton laid out on the ground at the edge of the town square. Jacob Matson knelt beside them, a pile of discarded repeller rifles at his feet, scattered alongside those dropped by Mick and Thom. Each man had been carrying an armful of weaponry. A small group, led by Doc

Lieber, broke off from the gathering and rushed to help the fallen men. Across the distance Duncan could not tell if they still lived.

Mungelson sneered. "Well, now, that's about the saddest attempt to fight back I ever did see."

Duncan looked to Joseph Matson and Finch for explanation. Both men's faces had gone pale. The marksman lowered his weapon "Damn sniper," Finch grumbled.

"I'm sorry, Stu. Dad thought Mick and Thom would get through with the guns, get the crowd spread out to defend the town," Matson said. "We set them up before we reported back to you. Figured it was worth a shot."

Duncan shrugged. "I suppose it was at that."

"Well, what's it gonna be?" Mungelson prodded. "As if I don't already know."

A knot tightened in Duncan's stomach. Every one of his muscles trembled with the desire to clutch Mungelson and beat him into silence. But there was nothing he could do. He hated his helplessness. If it had been only his own life at stake, he might have sacrificed it, so long as he could take Mungelson with him. But he had others to watch over and protect.

"Keep your shirt on, Mungelson. I may be ornery, but I know when I'm licked," Duncan said.

Mungelson's face broke into a wide, self-satisfied smile, but it faded fast.

A sanguine howl filled the moonless sky: a long, anguished accusation, answered by other voices joining it in a discordant chorus that rose together and meshed into a single outpouring of pain, injustice, and anger. It thinned the blood of all those who heard it. The tall, dry grass that grew off the trail rustled with movement beyond the range of the electric light. The guttural wailing continued, increasing in volume as it drew closer, and achieved a shrill, painful pitch before it ceased as abruptly as it had begun.

Mungelson seized Duncan by his shirt. "We got no time left!" he screamed. "Order your men to protect us. Now!"

Duncan ignored the poacher's frantic pleas. His attention fixated on the lithe form taking shape in the shadows by the rear of the Crawler. The towering figure stepped partway into the realm of the noonlight, where its powerful striped legs identified it as a Kuzzi warrior. The auburn embers of its eyes, still shrouded in darkness, conveyed its disposition. Muscles and sinew twisted and flexed and a bulky shape flew across the air. A poacher, his hands still wrapped around a bolt thrower, crashed to the dirt. A long spear angled with multiple blades and points protruded from between his shoulders.

A second Kuzzi joined the first, this one taller and stronger, its eyes enflamed with fury, its teeth bared and glowing in the dark. It stamped the dirt beside its wide taloned paws with the haft of its *purjung*, a spear identical to the one embedded in the sniper.

"Must be a hundred of them out there," said Finch.

"More," added Matson.

Guardsmen crouched behind the flimsy protection of the blockade, their weapons raised, their nerves buzzing with anticipation.

"Shoot! Shoot already," cried Mungelson. "What are you waiting for? You'll let them kill us all. Give the order, Sheriff, by the count of three, or I will have my man burn your town to extinction."

Mungelson leveled the repeller toward Duncan and began his count. He never finished it.

At "two," an explosion ripped across the air directly above the men, followed half a second later by two more. Even the noonlight paled in the sudden flash of colors that bit the men's eyes and turned their movements into strobed pantomimes of activity. In the increased illumination, Duncan saw the ranks of the Kuzzi spread out in semi-circles on each side of the trail, two or three deep in places, their lines stretching into the foothills and beyond sight. Their long, creamy fangs, slicked with saliva, protruded from black gums; the dark lips of their muzzles were drawn back in shallow snarls. Their eyes narrowed to bores of ferocity, and their shiny, black manes stood erect and pointed along the backs of their skulls and down the line of their spines. Each one clasped a twelve-foot purjung, arrayed with three or more blades.

There were not a hundred, but hundreds, possibly thousands stretching deep into the foothills, as if the entire Kuzzi nation had turned out in witness for the events of this dark night.

A gunshot cracked, but Duncan could not tell who had fired. The clashing glares tricked his vision. A second report snapped. He ducked in fear of stray shots, but no other gun spoke, and he crouched, uncertain whether to run or defend himself. He rubbed his eyes as the parti-colored flares faded, giving way to the steady clarity of the noonlight. What had happened had taken only seconds.

Mungelson lay sprawled in the trail, blood spattered across his leather tunic, his chest pumping in erratic gasps for breath as consciousness bled from him.

The poacher armed with the blisterbomb hung from the hatch of the Crawler, his rocket launcher lost in the dust beside the machine's tracks. Half a dozen men from the Guard, who had been further back and away from the full intensity of the explosions, had already surrounded and entered the vehicle, taking control from the stunned poachers inside. The men tried to ignore the fierce Kuzzi warriors, who watched and waited.

"You all right, Stuart?" someone asked.

A reassuring hand pressed Duncan's shoulder. It was Finch.

"Told you I had the bastard dead to rights," he said.

Duncan rubbed his eyes. "So you did."

"Your eyes will recover. One of those fireworks went off right over your head. Another practically set that man on top of the Crawler's hair on fire," Joseph Matson said.

Duncan scanned his men as his vision cleared and wondered who had ignited the fireworks. He thought he already had a pretty good idea, but he wasn't quite sure how he felt about it.

The Guardsmen led the poachers from the Crawler and lined them up in a row in front of the vehicle. There were five of them, all dirty and tired-looking, with expressions ranging from frightened to defiant. Duncan felt cold hatred for these men, who were themselves more like beasts than the Kuzzi they hunted. The hum of leathern paws scuffing brown grass and coarse dirt snapped Duncan back to the moment. The Kuzzi tightened their ranks, moving into the light and closing the half-circle they had formed around the Crawler. Duncan could not interpret their reserve during the brief firefight. Why had the Kuzzi not taken the opportunity to sweep in and overwhelm the men with their numbers? He searched their alien expressions, but no face among them divulged a single clue.

The tall one he had noted earlier broke ranks and approached him.

Better than eight feet in height, he loomed over Duncan, a giant of muscle and bone and fur, the kind of beast fit to spawn a thousand legends back on Earth. The Kuzzi nodded and dipped his muzzle in a traditional greeting and then it growled a low rumbling sound that rolled on for a full minute. The other Kuzzi echoed him. They stamped the posts of their purjungs against the ground, the dull thumping building to a thunderous roar as more and more of them joined in, found a common rhythm, and turned the arid plain into a massive, muted drum that throbbed with fury and heartache. And then Duncan understood their discipline, their purpose.

How Mungelson or anyone else could consider these creatures less than human was something he would never understand.

With all the power they needed to enforce their will at hand, the Kuzzi had chosen to make known their desires and then wait to see what their human neighbors would do. Duncan knew the people of New Dodge were being tested tonight in more than one way. The standoff with the poachers had been defused, and now the Kuzzi had laid their claim. The hunters had broken the law, and Duncan knew he could imprison them, hold them until the Rim Authority could send a transport to take them back to Earth to stand trial. But Earth law was not the only law they had transgressed. Certainly, it was not the first law they had broken. Didn't the Kuzzi have an even greater right to satisfy their need for justice? Kuzzi blood had been spilled, not human. The people of New Dodge had been unwilling players in the eternal conflict between hunter and prey, though Duncan could not say for sure precisely which role fit the Kuzzi and which the poachers. Not that it mattered. The way was clear to him now.

The sheriff crouched and retrieved the hide Joseph Matson had thrown to the dirt. He carried it to the Kuzzi leader, cradling it across his forearms, and then he knelt and presented the skin as though handing over the corpse of a fallen friend.

"My name is Sheriff Stuart Duncan, and I'm deeply sorry," he said to the Kuzzi, not knowing if the creature understood. "I'm sorry for all this, for everything men like these here have done to your kind. That must sound hollow, and I know it's no comfort, but these are bad men. We recognize that. They're outlaws and murderers, and we do not associate ourselves with them."

The Kuzzi took the hide and nodded once, a wet rumble rolling over in his lungs.

Duncan rose. "I imagine you have ones like them among your own people, ones you single out for punishment. I hope you understand what I'm saying."

He gestured for the men guarding the Crawler to stand down, and as they moved aside, Kuzzi warriors took their place. A line of Kuzzis entered the Crawler, and after a short time, reemerged, each one carrying a share of skins in their arms, the remains of their fallen. Other Kuzzi raided the rear storage compartments, producing more hides, and soon the lanky warriors were stealing away into the darkness, the striped furs draped across their shoulders and hands. They moved in silence. Duncan's heart sank at the number of skins reclaimed. He knew, measured in money, they would amount to enough to buy a city, but he could not comprehend that kind of bargain.

When the Kuzzi had completed their work, the sheriff ordered his men to take the empty Crawler into town and leave the poachers for their new captors. As he turned back to New Dodge, he found Jacob Matson blocking his way, the old man's chest bucking from his jog out from town square.

"You sure about this, Stuart?" Matson asked. "You remember that day out past Morgan's Bluff, back when we were charting the land? You know the place I mean? Way out on the edge of the frontier? Long time ago, I know, but we were both there. I can't believe you've forgotten. That's what you're sentencing these men to. You prepared to do that?"

Duncan had already considered the sheer rock of the bluff, the gentle, sloping valley beyond it, and the terrible sight it had contained. He and Matson had been with ten or twelve other men scouting the outlying reaches of the region on hovercycles when they came to it—a thicket of purjungs and sharp pikes planted in the earth and draped with the skins and bodies of dead Kuzzi warriors, laid out there by a rival tribe that most likely had ambushed them coming south along the bluff. The stink of rotting flesh had been repellant, but even worse were the faces, the flayed skin with eyeholes and muzzles still intact, flapping in the wind from the tips of broken spears.

"Yeah, I know what it means for them," said Duncan. "I'll never forget what we saw out there, but I'm not the one sentencing them. We're not the ones most wronged by these men. It's the Kuzzi, and the fate of these men is up to them. Way it's gotta be, Jacob."

"But it was horrible," prodded Matson.

Duncan looked his friend in the eye. Matson recoiled from the stark wetness he saw there. "More horrible than what they did to the Kuzzi?" Duncan asked.

The Crawler grumbled down the trail toward the vehicle shed. The poachers hollered and swore as half a dozen Kuzzi took position around them. They cursed the men for leaving them, but their pleas went wasted. Poking the men with the flat of their spears, the Kuzzi marched them toward the foothills. Soon only Duncan and the Kuzzi leader were left, face-to-face in the middle of the trail, their people withdrawing on both sides, stillness returning to the night.

"I hope neither of us ever meets men like that again," Duncan said.

The Kuzzi leader snarled, a low, throaty sound. His fur rippled and shimmered as he shifted his shoulders. "So do I," he spoke in a halting, feral tone. "For your sake as much as ours."

Duncan watched the leader join his tribe. The words filled him with a sensation that he could not identify, one that dulled the edge of the outrage and horror he still felt and stoked the hope for the future that smoldered inside him.

When he reached the town square, he found nearly the entire populace of New Dodge circled around a pair of picnic tables on which his son and his two friends stood.

They were entertaining the crowd with the story of how they lit the fireworks that had saved the day; how they tested the wind, measured the fuses, took careful aim, crossed their fingers, and watched the rockets burn. Doc Lieber had reported that Mick and Thom would pull through with some bed rest and careful medical care, and the settlers were already looking to find some humor in the night's events. When the boys finished their tale, Duncan waited for the laughter and cheers to subside before he stepped forward.

"Frankie, Grant, Colt," he said. "You boys played a bigger role in what happened here tonight than you know. Maybe one day you'll look back and understand it for what it was. As the sheriff of New Dodge, I want to extend the gratitude of the town to you for your fast thinking, your bold action, and your good humor through adversity. We might have been lost without it."

The boys beamed with pride, smiles creasing their mouths.

"But that doesn't change the fact that you broke the rules when you climbed the dew towers and that you broke them again, not an hour later, when you fooled around with Mick and Thom's fireworks. Starting tomorrow, you're all on three months duty digging trenches for the irrigation system," Duncan said. "And, dammit, I don't want to hear a word of complaint from any one of you the whole time."

Frank and Grant looked stunned. Their grins evaporated. Colt's shoulders slumped in resignation.

The people of New Dodge filled the square and the streets of their town with a typhoon of communal laughter.

"But tomorrow isn't here, yet, boys. So for now, get your butts off those tables and let's get on with the celebration!" Duncan boomed.

In response, a fiddle played and a horn blew, and the band picked up a jaunty beat as three young women dragged the boys into the center of the clearing and made them dance. Later that night, while the party wound to a close, the boys, tired and overexcited, puffed their cigars out behind the vehicle shed and grew dizzy on the potent smoke.

JAMES CHAMBERS' FICTION HAS BEEN PUBLISHED IN ANTHOLOGIES SUCH AS THE *Dead Walk, Sick: An Anthology of Illness, Weird Trails,* and *Warfear;* the chapbook *Mooncat Jack*; the magazine *Inhuman*; and in numerous other venues. His tale "A Wandering Blackness," published in Lin Carter's *Dr. Anton Zarnak, Supernatural Sleuth* received an Honorable Mention in The Year's Best Fantasy and Horror, Sixteenth Annual Collection. He lives in New York. He can be found online at www.jameschambersonline.com.

NOT BORN A MAN

John C. Wright

RHADAMANTHUS O'BRIAN WOKE CHOKING, WITH THIN SPIDERY TICKLES touching his face. During the night-watch, a cluster of fleshy, gray vines had crawled in through the window, breaking the thick, bottle-glass pane out of the crude wood windowframe, dislodging a stone or two from the wall. The gray vines fell in through the window, spread in a thicket over the bed. One vine had thrust a root-tip into his mouth as he slept, and reached down his throat; thin vine-twigs were clinging and crawling over the flesh of his face, groping blindly. The whole mass of wet vines was trembling with slow glee.

Rhadamanthus gave a gargling grunt of fear, and tore the root with both hands from his mouth. There was blood on the root-tip. The tendrils shivered and tightened, trying to catch him in their thicket. He slid from under the wool blanket to the floor-boards.

On a peg in the stone wall above his bed, next to his musket, hung his poison-sprayer. It was too far; the grotesque fleshy leaves were already beginning to stir and thrash, and several bulbous knots along the vine-lengths squeezed open, revealing pale round eyes. Stings and thorns, dripping venom, slid trembling out from the root-ends.

But beneath the bed was a bed-warmer, a long-handled pan filled with coals from the grate. Rhadamanthus swung the pan up and dashed the smoking coals into the tangle of vines across the bed.

The vines recoiled, shivering and thrashing in pain. During that moment, he was up, across the bed, and had the sprayer in his hand. He pumped the brass plunger vigorously; flammable poison sprayed across the vines. Where the poison splattered across the coals, thick smoke boiled up, and sparks and little darts of flame appeared.

With a grinding and slithering stir of motion, the vine mass pulled itself massively back out the window, releasing clouds of stinging insects as it did. Out the window, in the smoky red light of the unseen sun, Rhadamanthus could see where the vines had crept up across the garden-wall, snaked across the lawn, and thrust into the wall of the house. He saw where two goat-kids had died, no doubt by nibbling at the vines. They lay on their backs, spore-growths like sponges growing up from their mouths and eyesockets. He saw a second set of vines had thrust into the window of his brother Minos' room.

Beyond the garden wall rose a rounded bulk of gray flesh; presumably the intelligence directing the vines. Rhadamanthus wanted to leap out the window with his musket to pursue it, for, even as he watched, the gray bulk was dispersing into chunks of slime and starting to slide away down through the ferns and monoliths, down the mountain slope. But he could not leave; with one hand, he beat with his bed-blanket at the fire in his bed; with the other hand, he sprayed poison at the swarm of insects, holding the plunger in his teeth, and jerking the spray-can back and forth.

He was stung in several places before the swarm dispersed and died, and his head began to swim. Rhadamanthus stumbled to his night-stand. Here was a pitcher of chemical water standing in a bowl, next to it, the brass needles his brother Nemisis had made, coated with disinfectants and antidotes. Rhadamanthus found the one he wanted and stabbed his arm; the faintness passed.

In the mirror above the night-stand, Rhadamanthus saw his face; he was a gray-eyed, dark-haired young man, straight of nose and lean of cheek. One or two thin gray shoots had taken root in the flesh of his cheeks; he opened his shaving razor and scraped them out. The shoots had not been present long enough to spore. There was no time for a proper cleansing; he merely dumped the pitcher over his head and body, shuddering as the stringent chemicals stung his flesh. And, because the root had been in his mouth, he swallowed a mouthful of the horrid stuff from the bottom of the pitcher. It burned his throat; he spat and retched.

A moment later, a cloak thrown over his nudity and his musket in hand, he was dashing down the corridor to his brother's room. Over his shoulder he had flung the belt from which dangled his powder-horn and worm-box, and his little sack of musket-balls. As he reached the door to Minos' room, he saw one of his other brothers, Aeceus, wandering absentmindedly down the hallway, eyes glassy.

Since Aeceus seemed not at first to recognize him, Rhadamanthus turned his musket toward him. "Show me you are Aeceus, and not some thing which mocks his shape!"

Aeceus blinked. "I am a son of our Father. My blood is red, not gray."

"They have broken into Minos' rooms. Go! Rouse the house!" said Rhadamanthus, but Aeceus only gazed blankly at him.

Rhadamanthus threw open the door. The room beyond was a surging mass of glistening tentacles, which had thrown the enamel furniture asunder. There was no sign of Minos. Already, a clot of tentacles had formed in the center of the room with the crude and distorted outline of a human face and head. The grisly eyes rolled when Rhadamanthus opened the door; the misshapen mouth fell open, drooling, and gargled with slurred laughter.

But when Rhadamanthus drew back his hand as if to throw the entire contents of his sprayer into the room, Aeceus caught at his arm.

"Brother, wait!" Aeceus said. "We dare not anger them!"

"Are you mad? Unhand me!" Rhadamanthus said.

A group of tendrils was crawling across the floor toward the open door. By common impulse, both brothers thrust shut the door. Like all doors in the High House, the wood of this door was impregnated with many layers of disinfectant paint. The tendrils scraped tentatively against the wood—they heard the scratching—but the main vines did not try to press against the doorplanks.

Aeceus' eyes were wide and wild. He spoke in a rushed whisper. "You endanger us, if you resist them. We must appease them, the gray people."

Rhadamanthus said, "Have you forgotten that Nemisis was killed and replaced by a Shapethief? We still don't know how long it lived among us, learning our ways, reading Father's Books from Earth. Have you forgotten the hive of Impersonators we found inside Forseti's stomach when we autopsied him?"

"They are right to be angry with us! We used to help them, have you forgotten that? They did not have circulatory systems, or sugar energy cycles, till we showed them how earthlife did these things. We have so much wealth, so much knowledge. We can spare a few sheep! They cannot evolve without our help! They need us!" Even as he spoke, there came a rustling slither from behind the door.

"Unhand me, or I swear I will kill you," Rhadamanthus said.

Aeceus released, but continued to flutter his finger near his brother's face, as if he wanted to lay hold of him, but feared him. "Wait! Wait! Heed reason! The gray folk are many, and we are few. I think it is you who have forgotten, Rhadamanthus! Forgotten that we are the only humans here, stranded on this alien world, just Father and we children. Fourteen of us against the gathered might of all the world! We dare not even leave the mountain shadow! The dream-people told me..."

Rhadamanthus gave him a hard look. Aeceus shrank back, his hands before his mouth.

The dream-people were things Aeceus had invented during his hallucinations; he had tried to convince his brothers that the dream-people were real, that they whispered secret things to him his brothers could not hear.

Rhadamanthus pushed his brother up against the wall, and pulled his hands aside. Aeceus struggled feebly, but Rhadamanthus pried open his mouth.

Aeceus' tongue was gray and his teeth were slick with slime.

Rhadamanthus pushed him away. "You have been out in the sunlight. You have been down to the sea."

Aeceus mumbled, "The gray weed is special. It gives me dreams. The dream people told me that only they are real; that all this world is a false illusion." Aeceus hunched against the wall, pouting. "You can't understand these deep things."

"Forseti also ate forbidden food," said Rhadamanthus. "It absorbed the cells from the lining of his stomach, and learned the gene-combinations to make itself into the homunculi that killed him. This I understand. The thing beyond this door probably killed Minos, the same way the maggot-worms killed Hammurabi."

"No. Hammurabi was calling out in the distance. I heard him through the window. It was his voice."

"Hammurabi is dead. What you heard was not human."

"Minos heard it too. I saw him go down the mountain, following the voice. Minos has gone down to the sea."

Angrily, Rhadamanthus turned away from Aeceus. He tried to thrust open the door, but the creatures beyond had piled the bedframe against it.

Rhadamanthus put the nozzle of his sprayer into the doorlock, and pushed the plunger home. There came a bubbling shriek of hatred and pain from beyond the door, and the frenzied thrashing of tentacles. Rhadamanthus smiled coldly.

He went to the main hall vestibule and dressed. Rhadamanthus put on his tunic, waistcoat, and pantaloons, and pulled on the high black boots one needed to walk the outcropping of sharp basalt rock of the mountainside. From a tub in the vestibule, he took a dripping black cloak. It had been soaked in disinfectant, so that every fiber was swollen with poison. He squeezed and wrung the excess back into the tub, and slung the cloak over his shoulders.

He took a wide-brimmed black hat from the many hanging on pegs against the wall. Rhadamanthus saw Minos' hat still hanging on its peg. He grimaced. He had hoped Minos would resist the temptation to expose his skin to sunlight, that Minos would somehow find the fortitude.

From a jar, he took the thick brown cream which he spread upon his hands and face to protect him from the sunlight. Around his neck he slung the dark glass goggles. His brother Vindictus had done the glassblowing, but the lenses were warped and crude, and Rhadamanthus preferred not to wear them except in need.

He took a brace of worm-lock pistols and tamped powder and shot in to the enamel barrels, and thrust them through his belt. There was not enough metal to spare from the construction of Father's Revenge Weapon to forge pistol barrels; these barrels had been grown out of hard shell-like enamels by his brother Justinian.

He cocked back the hammer and fitted a worm from his worm-box into the clamp of the hammer. He touched the worm with his tongue to make certain it still was healthy. The worm jarred him with an electric jolt. He made sure the pistol's touchhole was covered by its lid; he did not want a spark from the worm to touch off the powder prematurely.

Now he ventured outside to find Minos. The motionless sun, smoldering red and dim, was hidden, as ever, behind the bulk of the mountainside. At the apex of the mountain gleamed the Weapon of Father's Revenge, a tall cylinder of steel, a metal Rhadamanthus had never seen any other place but built into the Weapon. On the other peaks were the domes of the countermeasure gear and dishes of the radar array, grown elaborately out of coral and bone, surrounded with the gray fibers of the worm-grass that housed the worms which powered the machines.

Rhadamanthus went to the garden wall and climbed it. To one side of him was the long, rambling wooden structure of the High House, the gardens and arbors in which green earth-plants grew. Further up on the mountainside were their other outbuildings and plots of ground, lawns for sheep to graze, pens for pigs, each surrounded by its wall of fitted gray stones. Little lambs frisked on the grass on the mountainside.

To his left, somewhat far downslope, was the house where his brother Lycurgus once had lived. He had once invited one of the emissaries of the Princes from the Sea to eat with him, to negotiate a peace. The chimney of the House of Lycurgus now was overgrown with moss and eye-weed. The roofbeam had cracked, and from the lower windows spilled many long gray trunks of flesh, and snakelike tongues which writhed and swayed, even when there was no breeze. No one knew what lived in the upper stories now in the house of Lycurgus, but occasionally one of the brothers saw lights glimmering in the upper windows, and heard violent gusts of laughter, screams, or the noise of strange music.

A broken and chaotic landscape of crags and deep valleys, narrow hills and crumbling cliffs fell away down the mountainside into the sea. In many places grew

the monoliths of bone that were one of the few fixed features of the terrain. To the west, a forest of spore-ferns had grown up since the last time he slept. Beyond them, a herd, or perhaps a forest, of pyramids of gray slime had migrated up from the lower slopes, leaving long trails of pulsating fiber behind them. The fibers ran all the way down the many hills into the sea. The pyramids were some agency of the Princes from Below the Sea. The Princes never came above the sea, but they could shape the flesh they touched to do their will; the things would be freed of the Princes' control if the fibers could be cut.

On a tall hill beyond the pyramids, half obscured by the smoke from the forges and smokeholes of the Deformed Ones who lived and stirred in the valley between, rose up the huge sphinxlike shape of the Northwest Watching Thing. The Northwest Watching Thing moved too slowly for human eyes to see, but measurements taken over a span of years by his brother Nemesis had proved the Thing was slowly creeping toward the house.

The Northwest Thing was crouching along the crest of its hill, its gigantic mask, frozen forever in a grimace of hatred, pointing this way. Its lidless eyes were larger than shields, and brighter than mirrors. Rhadamanthus defiantly saluted the Thing with a wave of his musket.

Turning to the east, he saw the flat hill on which the Northeast Listening Thing was crouched had been overgrown with a flock of funguses and writhing snakes. Its blind face was hidden behind the curtain of growth, but the great webs of ear tissue were unobscured.

Downslope from the Thing, clouds had blown in from the sea and formed a fog against the mountainsides. A dull haze hovered below the clouds. The clouds were composed, not of water vapor, but of seething airborn spores. They were raining swarms of insects, which mutated and recombined as they fell.

The forest of knotted shapes of bone and thorn that had covered the eastern slopes had apparently been poisoned and destroyed by this rain. Long bare shelves of rock now went down the hill-slopes to the sea. The monstrosities had apparently lost their consistency in the rain; where once huge behemoths had lumbered, now only pools of blood and floating gristle slid and crawled, mounds of jelly the size of ponds. It seemed a clear route to the sea.

Rhadamanthus was off the wall and running down the slopes of barren rock a moment later. He hurried down the hillslopes, trying to avoid the pools. He hurried because already some of the pools were collecting themselves back together, the organs and veins floating in their mass gathering slowly into knots in the center of the pools.

He crested a tall hill and found himself suddenly in the place his oldest brother Solon had been buried, back in the days before they cremated their dead, before Father realized how swiftly the gray creatures could absorb and mimic human genes.

The mound of the grave had been broken open by a tree of bone, hung with many blobs of faces shaped like his dead brother's face. Their eyes all opened when Rhadamanthus ran through the burial spot, and their mouths worked silently. All about the edge of the burial place, plants shaped like human arms and fingers, his brother's hands, had grown up in multitudes. Here and there, surrounded by veins, grew teeth, or intestines, or shards and joints of bone. The fingers caught at the edges of his cloak as his leaped over the thicket of them.

Then he was beyond that spot. Ahead was a forest of thick gray ferns and webs of ropy flesh, but these things shuddered and drew aside at the brush of his poisoned cloak. He pushed through them and found himself in a narrow valley leading to the shore.

Ahead of him, in the sand, were footprints, made either by a human, or something mimicking a human. Rhadamanthus climbed a small rise and saw the shore. Near him lay the black folds of an abandoned cloak: Minos' cloak.

Rhadamanthus looked back and forth across the ocean shore. There were no tide-lines. This world forever kept the same face turned toward the sun. Rhadamanthus was still in the shadow of the mountain. That shadow never moved, except that during the winter, the shadow crept a mile or two to the west, and, during summer, crept east again.

The terminator was not far from him. Rhadamanthus was not in the sunlight, but the red glow reflected off the sand was bright enough to send waves of strange drunk pleasure through his body. He felt a shivering of sickening intoxication tremble inside his groin and stomach. Rhadamanthus controlled his breathing, and recited the table of laws and edicts in his mind until the trembling stopped.

He still felt warm in his face, and strange, evil thoughts swam in his brain, but he was a man, and would resist.

Now he looked out. The ocean was gray and mauve in each direction, with high waves in some places, and the crests of those waves erupted into swarms of midges and flying worms. In other places, the consistency of the oceanic fluid had thickened, and mounds of gelatin held slowly squirming shapes. There were other mountains that rose up like this one from the sea; the mounds and schools of wormlike organisms tended to collect in the shadows of these mountains.

Rhadamanthus had been told that, in the early years, when Father first had been stranded here, the shadowed sides of the mountains had held no life. But now, the slopes of nearby mountains were covered by writhing forests and pools of creeping slime.

Only the organisms out of the sunlight, on the northern slopes, or below the sea, were stable, and kept their same shapes for many daywatches, or even several seasons. The things boiling the waves changed and fought and mutated and dissolved hour by hour.

On a tall rock overlooking the sea to Rhadamanthus' left stood the ruins of the altar which Forseti had maintained in secret, offering blood taken from his own veins to hungry Mimes and Shapethieves, and receiving the hallucinogenic gray weed in return.

Below the shadow of that same altar-stone, Minos now crawled through the tangled rocks toward a pool from the sea. Minos was out of the shadow of the mountain; his shirt was off, and his flesh gleamed strangely in the sunlight.

Rhadamanthus ran. More than once he lost sight of Minos, since the rocks below the altar stood in a chaotic cluster, like a labyrinth. But Rhadamanthus ran a twisting trail back and forth between the boulders, and came suddenly to where Minos was crouching by the pool.

Rhadamanthus stayed in the shadow of the rock, with a wall to either side of him, but the nearby beams of smoky sunlight dazed him with strange passions. He fought the desires back; he recalled that he was a man.

He looked, and suddenly he was not certain whether or not Minos was a man.

The thing that looked like Minos was kneeling by the pool and scooping inky slime into his mouth. The slime wriggled and stirred in his hands as he gulped it down. Now Minos threw himself on his belly and ducked his head beneath the pool.

Rhadamanthus raised his musket and drew back the hammer. "Minos! Stop!"

Minos startled, scuttled around from the pool, slime dribbling from his nose and mouth. He moved strangely, his palms and footsoles kicking sand, his elbows and knees jerking as he turned, and he never rose from all fours.

Minos cocked his head sideways. "I am the son of our Father. My blood is red, not gray." But the words were slurred, as if thick jelly clotted his throat. Or, perhaps, as if the words were made by organs not quite shaped like a man's.

"True men are poisoned by the gray food." Rhadamanthus said sternly.

Minos croaked, "A lie. The gray food makes me stronger; I feel it seething and spreading inside me like a thousand tickling strands. My dreams are filled with things which human words are far too weak to name. I hear the soaring words of those who lurk beneath the sea ringing in my brain."

"You are drugged. Come back with me. Stand up like a man, and walk. We will return to the house. You will see green grass and flowers, sit in a chair at our table by the fire like a man, eat wholesome food, quaff rich ale, and listen to music. You will remember what true humans must be."

"I will not return. The High House will fall one day; it is inevitable. Our ecology is too complex, too selfish to exist. Each predator cares nothing for his prey, each tree extends its roots to poison and to strangulate those all around it. The time will come when all the selfish germ-seeds of all earthly life will fail, and the Princes rise in triumph from the sea. On that day, all life will be made as one life, one homogenous gray slime, drinking sun and sea-water, and there shall be no more need for teeth or claws, or eyes to see."

"Or brains to think."

"Human thought is all the stuff of phantasies and lies. But I do not blame you, brother; your thoughts are no more than the secretions of the earthly flesh you wear. That flesh is not meant for this world; your thoughts are not apt for this world, and you can understand no truth. Kneel. Eat the slime, and your thoughts will rollick in your brain, and you will understand."

Minos, still crouching like a dog, reached back and scooped a handful of the stuff and proffered it to Rhadamanthus. To his horror, Rhadamanthus found he was attracted by the smell. He wondered what it would be like to force the cold slime trickling down his throat...

Minos flicked his wrist and tossed the slime-ball at him. The slime struck his shoulder and put out roots and tendrils, trying to cling. The disinfectants in the cloak-fibers made it lose its purchase. The slime slid off.

At that same moment, Minos drew his own pistol from his breeches. It was a foolish gesture; Rhadamanthus was the truest shot of all of them. His musket-ball shattered Minos' wrist and elbow. Minos flopped backward on the sand, spilling out black blood, yowling and gibbering. Rhadamanthus saw no tongue in the open mouth, but a white barbed claw. Where the bone was laid open on the arm, black worms and twisting roots writhed inside the muscles, and little midges spilled out amidst the blood, and began to spin strands of silk back and forth across the wound to close it.

Rhadamanthus dropped his musket, drew out both his pistols and stepped forward out of the shadow of the boulders walls.

A soft voice behind him spoke. *"Rhadamanthus O'Brian, kill not your brother."*

He turned. Two Princes from the Sea had been seated, one to either side of the rock wall, out of his line of sight till now.

The one on the left was human shaped, hooded and cloaked with soft layers of spun spider-silk. Nothing could be seen of this one except his mouth and chin, and small spiders fell out of mouth when he spoke, drifting on strands of silk.

"Your brother is as much a man as you, which is to say, not at all. True, you have found he is an imitator. So are you. So are all the sons of O'Brian. Have you never wondered how it was that O'Brian had no wife, and yet has sons enough to do his chores, to draw his water and hew his wood, and build his weapons of impossible revenge?"

Rhadamanthus pointed his pistol with steady hand. "I am a man. I am loyal to my Father."

"Do you recall your birth? You were not born a man."

Rhadamanthus said, "No man recalls his birth. Whatever I was born, I am now a man. I have made myself a man."

The Prince to the right was also human-shaped, dressed in skin of brown and oily leather, with a long cloak of fluttering black tissue flowing from his shoulders and sweeping many yards behind him. This prince had no face; to the front of his head was clamped a featureless bony shell. From the rim of the shell, armored legs and claws dug into his cheeks and ears, and the claws slowly opened and closed.

The faceless prince held up a wet and shiny organism shaped like a pair of blowing lungs, crowned with a tubelike membrane, opening up into lips and teeth and tongue.

The tube spoke in a breathy voice: "My master says there is no earth, no earthmen, no sky-ship of evil soldiers who stranded O'Brian here so many years ago. No sky ship ever shall return years hence. There will be no Vengeance. Your weapon will never fire. Your life is a lie. You are no more than the playthings of some master of the darkest deep, created and cast out from the waters to amuse him, but he has died, or forgotten you, and you have forgotten him, and think you are fallen from the sky. One drop of your blood will prove all my master says. Prod your finger. Black ink will come forth, not red blood."

Rhadamanthus pointed his pistols, one in each hand, at both princes; but now his back was to his brother. His only place to move, to keep all three before him, would be to step in the sunlight. He drew the goggles up from around his neck and donned them. During that moment, he was not covering the Princes with his pistols; yet they did nothing. He stepped into the light.

Rhadamanthus staggered when the red sun-beams smote him, and his brain swam with evil imaginings, as if he wanted to dance, or die, or scream, or dissolve. He gritted his teeth.

The hooded one spoke, and spiders floated up from his mouth, trailing silk. "You know our reproductive process. We are composed of colonies of independent cells. Our bodies must shatter and return to pools of slime to free the cells to divide. This division requires sunlight. Hiding in the gloom as you do, you can arrest the desire to reproduce, but only for a time. Your blood will show the truth in time. Look. Even now your skin turns gray. Can you deny that you are one of us?"

Rhadamanthus could see that his hands, clutching the pistols, were losing their color.

The hooded one spoke again. "Merge with us. We dissolve and slay each other, it is true, but our brain cells retain part of the knowledge they had learned when they were gathered together into webs of nervous systems. When enough brain-cells come together in our flesh, we wake. If we are eaten, not by lower creatures, but by each other, no continuity is lost. We die, but fragments of our memories endure. Join us, and your memories will not be lost."

The faceless one held up his lung-creature. "We will draw you down into the black depth, and take you in honor to our feast hall, and lay you on our table, and strike your skull asunder with a sharpened axe, and press our muzzles forward into the bleeding mass, each of us to swallow down some part of your brains. You will live in many bodies, your selfishness erased and blended all together with the swirl of our thoughts and passions. You will dissolve into the greater whole. Come. Join us. We see the thought is tempting to you. Lay down the burden of your individuality. Rest from futile thought."

The hooded one raised his face. Behind his eyelids there were no eyes, but squirming clusters of furry insect bodies, their many spidery legs wrapped all around each other.

"The greatest of us dwell at the very bottom of the deep, like huge mountain-shapes composed entirely of brain, intellects vast and slow beyond your reckoning. Our perfect gardens below the ocean are controlled and organized, free from the competition and selfishness of your ecology. Each living thing there eats and is eaten according to the grand design, and the weak are aided by the strong, not victimized. Can you dare to match or to oppose the tremendous philosophy of the Great Brains? They have discovered the futility of all conceptualization, the superstition of believing in causality. The universe is mad and random, and thought is selfish. But passions, desires, dreams, these things spring from the whole and serve the whole."

Rhadamanthus said angrily, "Is this why the seas above your perfect gardens ever are afloat with corpses, stale blood, rottenness, and filth?" But he was staring steadily at his hands. His flesh was now as gray as lead.

The faceless one gestured with his lung thing. "On the dark side of the world lurks a single super-organism, continents broad and miles deep. Soon it reaches out its miles-wide arms to crush all dayside life, and absorb us all back into primordial bliss and thoughtless unity."

The hooded one shouted, "We are the masters of all pleasure, the lords of all life. Living things will serve as we direct! Submit! Our slaves receive their due pleasures! Observe!"

A tongue of the sea surged forward, sending out sprays of insects, worms, and strands of flesh. A bubble of clear gelatin formed and rose to the surface. The membranes of gelatin slid aside to reveal within a nude woman of perfect face and figure, round-bosomed, narrow-waisted, full-hipped. Long golden hair framed her beautiful face. Her red lips curved in a sensuous smile; her green eyes burned with evil passion.

She looked like a woman from one of the pictures in Father's books, from earth. Rhadamanthus wondered how they had made her; perhaps by combining the sexual genes from two dead brothers, to produce an XX rather than an XY.

The woman turned toward Minos and extended her slim arms pleadingly to him. At once he was scrambling across the sand, ignoring his brother's warning cries. Minos fell into the arms.

Rhadamanthus, from the side, could see what Minos, seeing her straight-on, could not. The woman's back was open, and greasy veins and tubes and nerves and organs reached out from inside her skin into the gelatinous mass she rested upon, controlling her like a puppet, or part of a vast creature hanging below the black waves. It was as if they had constructed a woman, but could not discover how to fit all of her organs correctly within the confines of the flesh.

Rhadamanthus raised his pistol to fire at the hollow woman. But a spider, ejected from the hooded prince by his last shout, landed on the pistol barrel, and stung something into the enamel. The barrel twisted and darkened, and the wooden stock warped. It was too late to stop his finger; the trigger pulled, the hammer struck the worm into the touch-hole; the angry worm gave off sparks, touching off the powder. Rhadamanthus flung the gun from him as it back-fired and exploded.

The hooded one crowed. "Your metals and stone we cannot touch, but whatever was alive—enamel, wood, or bone—is not outside the orbit of our power!"

The membranes surrounding the woman folded around Minos as they embraced, drawing them both beneath the waves. There was a swirl of gray water; and Minos was gone.

The faceless prince, meanwhile, had stood, flinging wide his cloak. The black tissues of the cloak erupted into a cloud of filmy black wings, and flew out in a silent flock. Several of them fell on Rhadamanthus, and tried to sting him, but were defeated by the thickness of his poisonous cloak.

One landed on his face, and tried to drive its sting into his eye. The stinger scraped against the brown glass of the goggles. With his free hand, Rhadamanthus reached into his worm-box, drew out a handful of electric worms, and struck himself in the face.

He was jolted from his feet. The black flapping thing fell off his face, dead. The poison spray-bottle was in his hand. But the black things were in cloud all around him, and swarms of spiders were skittering across the sand toward him from beneath the hem of the hooded one's robe.

As he had done before, he took up his poison sprayer in his teeth and jerked the can back and forth. Drops of poison turned the winged membranes ash-gray where they fell. The black flock dispersed, disobeying whatever control the faceless one was exerting.

Now Rhadamanthus rose to one knee, and, pulling off the lid of the poison sprayer with his teeth, dashed the whole contents of the canister at the faceless one's body. The leather skins sagged and fell asunder; the whole body swayed and fell.

From beneath the pile of shivering skins, the hard mask darted forth, scuttling on its crab-legs, and ran across the sand into the sea. The pile of skins wiggled and spread out aimlessly.

The hooded figure stepped forward slowly, its many layers of filmy spider-silk spreading and floating as it came forward. "Now, loyal son of O'Brian, now you must deal with me. How will you destroy me with but a single musket ball? My brains and hearts are not kept in any single spot within my frame. I am not a single organism, but a collection of multitudes. You have cast your poison all away, but I, I need but land a single bit of my host upon your flesh to sting you into death."

Rhadamanthus dropped his aim. "I will not kill all of you. I will only shoot whichever of your legs steps forward first. Perhaps the organism of your legs are willing to make the sacrifice for the good of the whole."

The hooded one swayed. "Do not be foolish. You can not turn me against myself by so transparent a deception. I need but step forward..." But the Prince of the Sea was already dropping to the ground, as the flesh of his legs melted and slid aside.

The skin erupted as it fell, and swarms of spiders scuttled out in all directions. The bones of the legs were exposed, but apparently even these were made up of smaller creatures, and dissolved into clusters of small, white, hard, scuttling insects.

Rhadamanthus strode away, and the head and torso of the hooded one shouted terrible oaths and imprecations, snarled, and began to drag itself into the sea.

Rhadamanthus shouldered his musket. Only then did he stare at his hands, and squint, face cold and calm and terrible to behold, as if he fought in his mind against some nearly irresistible but utterly unspeakable temptation. After many minutes, the iron-gray hue left his skin, and his hands returned to a healthy pink color.

"I am a man," he whispered to himself.

He had returned home, and rested, and ate wholesome food. He listened to gentle music, while sitting upright in a chair, like a man, and studied a work on ethics by Aristotle.

Only then did he seek out his father, climbing the hillside to find the old man among the highest and oldest of the arbors.

Inside the wall protecting this arbor grew old and stately apple-trees. When the breeze blew, the scent of apple-blossoms floated on the air, and green leaves floated down to rest on green grass.

His father was white-haired and white-bearded, but unbowed by age, standing straight and tall. In one hand he held a thick wood staff. In the other, he held a clay jug.

The apple tree he faced had turned all gray and black, and it swayed and started pulling up its roots. Little hairs like tendrils writhed out from underneath the running bark. It began to wave its branches threateningly.

Father drove a sharpened funnel into the bark with a blow from his staff, and poured some fluid from the jug he held into the interior of the tree. He put his mouth near the bark and spoke soft, soothing words. In a few moments the tree grew motionless, still and calm, replaced its roots back down into the dirt, and stood once again, an apple tree.

Rhadamanthus had come up during this procedure, but stood silently aside till it was done. Now he spoke: "Father, Minos is dead. He was pulled beneath the sea."

Father nodded gravely, seeming sad, but not surprised. "Minos was smart, but not wise, and he did not trust his own thinking."

"The Princes from below told me I am like one of them."

Again, Father nodded. "They have known and forgotten this many times before. Their brains are savage and chaotic, and dissolve and recombine in unsteady combinations." Now he looked carefully at Rhadamanthus. "And what did you say to this news?"

"I told them what you have always taught us: that man is a creature of a self-made soul. That we have no instinctual knowledge, no automatic behaviors, and that what we think and what we do is a matter entirely of our own making. That we are born as mere clusters of animal flesh, but that we must make ourselves men."

Father nodded gravely. He pointed with his staff up to the mountain-peak not far above, where the weapon gleamed in its steel cylinder. "Not even all men can make themselves into men." Now he spoke in a voice like one reciting a ritual. Rhadamanthus had heard the speech many times before; nonetheless, he stood in a posture of careful attention.

"Even I was evil at first," Father recited, "when first I signed aboard the Robin Hood, eager to make war upon the innocent flower-creatures of a far star. But I repented halfway through the long decades of the flight, and so they stranded me here, where they had stopped to take on oxygen and water, and left me with nothing but a few supplies. This is the only other world, other than old earth, with free oxygen within its atmosphere. I know that they must stop here again, their hands still reeking with the blood of genocide of the innocents. To live, to grow food, to dig up uncontaminated water, and, especially, to make the weapon to avenge myself, I needed helping hands. This apple garden was the first place I stood when first I understood the way: I had thrown an apple-core away, and returned the next daywatch to find a beautiful orchard. Are you sorry that I brought you and your brothers into being? Do you regret that I have forced you to live as men?"

It was a ritual question; Rhadamanthus spoke a spontaneous answer, as fervidly as if he had not heard the question a thousand times before.

He said: "Never do I regret being a man. If I had been born in the sea, in the sunlight, like my ancestors, I would be one unfocused group of wandering thoughts and mad passions floating through a disordered collective consciousness. Now I am a creature with an ego, proud, self-reliant, independent. I will never yield my consciousness to another. You raised us and we love you, we alone of all creatures on this planet, know and love the one who brought us into being. Some of us have fallen away. Some of us have stopped thinking like men and returned to the state of imitators. But I will never give up. But you can trust me, at least, Father."

"I do trust you. I trust you most of all," the old man said. For a moment, his face seemed to darken, and his features blurred and shifted like plastic. The hair of his head and beard stood up and writhed and swayed. He doused himself with the fluid from the jug he held, and stood, breathing deeply, till his face grew pale and still again.

"I trust you most of all, and I am old. I would like you to take my place as Father after me, Rhadamanthus. I am not the first father, nor was the father before him, nor the one before him. Nor, I deem, shall I be the last. But whenever a father thinks he cannot hold away the temptation to return to the sea for long, that is when he should pass the mantle of fatherhood along. You are the hardiest and sternest of us; never allow us to deviate one inch from the principles the first father laid down for us. He was a true man, and came from the stars. His dream of vengeance has far outlived him, and woke to a life of its own. From such questionable beginnings, great good can come. Now then: Let us go into the lab; we will need a sterile needle to pierce into my brain."

"But what will you do?" Rhadamanthus asked, amazed.

The old man chuckled. "If I survive the operation, perhaps I shall become the next Minos. We always should have at least one Minos around here, to provoke debate, if nothing else.

JOHN C. WRIGHT IS A RETIRED ATTORNEY, NEWSPAPERMAN AND NEWSPAPER editor, who was only once on the lam and forced to hide from the police who did not admire his newspaper.

He presently works (successfully) as a writer in Virginia, where he lives in fairy-tale-like happiness with his wife, the authoress L. Jagi Lamplighter, and their three children: Orville, Wilbur, and Just Wright.

His novels include: *The Golden Age, The Phoenix Exultant, The Golden Transcendence, Last Guardians of Everness*, and the forthcoming *Mists of Everness.*